RANDOM HOUSE
LARGE
PRINT

One
Good
Thing

Also by Georgia Hunter
Available from Random House Large Print

We Were the Lucky Ones

One
Good
Thing

GEORGIA HUNTER

RANDOM HOUSE
LARGE PRINT

Original cover design: Nayon Cho
Design adapted for Large Print
Cover image: Bert Hardy / Getty Images
Map by Meighan Cavanaugh

The Library of Congress has established a Cataloging-in-Publication record for this title.

ISBN: 979-8-217-06748-0

https://www.penguinrandomhouse.com/

FIRST LARGE PRINT EDITION

Printed in the United States of America

1st Printing

The authorized representative in the EU for product safety and compliance is Penguin Random House Ireland, Morrison Chambers, 32 Nassau Street, Dublin D02 YH68, Ireland, https://eu-contact.penguin.ie.

For my parents, Tom and Isabelle,
and for my boys, Robert, Wyatt, and Ransom,
with love

Ferrara

Nonantola
Bologna

Florence

Castelnuovo
Berardenga
Assisi
San Terenziano
Torre del Colle
Todi

Scalo Teverina
Rome

Naples

N
W E
S

©2025 Meighan Cavanaugh

One
Good
Thing

PROLOGUE

She could carry the boy, but it would slow them down. He's too heavy. She grips his small hand as they run, trying not to fall. Twigs snap underfoot, the ground uneven.

"Faster," she tells him. "Pick up your feet."

A bullet lodges with a sharp thunk in the trunk of a pine a few meters ahead. Lili stoops reflexively, resists the urge to turn around, her breath ragged in her ears like an ocean in a storm. She isn't sure if it's a farmer shooting or another band of partisans or Mussolini's men from the Salò. It could be the Italian police or a German soldier. They'd scanned the field carefully, she and the others, before veering from the safety of the forest canopy to inspect the vegetable garden of what they thought was an abandoned farm. They'd unearthed five potatoes and were trekking back toward the tree line, giddy at the prospect of a meal come sundown, when the first shot was fired and someone up ahead—Ziggie, maybe—shouted. **Run.**

"This way," Lili orders, weaving to the right, the

group now scattered. "Jump!" She hoists the boy into the air. They leap over a log in unison and land without breaking stride, sprinting on, deeper into the woods, their dirt-caked palms sticky with sweat.

The lace of Lili's boot has come undone and a bright red gash blooms on her forearm from the scrape of a branch, she presumes, but she feels nothing.

Don't stop, she tells herself. Don't let go of his hand. Just keep going.

PART I

CHAPTER ONE

FERRARA

December 1940

Eight thirty-two. Lili slides a pencil from behind her ear and writes the time in her chart. "It's every seven minutes now," she says from her seat on Esti's sofa. "I think we should go."

Esti paces the perimeter of the room. She waves a hand. "My water hasn't broken. I'm fine."

"Are you sure? You don't look fine."

"Thanks," Esti says, making a face at Lili.

"Sorry. You don't look **yourself**."

"I hardly feel myself. But I refuse to sit around the hospital for days. My mother labored for forty-eight hours with me. Besides, Niko's not back yet. I don't want to leave without him."

Lili sighs. "All right. But when your contractions come five minutes apart, we're going. You know I'd do anything for you, Es, but please don't make me be the one to deliver your baby."

Esti laughs, emitting a deep bark of a sound, and Lili shakes her head.

"You're as stubborn as they come, you know that, right?"

"So my husband tells me."

"Speaking of your husband, where is he?"

"He didn't say."

Lili chews the eraser of her pencil. Niko's been out a lot in recent weeks, she's noticed, his whereabouts always vague. It's unlike him. "I'll write a note, then," she says, "in case we leave before he's home."

"Suit yourself," Esti says, then winces. She props herself in a doorframe and closes her eyes, pressing her forehead into the back of her hand as she breathes through another contraction. Lili checks the time.

"Six and a half minutes," she says when Esti straightens.

"Noted."

Esti resumes her slow lumber around the room, and Lili frowns, wondering how she might convince her friend she'd be smart to labor with a doctor nearby. But to argue with Esti, she's learned, is to waste her breath.

They'd met three years earlier, in Lili's first week at university. Lili had just moved to Ferrara from Bologna and didn't know a soul; she was missing home and trying to find her footing. When she slipped into the seat beside Esti's in her Modern

European Literature class, Esti turned and said hello and her smile was so warm and self-assured, Lili forgot to be shy. Esti's Italian was excellent—Lili had no idea, at first, that she was Greek. They struck up a conversation, making a plan to meet for lunch later that day, then every day after, and within a month, they arranged to share a flat on Via Belfiore, a short walk from school.

There were times in those early weeks when Lili wondered why Esti had chosen **her** to befriend. Lili was seventeen then, still girlish, reserved. She was most comfortable with a book in her hand or at the keys of her typewriter. Esti, in her third year at the university, was nearly twenty, and, in Lili's mind, every part a woman. Smart. Opinionated. Beautiful. With her smooth curves, cobalt eyes, and stylish wardrobe, she was the envy of most of the girls on campus. Perhaps it was the fact that they were so different, Lili told herself in the beginning, that they got on so well. Lili was a planner, careful in her ways; Esti a champion of spontaneity. But in the end, Lili realized, their differences didn't matter. They were inseparable. Lili has barely a memory from her years in Ferrara that doesn't include Esti.

Esti was there when Lili's first opinion piece was published in the **Corriere Padano**—she'd insisted they celebrate with dinner and dancing. **This is my writer friend Lili Passigli!** she told everyone they met that night. **You'll do well to remember her name, she's going to be famous someday.** It was

Esti who stole Lili away on her eighteenth birth-day for a weekend in Venice, where they got lost for hours in a maze of impossibly narrow alleys, feasted on fried sardines and tender green **moleche** crabs, and chatted up the gondoliers who gave them free rides back to their hotel by flat-bottom boat, the water glistening beneath them like pol-ished lacquer in the moonlight. Esti was there, too, on the afternoon when Lili received the telegram from Bologna with news that the cancer had finally taken her mother. She'd wept with her and boiled pasta for her, traveled back to Bologna with her for the funeral and the shiva, and later attended Lili's classes to take notes until Lili found the strength to return to her studies.

Esti was there, always, like the older sister Lili never had.

"Six minutes, twenty seconds," Lili says, the next time Esti muscles through a contraction. "Let's check your bag again, make sure you've got every-thing you need." She reaches for the canvas tote at her feet.

"It's all in there," Esti says, her face pinched. "You packed it, remember?"

Still, Lili rummages through, matching the contents of the bag to the inventory in her head: nightgown, slippers, underwear, a flannel blanket, a miniature white knit jumper and a matching hat. She's refolding the blanket when Esti makes a small sound, like a hiccup.

"Oh," she says, and Lili looks up. Esti stands stock still, a puddle between her feet.

"Oh!" Lili cries, knocking over the tote as she leaps from the couch. "I'll get some towels."

IT'S THREE IN THE MORNING WHEN THE DOCTOR finally gives Esti permission to push. Niko stands at the head of the bed, a hand on Esti's shoulder. He'd arrived at the hospital just after ten, panic-stricken at the thought of missing the birth of his child.

"The waiting room is just down the hall," the doctor tells him now.

Niko swallows and makes a meek offer to stay, his face pale, but Esti shoos him away.

"I'll be fine, love," she manages. "Lili's here."

"You sure?"

"I'm sure."

Relieved, Niko kisses his wife on her forehead then nods once at Lili, as if to wish her good luck before leaving. Lili returns the nod and steels herself, realizing how unprepared she is for what's about to come.

The minutes pass slowly. Lili presses a damp cloth to Esti's neck between contractions and offers up words of encouragement that feel entirely inadequate. The room is cold but Esti's skin is hot to the touch and slick with sweat. Dark tendrils of hair plaster her forehead. Every few minutes she moans as the pain builds, crunching her chin toward her sternum, and Lili has to hold back tears as Esti screams out in agony. She's glad Niko isn't here. It's nearly impossible to stand by, helpless—to watch her friend endure such pain.

"Just one more push," the doctor says from the foot of the bed.

Lili's certain that Esti has broken a bone in her hand by the time the sound of a baby's wail fills the room.

"It's a boy," the nurse calls out a moment later, and Esti, panting, lets her head fall back to her pillow.

"You are a hero," Lili says, kissing Esti's cheek. She smells of salt and lavender. They can hear the doctor giving orders at the foot of the bed, the snip of the umbilical cord.

Niko is called back once Esti has been cleaned up and the baby bathed, weighed, measured, and swaddled.

"Come meet your son," Esti says. She sits upright, her eyes bright, her cheeks flushed, the pain of her labor already a thing of the past.

Lili steps aside and Niko moves to his wife, staring at the bundle in her arms. All that's visible of the baby is his face—round cheeks, velvet skin, dark lashes, mauve, heart-shaped lips.

"I'll be damned," he stammers.

"Here," Esti says. "Take him."

Niko blinks. "Right now? He looks so comfortable."

"Niko."

"Are you sure?"

"Niko! Take him!"

Niko bends, maneuvering the baby gingerly into his arms, and Lili watches his hesitation meld to wonder and then joy. A broad smile stretches across his face, and he sways gently.

"Welcome to the world, little one," he says softly.

Lili smiles, too, her limbs heavy, as the adrenaline, the worry, begin to drain from her. Esti is okay. The baby is healthy. Niko is here. "I'll let you sleep," she says, making her way toward the door. "Give you all some privacy."

"What?" Esti shakes her head. "You can't leave now. The party's just started. Stay for a while, would you?"

Lili laughs, realizing the only thing missing from Esti's hospital bag is a bottle of prosecco. Sleep can wait, she decides, grateful to be a part of these first few moments, together as a family of four.

THE MATERNITY WARD IS QUIET, THE WORLD outside the window in Esti's room still dark. Niko is dozing, curled up awkwardly in a chair in the corner, Lili propped on her elbow beside Esti in the hospital bed. Theo, named after his paternal grandfather Theódoros, is asleep belly-down on Esti's chest. Lili studies him closely: the wisps of his eyebrows, the spiderweb of tiny pink capillaries threading through his eyelids, the paper-thin fingernails.

"I can't believe you **made** him," she says softly.

"I can't either."

"He looks like you."

Esti peers down at the top of his head, adjusts his cap over his ear. "You think?"

"Your faces are shaped the same."

Esti smiles. "I wonder what he'll be like."

"He'll be confident, like his mama. And playful like his papa."

"I hope so."

"I know so."

Esti strokes the back of one of Theo's fists with her index finger. "I've been telling myself for the last nine months the timing doesn't matter," she says after a while. "But now that he's here . . . Look at him. He's so innocent. So helpless."

Esti's right—it's a terrifying prospect, to raise a child at a time like this, with Europe at war and with the Racial Laws in Italy restricting their every move—but Lili isn't about to say so.

"I imagine there's no such thing as perfect timing," she says. "Look at us—you were born during the Great War; I was conceived on the heels of it. Our parents made do. And I'd like to think we turned out okay."

"Well, **you** did," Esti quips. "Your life is so **in order**. I can barely remember to turn in a paper or to make it to a dentist appointment."

Lili laughs. "As if any of that stuff matters. You're going to be an amazing mother, Es."

Esti raises her brow.

"The war is being fought across borders, not in

Italy. And anyway, it'll be over soon," Lili adds. "They're calling it a **blitzkrieg**, right?"

"The war may end, but what state will the world be in? And who says the Racial Laws aren't here to stay?"

Lili wants to argue but she can't. Mussolini put his laws into place a full year before Hitler sent his men into Poland. "Don't worry yourself with any of that right now," Lili says. "You've got more important things to think about."

Esti lets her eyes flutter closed, a hand resting on Theo's back. Lili watches her fingers rise and fall to the quick rhythm of his breath. At least they have access to private medical care, she thinks. Something the laws haven't taken away. She makes a mental note to write down the dates of Esti's follow-up appointments before she leaves the hospital.

THEO FLINCHES AND ESTI OPENS HER EYES. "I FELL asleep," she says.

"I'm glad," Lili says. "You should sleep more."

"I was dreaming."

"Oh?"

Esti smiles faintly. "Yes. About the day Niko proposed."

"It was a good day," Lili says.

She remembers it well, despite the fact that more than two years have passed since. Niko had come to her beforehand—**I want to make it special**, he said—and Lili had helped him to organize it all: the picnic in the park, the bottle of Taittinger, Esti's favorite sparkling wine. She'd even gone with him to pick out the ring, a simple gold **fede**, molded in the shape of two hands, clasped together at the bezel. The three had celebrated over dinner at their favorite trattoria, Al Brindisi, then walked through town with a bottle of half-drunk Lambrusco to the ancient **bastioni**, the massive stone wall encircling the city. They'd sat for hours atop the wall, admiring the shimmer of the canal below, faded and mist bound beneath the star-studded sky, talking about weddings and plans for once they'd graduated.

It wasn't until the end of the otherwise perfect night that the subject of Mussolini's **Manifesto della Razza** finally arose—it had just been announced, the week before. **Real Italians**, the manifest proclaimed, **are descendants of a pure, Aryan Race; Jews are descendants of an inferior race.** The announcement had blindsided Lili; she'd never considered herself Jewish **or** Italian, but both. She'd sat quietly that evening, her arms wrapped around her knees as Niko and Esti argued over the meaning of it. **Look what's happening in Germany,** Niko said, jabbing his cigarette north. **With the Nuremberg Laws. And with Il Duce sitting pretty in the Fuhrer's pocket . . . it feels like we're up against the clock.** Esti had rolled her eyes. **It's just a stupid piece of paper,** she countered. **Some sort of concession. A way of appeasing Hitler. Besides,** she added, the

pope is Italian! And he's human. He wouldn't allow it.

Esti was certain nothing would come of the decree. (**Easy for you and Niko to say**, Lili had argued, **when it's not your country issuing it**—Niko is Greek, too, and like Esti, had come to Italy on a student visa.) And for a while, it seemed Esti was right. Piazza Trento e Trieste still teemed with bicyclists pedaling home from work or out to dinner; the streets were still full of children chasing one another, cones of soft gelato in hand. Niko kept up his Sunday matches at the tennis club, and Lili and Esti spent their weekends perusing the market by Castello Estense for just-ripe peaches and bags of Vignola cherries, or meeting for a glass of wine and plate of **ciupeta** bread before heading to the cinema for a show. That September, Lili traveled to the island of Rhodes for Esti and Niko's wedding, where the friends spent five magical days swimming and eating and celebrating before returning to their classes in Ferrara. It felt entirely possible that their lives would continue on exactly as they always had.

They were living in a different reality then, Lili thinks now, her eyes tracing a crack in the plaster ceiling over the hospital bed. A delusional one, perhaps, but one she'd return to in a minute if she could.

"Thanks for making that day so special," Esti murmurs in her half sleep, and Lili warms. She'd never made a to-do over the effort she'd put into the planning; the day was about Esti and Niko, after all. Now, Esti's gratitude feels like a balm, smoothing the edges of her worries.

"Of course," she says, but Esti is still, her expression once again slack.

Lili watches her sleep for a moment, considering how rare it is for her friend to worry. Fretting over out-of-control things is Lili's area of expertise, not Esti's. No matter, she decides. They'll manage whatever comes their way. Together. And when the world feels like it's closing in on them, Theo will be just the distraction they need.

The room is silent, save for the gentle rasp of Theo's breath. Lili watches him for a while longer, letting the pull of exhaustion numb her thoughts. She nuzzles closer, her head heavy on the pillow, Esti's body warm against hers, and succumbs, finally, to sleep.

CHAPTER TWO

BOLOGNA

March 1941

Lili peers through the train car window, a worn copy of **Decameron** on her lap, her index finger tucked between pages to mark the place she'd left off. A speaker crackles overhead. **Bologna Centrale, cinque minuti.** Outside, the scenery of Emilia-Romagna scrolls by, a patchwork of pear and chestnut orchards, golden wheat fields, and terra-cotta rooftops. Her view looks as it always has. Idyllic. Serene.

The train's whistle blows and Lili gathers her things, stepping a few minutes later onto the station platform. She scans the crowd. It doesn't take long to spot her father striding toward her, waving his felt cap overhead. She waves back and jogs in his direction, and when he pulls her into a hug Lili closes her eyes, comforted by the familiar scent of his orange-menthol aftershave, by the sturdiness of his embrace.

"You look well," Lili says when they part.

Her father is handsome still at fifty-two—tall, with a full head of dark hair, olive skin, and eyes the same hazel green and almond shape as Lili's. His sideburns are speckled with more gray than she remembers, and the creases at the corners of his eyes have grown deeper, more permanent. Smile lines, her mother used to call them. The war has a way of doing this, Lili's noticed—weathering even the youngest at heart.

"And you look a little pale in the face, Babà," Massimo says, calling her by the nickname she'd earned when she was three years old and he caught her in the pantry, stealing bites of her mother's famous **babà** sponge cake. "You all right?"

"I'm fine," Lili nods. "Just a little woozy from the train." She kisses his cheeks. "I'm so happy to see you, Papà."

"Come, let's get you some fresh air." He checks his watch. "And a rest. We've a few hours before we need to be ready." Tomorrow, they'll visit Naomi's grave, as they do each year on the anniversary of her death. Tonight, though, they'd made plans to see a new film. It's opening night and, according to her father, the talk of the town.

Massimo throws Lili's duffel over his shoulder and takes her arm. They make their way through the station and beneath a vaulted stone portico to a side street where the family's old Fiat is parked.

"So. Tell me," Massimo says, turning the engine over. "How are things in Ferrara?"

Lili shrugs. "Not too bad. All things considered."

"And your students?"

When the Racial Laws banned Jewish children from attending public school in Italy, Lili's synagogue cobbled together a group of volunteers to give lessons in the basement of the temple; Lili teaches classes twice a week now in reading and writing.

"They're doing well," Lili tells her father, brightening. "It's amazing how quickly they learn."

"That's wonderful, Babà."

Massimo slows the Fiat to let a woman cross the street, a child in tow. She doesn't wave and Lili wonders if her husband was conscripted. Since Mussolini joined the war on the side of the Axis, there are hardly any men of fighting age on the streets anymore, she's noticed. Unless, of course, you were Jewish and not allowed to enlist.

Lili watches the young girl as she and her mother pass. "I just wish there was an end in sight. I wish I could tell the children at the synagogue that someday they'll go back to a real school." Even though there is no fighting in Italy, the country is at war now, and the prospect of a return to normal feels distant.

Massimo glances at her. "Life will resume as it once was," he says. "It always does. All of this, it's only temporary."

Lili wants badly to believe him. But with every passing month, it becomes harder to remember what normal is anymore.

As they motor on, Lili thinks back to the day she understood—or perhaps finally accepted—that things were about to change. She'd just returned from Esti's wedding in Rhodes and Ferrara had put out an order for all Jews, Italian and foreign, to report to the town registrar for a census and new ID cards. Lili's papers, which she's required to carry at all times, now bear a bold red stamp above her photo: DI RAZZA EBRAICA. Of the Jewish Race. Not long after, Jews with foreign passports were banned entirely from living in Italy. Lili had raced through the rain to Esti and Niko's apartment when the law was announced, certain they were about to be sent back to Greece, only to find Esti stretched out on her couch with a magazine, unfazed. **I won't allow Il Duce's theatrics to govern my life**, she declared. **We're happy here at the moment. If we move home, it'll be of our own accord.** A sympathetic dean at the University of Ferrara offered to enroll Esti and Niko in graduate school—a loophole to extend their visas, he told them behind closed doors. The plan had worked, but Lili still worries it's only a matter of time before the student exemption is repealed and they are deported.

The restrictions that followed that fall of '38 were endless. Suddenly, it was illegal for Jews to marry non-Jews, to work in government services or at a bank, to employ Aryans, to own a radio. The list went on. When Jews were banned from holding jobs in the media, Lili lost her part-time position as junior editor at the **Ferrara Daily. It's out of my control**, her boss said, but still, it came as a blow. Lili loved to write. She'd dreamt since she was a child of becoming a journalist, had spent years honing her craft. By the time she was let go, though, censorship and propaganda in the press had intensified to such a degree that even if she'd been allowed to stay on, there was no telling how her work would be presented. In the end, Lili told herself, it was just as well the paper no longer wanted her. She managed to find a job tending orchids at a greenhouse in the Botanical Garden. She spends her days taking soil samples or with a watering pail in hand, her fingernails rimmed with dirt.

Massimo steers the Fiat through a roundabout, and Lili is brought back to the present by the sound of a car horn.

"What about you?" she asks. "How are you getting on?"

Before the manifest came into effect, Massimo owned and managed several apartment buildings in Bologna. Now, he's no longer permitted to own properties, or to operate his real estate business.

"Actually, I have news."

Lili turns. "Good news, I hope?"

"Yes. I've officially signed my properties over to Settimo."

Settimo is a family friend who lives a floor down from Massimo and who happens to be Catholic. He lost his wife, too, not long after Naomi died.

"It's his name attached to the deeds now," Massimo says. "He'll sign the business back to me after the war."

Lili exhales. "That **is** good news." She'd worried her father's buildings would be confiscated by the government. That his life's work—and savings— would disappear, as it had for others.

"We've found a good rhythm, Settimo and I. He makes the rounds to collect rent, and I keep the books. I help when I can, with a broken pipe or creaky floorboard, that kind of thing."

"So . . . you're still managing."

"Not on paper," Massimo says with a wink.

Lili frowns. "Be careful, Papà. The police will punish you for it if they find out."

"I'm careful, love. Don't worry about me."

It's impossible, though, not to worry. Massimo has always been in good favor with his tenants, but now . . . Lili thinks of the handful of friends in Ferrara who've distanced themselves in recent months, who see her on the street and drop their gaze, rather than stopping to say hello. What if a neighbor were to report him?

"Here we are," Massimo says, pulling the Fiat into the alleyway beside their building. Lili feels her shoulders relax at the sight of the familiar brownstone exterior. Of home.

AFTER A QUICK NAP IN HER OLD BED, SHE FINDS her father seated on a stool in the den, paintbrush in hand, an easel before him. He's mentioned in his letters that he's taken up painting as a hobby, but Lili has yet to see his work.

"Papà. It's beautiful," she says, studying his canvas—a landscape of warm earth tones and pale blue sky. His brushstrokes are big, his colors bold. "Where is it?"

Massimo smiles at her over his shoulder. "It's from a memory—a trip your mother and I took to Tuscany, before you were born."

"And I always thought Mama was the artist."

Massimo laughs. "She was. I'm just playing around. I enjoy the process. Helps to turn the brain off, you know?"

Lili nods. "I love it."

"It's yours then, when I'm finished." Massimo drops his paintbrush into an old coffee tin half full of linseed oil. "We should head out," he says. "We'll want to get there early."

IN THE THEATER, LILI AND MASSIMO CHAT QUIETLY as the seats around them fill. Lili tells her father all about Theo, who's getting bigger every day.

"He's a good baby," she says. "Though he eats constantly. It's driving Esti mad."

Massimo chuckles. "You were like that too. The first few months are the hardest."

The lights in the theater dim and the crowd quiets. Cocooned in darkness, Lili settles back in her seat, runs her fingers along the red-velvet armrest of her chair, the prospect of being transported to another world—even if just for a short while—suddenly thrilling.

But the film, she realizes as the plot begins to unfold, is not at all what they expected. The protagonist is a Jewish man—a swindler who talks his way into the job of treasurer for a prominent German duke and whose brazen schemes wreak havoc on the dukedom, nearly causing a civil war.

Lili shifts in her seat. "Maybe we should—" she whispers to her father, but she's interrupted by a hiss from the row behind them. **Hush!** Lili stiffens, then starts as something falls into her lap. A note, folded in two. She looks up, trying to see who'd thrown it, but it's impossible to make out the faces in the balcony. She opens it. Though the penmanship is crude, the words are clear, even in the shadows. **Death to the Jews,** it reads. Out of the corner of her eye, she spots another paper being dropped from above, then another. She hands the note to her father. He reads it, crumples it slowly into his fist. She nods toward the exit, a silent plea to leave, but Massimo shakes his head.

And so, they stay, doing what they can to ignore the threats that continue to rain down from above as the film's Jewish lead is eventually sentenced to death for raping a Christian girl. When the curtain finally closes, the audience erupts in deafening cheers. Massimo stands. He reaches for his coat.

"Let's go," he says, his voice low.

They exit the building quickly, chins tucked into their coat collars, avoiding eye contact with the patrons around them. They don't speak until they're several blocks from the theater.

"Unbelievable," Massimo says, tugging at his tie to loosen it.

"Two years ago it would have been, maybe," Lili says. "Now . . ."

Massimo looks up, as if for an explanation, and Lili follows his gaze, staring at the night sky, thick with stars, tiny white pricks of light. The universe, once again, beautiful. Oblivious. "I'm so sorry," he says. "I had no idea."

"Of course you didn't." Lili loops her arm through his. "All of this . . . it's only temporary," she says. "Remember?"

Massimo looks down at her, cracks a reluctant smile. "Come on," he says. "Let's get home and put this night behind us."

LILI WAKES EARLY THE NEXT MORNING AND SLIPS into her mother's silk dressing gown, which she keeps in her closet for when she's home. She pads to the kitchen, pours herself a glass of water, then surveys the pantry, hoping her father still has a store of coffee. Last week, the owner of her favorite café in Ferrara told her his supply would soon be depleted. Normally, Marco would treat Lili to a little gift when she was there. **Un regalo**, he'd say, setting a **cannolo** or **crostata** at her table with a playful wink. But her last visit was different. **No cornetti today**, Marco sighed as Lili ordered her cappuccino at the bar. **Not enough flour. The army is taking most of our supplies. Pretty soon I'll be out of coffee too. I'll have to get creative to keep myself in business.** Lili assured him she'd drink whatever concoction he invented.

Massimo's shelves are spare, but his coffee tin, Lili is relieved to find, is a quarter full. She opens it and brings it to her nose, inhaling its rich spiced chocolate scent. Reaching for the Bialetti, she unscrews its base and fills it with water, then spoons two mounds of finely ground beans into the funnel and twists the top back on, setting the pot on the stovetop to boil. While she waits, she looks around, comforted by the familiar space—the old oak slab next to the sink with its checkerboard knife marks; the basil plant in the window; the shelf over the stove, home to a dozen mismatched espresso cups, collected from her parents' travels. When her gaze lands on her mother's recipe tin, she slides it to her and flips slowly through its contents, removing three thick, cream-colored note cards. Her mother's cursive is loose, effortless. **Spaghetti carbonara. Baked eggplant parmigiana. Sweet almond babà sponge cake.** Nostalgia washes over her, and Lili's stomach growls. She tucks the cards back into the box, vowing to someday learn to cook like her mother could, once provisions are again plentiful.

"**Buon giorno.**"

Lili looks up to find Massimo in the doorframe. His hair is tousled, his eyes still heavy with sleep. He kisses Lili's cheeks.

"**Buon giorno**, Papà."

"You look like your mother in that robe."

Lili smiles. "I'll take that as a compliment."

"It is. Sleep well?"

"I did, for a change." There's something about Lili's room, her old bed, that knocks her out, every time. She extinguishes the flame under the coffee maker.

"I thought we could walk the long way to the cemetery today," Massimo says, plucking two espresso cups from the shelf and setting them on the counter. "Through the Giardini Margherita."

Lili's favorite park. "Yes, let's."

THE MORNING IS COOL. THE SHOPS—THOSE STILL in business—are just opening, the street sounds swelling with the creaks of metal grates being lifted, the scratch of straw on cobblestone as doorsteps are swept clean. They enter the park and Lili absorbs the sights: the cedar tree whose low, twisted branch she'd climbed countless times as a child; the small pond, home to a family of stoic swans, their reflections marbled on the water beneath them; the catchy tune of a fiddler playing up ahead, an old fedora propped in front of him. Massimo places a few lire in the hat as they pass, and they walk on until they've reached the park's main square beside the Observatory. There, they buy a bouquet of calla lilies at a flower stand, arriving twenty minutes later at the tall brick entrance of the cemetery.

"Here we are," Massimo says.

They walk silently along a pebbled path toward Naomi's plot, and as they near, Lili's chest fills with a familiar, hollow ache. Four years. Some days it feels longer. Others, it's as if no time has passed at all. Her grief has ebbed since her mother's death, but there are times, still, when the emptiness sets in and the ground beneath her feels unsteady, as if she's just stepped off a boat and her equilibrium is shaky.

They slow to a stop at Naomi's plot. A simple granite headstone reads:

Naomi Giuliana Passigli
1885-1937
Beloved Wife and Mother

Below that, her favorite saying: **To live is to dream.**

Vivere è sognare

Massimo hands the bouquet to Lili. "Go ahead."

Lili kneels. She props the flowers carefully against the grave. Her throat closes as she presses her hand to the stone, its gray marble cold and smooth against her palm. **I miss you, Mama.** When she stands, she and her father take their usual places on a stone bench across the path.

It's quiet in the cemetery. They are the only visitors, save for a restless sparrow, branch-hopping in a cypress overhead.

"You're wearing the necklace she gave you," Massimo says.

Lili reaches for the pendant, rubs it between her fingers. "I was wondering if you'd notice."

She was home from university when her mother asked her, despite her protests, to fetch her jewelry box. Naomi's hands shook as she pulled the delicate gold chain from its velvet sack. **This one is special**, she said, dropping the necklace into Lili's palm. Lili hadn't seen it before. **My mother brought it back for me from Jerusalem.** Lili vaguely recalled the story of how her maternal grandparents, whom she'd never met, had traveled with a group of friends to the holy city before the Great War. **It's a coin, see?** her mother said. **The flower is the blossom of an almond tree. A symbol of hope. Wear this, my love, when you need a lift.**

Lili leans into her father, rests her head on his shoulder. He never talks about the void Naomi left behind in his life, but she knows it must be impossibly deep. She isn't an expert on marriage, or love—at least, she's never been in love—but what her parents shared was profound, of this much she's certain. Theirs was a quiet kind of love, constant as a river current. She could hear it in their gentle exchange of words, could see it in the way Naomi tilted her head when Massimo was talking so he knew he was being heard, in the way Massimo watched her go about her business from across the room, his eyes filled with affection.

"It gets a little easier in some ways, as the years pass," Lili says after a while. "But I miss her so much still."

Massimo takes her hand. His fingers are warm to the touch, as they always are. "So do I, Babá. So do I."

CHAPTER THREE

FERRARA

April 1941

A re you sure you want to hold him?" Esti asks, buttoning her blouse. "There's a good chance he'll spit up on you."

Theo, four months old, is propped on Esti's lap, his head at her knees. He looks up at his mother, eyes half-mast in a post-feed stupor. He eats on a civilized schedule now and sleeps through the night, and as a result, Esti has regained her sanity.

Lili's weekend bag is propped in the doorway. She and Esti are set to leave in an hour for a quick getaway to the beach. "I have plenty of spare clothes," she says. "And I don't mind a little spit-up."

"Well then, he's all yours."

Esti drapes a quilted cotton cloth on Lili's shoulder and passes Theo over. Lili cradles his head in the palm of one hand, his torso in the other, and brings him to her chest, feeling the weight of his cheek, the down of his hair against her collarbone. She pats his back to coax a burp from him, his malted-milk scent as inebriating as a glass of brandy.

"You can be more assertive than that." Esti laughs. "He won't break."

Lili pats a little harder, rubs a circle in the tiny space between his shoulder blades.

Theo's been winning the hearts of everyone he meets, friends and strangers alike, with his mother's deep-blue eyes and his father's wide, dimpled grin. Every few days, he learns something new. Most recently he's discovered that with enough effort, he can roll himself from his belly onto his back—after which he flaps his arms and legs in celebration, babbling with satisfaction.

Theo lets out a loud belch, and Lili feels his stomach soften. She lifts him overhead, triumphant. He laughs, and a spool of drool spills onto Lili's lap.

"Excuse you!" Lili says, nestling him into the curve of her elbow. She dabs his lips, then at her skirt, with a corner of the burp cloth.

"Sorry," Esti says, wrinkling her nose.

"No apologies. I volunteered for this."

Esti gives one of Theo's earlobes a gentle tug. "You love your Aunt Lili, don't you, **amore**."

"Especially after a feed," Lili says. Theo looks from his mother to Lili and then to his hands, staring at them wide-eyed. "Wait until you find your toes," Lili teases.

Theo claps his hands and Lili wonders how old

he'll be before he meets his grandparents. Esti had hoped to visit Rhodes last month to introduce Theo to her family, but travel is impossible now with another front of the war raging, this one between Italy and Greece. Tensions between the two countries are high. **Is the world trying to tell us we should be enemies?** Esti had mused at first, though the humor subsided when Hitler ramped up his troops in the Balkans, making a German attack on Greece seem imminent.

With a trip to Greece on hold, Esti suggested a weekend with Lili at the beach. **I'm desperate to get my feet in the sand**, she said. Lili jumped at the idea, booking them a room at a resort in Rimini where she and her parents used to holiday. Niko agreed to stay home with Theo, and Esti stockpiled enough milk through the black market to last him a few days.

"You sure Niko will be all right on his own?" Lili asks.

"I'm sure. It'll do him good."

Lili glances at Esti. Niko was out a lot before Theo was born; now, she's lucky to cross paths with him once in a week. She's wanted to ask about his strange absences but hasn't had the courage to do so. "Is everything okay with Niko, Es?" she ventures.

"What do you mean?"

"I don't know, I just feel like he's hardly around anymore."

Esti pauses, and Lili can see in the tight curve of her lips that it's a sensitive subject. "He's been busy."

"I don't mean to pry—" Lili starts, but Esti interrupts her.

"No, no, it's all right. I didn't want to say anything yet," Esti says. "He's been . . . trying to figure a way to move his family to Italy. He found an organization helping Jews cross the border. It's called Delasem."

Lili's heard of the group, the Delegation for the Assistance of Jewish Emigrants.

"Oh." Lili tries to mask the hurt in her voice. Why hadn't Esti told her sooner? "I had no idea."

"He's been discreet about it. And now with the fighting in Greece, it's all a mess. He's still determined to sort something. It's just . . . a lot more complicated."

"I'm sure," Lili concedes. But why, she ponders, would Niko want to move his family to Italy **now**, when foreign Jews without student exemptions like Esti's and Niko's are being incarcerated in the south—or forced to live **al confino**, under house arrest in small villages where they're forbidden to hold jobs and required to check in daily with the local authorities? Even if they could make it safely onto Italian soil, how would they be allowed to stay without visas? Would they need to hide?

"I thought Delasem was helping to get Jewish refugees **out** of Italy, not in," she says.

"For the most part they are. But Niko's gotten close with one of their correspondents, who seems to think he can help. We'll see."

A key rattles in the apartment door, and Niko emerges a moment later from the hallway, his knees streaked with dirt.

Esti stands to kiss his cheeks. "Hello, handsome."

Niko flops down next to Lili on the couch, and Theo smiles when he sees him, punching at the air. "Practicing your boxing again, I see, little man. Fierce one, aren't you?" Niko growls, baring his teeth, and Theo burbles, delighted.

"How was the game?" Esti asks.

It's the first warm Saturday in April, and as Jews are no longer allowed at the tennis club, Niko and a few friends had organized a game of pickup football at the Botanical Gardens.

"Muddy. But fun," Niko says, then adds, "Your boyfriend was there," winking at Lili.

Lili's cheeks warm. "Daniel is not my boyfriend."

Niko grins. "Depends who you ask."

A few weeks before, Niko and Esti had arranged a double date with Lili and one of Niko's friends from university. They'd met for dinner. Daniel is from Poland, staying on in Italy with Esti's and Niko's same student exemption. Lili had seen him a few times before on campus, had found him good-looking in an understated sort of way. They got along well at that first dinner. Daniel walked her home and kissed her goodnight, and Lili went to bed thinking how long it had been since she'd taken interest in a boy, how nice it had felt to be kissed. They'd met twice since then, for a movie and for a walk and a picnic on the **bastioni**, where they shared stories about their studies, their travels, their childhoods, and where Daniel confided in Lili his anxiety about his family back in his hometown of Lodz. Lili had listened with alarm as he spoke of how his parents and two young sisters were evicted from their home and forced to live in a walled-off Jewish quarter. A ghetto.

"Are you excited for your boys' weekend?" Lili asks Niko, eager to change the subject.

"We sure are," Niko says. He scoops Theo from her arms and stands, spinning him around in a circle.

LILI AND ESTI ARRIVE IN RIMINI JUST BEFORE SUN-set, in a borrowed convertible Alfa Romeo. They'd spent the first half of the drive motoring east toward Porto Garibaldi, the second with the radio blaring, pelting out the lyrics to Carlo Buti and Alberto Rabagliati hits as they sped south down the coast to on-again, off-again views of the blue-green Adriatic. By the time they pull into the circular drive of the Grand Hotel, their throats are dry and their hair a mess, but they don't mind. They're on vacation.

A bellman approaches, opens Lili's door, and greets her warmly as she steps out of the car. Underfoot, square gray paving stones align at perfect right angles, giving Lili a welcome sense of order. She takes a long, slow breath, savoring the salt-infused air, its familiar scent transporting her immediately to her childhood. Rimini's long, sandy shoreline is dotted every hundred meters or so with rows of parasols in red and yellow and green, depending on the hotel that owns them. Lili's family used to spend two weeks every summer at the Grand Hotel, until Naomi became too sick to travel, and without discussing it, their holidays in Rimini quietly ceased. Tomorrow, Lili decides, she'll wake early, as her parents used to, to claim a couple of chairs close to the water.

"I don't think I can wait," Esti says. "Let's go get our feet wet." She turns to the bellman. "Would you mind holding our bags in the lobby?"

Within minutes, Lili and Esti are barefoot in the sand, their blouses ballooning behind them in a steady breeze. They spread their arms and jog to the water's edge, leaping as the waves break at their toes, and then gather up their skirts and wade through the shallow surf, letting the cold splash up their shins.

"I feel better already," Esti says, tilting her head back and closing her eyes.

Lili threads her arm through Esti's. "Me too."

They watch the gulls ride the wind, taking turns to dive-bomb the sea. Esti cheers when one of them surfaces with a minnow pinned in its beak. Lili had packed her bathing suit and wonders now if she'll be brave enough to swim. The days have grown warmer since the start of spring, but the water is chilly. They could have waited until summer to come, though with everything in constant flux, Lili had figured it was better to book now. It's nice, she decides, to have the beach to themselves.

She spots a flat, round stone and picks it up, turns, and side-arms it into the sea as her father had taught her to when she was little. It skips four times before disappearing into the blue abyss beneath it.

"Impressive," Esti says, an eyebrow raised. She glances over her shoulder toward the hotel. "I'm hungry. Let's shower, have a bite at the bar. We can watch the sunset and pretend all's right in the world."

"THE NAME IS PASSIGLI," LILI TELLS THE CLERK behind the check-in desk.

"Certainly." The clerk smiles politely. "Could I bother you for your identification card?"

Lili slides her ID across the counter. "I called ahead to reserve the room," she says.

The clerk picks up the card, hesitates. "I'm . . . so sorry, Miss Passigli," he says, his smile suddenly strained. He pushes her ID back to her, motioning the bellman over. "As it turns out, we're full tonight."

"What? That's impossible," Lili says.

The clerk shifts his weight. "Again, I'm terribly sorry." He whispers something to the bellman, who disappears, then returns a moment later carrying Lili's and Esti's suitcases.

"Wait—there must be some confusion," Lili pleads.

But the clerk shakes his head. "I'm afraid not."

Behind her, Lili hears Esti laugh. "Unbelievable," she mutters, and suddenly Lili knows. The hotel isn't full. They're just not welcome. A small part of her had worried that they'd be turned away—there were public parks and private clubs closed now to Jews—but the Grand Hotel was **her** hotel. It catered to a Jewish clientele.

"This is ridiculous," Lili says. "My family's been coming here for twenty years."

The manager of the resort used to greet Lili's parents personally when they arrived. She racks her memory for his name, whispering it to herself as it comes to her. **Arturo.** "I'd like to speak to your manager," she says. "Where is Arturo?"

"Arturo doesn't work here any longer."

Of course. Arturo was Jewish. Heat rises up Lili's neck. How could she possibly sway this man? She could offer him some lire. Ask to speak with the new manager. But she knows her money, her words, are worthless. All that matters to him is the red stamp on her identification card. Beside her, Esti picks up a newspaper from the corner of the concierge's desk, the latest issue of **La Vita Italiana**. The headline at the top reads: BEWARE OF THE JEWS IN OUR HOME.

Lili glances through the glass doors, where their car is still parked, its trunk open, their luggage already stowed back inside. She returns her ID to her purse.

Esti moves to stand beside Lili. "We've come all

this way, **signore**," she tells the clerk. "What possible harm would it do to honor our reservation and take our money?"

"It's not my decision to make, Miss," the clerk says.

"Whose decision **is** it exactly?" Esti asks, her tone sharp.

The clerk tenses. "I already told Miss Passigli—"

"I heard exactly what you told her."

"I'm sorry, but—"

"But what? Show me the law that prevents us from being guests here."

The clerk stands a little straighter. "It's hotel policy," he says evenly. "You need to leave."

"Oh, I see!" Esti feigns surprise. "You've been brainwashed, like the rest of them. Do you think that makes you a better Italian? A better Christian? I feel sorry for you."

A pair of well-dressed middle-aged women appear in the lobby. Lili takes Esti's arm. "It's okay," she says softly. "This is my fault."

Esti shakes her head. "It's not your fault. And it is **not** okay. It's preposterous."

The women behind them, who'd been chatting, grow quiet.

The clerk motions to the door. "If you don't leave now, I'll call the police."

"On what grounds?" Esti balks.

"You are disturbing the peace."

Esti glares at the man, leans over his desk. "How do you sleep at night?"

The clerk blanches.

"Your stupid policies may mean something at this particular moment in time, but what do you think's going to happen when the war is over? You think any of your customers who are—**no longer welcome**—will come back? I have news for you, asshole: they won't."

Lili's legs go weak. "All right, enough," she says. "Let's go." She moves toward the hotel entrance, pulling Esti with her.

"To hell with this place," Esti fumes. She's still holding the newspaper. She waves it once overhead then drops it with a flourish into a trash bin by the door.

Lili looks over her shoulder, watches as the women stare, as the clerk reaches for his telephone. "I'll drive," she says once they're outside. She's shaking as she climbs into the Alfa Romeo. She takes a breath, willing her pulse to slow. "You can't do that," she whispers, staring through the windshield.

"Do what? Stand up for what's right?"

"You can't unleash like that."

"You expect me to just—sit back and let them roll over us? Their rules, their policies—it's sickening."

"I agree. But—" She glances inside. The clerk is at his desk, the telephone receiver still to his ear. A siren wails in the distance. **Merda**. They should leave quickly. She turns the ignition key, reaches for the gear shift, and the Alfa Romeo lurches forward. In her rearview mirror, Lili can see the bellman watching them go. Esti rolls down her window as they exit the hotel drive.

"Fucker!" she shouts, waving a fist. Lili steps on the gas.

She drives until the sirens have dissipated.

"You nearly got us both arrested," Lili says.

"He was never going to call the police."

"He had the phone to his ear."

"It was all a show."

"You don't know that. You heard the siren."

"We did nothing wrong, Lili."

"Don't you get it?" Lili cries, no longer able to contain herself. "It doesn't matter who's right and who's wrong! The streets aren't **safe** anymore. People are getting arrested and deported, for much less than shouting a profanity. For stating an opinion. They're getting **beaten**. In public. Last week I watched a pack of boys swarm a rabbi outside the synagogue and pelt him with rocks. The townspeople just watched."

"I'd have murdered them," Esti says.

"Exactly. That's my point."

Esti sets her jaw. "I won't live in a world where I can't speak my mind. I refuse to believe I'm unworthy. I won't raise my **son** to believe he's unworthy. What kind of a life is that?"

"Goddammit, Esti!" Lili slams the steering wheel with her palm, surprising herself, and Esti too. "It's not forever! It's just until all of this blows over. I'm as angry as you are. It's infuriating, what's going on around us. But nothing good will come of ranting about it in public. You have to understand that."

Lili's mind flashes to Esti, at a gelateria, chewing out the owner for not removing the graffiti by the door that read **No Dogs or Jews Allowed**; to Esti cursing at a woman at the table next to theirs at Café Savona when she overheard her claiming the Jews were an **evil race**; to Esti ripping an anti-Semitic poster from the facade of the town hall and tearing it in half as a small crowd of passersby watched.

"Please. Just try, for once, to think before you speak," Lili says. "To temper yourself. If not for your sake or for my sake then for Theo's. He needs you. You aren't just responsible for yourself any longer, Es."

Lili's words land like stones, creating a heavy barrier in the space between her and Esti. Esti stares out her window, and Lili wonders if she should apologize, though she'd meant all of what she said. She could have conveyed it in a kinder way, perhaps, but would Esti have heard her?

They drive in silence. Darkness begins to fall, and still, they don't speak. Lili switches on the car's headlights.

It's not until they're nearing Ferrara that Esti finally says, "I've never been good at keeping my mouth shut. You know this about me."

Lili glances at her, then back at the road. "I know. But you have to try. If you explode on the wrong person . . . it won't end well."

Esti sighs.

"Please tell me you'll try."

"I'll try. It won't be easy though."

Lili feels her grip on the steering wheel soften, the color return to her knuckles. "Thank you," she breathes. "I'm going to hold you to that."

CHAPTER FOUR

FERRARA

September 1941

It's the eve of Rosh Hashanah, a Sunday. Lili rolls a loose thread at the hem of her sleeve between the pads of her thumb and forefinger. She'd agreed to meet Esti and Niko at the synagogue, but they haven't arrived yet and the benches in the women's upstairs gallery are filling quickly. It's not Esti's seat she's worried about though—Lili's coat will do for now to hold it—but the pinch she feels at the base of her gut when she and Niko are late.

Every few days now, there is an incident—a Jew harassed in the street, a new swath of graffiti debasing a shop front. Last week, Lili bumped into an old school friend, Mia, whose older brother, Giorgio, was detained for no apparent reason; a few days later, he disappeared. They won't tell us anything, Mia said of the carabinieri who'd made the arrest, and all Lili could say was I'm so sorry.

Since their fight on the car ride home from Rimini, Esti, at least, has held true to her word, keeping her wits about her in public and airing her grievances only behind closed doors. It's Niko that Lili worries most about now. Not just because he's absent—he's still out all the time—but because when Lili's around him, he's a different person. She noticed the shift in April, when the German army invaded his hometown of Salonica. His parents wrote soon after. Life under Nazi occupation, they said, was unsustainable. To leave was impossible. Niko didn't take this news well. As the weeks passed and the letters from Salonica grew more dire, he retreated into himself. His features darkened. The sound of his laugh became a thing of the past. Now, unless he's bouncing Theo on his knee, he's stopped smiling entirely. He's scared. And angry. Lili's heart aches for him, and for his parents too—she'd met Stella and Otello at Esti and Niko's wedding, can picture them standing misty-eyed beside their son, glasses raised in a toast.

Originally, Niko's plan was to get Delasem to help bring his parents to Italy. Now, he's begun talking about going to Greece himself to retrieve them. This seemed to Lili a terrible idea. The risk involved in crossing into German territory—or out of it, for that matter—felt too great. But others were doing it, Niko argued. Daniel, for one. A few weeks ago, Daniel had told Lili he was leaving for Poland. **My father's been begging me to come home**, he said.

He has a sister in England, he's trying to secure a way out of the ghetto. He needs my help. They both knew it wasn't safe to travel across borders. He promised to write. They'd keep in touch, they said. Lili had written to him once, but she's yet to receive a reply.

She checks her watch. Behind her, the temple balcony is crowded, the benches full; a dozen women now stand at the back. She turns, keeps her eyes down to avoid glares, tells herself not to worry. Niko and Daniel are smart men. And who is she to judge their decisions to try to help their families? Her father is nearby and safe. She's lucky.

"There you are."

Lili looks up at the familiar voice and exhales, reaching for her coat as Esti shuffles toward her. "You made it," she says, tucking the loose thread back into her sleeve.

"Sorry to keep you waiting. Our neighbor offered to watch Theo, but he threw a fit when we tried to leave. Took us forever to calm him down."

"It's okay," Lili says. "Glad you're here."

Below them, the rabbi approaches the bimah and the congregation quiets.

"What a group we have here tonight," the rabbi says, taking a moment to look around at the unusually large gathering. His words, inflected with pride, echo beneath the white, barrel-vaulted ceiling. "These are difficult times, my friends," he continues. "But we are here, together, marking a holy day. Let us move forward as the Prophet Zechariah was called to do, with good will in our hearts. With a sense of unity and purpose. Have faith that God's spirit will bring understanding and justice. Have faith that His spirit will bring peace."

Faith. Purpose. Lili turns the words over in her mind. What do they mean, anymore? Her faith, which she's never questioned, has earned her a stamp on her ID that abolishes most of her rights. And her purpose? It used to be to write. Now it's to get by on a meager salary and her allotted rations. To learn how to disappear on the streets. She's still volunteering at the school, at least—her time spent with the children the most rewarding few hours of her week. **This will pass**, she tells herself, her father's voice ringing in her ears. **Be patient.**

Outside, from somewhere on the street, Lili can hear the muffled sound of shouting. She tilts her head, listening. Around her, women shift in their seats.

"Must be another rally," Esti whispers.

There have been a dozen demonstrations in Ferrara in recent weeks—groups of Fascists preaching about "Il Grande Duce" and the dangers the Jews posed to the country.

The shouting grows closer and the rabbi pauses, glances at the door, then continues, amplifying his voice over the commotion. But he's interrupted again a moment later, this time by the sound of metal striking wood. Lili stiffens. Whoever is outside, she realizes, wants to get in. The congregants a level below turn. The door is locked, Lili reminds herself. It's always locked these days. She's barely finished the thought when a loud **crack!** ricochets through the temple. Lili reaches for Esti's hand as the door crashes open. A band of men explodes into the synagogue, yelling over one another, their voices like thunder: **For the future of Fascism! For the power of the nation! Down with the Jews!**

The women in the gallery begin to shriek. Esti and Lili slip from the bench and push to the rail of the balcony, so they can see what's happening below. The men—there must be a dozen of them—are dressed entirely in black. Lili watches, holding her breath, as they topple the reader's lectern, then rush to the carved black cupboard where the ancient **sefarìm** are kept, pulling the scrolls from shelves and stuffing them into big, burlap bags. The men in the congregation yell; a few chase after the intruders, demanding that they stop, but are silenced when one of the youngest of the gang produces a pistol from beneath his overcoat. He points it at the ceiling, fires a shot. Lili screams. A slab of plaster falls from above. She and Esti drop to their knees, crouched in wait. When there are no more shots, they right themselves slowly. Beneath them, two feral men close in on the rabbi; he's at the bimah still, clutching a railing for support. They seize him by the elbows. Again, the congregation yells out in protest.

"No," Lili whispers. "Please, no."

The rabbi doesn't resist as he's dragged to the broken-in door. And then, as quickly as the intruders had come, they—along with the rabbi—are gone.

Lili and Esti scour the crowd below for Niko. "Can you see him?" Esti cries. But all Lili can make out is a sea of kippah-topped heads, moving in the wake of the mob toward the door.

"I can't."

Sirens howl in the distance. The **carabinieri**. Had they been alerted? Or just heard the commotion? Lili prays they come quickly, then realizes she's fooling herself: it's just as likely the police will be loyal to the mob. It's entirely possible no one is coming to help them.

"I've got to find him," Esti says. They throw on their coats and hurry from the gallery down a spiral staircase, following a throng of women onto the cobblestones of Via Mazzini. The street is narrow, choked with bodies.

"Something's burning," Lili shouts over the din.

She and Esti snake their way through the crowd until they reach a metal trash bin, alight in flames, a pile of scrolls and a Torah from the synagogue beside it. They stand by the burning bin, searching in vain for Niko. When the **carabinieri** arrive a few minutes later, they stride through the crowd with their batons raised, shouting for order. Lili watches, relieved, as a pair of officers extracts the rabbi, shaken, from the mayhem. One of his eyes is swollen but more disconcerting is the shine of his bare, bald head reflected in the light of a streetlamp—Lili has never seen him without his kippah. Another officer stands guard over the plundered artifacts. Several of the items, Lili notices, are intact. But the gang is still roaming the streets, and the **carabinieri,** it appears, have yet to make any arrests.

A scuffling up ahead draws their attention. "This way," Esti says, moving toward the melee.

"It's a fight," Lili realizes as they near, wanting desperately to turn around. But Esti ignores her, pushes on. They stay close to each other, slowing when they reach a crowd gathered in a circle. That's when they spot him.

"Niko!" Esti's voice cuts through the air, but Niko doesn't hear—or chooses not to. "Niko!" she cries again.

Niko is at the center of the circle. His arms are wrapped around something, someone. He's struggling to keep his balance. Esti fights through the crowd, and Lili follows, until they're close enough to see that the body Niko is wrestling belongs to the young boy with the pistol.

"Niko, stop!" Esti screams, and this time Niko turns. He looks at her with fire in his eyes, gives a violent shake of his head, then twists his torso. In an instant, he's on the ground straddling the boy, his knees pressed into his shoulders, a hand around his neck. The boy writhes under Niko's weight, but he's pinned, helpless. With his free hand, Niko fishes through the boy's trench coat, and in Lili's next breath he's holding the pistol. She watches, horrified, as he cocks it with his thumb, presses its black steel barrel to the boy's forehead. **Don't**, she wills. She pinches her eyes shut, bracing for a gunshot. But the only thing she can make out above the clamor is the bellow of Niko's voice, harsher and more guttural than Lili's ever heard it, but distinctly his.

"Who the fuck do you think you are?"

When Lili opens her eyes, the circle is broken, bodies are converged, and Niko is hidden from sight. Three **carabinieri** muscle through the pandemonium, shouting for order, hands on holsters, and the cacophony dims. Onlookers part as the police pull Niko off the boy. One rips the gun from Niko's hand. Another tends to the boy, still sprawled on the ground, blood dripping from his nose onto the collar of his overcoat. The **carabinieri** bark at the crowd, commanding order. The fight is over, but the air is electric, combustible.

"I need to help him," Esti says.

"What? Esti, no."

"I have to."

"Esti! It's not safe. Please!"

"Go to my place. Stay there until we get back." Esti fumbles in her purse, presses a key into Lili's palm.

"Wait a few minutes," Lili protests. "Let everyone calm down a little."

"Lili, I'm not asking. Go. Now."

Esti turns, approaches the officers, speaking first

to them, and then to Niko. Rooted in place, Lili tries to spot the boy, or the others from the band, but they've disappeared. What's stopping them from coming back? Is it safe for her to walk alone? She contemplates waiting. It feels wrong to leave her friends. But Esti will have her head if she stays, and her flat isn't far. She should go now, Lili decides, while the police are still nearby.

She threads her way through the thinning crowd, trying to comprehend what she's just witnessed. The raid. The fight. Niko. How strange he'd sounded, as if his body, his voice, belonged to someone else. How easily his fingers had moved as he cocked the pistol, as if he could have done it in his sleep.

The teeth of Esti's key dig into her palm. She turns down an empty street, looks over her shoulder, but all she can see are shadows. When one of them moves, she picks up her pace, resisting the impulse to run.

CHAPTER FIVE

FERRARA

October 1941

Lili bolts upright, eyes wide, ears straining. She waits, silent, blinking into the darkness. After a few seconds, she hears it again. **Tap-tap-tap-tap.** Someone is at her door. She pulls the chain of her bedside lamp, her breath quick as she squints at her clock. It's not yet six in the morning. Who would come this early? The knocks come again, louder, more persistent. She climbs from her bed and tiptoes silently to the hallway. There, she pauses, a hand on the wall to steady herself. She could pretend she's not home, she thinks. She stands, frozen in place, waits. And then, a voice.

"Lili, it's me!"

Lili's hand slides down the wall. Esti.

"Coming!"

She fumbles with the deadlock and a second later

Esti steps inside, Theo asleep in her arms. Lili closes the door, locks it behind them.

"What is it, Es? What's wrong?" Esti's eyes are filled with tears. She's never seen her friend so disheveled.

"It's Niko. He's gone."

Lili's mind turns to the synagogue brawl three weeks ago. She'd nearly fainted with relief when Esti and Niko finally returned home that evening. Esti was too upset to talk about what had happened, though, and Niko simply raised a hand when he saw the worried look on Lili's face, then retreated to the bedroom. They've barely spoken of the incident since. Meanwhile, the artifacts that escaped the fire after the raid were returned, the temple restored, though the ceiling still bore a crater where the bullet struck it. No arrests were made, no apologies issued. Niko had come out of the night unscathed, thank goodness, but he'd identified himself as a resister, attracted the attention of the **carabinieri**. Lili's wondered every day since whether the police would show up at his door.

"What do you mean, **gone**?" Lili manages. "Was he arrested?"

"No. He left. Of his own accord. An hour ago."

"Where did he go?"

"To Bari. By train."

"What?"

"He's hoping from there he can sail to Greece—if he can find passage. To his family."

"In Salonica."

"Yes." Esti looks pained. "He'd begun making arrangements to leave in two weeks. . . . I was going to tell you once they were firm. But then the **carabinieri** came last night, with a warrant for his arrest, and—"

"Because of the fight?"

"They accused him of being a communist."

"That's ridiculous."

"I know."

"But they didn't arrest him."

"He wasn't home when they came. They said they'd be back. I nearly lost my mind waiting for him to return to the flat. When he did, we stayed up all night talking about what to do. In the end we decided it was best for him to leave right away."

Theo squirms, opens his eyes, and Esti startles, as if she'd forgotten she was holding him. Lili moves closer, and when Theo sees her, he reaches for her and she lets him wrap a hand around her finger.

"Hello, angel," she says.

"I knew Niko would go eventually," Esti says, looking down at Theo. "He had to. You've seen him. He hasn't been himself for months. And then with the fight . . ."

"It was so unlike him," Lili says.

"It was. He said himself he didn't understand what came over him. But I understood. He was enraged. Over the raid, the news from home. My parents' reports from Rhodes are mild in comparison. The island isn't occupied. But the situation in Salonica . . . his parents are desperate. I can't imagine the torture of it. Part of me doesn't blame him for exploding."

Lili nods. She can't fathom how it would feel to receive such news from her own father.

"He was so relieved when we finally decided he should make the trip home," Esti says. "He seems certain he can help his parents find a way out of Greece, that he can bring them here. I didn't want him to go, of course . . ." She pauses. Her eyes fill with tears. "But who was I to ask him not to?"

"You had to let him go, Es. You did the right thing."

"I keep telling myself so. But then he left and now our flat feels so sad and empty. I had to get out."

"I'm glad you came," Lili says.

IN THE LIVING ROOM, LILI MOTIONS FOR ESTI to have a seat on the sofa. "Do you think he'll go back to sleep if you put him down?" she asks, glancing at Theo.

"Let's try."

Lili arranges two pillows and a throw blanket on the floor. "Here," she says. She takes Theo from Esti's arms.

Esti pulls a small knit lamb from her purse. "This will help him sleep," she says. Theo smiles as he takes it, brings it to his cheek, then holds it out for Lili to see.

"For me?" Lili asks, reaching for the lamb, but Theo retracts his arm, a game of keep away. Lili eyes him. "I didn't think so." She rocks him for a few minutes, then kneels and lays him down on the makeshift bed, tucking the blanket tight around him like a swaddle. Theo makes a cooing sound but doesn't protest. A few minutes later, he's asleep.

Lili moves to sit by Esti, curling her legs under herself.

"You're so good with him," Esti says.

"I don't know about that."

"You are."

"I just try to copy what you do."

Esti shakes her head. "I don't know if you should look to me as a role model. Sometimes I don't feel fit to be a mother."

"Stop that. No one's more capable."

The friends are quiet. Lili chews her lip. "Salonica is occupied," she says after a while. "How will Niko manage?"

Esti's shoulders rise and fall as she takes a breath, then another. She picks at a cuticle, considering her words. Lili sits up straighter.

"You know the group I told you about, that Niko's been working with?"

"Delasem?"

"That one. Well, the organization is technically backed by the regime. Ironic, right? Mussolini's interning Jewish foreigners on Italian soil, but his government supports a program whose goal is to help those same people cross into and out of the country. It doesn't make any sense." Esti pauses and Lili agrees. It does seem backward. "Niko's been trying to figure out how the organization might stay of service if . . . well, more like **when** Mussolini shuts them down," Esti says.

"Okay . . ."

"I didn't want to pull you into this, because I didn't want to put you in danger."

"Pull me into what? If Delasem is still function-ing legally, why would that pose any danger?"

Esti takes another long breath. "Well, that's the thing," she says, exhaling. "Some of the members are going underground."

"Underground."

"The government's so-called assistance is evapo-rating, and there's only so much they can do with a dwindling budget. This group that Niko's with . . . they believe the best way to get Jews across the bor-der is with the right papers."

"What do you mean **the right papers**?"

Esti is silent.

"Aryan papers?"

Esti looks pleadingly at Lili. "Please don't be mad."

Lili sorts the details, trying to catch up. "Is that how Niko's traveling to Greece? With false papers?"

Esti nods. "We've made documents for his family too."

"We?" Lili shakes her head. "Esti, what's going on?"

Esti swallows. "I'm sorry. I thought about telling

you so many times. When they found out I was a photographer, that I had a camera and access to a darkroom, and that I could take a good head shot, they asked me to help."

"To help make false IDs."

"I know it's dangerous, what we're doing. I don't take it lightly. But I made the choice to be a part of something, Lili, and I didn't want to put that on you. I told myself the less you knew, the better."

Lili looks down. Fragments of memories rearrange themselves in her mind, as the last few months begin to make sense.

"Say something," Esti pleads.

"How did Niko learn to fight like that?"

Esti scrunches up her brow. "What do you mean?"

"Outside the synagogue. The way he wrestled that boy to the ground, took a pistol to his head."

Esti looks at her lap, then back at Lili. "He wanted to be prepared to resist, when the time came," she says. "He's been training to be ready for whatever's in store for us."

Lili shakes her head. "Esti, the risks . . ."

"I know, believe me, Lili, but—"

"We can be arrested for **owning a radio**. For publishing our names in the phone directory. For placing an obituary in the paper! If Niko's caught carrying falsified IDs—if you're caught helping—"

"We've been careful. Painfully so."

Lili crosses her arms. "How many IDs have you made?"

"I don't know, a lot. I've lost count. I made one for myself, and I'm making one for you. Theo too."

"Why would I need an Aryan ID?" Lili asks. "We have no rights here in Italy, but we're allowed to live openly as Jews. Our lives aren't at risk.

"Not yet," Esti says. "Things are getting worse. I know it feels sustainable at the moment, but look at what's happening in Greece. In France. In all of eastern Europe. The sealed off Jewish quarters, the labor camps. Hitler's a madman. He's turned his back on Stalin—what will he do next? Everyone says he'll be stopped, but by whom?" Esti's cheeks begin to flush. Her words come quickly. "Think about it, Lili. Who do the Jews have on their side in Italy? Hitler and Mussolini are allies. Do you really think Il Duce will put up a fight when Hitler decides to throw **us** into the ghetto?"

"We have the pope," Lili says, though the argument feels weak. What has the pope done thus far to protect the right of his country's Jews?

"The **pope**? His only concern is not to upset his Catholic flock in Germany. The writing's on the wall, Lili. We need a safety net. We need IDs. A way out."

Lili blinks, absorbing this. Since the onset of the Racial Laws, her greatest fear has been that if Esti's graduate-school loophole was discovered, she'd be deported back to Greece. Was Esti right to expect the worst? "Esti, I . . ."

"I need your help," Esti says.

Lili blinks.

"There are secret meetings. Niko used to be the one to go, and he'd report back, bring home supplies. He asked last night if I would take his place while he's away, and I'd like to. But I've got Theo, and . . . the hours are strange." Esti pauses, licks her lips. She glances at Theo. "What if we moved in with you for a while, Lili? You could help with Theo in the evenings, and I wouldn't have to worry about the police returning to our flat in search of Niko. I'd be careful never to leave a trail to here, and I can support us. I've got some savings."

Lili's stomach turns as she considers what Esti is telling her, asking of her. Niko is gone. Esti is secretly forging IDs. And now she wants to move in with her. The thought of sharing an apartment with her best friend again is appealing, sure. But wouldn't living together make Lili complicit in whatever this thing was that Esti was involved in? Was she willing to take that risk? Never mind the thought of tending to Theo—she adores him, but she's no mother. Is she even capable of caring for a ten-month-old? The danger, the unknowns, are paralyzing. "I don't know, Esti."

Esti scoots closer to her on the sofa, so their knees are touching. "I know it's a lot to ask. But I can't be alone right now in that apartment. I'll go mad. And I don't think it's safe."

Lili gazes at her lap as she tries to think. Across town, a clock tower rings out, emitting six somber tolls. Lili looks up, meets Esti's eye. "Is there anything else you haven't told me?" She's been kept in the dark, and her feelings are hurt and part of her wants Esti to know this. "Be honest."

"Lili I . . . I haven't **lied** to you, just omitted some things. For your sake."

"Esti, come on. Since when are we not open with each other?"

Esti brings her hands to Lili's knees. Lili sighs, uncrosses her arms, lets her hands fall into Esti's.

"You're right," Esti says. "It's not who we are. And no, there's nothing else."

"You promise?"

"I promise."

"And from here on?"

"Full transparency. I'll tell you everything."

Lili feels herself softening. "Okay." She says the word quickly, so she doesn't change her mind.

Esti's eyes widen. "Really?"

"Really."

"Oh, Lili. That's—thank you!" She pulls her into a hug and Lili submits, letting her forehead rest on Esti's shoulder.

"I love you," Esti says into Lili's hair.

"I love you too."

CHAPTER SIX

FERRARA

September 1942

A Saturday evening, early fall. Ferrara is in full flower, the honeyberry trees dotting the city's stone walls thick with leaves, the gardens teeming with pink bergenia. Shop windows display mannequins in utilitarian dresses and wide-brimmed felt hats, and the streets are alive with women and children walking hand in hand, with old men pedaling their single-speed bikes along the cobblestones. Normally, Lili would bask in the change of season. She'd spend the evening on her sofa, perhaps, with the windows open, a record playing, or at an outdoor café with a favorite book in hand. Tonight, though, she's too antsy to sit, her mind consumed with the fact that Esti, who'd gone out hours ago with Theo for rations, hasn't yet returned. She should be back by now.

They're fine, she tells herself. **They're fine**. Her new mantra.

Almost a year has passed since Niko left Ferrara and Esti and Theo moved in. In that time, Hitler has gained momentum in the war at a terrifying pace, dropping a torrent of bombs on England and Northern Ireland, battling the British for control of northern Africa, and in what the papers were calling the bloodiest front of the war, invading its one-time ally, the Soviet Union. The fighting across the globe has escalated as well, thanks to a Japanese attack on a naval base in Hawaii, spurring the United States to enter the war on the side of the Allies.

So far, somehow, the Italian peninsula has still seen no fighting. Life's gone on. Lili has kept a low profile, spending her days at the orchid garden and teaching at the synagogue, her nights watching over Theo when Esti is out—a rather easy task it turns out, as most evenings he's asleep by seven. Her job pays little, but Esti has stayed true to her promise to support them with her savings and with a stipend from Delasem, and Massimo sends a small money order every month as well. They're hungry—rations are strict—but they're getting by.

It was March when a letter finally arrived from Niko in Salonica. Esti wept with relief, for in the months of his silence, she'd begun to fear the worst. But her husband was alive; he'd made it to Greece. He was with his family, Niko wrote. His father, however, was ill. They would try to return to Italy as soon as Otello was well enough. **Please, stay where you are**, he signed off; **you are better off there. Send me some good news. And a photo of my dear boy.**

Esti writes to Niko every few days, and in the meantime, in his absence, she's doubled down on her commitments to the underground, often staying out past midnight in order to meet a growing demand for IDs. She's careful, she insists, but still, Lili worries. Ferrara is a small city. If Esti is churning out papers at the rate she says she is, how clandestine could the enterprise be? How long before someone discovers what's happening and reports Esti, or follows her back to the flat? Lili keeps a brave face most days—it's Esti who's putting herself on the line every day, after all—but her nerves have begun to fray. It doesn't help that Esti's student visa has expired, that she's living illegally in Italy now, with nothing but her false ID keeping the authorities at bay. Nor does it help that Mussolini's presence is felt more than ever in Ferrara. His portrait is mounted on every corner, his propaganda force-fed through all possible avenues, his anthem blasted on loudspeakers from windows: **Se avanzo seguitemi. Se indietreggio uccidetemi. Se mi uccidono vendicatemi!** If I advance, follow me. If I retreat, kill me. If they kill me, avenge me.

IT'S DARK WHEN ESTI AND THEO FINALLY RETURN to the flat.

"I was worried," Lili says, taking a small bag of turnips from Esti so she can deposit Theo onto a chair at the kitchen table. Lili senses that they've come from one of Esti's covert meetings, not from the market. Her hunch is confirmed when Esti sits, her expression serious, motioning for Lili to join her.

"We have to talk," she says.

Lili lowers herself tentatively onto the chair across from Esti's. "Tell me."

Esti props her elbows on the table. "There's an abandoned villa south of here housing Jewish children. Refugees. Delasem has asked me to go, to help settle them, and to make them IDs in case they need to cross again into German-occupied territory."

"Refugee children?"

"Yes. Orphans, mostly. We believe their parents were either killed or sent away."

"Where are they from?"

"All over. Germany. Austria. Poland. They were hidden first in Yugoslavia but had to run when Hitler invaded. They crossed the mountains of Slovenia on foot and were smuggled into Italy by train."

"So they're fugitives."

"Exactly."

Between them, Theo traces an index finger in the shape of a circle around a water mark left on the table. He will be two in December.

"They have no one, Lili. All I can think about is, what if it were my own son, orphaned in a foreign country . . ." Esti nods, as if reaffirming her decision in her mind. "I have to go."

Lili stares at Esti, her thoughts churning. She can barely comprehend what it's like for Jews in German-occupied Europe. A month ago, she'd received a single letter from Daniel—he'd made it back to Lodz and confirmed Lili's assumption that life in the ghetto was miserable. **There's barbed wire and disease and starvation,** he said. **And rumors now of entire populations being sent to forced labor camps in the east.** Lili had replied right away—**Have you been able to reach your aunt in England?** she asked—but the letters have stopped. She hates to think that Daniel and his family could be among the deported.

"How long would you go for?" Lili manages.

"I don't know. Weeks. Maybe months."

"This is so sudden, Es. And—it feels a little crazy."

Esti shakes her head. "What's crazy is that the children all survived. They were nearly captured, twice. Now they're here, and they need our help."

Lili knows that to argue would be futile. She swallows. "When would you go?"

"Tomorrow."

Lili's eyes widen. "Tomorrow?"

"Come with me, Lili."

"What?"

"Please. We have to stay together."

Lili sits back in her chair, processing a now famil-iar predicament—her best friend asking her to take a risk, pushing her past the boundaries of her comfort. Life in Ferrara is monotonous and miserable in many ways, but there is consolation in the routine of it all. She's getting by. Her instinct is to stay put. Wait for the fighting in Europe to be over. The United States has finally come to the aid of the Allies. With all their firepower, surely Hitler will soon be stopped. It feels like only a matter of time.

"Where exactly is this abandoned villa?"

"It's called the Villa Emma. It's in Nonantola, an hour and a half from here, but closer to Bologna. We wouldn't be far from your father."

Lili pulls the sleeves of her sweater down over her hands, balls the hems up in her fists as she ruminates on the idea, contemplating the risks.

"Look." Esti's voice is calm. "We have no way of knowing when the war will be over or how much worse it will get first. In Nonantola, at least, nobody knows us. It's a quiet village, too small for the Fascists to worry about. It's not far. We can return to Ferrara if we need to."

Theo drums the table with his fists, babbling to himself. It makes sense for Esti to go, Lili realizes. Her presence in Italy is against the law now, and while she's not officially traceable to Lili's address, the authorities know her face from the incident with Niko. If she's safer in Nonantola, Theo will be too. Perhaps, Lili admits, the change of scenery would be good for all of them. She'd be close to her father—this much appeals.

"What about my flat?" she asks.

"We can sublet it," Esti says quickly, sensing an opening. "Save some money. My colleagues have already found us a place to stay, not far from the villa. It's big enough for the three of us."

"The three of us."

"Always," Esti says.

Lili looks at Esti. "It sounds like your decision's already been made."

"Come with us, Lili. I need you."

"You don't need me."

"I do."

Lili takes a long, slow breath. "Dammit, Esti," she says as she exhales, but her tone is soft.

Esti tilts her head back and laughs, and the sound is like sunshine.

LILI SPENDS THE REST OF THE EVENING ARRANGING and rearranging her belongings into piles on her bed—skirts, sweaters, pants, blouses, shoes, socks, and undergarments, her cotton dressing robe. A silver boar-bristle hairbrush, a small velvet pouch containing a few pieces of jewelry, a fountain pen and some stationery, a book of photos. It's nearly ten when she steps away, surveying her work. Not wanting to draw attention to their plan, she and Esti had decided to pack only the essentials. But figuring what to bring was exhausting—one sweater or two? A lightweight jacket or her warmest winter coat? She'll dress in layers when they make the trip tomorrow. She'll wear two shirts and two pairs of underwear and her winter shoes; but still, there is too much.

Lili reaches for her photo album, runs her fingers over the gold-embossed initials on the cover, her mother's. The book makes a cracking sound as she opens it. Inside, the thick black pages smell of must and cedarwood. She flips through them, pausing at an image of herself as a baby, nestled into the crook of her mother's arm, eyes alert. Her mother is peering down at her with gentle poise, a languid smile. **Oh, Mama. What a time we're in.** Lili slips the picture from its mount, sets it aside, pulls four more from the album. These five, she decides, will come with her.

Retrieving her valise from under her desk, she opens it at the foot of her bed, cringing at the size of its cavity. **Only the practical things**, she reminds herself, removing a dress, chartreuse green, with a fold-over collar and flutter sleeves—the one Esti had picked out for her to wear to dinner the night before her wedding in Greece. She brings the dress to her nose, burying herself in the cloth, and the faint scent of Esti's lavender perfume sparks a memory.

They were seated at a rooftop restaurant on the water in Rhodes, Lili and Esti opposite each other, the table piled with platters of grilled squid and lobster pappardelle, baskets of thick-crusted bread, and shallow bowls of olive oil as green as sea grass.

Overhead, the night sky was velvet black, pricked white with constellations. Esti's father, Lazar, had just made a toast. **To my beautiful, stubborn, big-hearted daughter, and to Niko, whom I am proud to call my son. Here's to a future as bright as the stars.** Glasses were raised to a chorus of l'chaims and **saluts**, and when Lili looked across the table, she found Esti smiling at her, a hand outstretched, palm down on the tablecloth between them. Lili laughed. She'd told Esti once that at mealtimes, her mother liked to slide a hand toward hers, an invitation for Lili to lay her own on top. Often Massimo would follow suit, sandwiching Lili's palm between his and Naomi's. It was a small thing, and Lili used to roll her eyes at the sappiness of it, but Esti found the gesture so endearing, she took up the habit herself. Lili's eyes were damp as she reached across the table, resting her hand atop Esti's, and the two were still for a moment, candlelight dancing across their faces.

The memory lingers as Lili moves to her closet, hangs up the dress. She'd do anything to go back to that moment—when food was plentiful; when outfits were chosen for fun and not for necessity; when her only worry was for an exam or a looming deadline. When she and Esti could sit across the table and simply enjoy each other's company, their futures as bright as the stars.

PART II

CHAPTER SEVEN

NONANTOLA

March 1943

Lili rubs her hands together for warmth. It's been a long winter; she can't shake the numbness in her fingertips. Reaching for her fountain pen, she slides it from its case and unscrews the top, admiring the weight of its mother-of-pearl body. The pen was a graduation gift from her father. She'd planned to visit him in January, but there are rumors now of a German invasion. Travel feels unsafe. And so, she writes.

Every week, she sends a letter, cherishing the replies that come in return, even though she and her father both choose their words carefully to avoid attention by the government, the mail now censored by the authorities. Despite the relentless cold, Massimo said recently, he's managing all right in Bologna. **Settimo and I have taken up the game Rumino—we play** every Sunday—have you played? If not, I'll teach you when I see you next.

Lili wishes she could tell her father the story of Villa Emma. But the subject of the children is off-limits, so she fills her letters instead with details about her life in Nonantola. The town, she told him, is walkable from end to end in minutes, the streets cobbled and quiet, the shops and residential buildings modest. The most impressive of Nonantola's monuments is the towering redbrick Abbey of San Silvestro at its center. The village, she said, is a place where everyone knows everyone. She omitted the fact that, as a newcomer to such a tight-knit community, she feared she would be looked upon as a stranger who couldn't be trusted when she first arrived. That, thankfully, hasn't been the case. The local priest, who works closely with Delasem, introduced Lili and Esti as missionaries sent from the Church to help care for the children at the villa, claiming that Theo himself was an orphan. The story stuck, and the locals, most of whom are peasant farmers or cattle breeders, are friendly. They know of the children at the villa, welcomed them even, with gifts of fruit from the orchards, clothing, and toys. Whether or not they are aware that the children are Jewish is uncertain. **If they know, they haven't said a word,** Esti claims. **I don't think it matters to them.**

When Massimo inquired about her apartment, Lili replied simply that it had everything they needed. In fact, the space is cramped and dark and spare. There's a kitchen with a sink the size of a mixing bowl, a single-burner stove, a rickety side table where they take their meals, and a bedroom with two skinny beds, which Lili and Esti have pushed together so Theo can sleep between them. The living room is just big enough for a love seat and the desk where Lili's seated now, the washroom down the hall, shared with the other boarders. Most nights, there is no hot water.

I miss you, Lili writes. **How are you? We're fine here. Nino is still away** (she never uses their real names). **He says he's managing. Evie and I are working the same job, mending uniforms from the front.** This is a lie, of course, an attempt to come off as patriotic in the eyes of her censors. In reality, Esti spends her days at the villa creating IDs and, when Lili isn't helping with Theo or tutoring the refugee children in reading and writing, she works at a blacksmith's shop in town, holding the horses while they get their hooves trimmed. The job provides her with a little income, and she's found being around the animals—running her hand along the velvet fur on their necks and talking to them gently when they get skittish—to be surprisingly soothing. **Sewing is tedious work, but calming in a way. The true highlight of my day of late though is my time spent with Tito. He is coming into himself, Papà, and it fills me with joy to watch him grow. You should see him, running**

(not walking) now, and showing off a mouthful of teeth whenever he smiles, which he does, often. He still carries around the silver rattle you sent for his birthday. He loves it, and it makes for a fine way to keep track of where he is when we lose sight of him. Esti had taken a photo of Theo on his second birthday, holding his rattle. Lili sent it to Massimo with a description of the celebration they'd had, which was complete with streamers cut from an old newspaper and a chocolate cake the size of a pack of cigarettes, procured from the black market. Please write soon to let me know how you are, Lili concludes. Next week is your birthday—I hate that I won't be there to celebrate with you. She signs off with the obligatory, Vinceremo! We shall conquer! then fastens the top to her pen, folds the letter into thirds.

A door opens and closes in the foyer, followed by the quick drum of footsteps in the hallway. A moment later, Theo bolts into the room.

"Zia!" he calls, stumbling into Lili's arms and smelling of winter and wool. He hasn't mastered his l's yet, so for now he affectionately calls her aunt. She wraps him in a hug.

"Did you have a good day, my sweet?" she asks.

Theo nods, his cheeks pink from the cold. He unfolds a mittened hand to reveal a small gray pebble nestled in his palm.

"Wow," Lili says, her tone serious. "That looks special. Who gave it to you?"

"Owber," Theo says.

Lili knows most of the children at Villa Emma by name. Albert is a new arrival. He came to Nonantola a week ago, with a second group of refugees from Croatia. The children number seventy-two now. Lili worries for them, wondering if they're hungry with rations so strict (though she's never heard them complain about an empty stomach), or if they're missing their families. She worries about their parents, too, and what's become of them. But the children seem comfortable at the villa. Happy, even. Lili often spots them mingling with the local children, who seem thrilled to have new playmates in town. In addition to reading and writing, they're offered courses in music and mathematics and philosophy. Once, Lili helped to arrange a visit to the cinema, so they could watch **The Jungle Book**.

An entire staff, mostly volunteers, tends to the children's needs at the villa. Lili has met them all: the town physician and his wife, Doctor and Signora Moreali, who come when a child spikes a fever; Goffredo Pacifici, affectionately nicknamed Chi Chi-Boo, a businessman who left his job to help smuggle the children into Italy; Emilio, the cook, who works magic in the kitchen day after day with his meager allotments of rice, potatoes, and beans. Lili is comforted to know the children are in good hands and in good spirits, despite the circumstances.

"May I hold it?" Lili asks, gesturing to the pebble in Theo's hand.

Theo shakes his head. "**Mio**," he declares, then turns and races back up the hallway. Along with **Mama**, Theo's favorite word at the moment is **mine**. Lili laughs, listening to his footsteps recede. When she looks up, her smile fades. Esti is in the doorway, eyes swollen and red. Lili stands.

"Oh, no. What's happened?"

Esti rakes her fingers through her auburn hair. "A report came in just before I left the villa, through Radio London. From Salonica. There's been another roundup."

"No."

Esti nods, dazed.

"Able-bodied only? Or the elderly too?"

"The entire Jewish community, apparently."

"Oh, Esti."

Over the summer, Niko had written about how he'd been called up by the Germans, along with thousands of Jews under the age of forty-five, for forced labor; how he'd stood for hours in Eleftheria Square while men were pulled from the crowd at random, forced to perform push-ups and jumping jacks; how several fainted, and those who resisted were beaten unconscious. The Germans finally sent off some two thousand men for labor, he said; the rest—Niko included—were held for ransom. The Jewish communities of Salonica and Athens managed to scrape together every drachma they could in order to raise the sum the Germans demanded. They went so far, even, as to sell Salonica's Jewish cemetery, which the Wehrmacht began dismantling immediately, intent on using its headstones to construct a road outside of the city.

"Did they say where they were taken?"

"No."

After the roundup in Eleftheria Square, Niko's accounts grew dire. The city's Jews were made to wear yellow stars on their arms; there was talk of confining them to a walled ghetto in his neighborhood of Baron Hirsch. Some of the families he'd known all his life had been deported—where to, he had no idea. In her replies, Esti implored Niko to leave at once, to use his Aryan ID to return to Italy, to join them in Nonantola. **You can go back for your parents. Please, find a way**, she begged, even though she knew leaving Nazi-occupied Greece, with or without his parents in tow, was likely impossible.

"There has to be something we can do," Lili says. "Through your contacts? The underground?"

But Esti's eyes have clouded over, and in the concave slope of her shoulders, Lili knows. There is nothing they can do but wait.

CHAPTER EIGHT

NONANTOLA

July 1943

The bricks of the village clock tower glow bronze in the liquid light of a dipping sun, and the summer breeze carries the welcome scent of cut grass, but the streets of Nonantola are deserted.

"Where is everyone?" Lili wonders aloud as she and Esti walk back to their apartment from the villa.

Esti checks her watch. "I don't know. It's strange."

Theo runs up ahead, poking a twig between two cobblestones. "Found some!" he calls. He's been hunting for ants since they left the villa.

"Don't hurt them, love," Esti reminds him.

It's not until they've reached the center of town that they glimpse a sign of life—a group of locals gathered around a radio propped on a table outside a café.

Lili shudders. "What now?"

The war has finally come to Italy. Two weeks ago,

Allied forces—American, Canadian, and British—invaded the island of Sicily with hopes, the papers reported, of securing the peninsula, and with it, a path to Europe. The invasion prompted Hitler to begin sending German divisions to protect the mainland. Italian soldiers, who'd been fighting overseas alongside Hitler's army, were called home to join the Germans in the fight. In response, the Allies took to the skies, launching full-scale attacks from the air to cut off German supply routes from the north. First, Rome was targeted. And then, a few days ago, Lili listened in horror to reports of British air raids over Bologna. The bombs were aimed at power plants and freight terminals, but many missed, landing instead on homes and businesses. Lili had spent the day in a frenzied panic, her throat filled with the acrid taste of bile as phone calls and telegrams to her father went unanswered. When she finally received word that he was safe, she collapsed in tears. He was lucky; others on his block, Massimo said, were not so fortunate.

Meanwhile, Esti continues to write every week to Salonica—to family and friends, to distant relatives, to embassies and relief agencies—anyone who might have some news on Niko's whereabouts, but she's received nothing in return. The lack of information is driving her mad; Lili can see it in the divot between her brows when Esti returns home empty-handed from the post office. **Nothing today?** Lili asks, and Esti shakes her head. She's careful not to talk about Niko in front of Theo, who has no memory of his father. **He's better off not knowing**, Esti says, **for now at least**.

"This way," Esti calls to Theo. He skips over, takes his mother's hand. They approach the café and Lili recognizes the voice on the radio as that of King Vittorio Emmanuel III. She glances at Esti, then back over at the townspeople, all leaning in to hear. Someone adjusts the radio's antenna, dials up the volume.

"I'm bringing you today a special announcement," the king's voice calls through the static. The small crowd outside the café goes silent. "After more than two decades in office, Benito Mussolini has stepped down."

Lili stares at the radio. Mussolini. Out of office. Someone lets out a whoop of approval.

"As your king, I will retain full constitutional powers," Vittorio continues. "The world is at war. **We** are at war. But have no fear—Italy is in good hands. We will find the way to recovery. I have appointed Marshal Pietro Badoglio as head of the government," he concludes. "You will hear from him shortly."

The crowd buzzes. Cheers float from open windows. Lili turns to Esti.

"What do you make of it?"

Esti frowns. "I don't believe it."

"Which part?"

"Mussolini. He doesn't have it in his blood to resign. His ego would never allow it."

"But he's out. That's a good sign, right?"

"I guess. I just feel like there's more to it."

Badoglio's voice spills from the radio a few minutes later. "The war will go on," he declares. "We remain faithful to our German allies, and we must rally around the king. Be warned, any attempt to disrupt public order will be dealt with severely."

When the bulletin is over, it's followed by a song— and not the usual **Giovinezza,** the official hymn of the Fascist Party, but the unmistakable B-flat major of **Fratelli d'Italia,** Italy's former national anthem. The selection is a statement, a small one, but it's something, Lili thinks.

Cheers float from open windows as locals begin to file onto the street. Some carry flags overhead, red, white, and green silk flapping behind them like sails. Others pump their fists in the air. A man wearing a baker's apron produces a harmonica, and beside him, an elderly couple link hands and dance. Lili marvels at the joy in the townspeople's faces, wondering how Italians elsewhere are responding to the news of Mussolini's resignation. Nonantola is decidedly anti-Fascist. Most have been awaiting the dictator's demise for years. Whether he stepped down of his own accord or was removed from office doesn't seem to matter to them as it does to Esti. But were the people in more Fascist-friendly cities like Ferrara cheering in the streets as well? In Bologna?

Part of Lili wants to linger in the piazza, to pause for a moment amid the revelry. But it doesn't feel right to celebrate. Not with Italy at war. Not with Niko unaccounted for. They walk slowly back to their apartment.

"Happy," Theo says as they leave the square. He smiles up at his mother, not used to such festivity.

"Happy," Esti says, though there is no cheer in her voice.

"Don't you think something good will come of this?" Lili asks, hopeful. "Il Duce out of power? Haven't we been dreaming of it?"

Esti looks at her. "Mussolini may be out of power, but you heard Badoglio—Italy is still loyal to Germany. Do you really think Fascism will end just like that?"

"No," Lili concedes. "Probably not. But maybe it's the beginning of something."

"People are set in their ways," Esti says.

Lili nods, not wanting to argue.

They round the corner to their apartment. "In we go," Esti tells Theo. "All this commotion is hurting my ears."

CHAPTER NINE

NONANTOLA

September 1943

Lili is at the villa conducting a lesson in Italian literature when Chef Emilio rushes into the room.

"**Scusate**," he says, agitated. "**Maestra** Passigli, you are needed."

Lili pauses, then instructs her students to work on their writing assignment until she returns. In the foyer, she finds Esti among a group of staff and volunteers. Everyone is talking at once.

"What's going on?" she asks, touching Esti's elbow.

"Another radio announcement."

There have been so many—it's all Lili can do to keep up. First, there was the report that Mussolini hadn't actually resigned but was arrested on the king's order. **I told you!** Esti cried. **I knew he would never step down.** Then came the news that the dictator was being held in a prison somewhere up in the Apennine Mountains. With Mussolini incarcerated and stripped of his dictatorship, Lili—along with the rest of the country—wondered what would come of Italy's alliance with Germany. Would the king stay loyal to Hitler?

"What is it?" Lili asks.

"Badoglio's surrendered to the Allies," Esti says.

"Surrendered!" Lili's heart leaps, then falls as she contemplates the implications of this turn of events. The fact that Germany is now the enemy.

Goffredo, who'd helped to smuggle the children at the villa into Italy, is at the center of the group. He's been living at the villa since the children settled there, and has shifted naturally over the course of his stay into the role of leader among both the kids and the staff at Delasem. He clears his throat, holds up his hands to quiet the others.

"Friends! Listen, please!" A hush falls over the room. "Italy has capitulated," he says. "There is much we still don't know. But one thing we can be certain of is that we are now at war with Germany. And their army is close. I've just met with the chief of police, and he confirmed that there are Wehrmacht already in Modena; he thinks they could reach Nonantola as soon as tomorrow morning. When they do, they will not be sympathetic to any of us Jews, young or old—or to those caught helping. We're all in danger of arrest."

A chill runs the length of Lili's spine. She wraps her hands around her elbows, cradling her arms tight to her waist.

"We have false IDs for the children," Esti offers.

"Yes, and we've distributed them. But even so," Goffredo says, "they are too large a group. It's too suspicious. Our only choice is to evacuate them from the villa, get them into hiding. I'll go now to speak with Rector Pelati at the abbey. He may be able to hide a handful of the children, but the others . . ."

"We split them into groups and go door-to-door," Esti says. "Ask the locals to take them in."

Goffredo takes a breath, then nods. "I don't see what other option we have. Tell them to pack their belongings. I'll return by dusk with news." He checks his watch. "We should wait until dark to move them. Meanwhile, they must not leave the villa for any reason."

Goffredo turns and Lili watches him jog toward the abbey as the door to the villa swings closed behind him. Germans. In Nonantola. As early as tomorrow. She has questions, but Esti is by her side, talking quickly.

"I'm going to stay here to help organize the children. Theo's up in the boys' quarters. Take him home. I'll come for you as soon as I can."

Come with us, Lili wants to say. **Let the others help.** But it's a cowardly, selfish idea; she feels shame at having thought it.

"I'll stay too," she says instead. "I want to help."

Esti looks up. She considers Lili for a moment.

"You have your papers on you?"

"I do." Lili keeps the ID Esti made her in her

purse. The new card looks just like her old one. Her name is the same but her address reads Lecce—a town in the south now occupied by the Allies, who have gained control of Italy's toe—and the card no longer bears the mark of RAZZA EBRAICA. All traces of her Jewishness have been erased.

"All right," Esti says. "Theo can stay with us."

"My class," Lili starts, having nearly forgotten about the students she'd left in wait. "What should I tell them?"

"Tell them to pack up. Tell them we're leaving."

GOFFREDO RETURNS TO THE VILLA AT DARK OUT OF breath, his forehead damp with sweat—he'd jogged from the abbey. "Rector Pelati can take thirty," he tells the group. The curtains are drawn and half a dozen candles cast trembling shadows beneath the tall, frescoed ceilings. The children sit, jammed together along the grand staircase in the foyer, a small army awaiting orders. Goffredo produces a map of Nonantola and spreads it out over a credenza by the door. The staff huddles around him.

"I'll take the youngest with me to the abbey," Goffredo says. "The rest we'll split into groups."

Chef Emilio is there, along with Doctor Moreali. They, along with Esti and Lili, it's decided, will each take ten children.

Goffredo runs a finger along the map. "Emilio, **Dottore**," you start with the streets west of Via di

Mezzo," he instructs. "Esti and Lili, you two try these streets here, to the east. Knock on every door you see. Some may be willing to take more than one. Others will refuse. Whatever the case, make no mention of their Jewish identity, and move quickly. Once the children are hidden, we'll meet at the abbey."

The group murmurs in agreement as Goffredo folds the map, tucks it into his coat pocket. He glances at Esti.

"I can take Theo with me to the abbey," he says.

"Oh, I—do you think that's best?" Esti looks up at Theo, seated beside Alfred on the stairs, playing a game of Rock Paper Scissors.

"I do."

Esti swallows.

"I'll keep him safe," Goffredo promises.

Esti nods. "All right. Thank you."

"Good luck, everyone," Goffredo says. He turns to the staircase. "**Ragazzi**. It's time. Follow us, please."

As the children file down from the staircase, Esti moves to Theo, lifts him to her hip, and they all funnel through the villa's heavy door and onto the lawn.

"You ten, you're with Emilio," Goffredo says, herding a knot of bodies in the chef's direction. "**Dottore**, this group belongs to you."

Without a word, Emilio and Moreali set off into the night, the children trailing behind, their suitcases swinging beside them.

"You all are with me," Goffredo says, marking

off the group that will go to the abbey. "You, too, young man," he tells Theo. Esti whispers something in his ear and sets him down, giving him a nod as Goffredo takes his hand. "Esti, you and Lili can take the rest."

Lili and Esti wrangle the remaining twenty children into two lines. Lili searches their faces, trying to decipher their expressions, but the moon is at their backs, and all she can make of them are their silhouettes, the faint whites of their eyes.

"Let's go," Goffredo calls. Theo looks once behind him, and in the next moment he, Goffredo, and the thirty smallest children turn and move quickly through the shadows, away from the villa.

Esti watches them for a beat, then straightens.

"This way," she instructs. "Stay close."

Lili can hear the shuffle of feet, the soft whisper of voices behind her as they set off.

"We'll walk together to start," Esti says, and Lili wonders how her friend is so calm. She links elbows with Esti, wishing there were a scenario where she wouldn't have to let go. But there is not. A few short minutes later, Esti squeezes her arm and wishes her luck, then splits off down a side street, and Lili finds herself alone, a band of ten children at her heels.

"Let's walk a little faster," she says.

They pass a park and a church before approaching a small two-story stone apartment building. Lili slows. "We'll start here," she says. She turns to the young girl at the front of the line, whom she recognizes as one of her students. "Jelena, right?" The girl nods. "Come with me."

"**Si, Maestra.**"

"The rest of you—don't move and don't make a sound."

Lili and Jelena climb a small set of stairs and step through an arched doorway to the building's narrow entrance hall. There are four apartments, two doors on each side of the hallway. Lili moves to one of them, takes a breath, and knocks. When no one answers, she knocks again, flinching as the sound ricochets off the low stone ceiling. Any louder and she'll wake the whole building. She's about to knock a third time when she hears the clip of footsteps from inside. She takes a reflexive step back as the door opens.

The old man who fills the frame wears a pair of white sleep shorts and a matching shirt. Lili raises a hand in greeting—**I come in peace**, she hopes to convey—but he squints his sleep-crusted eyes at her, wary.

"**Signore.** I'm so sorry to wake you at this hour."

"What do you want?"

"I have a child here," Lili says, looking down at Jelena. "And she's in trouble." The man leans from his door, peering over Lili's shoulder, and Lili wonders if he can see the rest of the children outside the entranceway. He says nothing. "I'm here to ask a favor," Lili says. She glances up at him. There is no sympathy in his eyes. Lili clears her throat. "Would you take this girl in, **Signore**? Just for a little while?"

The man frowns.

"I'm not sure if you've heard the rumors," Lili stammers, "but the chief of police told me—us— this evening, that he believes the Germans may arrive in the morning. The girl is an orphan. I—fear she is not safe."

"The Germans are coming," the man says, processing this news. "To Nonantola."

"That's what I heard, yes."

He scratches at the back of his head, turns his gaze to Jelena, stares at her for a breath, then two. "You are from Villa Emma," he says. It is not a question.

Jelena nods.

"She has papers," Lili offers, but the man ignores her.

"How old are you, girl?"

Jelena's voice is barely above a whisper. "Eleven."

The man cocks his head. "My granddaughter's age," he says. "Maybe you know her."

Jelena blinks. "Maybe."

"Well then." The man steps aside, motioning for the girl to enter, and Lili feels her shoulders fall away from her ears.

"It's okay," she says, a hand on Jelena's back. "You'll be safe here. You can go." Jelena disappears into the apartment. "**Grazie**," Lili offers, as the man pulls the door closed behind him.

He took her in, Lili marvels. She gives her arms a shake to ease her jitters, then returns to the rest of the children, waiting patiently in the dark. "Henrik. Come," she says. She extends a hand, and the boy at the front of the line takes it. They climb the stairs and approach the next door in the entrance hall. Lili pulls her shoulders back and knocks.

CHAPTER TEN

NONANTOLA

September 1943

The next day, Lili, Esti, and Goffredo are huddled in the hallway of the abbey, talking in whispers.

"Do you think someone tipped them off?" Esti asks.

Goffredo furrows his brow. "Rector Pelati said the Germans raided the villa as soon as they arrived, that they've been searching homes and businesses in the village since. **Someone** must have informed them of the operation."

"The children," Lili says. "Have any been discovered?"

"I don't think so, but—I can't be sure."

As the chief of police had predicted, the Wehrmacht arrived in the village just after sunrise—less than an hour after Lili and Esti had placed the last of the orphans in homes—their jeeps and motorcycles and horses thundering in from the west.

They'd crowded the streets, claiming Nonantola as their own, their emphatic **Heil Hitlers** audible through the thick stone walls of the abbey, where thirty stowaways from Villa Emma were hidden in an underground vault.

"Do you think we're safe here?" Lili asks.

"I hope so," Goffredo says. "The vault is well concealed. Even if the abbey is searched, you'd have to know it's there to look for it."

"The children can't live here forever," Esti says. It's been only a day and already they've grown restless, not used to being confined to such a small space. The nuns have brought food, have cleaned the pails they use to relieve themselves, but life underground isn't sustainable. "We have our papers. We can be helpful aboveground. Bring more food, and news. Try to find more places for the children to stay."

"That's good of you to offer," Goffredo says. "But it's too soon. Too dangerous. Let's give it a little more time."

FIVE IMPOSSIBLY LONG DAYS PASS BEFORE LILI AND Esti gather the courage to venture from the abbey. When they do, the village is barely recognizable. German soldiers fill the streets and shops and cafés, and tall banners hang from second-story windows, red and black and emblazoned with swastikas. Even more disturbing are the notices taped to the city walls, calling for all Jews to report to the town registrar. **Those found aiding a Jew will face arrest**, the flyers read. If they're arresting the locals for helping a Jew, Lili thinks, what do they have planned for the Jews themselves?

"Don't make eye contact," Esti says as they walk from the abbey to their apartment, their cadence brisk. Theo hurries along between them, holding their hands, taking three steps for each of their two. Lili keeps her gaze steady, forward, but her stomach is tight, her breath shallow. She thinks of her father in Bologna, wondering if the streets of her hometown feel as foreboding as Nonantola's. Wondering if he is safe.

She spends the next week with Theo in the apartment, leaving only once for provisions and to send a letter to Massimo, promising to visit soon. Esti has made him an Aryan ID, and Lili is intent on getting it to him. Esti goes out more often, to inquire about the well-being of the orphans and to make lists of names and addresses of locals willing to take a child from the vault into hiding. If there are any Jews living in Nonantola, she tells Lili, they aren't reporting to the registrar, and town officials aren't offering up census details that could incriminate them. As far as she knows, no arrests have been made. The Germans, though, are determined in their search.

A few days after leaving the abbey, Esti had returned home shaken, her cheeks pale. She was visiting a local safehouse, she told Lili—asking if the family would be willing to harbor a second child, maybe even a third—when a pair of Wehrmacht soldiers showed up, pounding at the door. Margo, one of the young girls from the villa, slipped behind the living room curtain at the sound of their knock. The Germans ransacked the apartment, turning over chairs and mattresses. Margo never moved or made a sound, but if you looked closely, Esti said, the toes of her shoes were visible in the space between the floor and the hem of the curtain. It was the one place the Germans didn't think to search.

IT'S NEARING CURFEW WHEN GOFFREDO PAYS LILI and Esti a surprise visit at their apartment.

"What's wrong?" Esti asks. "Are the children okay?"

"Yes, yes." Goffredo says. "As of today. But they can't stay here in Nonantola with the Germans still occupying the village. We've made a plan to move them."

Lili and Esti exchange a glance.

"Where will you take them?" Esti asks.

"We're going to try to smuggle them into Switzerland."

"Switzerland is far," Lili says.

"Yes. But it's neutral, still. They'll travel in small groups, and in disguise. The townswomen are sewing them matching uniforms, so they'll look like they're on a school trip."

"That's . . . brilliant," Esti says. "How can we help?"

We. Lili straightens, unsure if she's thrilled or terrified at the fact that Esti has lumped her in to the offer.

"Actually, that's what I've come to talk to you about," Goffredo says. "I have a colleague in Florence desperate for counterfeiters. He's in direct collaboration with us, and with the underground. I've told him how capable you are and he's asked to meet you."

Esti cocks her head. "Surely there are other counterfeiters with more experience—"

"I think you should go," Goffredo says. "The three of you. You'll be safer in Florence; you'll blend in more easily. And what you lack in experience you make up for in skill. You're one of the best, Esti. With the children leaving, you'll be of more critical use there than you will be here."

Esti rubs at the back of her neck, quiet for a moment. Lili glances at her, still digesting the news herself, the risk of a move, of an even greater role for Esti in the underground.

"I know the jeopardy this puts you in," Goffredo says gently. "But there are thousands of Jews in Florence. Every ID can save a life. Think about it."

Esti looks at Lili and Lili nods, gives her a look to say, **I support you.**

Esti returns the nod. "All right," she tells Goffredo. "We'll go."

CHAPTER ELEVEN

BOLOGNA

September 1943

Breaks hiss as the train slows to a stop at the Bologna station. Esti stands, moves along the narrow car corridor, Theo on her hip. Lili follows close behind, a tight grip on the handle of her valise. At the door, the friends pause. Below them, the platform is jammed with German uniforms. Wehrmacht. Esti turns to Lili and raises her chin slightly.

"Ready?"

Lili swallows. "Ready," she lies.

They'd left Nonantola early that morning, their plan to stop in Ferrara, then to make their way to Bologna, where they'll spend the night with Massimo before continuing on to Florence. Their time in Ferrara was brief. The city, like Nonantola, was overrun by Germans. They moved quickly, carrying their false IDs and praying they wouldn't be recognized. Theo was mercifully quiet and cooperative, somehow sensing the urgency of the undertaking. They terminated Lili's lease and donated their clothes to the synagogue after restocking their valises with spare socks, fresh underwear, and anything of value—real and sentimental—that fit. Lili packed a set of her grandmother's silver, a heart-shaped, glass paperweight Esti had bought for her on a visit to Murano, a worn book of Rilke poetry that once belonged to her mother, and her father's Tuscan landscape, removed from the frame he'd sent it in and rolled in brown paper to make it easier to carry. Once the apartment was sorted, they hurried back to the train station and bought one-way tickets to Bologna. So far, they've managed to maneuver their way from one city to the next without incident.

"Try to look confident," Esti whispers now as they weave their way across the platform. They're wearing their best attire—shin-length dresses, polished shoes, and coats belted at the waist. Lili's hair is pinned up beneath a maroon felt beret, Esti's wrapped in a stylish navy turban. They've even applied lipstick. Theo is wearing his nicest clothes, too, his curls tucked beneath a flat tweed cap. **The better we present ourselves,** Esti said as they dressed that morning, **the better we'll feel. And the better we feel, the less chance we'll have of being questioned.**

"How do I look?" Lili asks.

Esti glances at her. "Like you've seen a ghost."

Lili frowns, tries to square her shoulders, but as they near the exit she registers that, in order to leave the building, they'll have to pass through a checkpoint. They'll have to present their papers.

"It's routine," Esti says when Lili slows. "They're stopping everyone. We'll be fine."

Lili watches, eyes wide, as a young man is escorted away from one of the checkpoints. "Let's find a different way out," she says softly, taking Esti's arm.

"Too late for that," Esti whispers. "Just breathe." An almost impossible task.

"**Papiere!**" a Wehrmacht officer snaps as they approach.

Esti hands the man her and Theo's IDs with casual confidence. Lili sets down her valise to retrieve her own, willing her fingers not to tremble, but it's no use—the card shivers as if caught in a breeze as she passes it over. She tucks her hands quickly into her coat pockets, fixing her eyes on the eagle engraved on the steel plate hanging from a chain around the officer's neck. He examines Esti's cards first; after a few long seconds, he hands them back. Lili glances up at him as he looks from her to her ID. His eyes narrow. **This is it**, Lili thinks. **It's over**. She shifts on her feet, holds her breath. And then, beside her, from Esti's hip, Theo lets out a loud, wet sneeze. A drop of spittle lands on the officer's lapel, and he takes a step back, his mouth puckered in disgust.

He returns Lili's card at arm's length, and motions the threesome along.

AN HOUR LATER, LILI IS SEATED AT HER FATHER'S dining table, cradling a mug of barley coffee— even chicory is hard to find now. She winces as she sips from her mug, the coffee bitter on her tongue. Down the hall, she can hear the murmur of Esti's voice as she puts Theo to bed.

Over a dinner of dried fish and watery soup, she and Esti had caught Massimo up on all that he'd missed, beginning with the Villa Emma. They told him how the children had been smuggled into the country and hidden at the villa, only to be smuggled out of the villa and into the homes of the villagers, and if Goffredo's plan has worked, were currently being snuck over the border to Switzerland. They told him about Niko's reports from Salonica, how they were in touch for a while but how, after the last roundup, they'd lost contact; about Esti's role as a forger for the underground (swearing him, of course, to secrecy); about Theo's well-timed sneeze at the station. Massimo had listened intently, his gaze volleying between Lili and Esti as he tried to make sense of it all.

Lili looks up as Esti returns sock-footed to the dining room, rubbing her eyes. She lowers herself into the seat beside Lili's.

"You girls must be exhausted," Massimo says. "Can I pour you some coffee, Esti?"

"I'm all right, thanks."

"Good choice," Lili says, wrinkling her nose. "No offense, Papà," she adds.

"None taken."

Lili reaches for her purse at the back of her chair and fishes through its contents. "This is for you." She slides an ID across the table. "I know what you're going to say, but please just take it. You're not safe any longer. None of us are."

"You overestimate my pride, Babà."

"Good. You're Aryan now. And you're from Lecce, like us."

Lili wonders how her father will feel about carrying his new ID. She'd felt strange about her own in the beginning—guilty even, as if in erasing her religion she was denying a piece of herself, her ancestry. But, she reminds herself now, an ID is just an ID, ink on paper. It has nothing to do with her beliefs or her religion or who she is on the inside.

Massimo looks the card over. "Where did you find the photo?"

"In an old album of Mother's. You'll have to work on your Puglian accent."

A stack of newspapers sits at the center of the table. Lili slides one over, skims the headline. GERMAN PARATROOPERS FREE MUSSOLINI FROM PRISON ON LAKE GARDA, it reads, and beneath it: MUSSOLINI

DECLARES NEW SOCIALIST REGIME, CLAIMING ALLEGIANCE ONCE AGAIN TO HITLER.

"It's day-to-day now, isn't it?" she says.

Esti holds a mock microphone to her mouth, puts on her best radio announcer voice. "Il Duce is dictator! Il Duce is arrested! Il Duce is freed! Germany is our ally! Germany is our enemy. The Allies are here to save us! The Allies are reducing the north to rubble!"

Lili and Massimo laugh.

"It's hard to keep up," Massimo agrees, shaking his head.

The period of celebration after Mussolini was arrested was short-lived. Hitler sniffed out Mussolini's whereabouts, sent a team of paratroopers to free him from captivity, and restored him to power. Now the country, occupied by the Allies in the south and by the Germans in the center and the north, is in complete disarray. Italian soldiers who'd put down their arms when Italy first surrendered have been pressed back into service. Amid the confusion, thousands deserted, preferring prison to the prospect of fighting alongside Hitler's army. Others fled to the mountains or joined the Communist Garibaldi or the Socialist Matteotti or one of the smaller arms of the Italian resistance, whose mission, from what Lili understands, is to sabotage the German occupation.

Meanwhile, if you were a Jew living in the center or the north of Italy, you were at risk of arrest, or worse—deportation. If you lived south of Italy's ankle, the area under Allied occupation, you were free, protected. The distinction was drastic, and had led Lili and Esti to contemplate whether they should try to venture south. But to travel such distance through German-occupied territory, especially with Theo, felt far too dangerous.

Lili swallows another mouthful of coffee, wondering how she'll manage another train tomorrow for Florence, another checkpoint. It feels good to be home, the idea of resting her head at night in her familiar bed, of combing her hair in the old gilded mirror over her clawfoot dresser when she wakes, a comfort. Most of all, it feels good to be near her father. She doesn't want to leave him again. But Esti is expected in Florence—she's been instructed by Goffredo to contact the archbishop himself, Cardinal Dalla Costa, when she arrives— and she'll need Lili's help with Theo, at least until she's established a role and a routine. In Florence, Lili tells herself again, they can start over with their new identities and a new address. Details that can't be traced back to a census. Perhaps, she rationalizes now, her father will decide to join them. She'd made the suggestion once already, even though she knew he wouldn't take her up on it.

"I wish you would come with us tomorrow," she tells him now.

He reaches for Lili's hand. "This is my home, Babà. I've done all right so far on my own, I'll be fine."

"But it's different now, with the occupation. You said there were arrests."

"Just one, that I know of. Friedelman. He refused to give up his bakery when the Germans tried to confiscate it."

"They have your address, from the census. Your religion."

"That was an Italian census. Not a German one."

"Aren't they one and the same now?"

"I have an Aryan ID now, Lili. Thanks to you two. I'll tell the authorities I'm renting the place if they ask. And I've got Settimo to keep me company. I'll come to Florence if it gets much worse here, I promise." Massimo squeezes her hand. "Don't worry about me, love. I barely leave the house as is, except for rations. I can manage." He could ask her to stay in Bologna, Lili realizes, though, to her relief, he doesn't. As much as she longs to be close to her father, she can't imagine a reality in which she and Esti part ways. Not now, at least, after they've been each other's constants for so long. Her father knows this.

"I'll write as soon as we're settled, with an address," she says.

Massimo smiles, pleats forming at the corners of his eyes. "We'll get through this, Babà. Just like your mother and I got through the last one. It feels interminable. I know it does. But it will end eventually. It has to."

A familiar refrain. Lili nods, though she isn't sure any longer if she believes it.

CHAPTER TWELVE

FLORENCE

September 1943

As she leaves the Mercato Centrale in Florence, Lili surveys the street. There are two enemies to watch for now: German and Italian. King Vittorio may have surrendered to the Allies, but Mussolini, with his new Salò regime in northern Italy, still commands an army—Blackshirts, they are called— a Fascist, pro-Nazi militia that works arm in arm with the Wehrmacht. Lili's learned to spot the jet-black and bottle- green of both uniforms from afar, and to do what it takes to avoid them. With none in sight, she sets off, heading east.

They've been in Florence for a week, staying with an elderly priest named Aldo, at the suggestion of Cardinal Dalla Costa. Father Aldo, chalk-haired but still spry for his age, spends most of his days leading services at the Basilica di San Lorenzo in the market district and teaching theology at the University of

Florence. His home is thirty minutes by foot from the city center. The A-frame attic where Lili, Esti, and Theo sleep is tiny, the air thick with the fug of dust and decay, the bed a flimsy construction of burlap and straw. It's far from comfortable, but the priest has made them feel welcome and encouraged them to use his downstairs space—the kitchen, the bathroom, the living area with its simple furniture, wireless radio, and plaster Virgin Mary—as if it were their own.

Lili loops the straps of her canvas sack around her wrist to keep its contents from jostling against her thigh as she walks. She'd hoped to bring home something appealing, but today her ration card was good for only a pair of sad potatoes and a handful of dried beans. What she would do for a plate of her mother's spaghetti. Naomi. Lili thinks of her now as she nears the Ponte Vecchio, taking in the view of the terra-cotta-tiled Duomo over the skyline. They'd visited the cathedral once, she and her mother. Lili was eleven, maybe twelve. It was summer, and Lili can still feel the rush of cool that greeted them as she and Naomi stepped inside the marbled interior. They'd climbed the steep, claustrophobic steps to the cupola where, hearts pumping from the exertion, they were rewarded with a bird's-eye view of the city stretched out before them, a kaleidoscope of clay rooftops tucked beneath the rolling, blue-green peaks of the Apennines.

As she walks, Lili considers how, on the surface,

little has changed in Florence in the decade since she and her mother visited. The Duomo still stands proud over the city. The Ponte Vecchio is crowded with shops. The Rialto presents Shakespeare and Chekhov, the cinema, Totò's **The Happy Ghost**. Life, in the daylight hours, goes on as usual. But Florence, once you peel back the layers, is nothing like the city she remembers.

First, if you are Jewish, you live in constant dread. The Germans have begun making lists. Taking names. Checking IDs. Checking addresses. Their methodical efficiency feels sinister. Most have heard rumors about deportations of Jews from cities in the north, though no one knows what to expect or what to believe. Hundreds, if not thousands of Florentine Jews, Esti was told through the underground, have gone into hiding. Some have escaped—to Switzerland, to the forest.

There's also the ongoing threat of Allied bombs, prompting many, regardless of religion, to flee the city for refuge in villages away from the likely targets of air raids. Others have stayed, refusing to leave their homes, refusing to that believe the horrors reported across borders—if there is truth to them—could ever unfold in Italy. Evenings are spent huddled at home with the windows covered carefully, so as not to allow through even a flicker of light.

And then there is hunger, deep and unabating. In the country, and in small rural villages like Nonantola, surrounded by farmland, supplies are better. But in Florence, even as swaths of city parks have been repurposed into orchards, football fields into vegetable gardens, the portions are scant, the food itself barely edible. Most breads are made now from a lumpy mix of potato, maize flour, and to Lili's horror, **insects**. It's not uncommon to spot old men rummaging through the garbage, or with a pocket knife in hand, skinning a dead cat.

Under the German occupation, only Italians with Aryan IDs can register for ration cards. Lili is lucky. Her false ID allows her provisions, and she has the means to buy extra food if she needs to. Her father had sent her off from Bologna with three thousand lira and a pair of his gold cuff links, which she'd sewn into the lining of her valise with her jewelry and her grandmother's silver, vowing to keep her valuables safe, to use the money sparingly. So far, she's resisted the temptation to purchase a quarter liter of olive oil or a slab of meat on the black market; the cost is exorbitant. She could spend all that her father gave her in a week, and for what? A few good meals? It's not worth it.

Lili worries incessantly about the Jews in the city without access to rations. How do they survive? The question gnawed at her until she gathered the resolve to ask Esti if she could help with her IDs. **I know it's risky**, she said, **but it's a risk just to walk the streets now. I can't stand knowing there are others starving.** Esti, of course, shut down the idea right away. **No. It's too dangerous. If you're caught,** you'll be arrested. Worse. Your father already lost your mother. I can't be the reason he loses you too. Lili had simply nodded, knowing better than to argue.

A few blocks past the Ponte Vecchio, Lili slows at the sound of a diesel engine behind her. She turns, curses under her breath at the sight of the open-topped vehicle motoring in her direction, taupe brown with bucket seats and a tire secured to its hood—a German Kübelwagen. Four men in green uniforms fill its seats. She looks for an alley or an open storefront, anywhere to duck out of sight, but the closest street corner is twenty meters ahead and the shops have already begun to close, preparing for curfew.

With nowhere to move but forward, she walks on, her ears tuned to the growl of the truck drawing nearer. She doesn't allow herself to turn again until the vehicle is beside her. Glancing over, she meets the eye of the soldier riding in the front, on the passenger side. They are close enough that, if they were both to extend their arms, their fingers would touch. Lili nods once in his direction, in what she hopes looks like a show of respect. He stares, and the driver slows so the Kübelwagen matches her pace. Lili counts her steps to keep from speeding up. The soldiers have no reason to question her, she tells herself, but she rehearses her story nonetheless, her insides roiling. **I am a widow, my husband was recently killed on the front; I've come to Florence**

to care for an ailing grandmother. Since leaving Nonantola, she and Esti have taken turns interrogating each other on the details of their Puglian addresses, sometimes even waking each other out of sleep: **Tell me, straight away—where do you live?** The response has become second nature. **Via Raffaello Sanzio 14, Lecce.**

After a few long seconds, the Kübelwagen picks up speed, its engine popping in protest, and Lili exhales. As it rumbles by, she spots a fifth figure, small, white-haired, hanging from the back—she hadn't noticed him before. A priest, she can see from his robes. He brings a hand to his heart, and Lili juts her chin, squinting after him. Father Aldo had mentioned once that he sometimes hitched a ride home from the Germans, but he liked to spin a good story and Lili had chalked it up as yarn. She returns the wave, smiling to herself as Aldo's figure grows smaller, the tail of his long, black cassock billowing like a sail behind him.

CHAPTER THIRTEEN

FLORENCE

September 1943

How's it going?" Lili asks, peering over Esti's shoulder. "You look exhausted. Can you take a break?"

It's late on a Friday evening. Esti is hunched at the desk in Aldo's attic room. Lili had put Theo to bed so Esti could make some headway on a new batch of IDs she'd promised Dalla Costa by morning. Normally, Esti does her forging from safehouses in the city. But she's fallen behind—or, rather, demand has tripled—and because it's illegal to be out after curfew, she's begun bringing supplies home with her so she can work through the night. She hardly sleeps. Lili often wakes in the morning to find her passed out at the desk, wearing her clothes from the night before, her head in the crook of an elbow.

Esti works out of a sense of obligation, Lili knows, but also to keep her mind from things. From Niko, still missing. From her parents, whom she hasn't heard from for months. Lili, at least, is in contact with her father. Her heart aches for Esti. For how it must be to face the fear, day after day, of losing touch with the people who mean the most to her.

"It's going," Esti says, dipping a small paintbrush into a glass bottle of glue and applying it to the back of a thumb-size photograph. Lili glances at a pile of blank cards on the desk—double the size of the finished ones. She'll be at it for hours.

Esti had explained to her once, the steps in making an ID. First, there are the blank forms, stolen by a conspiring city clerk or slipped from a printing press for a fee. Next, personal information (name, age, address, eye color) must be collected and handwritten on each card. People with names like theirs, Ezratti and Passigli, can pass—but if they sound too Jewish, they have to be changed. A Feistmann might become a Fiano. Adler an Amadeo. **We keep the first letter the same,** Esti told Lili. **Makes it easier to remember that way, allows more room for error if you slip up at first.** Addresses are plucked from a phone book, from cities in the south—anywhere not occupied by the Germans—photos, taken by Esti at a safehouse, or for people living outside of Florence, delivered by Dalla Costa's courier. Lili once asked if Esti had ever met the courier, but Esti shook her head. **Dalla Costa won't say who it is— it's all very secretive—just that he presided over the fellow's wedding a couple of years ago.** The municipal stamps, bearing the name and seal from the city where the IDs are supposed to have been issued, are the hardest to come by. Most are stolen, others made by hand, some pirated from old IDs using, of all things, a just-peeled hard-boiled egg, whose skin has the ability to lift ink from paper. And then of course there's the task of distribution, of getting the IDs into the hands of their new owners. Esti's job is to assemble the data—to write in the correct information, to affix the headshots, the stamps, all the appropriate markers. If she makes a mistake, which she rarely does, she starts over, for one missed letter or imperfect stamp could lead the authorities to call an owner's bluff.

Lili pulls two old crates from the corner of the attic and stacks them beside Esti's chair to make a stool. "Let me help. Theo's asleep. I've nothing else to do."

Esti looks at her. The whites of her eyes are rimmed in red, the skin beneath them translucent purple.

"I know you don't want me involved," Lili says, before she can object. "But no one will ever know. You'll be twice as productive with two sets of hands. Please."

Esti draws a long, slow breath. "All right. Fine." She scoots her chair over to allow Lili some space. Lili's heart skips. "You can glue. Just a tiny dab on each of the corners is all you need," Esti says, demonstrating. "The hard part is laying the photo down perfectly straight. You only get one shot at it; the glue dries fast."

"Got it."

Esti slides a bottle of glue and a paintbrush over to Lili and hands her an ID card and photo. Lili takes the photo by its edges, stares at it for a moment. A young woman stares back with dark, serious eyes, finger-waved hair, cat-eye glasses, a small dimple in her chin. **Maryla**, her ID reads. She turns the photograph over, reaches for the paintbrush, and pats a tiny drop of glue to its corners. Triple-checking her alignment, she exhales fully then presses the photo carefully to the card. **Good luck to you, Maryla**, she thinks, blowing on the card and setting it aside to dry.

"Next," she says.

Esti gives the ID a quick glance, nods her approval. "You're fast," she says.

Lili feels her chest warm as Esti pushes another ID in her direction.

CHAPTER FOURTEEN

FLORENCE

September 1943

They're seated around Father Aldo's dining table, eating a cobbled-together lunch of leek and parsnip soup, when Theo points his spoon at the ceiling.

"**Zanzara**," he says.

"Keep eating, love," Esti prods.

But Theo is still, his head tilted to one side. "**Zanzara**," he says again. Mosquito. He's nearly three, spouting new words every day.

Lili stops chewing and listens. At first, she hears nothing, but a moment later, she catches it—the far-off whine of an engine. "I hear it," she says.

"Do you hear it, Mama?" Theo asks.

Esti puts her hand on his shoulder. "Shhh."

When the buzzing grows louder, Aldo stands and moves to the window, pulls aside a muslin curtain. "It's too cloudy, I can't see anything. We should get downstairs."

Lili watches the curtain float back into place. "It's the middle of the day," she says. Surely if there were Allied planes overhead, they'd have heard sirens, a warning.

Esti takes Theo's spoon and sets it down by his bowl. "You have very good ears," she says, and he grins at the compliment. She lifts him from his chair.

Aldo reaches for a candle on the credenza and Lili and Esti follow him through a door by the kitchen down a flight of steps to the basement. There, enveloped in darkness, they pause, disoriented.

"Hold this," Aldo says, pressing the candle into Lili's palm. He lights a match and the wick catches, illuminating the space in a flickering halo of light and filling Lili's nose with the sharp scent of sulphur. She looks around. The ceiling is low, the floor packed dirt. It smells of earth and mildew. She hands the candle back to Aldo, and he guides them to the far wall, where they take a seat on a bench made of cinderblocks and plywood, Aldo at one end, Esti at the other, Theo and Lili between. Theo kicks his feet, his eyes flashing in the candlelight as he takes in the dark, sunken room, the sudden change of scenery. The minutes pass slowly as they wait in silence, straining for a sound.

"I don't hear anything," Theo whispers after a while.

"Keep listening," Esti says, pointing to her ear.

Another minute passes, then another.

"Can we go now?" Theo asks.

"Not yet."

"Why not?"

Esti cradles a hand around his thigh. "We need to stay here for a while longer. Just to be safe."

Theo quiets and Lili wonders if the boy has any concept of what he's hiding from. He knows about the war, vaguely. He understands there is fighting, and that there are certain things they do now to protect themselves, but Esti has shielded him for the most part from the specific dangers they might encounter—an air raid being one of them.

"Count to ten with me," Lili whispers, and Theo, who's been practicing his numbers, joins her as she begins counting slowly, from one.

"I hear something," Esti whispers, shushing them.

This time, they all hear it right away: a whistle, its pitch high, descending. And then a deep clap, like thunder.

"Is that—" Lili starts.

Another whistle, louder this time.

"That's close. Too close. Put your arms over your head," Aldo says, but his words are swallowed by a third whistle, and a fourth. Soon the thunderclaps roll into one, the air hums around them. Esti pulls Theo onto her lap, cocooning him with her torso, and Lili slides over to sit closer to Esti. Aldo snuffs out the candle and the space around them fades again to black.

Bits of dust and debris crumble from the ceiling with each explosion. Lili leans her chest over her knees. Her mouth goes dry and her heart slaps at the tops of her thighs. She presses her leg to Esti's—a reminder that, if the room caves in on them, she won't die alone. The detonations grow louder. Pinching her eyes shut, she thinks of her father as she listens to the bombs fall, to the sound of her breath in her ears, quick and urgent.

HOURS LATER, WHEN THE BARRAGE HAS FINALLY ended, Lili, Esti, Theo, and Aldo emerge from their basement hideout shell-shocked and parched. They return to the dining room, blinking into the afternoon light filtering in through the windows, soft and gray, like something out of a photograph. Dust films the table. There is plaster in their soup. They throw it away and set to work cleaning up with brooms and wet rags.

"What happened, Mama?" Theo asks.

Esti takes his hand and crouches down beside him, and Lili wonders how Esti will begin to explain.

"The mosquito you heard was an airplane," Esti says.

"There was thunder." Another new word.

"Those were bombs."

"**Bombe?**"

"Something that explodes when it hits the ground. They were dropped from the airplanes."

Theo is rapt. "Who dropped them?"

"I'm not sure, love."

Theo presses for answers, but Esti doesn't elaborate. "I'll explain more later," she says.

AT DUSK, LILI STEPS OUT WITH ALDO TO SURVEY the damage. Aldo's street corner is intact, but the neighborhood has been hit hard. The scene is haunting: homes without roofs, their insides splayed like gutted fish for all to see; a sofa, resting on its back; a piano pressed haphazardly against a smoking oven; an open book, its pages turning in the breeze. Amid the rubble there are corpses. Lili has read about the innocent lives the war has taken, but she can't bear to look at the bodies with their limbs strewn in odd positions like rag dolls. Her stomach sours and she averts her eyes. They walk around meter-deep craters pockmarking the streets and pass a pharmacy, flattened entirely. At the remains of a school, they stop to help a small group of desperate parents rifle through a pile of bricks and broken desks, and Lili holds her breath, unsure of what she'll do if they pull a lifeless child from the debris. But the effort is fruitless. More people rush to the scene, and Lili and Aldo continue on. Lili returns home pale and nauseated, the cries of desperate mothers in her ears.

According to the radio, the Allied bombs weren't meant to land on civilians. They were meant to destroy a rail station a few blocks from Aldo's cottage, to sever the German supply chain in Florence. But, thanks to the cloud cover, the Allies had missed. Hundreds were killed. **How could they be so careless?** Lili fumed. And the more ominous question: **Will it happen again?**

She and Esti stay up late that night, too disturbed to sleep.

"Do you think there will be more?" Lili asks.

"There could be."

Lili chews her lip. "The streets are barely walkable. Maybe we should leave. Find a safer place."

Esti is quiet. "We're being targeted from the skies and on land. I don't know if anywhere is safe. Here at least we have a roof over our heads."

Lili considers this. "Still," she says. "The rail station is only three blocks from here. It feels risky to stay."

Esti nods. "I think you're probably right. I'll talk to Dalla Costa tomorrow. Maybe he can help."

Esti has grown close to the cardinal since arriving in Florence. **A kind soul**, she said, when Lili first asked her what he was like. **As pious as they come. And staunchly anti-Fascist. Just my type.**

THE NEXT MORNING, ESTI SETS OUT FOR THE CARdinal's residence—a palace adjacent to the Cathedral of Santa Maria del Fiore.

"Be careful," Lili calls after her as she leaves.

"I'll be back by lunchtime," Esti says.

While she's out, Lili and Theo pass the hours with a ball of twine, tossing it back and forth in a game of hot potato, then unraveling it to make a cobweb through which Theo crawls, pretending to be a spider. When Esti returns a few hours later, her spirits are up.

"Good news," she says. "I think."

Lili is seated cross-legged on the floor with Theo. "Tell me."

"There's a Franciscan convent in Piazza del Carmine hiding Jewish women and children. It's just across the river from the city center, but far away from German supply lines—Dalla Costa thinks we'll be better off there. We'd have more room, too, to move around. We can go today."

"A convent?"

"We'll pose as nuns."

"Nuns!" Lili nearly laughs.

"I know. The irony of it."

"And Theo?"

"He'll be an orphan."

Theo looks up as he army crawls beneath a low-hanging string. "What's an orphan?"

"An orphan is . . ." Esti pauses. "Someone without parents, love. But you'll just be pretending. **Zia** Lili and I will be there with you the whole time."

"Like Owber," Theo says.

"Yes," Esti says gently. "Like Albert." She looks to Lili. "What do you think?"

Lili doesn't need convincing. She'd barely slept the night before—so certain she was that every noise was an approaching plane. "Let's do it," she says.

Esti claps her hands together, putting on a bright face for Theo. "Okay then—it'll be an adventure. Let's get packed."

It doesn't take long to gather up their things. When they climb down the attic ladder, valises in hand, they find Father Aldo in his living room, reading the newspaper. They apologize for leaving in such a hurry, and thank him profusely for letting them stay, for sharing his food.

"Be safe," he tells them as they go, and Lili's chest grows heavy. As much as she can't fathom staying, she will miss the priest, she realizes—his generosity, his calm protectiveness. She wonders if she'll ever see him again. She looks back at the cottage once as they set off, then down at the sidewalk as they pick their way through the debris littering the street.

"Broken," Theo comments, jumping over a mound of bricks.

"It is," Esti says. "It'll take some time to rebuild, but they will."

Theo looks up at the lavender sky, eyes wide, searching. Lili and Esti follow his gaze. "No mosquitos," he says.

"No," Esti says.

"I have good ears," Theo says. "I'll listen for them."

"I'll tell you what," Esti says. "We'll stay on the lookout together. I'll be the eyes and you be the ears. Tell me if you hear anything, okay?"

"Okay." Theo looks to Lili. "What will **Zia** be?"

"Zia? She can be the nose. Lili, tell us if you smell anything fishy."

"I will," Lili says, playing along, though the only smell filling her nose is that of scorched earth. They walk on in silence.

After a while, Theo sniffs. "Do you smell that, Zia?" His eyes sparkle in the sunlight.

"Smell what?" she asks.

Theo giggles. "I tooted."

CHAPTER FIFTEEN

FLORENCE

November 1943

The convent is shaped like a rectangle, with a courtyard in the middle. Covered walkways run the perimeter of it. Lili and Esti are huddled on one of the walkways, dressed in their nun's habits. Lili wears her winter coat. There is no one else under the portico, but they keep their voices low.

"Are you sure you're all right with this?" Esti asks.

"I'm sure."

"Don't stray from the route," Esti warns.

Lili reaches into her coat pocket, feeling for the map Esti drew for her earlier. "I won't."

"Remember," Esti says, squaring her shoulders, and Lili straightens.

"I know, I know."

"Proud chest," they say together in a half whisper.

Esti kisses Lili's cheek. "Thanks for doing this."

"Of course."

Esti turns. She waves, nods, then hurries off.

Earlier that morning, one of the nuns at the convent handed Esti an envelope with an urgent request from Cardinal Dalla Costa to meet him in the courtyard of his residence at three o'clock that afternoon. **Time is of the essence**, he wrote. He included an affidavit, explaining her made-up mission—to secure food from the cardinal's stores for the Catholic children at the convent—should she be stopped and interrogated along the way. But Esti had promised her contact in the underground that she'd have a batch of IDs ready for him that day; they'd made plans to meet in an alleyway behind the convent at dusk, and Esti feared if she didn't finish the IDs and deliver them as promised, she'd be putting lives at risk.

Now, Lili wishes she hadn't been so quick to offer to meet Dalla Costa in Esti's place. She runs her palms along the front of her habit, which she's worn since she arrived at the convent several weeks ago. **Welcome**, the mother superior said when she handed Lili and Esti the disguise. Sister Lotte had a no-nonsense demeanor, but her eyes were kind and her voice steady as she explained the correct way to wear the heavy woolen garment. Each of the twenty-some young Jewish women in hiding was given one. **Wear it at all times while you're here. Just in case**, the nun instructed. **Just in case what?** Lili had asked. **In case of a raid.** When Lili asked who would raid a convent, Sister Lotte replied flatly, **Carità. Nazis. Blackshirts. It's happened before. Not here, but it's happened.** This didn't sit well with Lili. She's heard whispers of the gang life in Florence. Mario Carità's band, for one, is infamous for its violence—against anti-Fascists, partisans, Jews—against anyone deemed an enemy to Mussolini and his pro-Nazi Republic of Salò. The men are rumored to play recordings of Schubert symphonies to cover the screams of their victims as they are shocked and beaten, their fingernails ripped out with pliers. So far, though, the convent has proven safe, quiet. Esti has continued her counterfeiting work, and Lili, for the most part, keeps to herself. The days are monotonous. Or they were, until Dalla Costa sent his message.

Lili suspects his request is regarding a new assignment in Assisi, a town two hundred kilometers south of Florence. He'd mentioned the opportunity to Esti a few days before, telling her about a shop secretly printing identification cards for Jews. His contact in Assisi has been arranging for many of the IDs to be couriered to Florence, but demand is high, and the shop needs help. **I thought of you right away**, he said.

Lili likes the idea of relocating to Assisi. It makes sense that they continue south, in the direction of the Allies. Assisi, while still technically part of German-occupied Italy, is a speck of a town, known for its churches and art and devoid of factories and industrial warehouses and military posts—in other words, a place with fewer Germans roaming the streets and even fewer reasons for the Allies to bomb it. A move would mean putting a greater distance between herself and her father, but Massimo had written recently to let Lili know he was planning a move as well—to Switzerland. He'd survived another Allied raid in Bologna, **narrowly**, he said, and enough was enough. When a telegram came from his uncle urging him to take refuge with family in Lausanne, he decided it was time. **Think about joining me**, he wrote to Lili. **You could bring Esti and Theo.**

Lili and Esti had talked at length about the idea of a move to Switzerland, but in the end decided that to attempt a border crossing with Theo was too dangerous, and anyway, Esti was too involved with the underground to leave the country. Lili had felt guilty at first, refusing her father's offer, but told herself that if Massimo could make it safely to Switzerland, he would be better off—and that as long as she, Esti, and Theo stuck together, they'd manage. They were family now, the three of them. And so it was decided: if Esti was needed in Assisi, Lili would go with her. She wrote to her father begging him to be safe and to send word as soon as he could, and she wonders now whether he's yet to leave Bologna.

Perhaps, Lili thinks as she paces, her footsteps echoing beneath the stone ceiling of the walkway,

Dalla Costa has arranged their passage to Assisi. Perhaps this is what he wants to talk about with Esti.

"Zia!"

Lili turns to find Theo walking toward her, the first in a line of children, Sister Lotte at the helm. Theo is the smallest of the group, by a head. Lili waves and Sister Lotte slows as she nears.

"You look pale," the nun says, in the unembellished tone Lili has come to expect of her.

"I'm off to meet the cardinal. I'm a bit nervous to venture out on my own."

"Ah." Sister Lotte nods. "Don't worry. You'll be all right."

"I hope so."

"You will." The nun brings her fingers to the cross hanging at her neck. "We nuns are bulletproof," she says, her eyes wrinkling slightly at the edges.

Lili gives a wary smile. She turns to Theo, tousles his hair. "How were your lessons, kiddo? Did you learn anything new?"

"I learned the rosary," Theo says, saying the words slowly. He looks up at Sister Lotte for approval.

"I taught him the sign of the cross today," the nun explains. "Remember, Theo?" She taps her fingertips to her forehead and Theo does the same, recites the words along with her: **Father, Son, Holy Spirit.** "And at the end?"

"Amen!"

"Well done, Theo!" Lili says, smiling. "You're

such a smart boy." It feels strange, she realizes, to congratulate Theo on pretending to be Christian, but she stops herself from overthinking it. He's too young to understand what it means to lie about his religion. A blessing, Lili supposes.

"He is," Sister Lotte agrees. The children fidget in place, growing restless. "I'd better move along. It's lunchtime."

"Yes. Enjoy your meal," Lili tells Theo.

"Be safe," Sister Lotte says, looking Lili in the eye.

"I will," Lili says, and Sister Lotte turns, calling for her flock to follow.

Lili watches them march toward the refectory. She pulls her shoulders back and adjusts the white cotton of her wimple so it hangs evenly across her torso.

AT TWENTY MINUTES TO THREE, LILI LEAVES THE convent, following the dark water of the Arno River to the Ponte alla Carraia, her map in hand. **The Carraia bridge will be quieter than the Ponte Vecchio**, Esti had said, in helping her plan the route. In other words, **safer**. Lili crosses the river, then continues along Via del Moro, unbuttoning her coat to make her habit more visible, grateful the November day is milder than most. She passes a few civilians, women, mostly, and elderly men. Some acknowledge her with a nod, but most seem to look through her, and Lili marvels at the cloak of invisibility her ensemble offers.

She's nearing the cathedral when four men in dark uniforms round the corner behind her at a sprint, hands on rifles, leather boots clapping hard on the cobblestones. Lili turns. Blackshirts. The soldiers brush past her, then disappear down a side street, and all is quiet again. **What** was **that? Why were they running?** Lili glances at her watch. It's five to three. She's only two blocks from the cardinal's residence. **You're nearly there,** she tells herself. She walks on, quickening her pace.

And then, a new sound. Shouts, from up ahead. In German and Italian. **Achtung! Attenzione!** Lili slows, listening. Behind her, the street is empty. She can be back at the convent in fifteen minutes if she turns around now. But she thinks of Esti, of how she'll feel to return without any news from the cardinal, and she thinks of Dalla Costa, awaiting her arrival. She presses on, turning onto Via degli Agli, then stumbles to a stop. The street is filled with army trucks and militia—SS and Blackshirts—dozens of them. They move quickly, efficiently, shouting orders. Lili ducks into a nearby doorway.

"Everyone outside!" one of the Blackshirts yells. "Take nothing! You have two minutes!"

Beads of sweat gather on the bridge of Lili's nose. She watches as a door to an apartment building swings open and a family stumbles out, prodded on by the butt of a German rifle. The oldest is stooped, with a kippah and a cane, the youngest an infant wrapped in its mother's arms. The family stands in a tight cluster on the sidewalk, and even from a distance Lili can feel the terror in their bones.

A pair of Blackshirts approaches, separating a toddler and two siblings who look no older than eight from the group. When one of the militiamen tries to pull the baby from the mother's arms, Lili stifles a scream. The woman resists, shrieking, and it's not until the second Blackshirt puts a rifle to her head that she finally relents, sobbing as the baby is taken from her and the children are herded into a nearby truck.

No. No, no, no. This can't be happening. Lili's eyes travel east along the length of the street, toward the cardinal's residence—she can see it now. There, a similar scene transpires: Blackshirts wrenching families from their homes and hiding places, loading them onto trucks—adults in one, children in another—at gunpoint. She looks away, her chest heaving.

Lili had heard about roundups in other cities—in the old Jewish quarter of Rome, in Trieste and Genoa. She'd read, repulsed, about the young boy who washed ashore on the Swiss bank of Lake Maggiore, spurring an investigation that led to the discovery of some fifty others, all Jews, mutilated, murdered, and—in an attempt to cover up the massacre—bound with rope and bricks and sunk to the lake's bottom. But those atrocities she blamed on the Germans. To watch Italian officers carrying out such brutality . . . to hear the rough thud of tailgates being slammed shut, their human cargo locked inside—**Where will they be taken?**—she didn't think her own countrymen capable of such betrayal. Had Mussolini himself given the orders? Lili's eyes fill with tears, horror bending to sadness and, in the next breath, fury.

Another commotion erupts and, in her periphery, Lili spots a moving figure. A civilian, running. The German officers behind him shout, several lift their rifles. Lili pinches her eyes shut as a gunshot sounds, its sharp **crack!** nearly bringing her to her knees. When she opens her eyes, the man is crumpled on the cobblestones. Lili reaches for the wall to keep her legs from buckling.

At the sound of a baby's wail, whatever sense of purpose or willpower Lili had drawn upon to make it this far dissolves, all at once, like ice dropped into boiling water. She claps a hand to her mouth but it's too late. Her vision goes dark. She gags, bending at the waist, and her vomit lands with a wet slap on the cobblestones at her feet. It takes her a minute to find her balance, to see straight again. Eventually, she rights herself, wiping her mouth with the back of her hand, and as she does, she hears a voice, her own. **You are not bulletproof. Get out, before it's too late.** She turns, looks once over her shoulder, and runs.

CHAPTER SIXTEEN

FLORENCE

November 1943

Lili rolls over in her bunk. She's barely slept in the week since the roundup on Via degli Agli. She closes her eyes and it's all she can see, all she can hear. When she's not reliving the barbarity, she's obsessing over what became of the families who were separated. Where are they now? Who's caring for the children? Are similar roundups happening in Bologna? Had her father made it safely out of the city? It kills Lili not to know.

"Are you up?" Esti whispers from below.

"Yes." Lili hears rustling.

Esti climbs the ladder to Lili's bunk. They haven't tried to see Dalla Costa since Lili's first attempt. It feels too dangerous to leave the confines of the convent.

"Move over," she says. There's barely room for one let alone two in her bed, but Lili slides over nonetheless and Esti crawls in, lays her head on the pillow, a dark mane of hair framing one side of her face in the shadows. They face each other and their knees knock together, their noses nearly touch. Lili doesn't mind the closeness.

"Can't sleep?" Lili asks.

"No."

"Me either."

"I've been thinking," Esti says. Her breath is warm on Lili's nose. It smells faintly of peppermint toothpaste.

"About the roundups?"

"About Assisi. What if we go at dawn?"

"Without meeting with Dalla Costa first?"

"He made it clear there's work to do. And I know the name of the monk I'm supposed to contact. Niccacci."

"Assisi is far," Lili says. "Isn't it some two hundred kilometers from here?"

"A hundred and seventy-five. It'll just be a few days travel. Less if we take the train. I think we'll be safer there than we are here."

"The convent is sacred ground," Lili says. "It's one thing to arrest Jews on the street, another to breach the walls of a nunnery."

"Sister Lotte says there are rumors now, of the church harboring Jews. And—you saw it yourself—the Nazis, the Blackshirts, they'll stop at nothing to find us."

Lili frowns. Until recently, they'd felt they were safe in the guise of nuns at the convent. Now, the protection of their Aryan papers is far from certain.

"At least here we have somewhere to hide," she offers. After hearing news of the roundups, Sister Lotte had helped them find places in the convent to conceal themselves, in case of a raid. Lili and Esti's spot is behind a rolling bookcase in the library, where a false wall opens to an alcove just big enough for the two of them to stow away.

Esti's hands find Lili's under the blanket. "Florence hasn't been kind to us. I think we should go."

Lili peers at Esti in the darkness, at the whites of her eyes, and though their faces are barely visible in the shadows she can feel the certainty in Esti's gaze. Perhaps her friend is right. Perhaps they'd be smart to leave before things in Florence get worse. "Maybe it's time," she relents.

"As long as we're together, we'll be all right," Esti says.

Lili smiles, bolstered by the thought. "We'll go to Assisi then."

THE FOLLOWING MORNING, HOWEVER, THERE ARE reports of violence on the streets, and the morning after, and the morning after that. Lili and Esti pack their things, so they can be ready to leave as soon as they see an opening. On the fourth morning, they're in the cloister when an elderly nun appears in the doorway.

"Raid!" she barks.

Lili drops her pen. "What?"

"Here? Now?" Esti scrambles to her feet.

"Yes! Hide!" In a panic, the nun disappears.

Esti and Lili lock eyes. Voices, distant, carry from outside the cloister. Italian. Lili can make out only fragments.

Jews! We know you're here . . . Come out or . . .

"Theo!" Esti's eyes are frantic.

"The children—" Lili checks her watch. "They're at lunch."

The refectory, where the children take their meals, is at the south end of the convent. Lili and Esti sprint across the cloister down an impossibly long walkway to reach it. They arrive at the refectory just as the nuns are locking the doors.

"Go!" Sister Lotte shouts, shooing them away. "The children will be safe with us, but you must hide. Go! Now!" The doors slam shut, and Lili hears the rattle of a chain, the sound of a dead bolt sliding through metal.

Esti grabs Lili's hand. They race back in the direction from which they'd come, the hems of their habits flapping behind them. When they reach the door to the library, they skid to a stop.

"What are you waiting for?" Lili says, panting, but Esti says nothing. She stands motionless, listening.

From somewhere nearby but out of sight, the shouting swells. The voices are men's, mostly, but a woman calls out too. **Aiuto!** Help me.

"Esti," Lili begs. She steps inside the library, pulls

Esti's arm, coaxing her to follow. "We have to hide. Now."

But it's too late. Two men emerge from around the corner, a woman in a habit sandwiched between them. Lili recognizes her right away. Sara. Her husband, also a Jew, had joined the resistance and was killed the month before in Piombino. Her daughter is a year older than Theo.

Sara writhes to free herself but the men have her by the elbows, her strength no match for theirs. "Let me go! Please!" she shrieks.

"We have to help her," Esti says, staring. "They'll kill her."

"They'll kill us too," Lili pleads. But Esti has already made up her mind. She jerks her arm from Lili's and moves toward Sara and her captors. Lili watches, motionless, as the men slow to a stop, glaring. Her gaze travels from Esti to Sara to the library door. She could duck inside; she could hide. If she pulls the bookcase into place as Sister Lotte had shown her, perhaps they won't find her.

Esti's voice, commanding, reverberates down the hallway. "Let her go!" Lili can't see her face, only the back of her, tall and narrow, her arms stiff by her side, her hands cinched into fists.

One of the captors laughs, his voice like gravel. "Look, Gio, one for each of us."

Go to her. Help her, Lili tells herself, but she can't bring herself to move. Should she yell for help? Or will that only attract others? A scream echoes from somewhere within the convent, and then another. Lili watches as the men, still clasping Sara by the elbows, take a step forward, as Esti takes a step back. Sara thrashes, cursing. The men hold on to her, but from their shuffling gaits, their strained expressions, Lili can see it's becoming an effort not to let her slip from their grip.

"Bastards!" Sara yells, her face red. She lurches and the men yell at her to settle down, but she won't. She whips her torso, flailing like a trapped animal, and in an awkward motion, the back of her skull collides with one of the men's noses. He howls, releasing her arm to cup a hand over his face, and in the chaos, Esti lunges, seizing him by the shoulders. She knees him, swift and hard, in the groin. The man yells again, and this time, crumples.

"You little bitch," the one still standing hisses. Sara bats at him with her free arm but her punches deflect from his frame. He glances at his partner, shakes his head, and begins pulling Sara back down the hallway, in the direction from which they'd come.

Lili watches, paralyzed, as their figures recede. As the man on the floor crawls to all fours, tries to stand. Esti takes a step in his direction and kicks him hard in the side of the head. He keels over again, his face to the wall, moaning.

"Esti!" Lili screams. "Please!"

Esti looks back at her, motioning with her eyes to the library. "Go!" she shouts.

Sara and her captor disappear around the corner at the end of the hallway. "Lili, now!" Esti cries.

Lili's body is numb. She turns, trusting, praying that Esti will follow, but when she looks behind her, she sees Esti duck into an open doorway, emerging a moment later with an iron fire poker in her hand.

"Don't!" Lili calls, but Esti is running now, away from the bloodied, floundering man, away from the safety of the library, away from Lili.

FOOTSTEPS RATTLE THE FLOORBOARDS BENEATH her. Lili tenses, blinks into the darkness. The muscles around her spine are searing. She's been sitting like this, her back pressed to the wall behind her, her knees pulled to her chest, hands clasped together at her ankles, for two, maybe three hours—it's impossible to know how long, exactly, and too dark to read the hands on her watch. When she first folded herself into the tiny chamber, the sound of her ragged breath helped to drown out the muffled screams from outside the library. But then it grew quiet, and the silence was worse. Still, she didn't dare move.

Now, the footsteps grow closer. When it seems they're beside her, they pause. Lili sits stock-still, silent. She'd secured the false wall behind her, but the bookcase was still several centimeters from the wall—she hadn't been able to pull it flush. **Please let it be Esti.** Her jaw loosens at the sound of knuckles rapping against wood—five quick, three slow, code for it's safe to open—then fumbles for the latch on the door. When she climbs from the cramped space, she sees it's not Esti but Sister Lotte, her expression drawn, her skin as pallid as her ivory coif.

"You're here," Sister Lotte says.

Lili looks around. The room was bright when she entered it. Now, the light sifting through the window is a murky gray. "Where's Esti? And Theo?"

"Theo is in the refectory with the other children. He is safe."

Lili exhales. "And Esti?"

Sister Lotte pauses. "She's this way. Come."

Lili follows her from the library, down the hallway in the direction Esti had run. They round the corner, stopping at a door she's passed on several occasions but neglected to notice until today. Sister Lotte reaches into her robe for a ring of keys and slides one through the lock. When it catches, she pushes the door open, closing it quickly behind them.

The room is small and windowless and smells sharply of antiseptic. Lit by a single lantern, it takes Lili a moment to realize it's some sort of storage closet, retrofitted with beds, one on top of the other, like the ones in the dormitory. In each bed, there is the silhouette of a body. Most lie motionless. One turns over, whimpering.

"My God," Lili whispers.

Sister Lotte leads her to a low bunk at the far end of the room, and Lili's heart lurches. **Esti.**

Her friend is nearly unrecognizable. Her hair is a mess of tangles, her cheeks swollen and bruised, her forehead wrapped in a bandage stained with blood. One of her eyebrows is split open with a gash the length of Lili's little finger. An arm rests across her chest in a sling, a leg in a wooden splint.

"Esti, **amore**," Lili says, sinking to her knees, reaching for her free hand, taking it tenderly into hers. Esti's eyes flit open at the sound of Lili's voice.

"You're okay," Esti says through cracked lips. Her voice is hoarse.

Tears well in Lili's eyes. She blinks, trying to pinch them off, but she can't. "I'm okay." She turns, aware of a weight on her shoulder. Sister Lotte's palm.

"I'm going to check on the children," the nun says. "I'll lock the door behind me when I go. Stay here until I return."

Lili nods, wipes the wet from her cheeks. "Thank you, Sister." She turns back to Esti. She doesn't know what to say.

Esti shifts on her pallet, winces. She speaks slowly. "I couldn't watch them take her, Lili," she starts. "I . . . I don't know what I was thinking . . ." She trails off, and Lili can tell from the cadence of her breath she's trying not to cry. She pushes a strand of hair from Esti's cheek.

"You were trying to help," she says. "I should have followed."

"No, you were smart to hide."

"Esti . . . what happened?"

Esti blinks up at her. "I thought . . . I could knock the guy out. But by the time I caught up to him there were others. There were so many of them, Lili."

Lili swallows. "Did they—" but she can't bring herself to say the word.

"They tried. I fought them off. And then there were sirens and they ran."

Lili looks around the room, trying to decipher who is who. "Is Sara here?" she asks, but Esti looks away, shakes her head. "You tried to help her," Lili whispers.

"It wasn't enough."

The friends are quiet for a moment. Lili lets her eyes travel the length of Esti's body. "Can you walk?"

Esti shakes her head, grimaces. "My ankle is broken, I think."

"Oh, no. You must be in so much pain."

"I wasn't at first. I'll be okay."

Lili's insides hurt at the thought of Esti suffering. "What do you need, Esti? What can I do?"

Esti closes her eyes and goes still, and Lili wonders if she's drifted to sleep. When she opens her eyes, Lili can feel a shift in her energy, a toughening of sorts. Esti fixes her gaze on Lili. "I've been thinking, actually. Of a way you can help."

"Anything."

Esti licks her lips. "You can leave the convent. And take Theo with you."

"What?"

"It's not safe here, Lili. You should go. As soon as you can. Tonight."

"What do you mean, **go**? Go **without** you?"

"Yes."

"Esti, you know I can't do that—"

"Lili, please, listen to me. These men, they know we're Jews. They'll be back, and they are monsters."

"How? How do they know?"

"Someone must have tipped them off."

Lili feels her temperature rising. "Why would they come back?"

"They said as they were leaving that they had **unfinished business**, that they would return. I believe them."

"Who would do this? Who?" Lili's voice is unnaturally high.

"Carità. Lili, I've seen . . . I know what they're capable of. I'm telling you, they are savages."

Lili straightens. "Esti, I can't leave you here. Not like this. We'll get out together, in a few days, once you're stronger. I'll carry you out if I have to."

"You don't understand!" Esti cries, her voice sharp. The woman on the pallet above stirs. Esti props herself on her elbow, winces as she brings her battered face closer to Lili's, lowers her voice. "You need to leave **tonight**," she says. "At dark. There's no time to waste. It'll be a week—maybe weeks—before I can walk. And . . ." Esti falters.

"And what?"

"They took my papers."

"Your false papers?"

Esti lets herself fall back onto her pallet, the exertion of the conversation catching up with her. "My ID was in my wallet. I was carrying it and they took it. I can't travel without it."

"We'll make another one then," Lili argues. "I'll make one."

Esti's eyes once again meet Lili's, her expression wide and imploring. "You know I'd never want to put you or Theo in danger, right?"

Lili nods.

"Which is why I'm begging you. Please. **Go.** Take my son. Go to Dalla Costa. He can help you find a way to Assisi. I'll meet you there, as soon as I'm able. Please, Lili. You have to trust me. You have to do this for me."

Lili is silent. How could she possibly leave now? Without Esti? Even if she **did**, would she make it to Dalla Costa? And Theo! What if something were to happen to him? How would Lili ever forgive herself?

"Esti," Lili begs. "You're in shock. You're not thinking clearly. Let's give it a night, at least—we can talk again in the morning."

But Esti has made up her mind. "Lili, I've never been more certain of anything in my life," she says.

"You asked how you can help. You said you'd do anything for me. Listen to me. This—this is how."

Lili's throat closes, her eyes fill again with tears. "I can't," she says, her voice small. "You **know** I can't. I've never been as strong as you. Please don't ask me to do this. There are places for us to hide in the convent. You said it yourself, we can do anything if we stick together. We've come this far. Please."

Esti squeezes Lili's hand. "You **can** do it, Lili. You can. If I didn't think you capable . . . if I didn't think it was the right thing, the **only** thing to do, I wouldn't ask."

"But Theo . . . I'm not his mother. I don't know him the way you do. What if he doesn't listen to me? What if he's inconsolable?"

"Lili, you've been as much of a mother to Theo as I have."

Lili's shoulders begin to shake. She closes her eyes, lets her chin hang heavy toward her sternum as, in her mind, she spells out the countless reasons she should stay. She imagines herself reeling these arguments off to Esti, but the words don't come, just a thought, lodged deep in the folds of her heart, an inescapable truth: Esti would do it for her. A tear slides down her cheek.

"You're sure?" she finally whispers. "This is what you want?"

"I'm sure." Esti says.

Lili nods, and Esti reaches for the back of Lili's

neck. She pulls her into a hug and holds her close. They stay like that for a while, cheeks pressed together, listening to each other breathe.

"Thank you, Lili." Esti says. "Thank you."

When Lili sits up, her head is heavy. If only she could erase the last twelve hours, curl up beside her best friend, close her eyes, and surrender to a deep and empty sleep. **You don't have to do this**, a familiar cautionary voice inside whispers. **Take it back.**

A key in the lock.

"It's me," Sister Lotte whispers. A dim shaft of light follows her inside, then disappears as she closes the door behind her.

"How are the children?" Esti asks.

"They're fine."

"And Theo? How is he?"

"He's asking for you."

"I need to see him."

Lili eyes the gash on Esti's brow. "Will he be all right seeing you like this?"

"I can't send him off without telling him good-bye. And I think it's important for him to hear it from me, that it's safe for him to leave."

Safe. Nothing about their plan feels safe.

"Sister, can you bring my son here?" Esti asks.

"Yes, of course."

"I can get him," Lili says. "I'll . . . gather our things and I'll stop at the refectory on my way back."

One of the women in the room moans, and Sister Lotte moves toward her. "Use the knock," she says over her shoulder, "when you get to the refectory. And when you return. So we know to let you in."

"I will." Lili stands.

THEO IS PERCHED AT THE EDGE OF ESTI'S BOTTOM bunk, both of his small hands holding on to one of hers. Lili sits at Esti's feet, her valise waiting by the door. When they arrived, she moved the lantern to the opposite corner of the room, in hopes of concealing Esti's wounds in the shadows.

"I don't want to go without you, **Mama**," Theo argues. The bed is low to the ground, but his feet don't touch the floor. His posture is stiff, and Lili wonders if he can feel the pain, the anxiety in the room.

"I know you don't, my precious boy," Esti says. "But it'll be okay, I promise. Your **Zia** will be with you the whole time. She'll take good care of you. And I'll be there, too, as soon as I can. You'll barely miss me."

Theo kicks his feet. "When will you come?" he asks.

"In a few days, **amore mio**."

"Two days?"

"It won't be very long."

Theo is quiet. After a while, he asks, "Can I bring Nello?" Nello is short for **agnello**, lamb—the name he'd chosen when he finally learned to pronounce his l's. He's become more and more attached to the woolen creature since they arrived at the convent, though Esti has insisted he leave it in the dormitory, for fear that the older kids would poke fun at him for carrying it around, or worse—that he'd lose it.

"Of course you can!" Esti says. "Nello is excited to go with you. He told me this morning. He can stay with you always." Theo cracks a thin smile.

At the foot of the bed, Lili brings a hand to the center of her collarbone where, hidden beneath her habit, her mother's pendant rests. She's found herself reaching for it often in the last week, the gold coin a beacon of hope, of strength, amid the chaos and uncertainty. **Wear this, my love, when you need a lift.** She's glad Theo will have his own talisman to carry with him, for comfort.

"Theo, this isn't easy," Esti says. "I understand that. It's hard to live this way, always moving. And it's okay to be scared. But you know what?"

"What, Mama?"

"You are a brave boy. In fact, I've never met a braver one—and I've met a lot of little boys! So be strong, my love. Do exactly as **Zia** tells you, all right? And everything will be okay."

Theo nods and his hand drifts to the dark stain on the bandage over his mother's brow. "Does it hurt?" he asks, frowning.

"No."

Theo studies her. "Here," he says, kissing his first two fingers and letting them rest on the spot of blood on the bandage—a gesture Lili has seen Esti use often, when Theo comes to her with a stubbed toe or a scraped knee. "All better," Theo whispers.

Esti's eyes shine. "Thank you, Theo," she says. She takes his hand, peels his fingers back. "This one is for you." She kisses his palm, then closes his fingers around the kiss, into a fist. "Hold on to it, okay?"

Theo nods. "I will."

"Come here," Esti whispers, and Theo wraps his arms around her, nestling his cheek into the hollow of her neck. Esti closes her eyes. "I love you," she says, running her hand through the loose brown curls at the back of his head. "I love you so much."

When she opens her eyes, she looks to Lili and nods once, almost imperceptibly, and Lili knows. It's time.

"Here," Esti says, holding out a fist as Theo stands. She drops something small and round into Lili's palm. Her wedding ring.

"I can't," Lili starts.

"You must."

Lili slides the gold **fede** onto her finger.

"Keep it safe until we meet again," Esti says.

Lili knows if she speaks, she'll cry, and she doesn't want to do that in front of Theo. She kisses her friend one last time, takes Theo's hand, and then they are gone.

PART III

CHAPTER SEVENTEEN

FLORENCE

November 1943

Theo makes it only a few steps down the hallway of the convent before crying out. Lili, hoping Esti can't hear, wraps her arms around his small, shuddering frame, shushing him and holding him tight until the sobbing stops.

"Here," she says. She pulls his lamb from her coat pocket and dries his eyes with the pads of her thumbs. When he finally calms, she helps him into his mittens and hat, then leads him to the refectory, where Sister Lotte is waiting.

"This way," the mother superior says, guiding Lili and Theo through the kitchen to a door that opens into a narrow alleyway. It's well past curfew, the city cloaked in darkness. "Godspeed," Sister Lotte whispers as they step out into the black, and Lili tries to thank her but her mouth is too dry for words so she just nods.

She keeps a firm grip on Theo's hand as they move north toward the Arno, listening for the sound of a motor, of voices, of the first rising note of an air-raid alarm—anything that might signal danger—but all she can hear is the steady clip of their shoes on the cobblestones underfoot. She'd made the same trip in her last attempt to reach the cardinal, but that was in the daylight. Now, she's disoriented, and it's too dark to read from her map. She follows her nose, praying she's not lost. With every step away from the convent, her anxiety builds, twisting like a rope around her rib cage, making it difficult to breathe. **You're doing the right thing**, she tells herself.

Fifteen minutes pass, then twenty, and Lili nearly weeps with relief when she finally spots the cardinal's palace. "Theo, look!" she whispers. "We've made it."

In the courtyard, she finds a large door flanked by two smaller ones. **Try the small door on the right**, Esti had instructed. Lili sets down her valise, takes a breath, and knocks. She'd met Dalla Costa only once before, when she and Esti first arrived in Florence. But Esti was with her, and the cardinal was expecting them. What if he's asleep? What if no one answers? What then?

Finally, a sound from inside.

"Oh, thank God," Lili says when the door swings open.

Dalla Costa's tall, thin silhouette fills the frame. He holds a candle and wears a crimson robe, a gold cross necklace, and a small round **zucchetto** cap. His broad forehead and angular features, accentuated in the flickering light, give him an air of gravity. He narrows his eyes, taking in the sight of her.

"May I help you?" he asks.

"Cardinal, we've met. I'm Lili Passigli. This is Theo. You've been working closely with his mother, my friend Esti Ezratti." The words tumble out quickly.

"Esti," Dalla Costa says. His gaze softens. "Yes, of course. She was meant to visit me. On the day of the roundups. When she didn't come, I worried. Is she all right?"

"She's . . ." Lili glances at Theo, swallows.

"Please," Dalla Costa says "Come in."

Inside, Lili tells the cardinal about the attack on the convent. For Theo's sake, she leaves out the worst of the details, but Dalla Costa seems to understand. He listens carefully, his silver eyebrows bent in the shape of an arrow trained at his nose.

"Esti had to meet with one of her colleagues on the day you requested to see her and asked me to come in her place. I made it as far as Via degli Agli before realizing what was happening and turning around."

"I'm glad you didn't get caught up in the violence," Dalla Costa says. He pauses, shakes his head. "You've seen the worst of humanity, Lili."

Lili thinks of the families being torn from their homes, of the man shot dead on the street, of the battered women cowering in hiding at the convent. It's true, she thinks, biting down on the inside of her cheek, trying not to cry.

"Are you hurt?" the cardinal asks.

"I'm not. I'm just . . ." **Scared**, she wants to say. "Esti told me you'd talked to her about a move to Assisi; she said there was work for her there. She's not well enough to make the trip at the moment, unfortunately. But she wants me—us—to go ahead of her. She thought we'd be safer there."

"I see."

"Do you think it's a good idea, Cardinal? For us to go?"

Dalla Costa glances at Theo. "I do. You'll be better off in Assisi."

Lili feels her shoulders drop a degree. The cardinal fetches a thick wool blanket and a candle from his study, and Lili and Theo follow him down a corridor to a small chapel where, behind a simple wood lectern, a worn Persian rug covers the floor. "I wish I had a bed for you. But this will have to do."

"It's all we need," Lili says.

Dalla Costa hands her the blanket and places his candle on the lectern. The room is cold and smells of must and melted wax. "Raphael's **Madonna dell'Impannata**," he says, when he notices Lili eyeing the painting over the altarpiece—an oil on panel depicting the Virgin Mary, a baby Jesus, and a naked boy at the periphery.

Lili nods, averting her eyes from the boy's unnerving stare.

"You should be safe here tonight," the cardinal says. "I'll do what I can to arrange passage to Assisi in the morning. For now, though, sleep. You'll need your strength for the journey." He turns and Lili catches his elbow.

"Cardinal?"

"Yes?"

"Is there anything more the church can do to help? I mean . . . officially?" She's grappled with the question since the onset of the Racial Laws— and now, with the German occupation, it's been weighing on her. She hopes she hasn't offended the cardinal in asking it. But in the confines of his palace, it seems obvious: surely, if the pope were to publicly condemn the barbarity unfolding around them, it would help to quell the violence—or at the very least, to temper the acts committed by his own Italian followers.

A flash in Dalla Costa's eyes. "We're doing all that we can," he says, and Lili can hear the frustration in his tone, though she senses it's not with her. She recalls Esti's description of the cardinal: **as pious as they come.**

"Yes. Of course," Lili says quickly. "Thank you again, Cardinal."

"Get some rest," Dalla Costa says as he leaves.

Lili spreads the blanket over the rug. She checks

her watch. It's nearly midnight. The adrenaline circulating through her has begun to wane, and she's struck, suddenly, by a rush of exhaustion.

"Are you hungry, love?"

"No," Theo replies. He's still holding his lamb. Lili takes it from him and removes his mittens, then returns the lamb. He rubs at an eye with a fist.

"Do you need to use the restroom?"

Theo shakes his head. "Will I see Mama tomorrow?" he asks.

A pang in Lili's chest. "Not tomorrow, love. But soon, I hope."

She removes two sweaters from her valise to use as pillows and blows out the candle. They lie down, fully clothed. Lili pulls the blanket over them, wondering if Theo will complain about the cold, or the hard surface beneath them, but he rolls onto his side, his back to her, brings a thumb to his mouth, and stills. A few minutes later, she can tell from the sound of his breath that he's asleep.

Lili can't recall drifting off, but some hours later she jerks awake. It takes her a moment to gather her bearings. She sits up, her body rigid, then startles again. **Theo.** Groping into the darkness, she calms when she feels the lump of his body beside her. He makes a sound at her touch but doesn't wake. **You are in Dalla Costa's palace. You are okay.** How long had she been out? Her sleep had come in fits, her dreams a spool of garish scenarios: Esti at the convent, one of Carità's men dragging her from the storage closet by her ankles, deaf to her screams; Lili at the Florence train station, a Blackshirt confiscating her ID and ordering her in for questioning; a silent Nazi raid on the cardinal's palace, Lili waking to find the spot where Theo had fallen asleep next to her empty.

She eases herself back down to the chapel floor and takes a breath, then another, resting a hand on her stomach as her father taught her to do when she was younger, a trick to help quell her nerves before a piano recital, a final exam, a leap from the three-meter platform at the city pool. Belly breaths, he called them. In, out. In, out. In her mind, she pictures her father beside her, his smile reassuring. **You could go back**, she tells herself. It wouldn't take long. She could carry Theo in his sleep, retrace her route to the convent. They could wake with Esti by their side and sort a new plan. A better plan. She breathes in deeply, feeling her abdomen expand beneath the weight of her palm. She thinks of her promise, of the relief in Esti's eyes when she'd agreed to her request. **You can't turn around now**, she realizes. **You made it here; you can make it to Assisi.**

Staring up at the ceiling, she searches for a sliver of light, a glimpse of the Virgin Mary—something, anything, to ground her in time and space, to quiet the seed of panic germinating in her gut, but the room is too dark; she can make out nothing.

Her stomach growls and her mind turns to the food Sister Lotte had prepared for them—a hard loaf of bread, two boiled eggs, a slab of fried polenta wrapped in waxed paper. Even if she doles it out sparingly, she'll have to buy provisions soon. She has savings, she reminds herself. The money from her father, and some cash Esti kept hidden in a sock and insisted she take. With her Aryan ID, she should also be able to receive rations, although her ration card still has Aldo's Florence address on it; she'll need to apply for a new one. A predicament for another day.

Shivering, Lili pulls the blanket to her chin and turns onto her side to face Theo, nestling her head in the fold of her elbow. She wears her wool hat and a thick coat, but the chill is inescapable, even indoors. She considers rummaging through her valise for an extra layer, but it's too dark to see, and she doesn't want to wake Theo. Instead, she takes a mental inventory of the items she brought.

She was in a hurry when she repacked her valise at the convent, but she tried to do so purposefully, removing a few of her belongings to make room for Theo's. She prioritized warm clothes and the things that might be of comfort for Theo: his **Pinocchio** book, his treasured marble. She considered bringing his silver rattle, then thought better of it—he loved the toy but it was noisy and would only draw attention, which was exactly what they didn't need. She brought her fountain pen and some paper, the photographs from her mother's album, her jewelry and her grandmother's silver, her hairbrush, their toothbrushes, a sewing kit. The glass heart from Murano she left with Esti's things, along with a note: **Return this to me in Assisi!** She'd slipped Esti's ring onto the chain of her mother's gold necklace; it hangs now next to the Jerusalem coin.

Stop thinking and sleep, Lili orders, recalling Dalla Costa's words: **You'll need your strength.** Edging closer to Theo, she presses the curve of her body to the round of his back and drapes her arm gently over his side, willing the slow rise and fall of his ribs to lull her back to sleep.

CHAPTER EIGHTEEN

FLORENCE

November 1943

Daylight filters through a stained-glass window in the chapel, filling the space with a hazy, purple hue. Lili stares up at the stucco ceiling. Her left side is numb. Her temple throbs, and her stomach yawns with a hollow ache. She's been awake for hours, too agitated to sleep, her famished state exacerbated by the gnawing question of how she and Theo will get to Assisi. She checks her watch. It's just past six.

When Theo stirs, she gives his shoulder a gentle rub, not wanting him to be jarred when he wakes by the unfamiliar setting.

"Good morning, sweet boy," she whispers.

Theo sits up, looks around. "I'm hungry," he says.

Good, Lili thinks. A problem she can solve. She offers him an egg and some bread and allows herself a bit of polenta, though it does nothing to satiate her. Ignoring her hunger, she folds the blanket and returns their sweater pillows to her valise, glancing again at her watch and wondering how long it will be before Dalla Costa comes for them.

Theo sits at a bench in the first row of the chapel's pews, his expression sullen.

"Shall we play a game?" Lili asks. A distraction, she hopes, might help his mood. She finds his marble then settles down beside him on the bench and holds out her fists for him to guess which hand it's in. He plays along for a few minutes, then slumps and starts to cry.

"I want my mama," he stutters.

Sadness wraps around Lili's heart like a fist. She pulls him into a hug. **I want her too.** She waits for him to stop crying.

"Let's read **Pinocchio**," she suggests. She fetches the book from her valise, then returns to the bench and props Theo on her lap, trying to relax into the rigid seat back behind her. They're partway through the book when Theo swivels to face her.

"Can we go back now?" He looks up at her, his eyes wide. "Please?"

A sting at the back of Lili's eyes. She takes a breath. "We're going to stay here until the cardinal comes—the nice man from last night, remember?" She pushes a curl from Theo's forehead. "And then we're going to go to a place called Assisi. It's a beautiful little town, from what I know. Your mother will meet us there."

Theo turns away from her, looks down at his lap.

"I want my mama," he says again, and Lili wonders how many times she'll hear those words in the coming days. She kisses the back of his head.

"I know you do," she whispers, then reads on slowly, to keep her voice from breaking.

IT'S NEARING TEN WHEN DALLA COSTA FINALLY appears, a well-dressed man by his side.

"Lili, this is an old friend of mine, Adelmo Giardini," he says.

Lili stands and smooths her habit. "**Piacere**," she says.

Adelmo tips his cap. He has a long face and kind eyes the same copper brown as his carefully groomed hair. He looks like a man of stature.

"Adelmo lives halfway between here and Assisi, in Castelnuovo Berardenga. He's offered to accompany you and Theo to his home."

"Oh," Lili breathes. "That's—that's extremely kind of you," she tells Adelmo.

"We'll take the train to Sienna," Adelmo explains. "From there, we'll ride by bus to Castelnuovo Berardenga. Once we arrive, you can stay the night—or for a few nights, if you'd like—then make your way to Assisi."

Lili wishes she had a map so she could better visualize the route.

"You think we'll be okay riding the train?" she asks Dalla Costa, realizing too late that Adelmo may not be aware of her Jewish identity. But the men exchange a look, and Lili can see it in Adelmo's expression—he knows.

"The last names on our IDs don't match," Lili says. "I'm not sure how I'll explain myself to the authorities at the station if they ask to see our papers."

"Where do your IDs say you are from?" Dalla Costa asks.

"Lecce."

"You can pose as Adelmo's niece, then," Dalla Costa says. "And Theo can be a cousin of yours, who you are tending to. If you're asked about your address, tell the authorities you spent your school years in Florence—that will explain why you are here."

Lili repeats the story in her head to remember it. Another alibi. She's no longer Lili from Bologna, but Lili from Lecce, who, depending on the moment, is a widow, or someone's niece, or a traveling nun.

"My friend, Father Rufino Niccacci, is expecting you in Assisi," Dalla Costa tells her. "Well, he's expecting Esti, but you can explain once you get there. He is the head of the San Damiano monastery there. A good man."

"Esti's mentioned his name. Thank you," Lili says. "Both of you. Truly, I can't tell you how grateful we are for the help."

"You should have matching IDs made as soon as

you get to Assisi," Dalla Costa says. "In the meantime, you'll be safer at times in religious attire, and
other times in civilian clothes. With Adelmo, you
won't need your habit."

Lili nods. "Understood." She glances at Theo.
"When Esti makes it here to the palace, would you
send word to Father Niccacci, Cardinal? We'll be
eager to reconnect with her."

"Of course," Dalla Costa says. "Do you have some
food for today?"

"Yes, the nuns at the convent sent us off with a
parcel," Lili says.

"Good. The Giardinis will be able to offer you
more when you arrive. Do you have some money
for your journey?"

"I do, Cardinal."

"All right. Good luck to you. I'm sorry to be so
brief, but time is a luxury I seem to have lost."

AT THE FLORENCE TRAIN STATION TICKET OFFICE,
Lili, Theo, and Adelmo are asked for their papers.
They show their IDs, and Lili exhales as the clerk
hands them back, no questions asked. On board,
they find their seats and stow their belongings. Lili
sits at the window with Theo beside her, Adelmo
across the aisle. The train pulls away, rocking gently
on its tracks, and Theo lies down, folds his knees
to his chest, and rests his head on Lili's lap. Before

long, he's limp with sleep. Stroking his hair, Lili watches as the metropolis of Florence gives way to rolling hills and stone hamlets. The Tuscan scenery is bucolic, but the only thought in Lili's mind is of the distance between her and Esti, drawing wider still.

After an uneventful transfer to the bus in Sienna, they arrive finally in Castelnuovo Berardenga, where, outside the station, they are met by a group of **carabinieri**.

"It's all right," Adelmo whispers to Lili. "I know them."

"**Signore. Buona sera.** Who's your friend?" one of the policemen asks.

Adelmo takes Lili's arm. "This is my niece," he says. "She's lost her family in an Allied bombing and will be staying with me indefinitely." He mentions nothing of Theo, and Lili wonders if the policeman will ask. But he simply pats Adelmo once on the shoulder, gives Lili a curt smile, and walks on.

"I'm afraid we'll have to travel the rest of the way on foot," Adelmo says. "The Bertone's been out of petrol for weeks. Here, let me help you with that." He reaches for Lili's valise.

"Some fresh air will do us good," Lili says, her tone upbeat despite the fact that the sleepless night, the day's travel, have depleted her. She hands her suitcase over with a grateful nod and glances at the sun, low in the sky. "Won't it, love?" She turns to Theo, waiting for him to protest, but his expression is blank. He's barely spoken since leaving Florence. She pulls his wool hat down low over his ears, takes his hand. When they arrive an hour later at the Giardinis' home, their fingers and toes and noses are numb with cold.

The house, Lili marvels, is a grand estate of stone and stucco, the property sprawling, well tended. There isn't another home in sight—a relief. Adelmo's wife, Eva, greets them at the door.

"Come in," she says, "you must be freezing."

As Adelmo explains the situation, Eva helps Lili and Theo out of their coats.

"Some tea?" she asks, as if Lili were a guest she'd been expecting.

"Tea would be lovely, thank you," Lili says. "But could we bother you first for a bathroom?"

"Of course."

Eva is Lili's height, with the same lean build. Her hair has just begun to gray. She's dressed in belted, wide-leg slacks and a soft wool sweater, with pearl earrings and a silk scarf tied loosely around her neck. She carries herself with her husband's same grace, and Lili finds that around them both, despite having just met, she's at ease.

"I'm not sure how long you're planning to stay," Eva says as they pass the kitchen, "but through there is a door to the back side of the property. You're safe to walk around, though if someone should drop by while you're out, I'll hang a red shirt in the kitchen window, so you know to wait before coming back inside." Lili nods, getting the sense that she's not the first person to take refuge in the Giardinis' home.

THAT EVENING, AFTER A MEAL OF ROASTED LAMB and potatoes with rosemary—the most robust, savory dinner Lili and Theo have eaten in months— and a warm, soapy bath, Lili sinks into a bed beside Theo's. Esti would be happy to know they've made it this far, she thinks. That they're in good hands. The home, the Giardinis—it almost feels too good to be true, Lili realizes, though she's too tired to worry on it. She's awake only long enough to notice the clean scent of lavender and sweet bay on her pillowcase, a delicate reminder of the herbs her mother once used in the **Havdalah** prayer, at the end of the Sabbath.

CHAPTER NINETEEN

CASTELNUOVO BERARDENGA

November 1943

Theo marches through a meadow behind the Giardinis' home, slicing at the waist-high grass with a long stick as if it were a sword.

"This way, kiddo," Lili calls, waving for him to follow. She's wearing a pair of thick tweed pants and her warmest wool sweater beneath her winter coat, but still, she can't shake the cold. "Let's get inside, before we turn to ice."

Lili had planned to stop over with the Giardinis for only a night, but then news trickled in of a second roundup of Jews in Florence—this one even more brutal than the first—and Eva convinced her to stay. Lili knew it would be weeks, possibly, before Esti would be able to move around again freely, so she didn't see the rush in getting to Assisi, where there was no telling what awaited her. With the Giardinis, she reasoned, they had comfortable beds, hot water, and ample food on their plates. They'd stay for a few days, she told herself, to rest and refuel, and then head on. That was a week ago.

Theo looks up. "Five more minutes?"

Lili wraps her arms around her chest, shivering. "Two," she says.

Theo is his best self, she's noticed since they arrived, when he's outdoors. Inside, he mopes. Or peppers her with questions.

When will my mother come?

She'll meet us in Assisi.

Can we go to Assisi now? Today?

Not today, but soon. I promise.

Why not today?

Because it isn't safe.

Is Mama safe?

Yes, she's at the convent. She's resting.

In truth, Lili has no idea if Esti is safe.

Her boo-boo is all better?

I'm sure it's getting better, yes.

Will she come here to Adelmo's house?

No. I told her we'd wait for her in Assisi, remember?

Why?

Because she asked us to.

So can we go to Assisi?

We will, Theo, soon.

When?

Soon.

It takes all of Lili's energy sometimes not to lose patience. But she doesn't. She can't. The boy misses his mother. And for him, the concept of time doesn't exist. Tomorrow, or in an hour, they're just words. For Lili, it's the opposite. Every hour, every day—and every thought and decision along the way—is carefully measured, carries so much weight. The minutes move slowly. It's a strange and frightening way to live, she realizes. How different life was before the war, how quickly the days passed.

"All right," Lili calls, clapping her hands together. "It's time."

"Can we come out later?"

"Sure. Let's see if Eva will make us some cocoa, yes? To warm up our fingers?"

The back door leading to the kitchen creaks loudly as Lili pulls it open. "In we go," she says, then stops short. A red shirt is draped on a clothesline over the sink, visible through the window. Eva's signal. She'd missed it. Someone is there.

"Theo," Lili whispers, closing the door as quietly as she can behind her and wincing as it lets out a catlike whine. "Come here, quickly." She brings a finger to her lips, holding Theo's gaze as she listens, and soon she can make out voices. Eva's. And a man's. She could go back outside, Lili thinks, hide in the shed, or in the woods, but the kitchen door—it's so loud. And how long would they last out there before they couldn't take the cold any longer?

She'll find a place to hide inside, she decides. She takes Theo's hand and tiptoes across the room to the pantry closet, glancing behind her to make sure they haven't tracked in any dirt. The door to the pantry is open, mounted from above on a rail. She steps inside. Theo follows. They turn around, careful not to knock any jars from the shelves, and slowly, soundlessly, Lili slides the door shut.

"We're going to play the animal game," Lili whispers, her hands cupping Theo's shoulders. "Silent as a—"

"Mouse," Theo whispers. He knows the game. They've been practicing. Some days he's a snake, others a fox. But mostly he's a mouse.

"Good boy. Silent as a mouse. Don't move, and don't say a word." She half expects Theo to ask **why**, but he doesn't. A few long minutes later, voices approach from the hallway.

"Grappa?" she hears Eva ask.

"It's a bit early for that. Even for me," the male voice chuffs.

"Some tea then."

"Just water is fine."

Lili can hear the sound of a faucet running, a glass filling.

"Anything to eat?"

Lili swallows. **Please, not something from the pantry.**

"Thank you. I'm fine. I'll only be a minute."

"All right then, tell me. What is it, Sandro?"

The visitor—Sandro—clears his throat. "I'll get right to it, then." He sounds uncomfortable. "We were issued a new order today, from the government."

"What kind of order?"

"It's from the ISR."

Lili blinks, registering this. The Italian Socialist Republic. Mussolini's Salò regime.

"And?"

"I brought you a copy. It calls for the immediate arrest of all Jews in Italy."

A pause.

"Well, nothing new about that. Haven't the police been arresting Jews since the Germans invaded, two months ago?"

"Yes, but now it's a mandate. Now it's our job to hunt them down, hand them over. There are penalties for failing to do so."

"Hunt them down?"

"Il Duce's words, not mine."

"Ah."

"And Eva . . . I have to tell you, people are talking. Your niece. The little boy. There are rumors. Not just in town but at the station. I just—wanted you to know. As a friend."

"Sandro, I told you, the girl—"

"Look, I believe she's who you say she is. But there are others who are skeptical. Some, I'm sure, who are eager to collect a reward."

A sigh. "Well, thank you. I appreciate your concern. We have nothing to hide here, but I suppose it's helpful to know that people are talking."

"Is she home?" Sandro asks, and Lili stiffens.

"She's out for a walk with the boy," Eva says.

"Would you like to meet her? I'm sure she'll be back soon."

Another pause.

"That's all right. I'll be on my way. It's always good to see you, Eva. Give my regards to Adelmo."

"I will," Eva says. "I appreciate your stopping by."

Their footsteps recede, and a moment later the front door opens and then closes. It's not until Eva returns to the kitchen that Lili lets her hands fall from Theo's shoulders, unaware of how tightly she'd been gripping them.

THAT EVENING, ONCE THEO IS ASLEEP, ADELMO asks to see the order again. Eva hands him a memo typed in bold black ink.

"Sandro gave this to you?"

Sandro, Lili has learned, is a member of the Castelnuovo Berardenga police, and a close family friend of the Giardinis' son Pietro who, last they'd heard, was fighting with the Italian army in North Africa.

"Yes. He says it's now in the hands of police departments in every province of Axis-occupied Italy."

Lili's read it three times.

POLICE ORDER NUMBER 5: ALL JEWS, WHATEVER THEIR NATIONALITY . . . SHALL BE ARRESTED AND SENT TO DESIGNATED

CONCENTRATION CAMPS, AND ALL THEIR
PROPERTY, FIXED AND MOBILE, MUST BE
IMMEDIATELY SEQUESTERED.

"So . . . the Germans have nothing to do with this?" Lili asks.

Adelmo rubs his chin. "It's from the ISR. But I'd be willing to bet Hitler gave Mussolini the order to issue it. Hard to know how strictly it will be enforced, with the country so divided."

Lili's mind returns to the roundup in Florence. "I saw them," she says quietly. "In Florence. Italians. Blackshirts. Working alongside German soldiers to evict Jews from their homes."

"Turns out our countrymen are capable of anything," Adelmo says, his voice bitter.

"Not all," Eva objects. "I imagine there will be some who take the mandate to heart, and some who quietly ignore it. We know plenty of good men in the police force, Sandro being one of them."

Adelmo props his elbows on the arms of his chair, tents his fingers. "This is true. Others, I fear, have forgotten what it is this country stands for. To persecute our own, it's . . ." He trails off.

"Either way," Lili interjects, "I should continue on. My friend—Theo's mother—is planning to meet us in Assisi as soon as she can, and I'm certain with news of this order she'll do everything possible to get out of Florence at once."

Eva looks worried. "I wouldn't be so quick to

leave, with the police on high alert. Why not wait a few more days, until we have a better sense of what will come of the order."

"Sandro said people are talking," Adelmo counters. "Perhaps he's warning us the situation is more serious than we think. If that's the case, we may be in trouble. All of us."

Lili weighs her options. If she leaves, she'll be on her own again, this time with only a false ID between her and direct orders for her arrest. If she stays, she puts the Giardinis at even greater risk.

"You've been so kind to welcome us into your home," she says. "But I think it's best we go." Her voice catches at the word **go.** She clears her throat. "Thank you, both of you, for letting us stay. I hope very much I can repay the favor someday."

"It's your decision," Eva says. "But sleep on it, at least. We can talk again in the morning."

"All right," Lili concedes. It's the right thing to leave, she knows. But the thought of abandoning the comforts of the Giardinis' home, of stepping out again into the unknown, makes her queasy.

Eva touches Lili's elbow. "Not everyone could do this, you know."

"Do what?"

"Take to the road with a false identity and a little boy in tow. It requires a great deal of strength to step into your shoes."

Lili nearly laughs. She doesn't feel strong. "I'm just treading water, trying to stay afloat," she says.

"I'd drown without the compassion of people like you."

"All we've done is put a roof over your head," Eva says.

"You've done so much more." Lili stands. "I should gather our things."

"Wait," Adelmo says, raising a finger. "I have a friend who lives just north of Assisi—a weaver who comes to Castelnuovo Berardenga the start of every month to deliver his goods. Cenzo. He always stops by for a visit on his way to town. Tomorrow is the first of December. Why don't I ask if you can ride with him on his return—it wouldn't be far out of his way to drop you in Assisi."

Lili had assumed she'd take the train. But the idea of avoiding station checkpoints sounds far better. "Would your friend be—open to that?"

"I think so. If you go by train, you'll have to transfer in Terontola," Adelmo says. "I was just there and Terontola is crawling with Germans."

"I suppose it couldn't hurt to ask, then," Lili says. "Thank you."

"That reminds me," Eva says. She excuses herself, returns a moment later carrying a coat over her arm. "Your jacket isn't adequate for this cold." She holds up the coat by the shoulders. "This one's been collecting dust in my closet for years—the color is perfect for you."

The coat is sewn from a rich purple merino wool, with a fur collar and lining dyed to match.

"Oh, Eva. I can't possibly take that," Lili protests.

"Please, you'd be doing me a favor. I insist." Eva steps behind Lili and holds up the coat. Lili slides her arms into its sleeves, runs her fingers along the buttery-soft trim.

"It's rabbit," Eva says.

"It's beautiful." Esti would go crazy for this, Lili thinks.

"Fits you like a glove. It's yours."

"This is incredibly generous of you," Lili says, but Eva waves the words away.

"It's nothing," she says.

But it's not nothing, Lili thinks, her heart full with gratitude. It's everything.

CHAPTER TWENTY

UMBRIAN COUNTRYSIDE

December 1943

"Doing okay back there?" Cenzo calls.

Lili's breath puffs from her taxed lungs in little white clouds. She's wearing Eva's coat, and beneath that, her habit, gathered up at her waist so as not to interfere with her pedal strokes, and beneath that, a sweater and pants. She'd opted to pack her wimple and to wear her winter cap but perhaps, she thinks now, she should have worn her hat **over** the wimple, as ridiculous as that would've looked, to cover more skin. "I'm fine!" she fibs. "Theo, are you warm enough?"

"Sì!" Theo yells from his perch on Cenzo's handlebars, and Lili can hear the smile in his voice. He'd squealed when Lili told him of the plan to ride bicycles to Assisi, and he's spent the last hour begging Cenzo to pedal faster. Cenzo, whose legs are as thick as tree trunks, seemed happy to oblige. At least they're enjoying this, Lili thinks.

Cenzo's truck had run out of petrol on the outskirts of Castelnuovo Berardenga—he'd arrived at the estate by the Bianchi he kept in his truck bed. With fuel almost impossible to come by now, Adelmo suggested he and Lili return to Assisi by bike. The Giardinis had an extra—their son Pietro's. **Keep it while you are in Assisi,** Adelmo said, **Cenzo can return it when his truck is running again.**

Lili wasn't sure what to think of the idea of traveling on two wheels and was surprised to find the first few kilometers of the ride tolerable. Fun, even. It had been years since she straddled a bicycle, and despite the December chill, it felt good when they set off, the wind on her face, the foothills of Umbria's Apennine Mountains stretching out before her, wilder and more rugged than the vineyard-clad countryside of Tuscany. But then the punishing cold set in, and the exertion required to climb the first hill nearly made her sick. She's underweight and horribly out of shape. Just keeping her balance is a challenge, with her heavy valise strapped to a metal rack over the back tire, throwing her off kilter at every turn.

They round a bend and a town materializes in the distance, a cluster of white stones clinging to the side of a mountain.

"Is that it?" Lili wheezes, pedaling up to ride beside Cenzo.

"That's Assisi! The mountain is called Subasio.

That church there, the massive one, is the Basilica of Saint Francis. Looks a bit imposing from here, but it's quite pleasing up close."

Lili coasts for a moment to catch her breath, her exhaustion tempered by a flicker of hope—by the chance that Esti was there, now, waiting for them somewhere amid the small knot of hillside churches and monasteries. Theo had asked if she would be, and Lili told him it was possible but unlikely. She didn't want to get his hopes up. Or hers. But now, seeing the town—their meeting place—she can't help but allow herself the possibility.

Fifteen minutes and several long ascents later, they glide to a stop in a grove of olive trees abutting a monastery just outside the town wall.

"Here we are," Cenzo announces. "San Damiano."

Lili dismounts and peels her fingers from the handles of her bike, leaning it carefully against a tree. She unstraps her valise and sets it on the frozen ground, then helps Theo down from Cenzo's handlebars.

"Thank you again, for showing us the way," Lili says. "And for the lift," she adds glancing at Theo. She'd offered to pay Cenzo at the start of the ride but he refused.

Cenzo does a little bow and smiles, showing off a gap between his two front teeth. "It was a pleasure," he says.

Lili taps Theo on the shoulder. "What do you say to **signore** Cenzo?"

"**Grazie mille!**" Theo cries, and Cenzo laughs, then waves as he pedals away.

Lili watches him, a pit forming in her stomach, wishing for a moment he'd stay. A curious feeling, considering she'd barely met the man. The routine of parting ways has begun to wear on her, she realizes. First it was Pacifici and his colleagues and the children at Villa Emma, then Aldo and Sister Lotte and Dalla Costa in Florence. Then Adelmo and Eva and now Cenzo. She hadn't thought much of the goodbyes at first, her sole objective to keep going, to make it safely to wherever she was trying to get to next. Perhaps what bothers her is the realization that, in all likelihood, she won't cross paths with any of these people again. And they are all good people. Not so much friends but kind souls whose orbits had intersected with hers, just briefly, before she was forced to hurtle off in a new direction. It's debilitating, all this moving around, she thinks, taking Theo's hand.

They walk beneath a brick portico to a large, arched wooden door. There, Lili pulls her shoulders back and knocks.

"Oh," she starts, when the door opens. "I'm looking for Father Niccacci?"

The young man in the doorway is broad-shouldered and chisel-jawed, with a helmet of thick, dark hair. He wears a brown cassock, tied at the waist with a long white rope. "You've found me," the monk says.

"**You're** Father Niccacci?"

The monk smiles, raising a pair of caterpillar eyebrows. "Last I heard," he says. "Come, you'll catch frostbite standing out there." He takes her valise, and she follows him inside.

Lili introduces herself as a friend of Cardinal Dalla Costa's in Florence, and also of Esti's. "The habit is . . ." she gestures to the coif at her neck.

"A disguise," the monk says simply.

"Yes. And this is Theo." Lili picks Theo up. He wraps his arms around her neck.

"Pleasure to meet you both. Is that your bike out there?"

"It is. Or rather, it's a friend's."

"Where did you come from?"

"From Castelnuovo Berardenga."

"That far!"

"It was . . . challenging," Lili says, realizing suddenly how spent her legs are, how windblown she must look.

"Can I offer you a water and some bread?"

"That sounds wonderful. Thank you," Lili says, still reconciling his appearance with that of the older, feebler Father Niccacci she'd imagined.

"This way."

Lili trails the monk down a hallway, letting her gaze jump over his shoulder, half expecting—hoping—Esti might step out of the shadows to surprise them.

The refectory is a room of white stone and

burgundy walls. Lili and Theo sit at one end of a long, weathered oak table, beneath a life-size painting of Jesus on the crucifix.

"So you're a friend of the Ezratti girl," Father Niccacci says, setting a wedge of peasant bread and a cup of water before her.

Lili brightens. "Yes! Esti."

"Dalla Costa speaks quite highly of her," Father Niccacci says. "It sounds as if she's been a great help to him."

Lili's heart skips. "She promised to meet us in Assisi. Is it possible that . . . she beat us here?"

Father Niccacci shakes his head. "I've been awaiting her arrival," he says, and Lili deflates, cursing under her breath.

"Sorry," she says, eyes wide as she realizes her mistake.

Father Niccacci laughs. "These are trying times," he says.

"Mama is not here?" Theo asks Lili.

"No, not yet."

Theo's shoulders sag. Lili removes his mittens and hat, then fishes in her coat pocket for his lamb and hands it to him. "Are you hungry for some bread, Theo?"

"No."

"If you're tired you can close your eyes, love." She pulls him onto her lap, and he leans back, lets his head rest heavy on her chest.

"Has the cardinal sent any word from Florence?" Lili asks the monk.

A shadow passes briefly over Father Niccacci's face. "I was with him a week ago, actually."

"You were in Florence?"

"Yes, I went to visit him. My timing wasn't so good though. When I arrived the city—" He glances at Theo. "I've never seen anything like it."

"I heard there was a second roundup," Lili says softly. "I was there for the first."

"I'm sure you saw what I saw then." Father Niccacci glances up at Jesus on his altar and crosses himself.

"How did it get so bad?" Lili wonders aloud.

"I keep asking myself the same."

Theo twitches.

"Is he asleep?" Lili whispers.

"Out cold."

Lili takes a breath. "I didn't want to ask in front of him—but did the cardinal mention anything of the women and children at the convent across the river on Piazza del Carmine? That's where Esti was. Is. Where I left her."

"He didn't, I'm sorry. It was chaos."

Lili wraps her arms a little tighter around Theo's frame. Her patience is waning. The waiting, the speculating, the worry—it's debilitating, like a poison in her veins. "I've sent two letters since I left Florence," she says, "but they've gone unanswered."

"The mail is slow. And unreliable. You'll find her. Have faith."

That word again. Lili recalls the rabbi's advice in Ferrara, at the Rosh Hashanah service, on the night the temple was raided. She wonders how the rabbi feels now, about his own faith.

She reaches for her water. She'll save the bread for Theo.

Father Niccacci tilts his head. "What has Dalla Costa told you about what we're doing here?" he asks.

Lili isn't sure how much she's supposed to know about the printing operation in Assisi, or how much Father Niccacci will be willing to share with her. She decides to tell the truth. "He said you were helping to print and distribute false identity cards. For Jews."

The monk weaves his fingers together, rests his hands on the table. "The cardinal trusts your friend, so I feel like I can trust you," he says. "But all of this is confidential, extremely so. My colleague, the printer, he hasn't even told his own son of his operation."

"Of course."

Father Niccacci holds her gaze for a beat, then continues. "There are scores of Jewish refugees hiding here in Assisi—at least three hundred, last I counted, although the number is always changing."

"That many. I didn't realize."

"We keep them hidden well. And until recently, we were able to help many find safe passage out of the country, mostly through Genoa, where Delasem—you are aware of the organization?"

"I am."

"Where Delasem was arranging travel by sea to Palestine or to the Americas or even as far as Shanghai. But the port in Genoa is overrun now by Germans. The city's no longer safe, even for those lucky enough to have Aryan IDs."

"Have you considered finding refuge for them in Switzerland?" Lili asks, thinking of her father. She'd do anything to know if Massimo had made it across the border as planned.

"Entering Switzerland is nearly impossible now. The border is heavily patrolled by the Salò and by the Germans. Where there aren't checkpoints, there are electric fences."

Lili lets this information settle. It's not what she was hoping to hear. "I've heard it's possible with a guide," she says.

"It is. If you can find a trustworthy one."

"My father fled to Switzerland," she says. "About a month ago."

"I see. His chances were better then."

Lili grasps for comfort in Father Niccacci's words. "There were some children who attempted to cross the border as well," she says.

"From the Villa Emma, yes. How do you know about them?"

"We spent some time in Nonantola. Esti helped with IDs."

"Ah. I see."

"Do you know if they made it across?"

Father Niccacci shakes his head. "No. But no news is good news, I think."

Lili's thoughts turn to the plan she and Esti had discussed—of finding their way into Allied territory. "Have you thought about moving people south?" Lili asks. "Toward the Allies?"

"Yes. That's the goal, eventually. Our focus at the moment is to get papers to those left in hiding here and in the bigger cities, like Florence and Rome."

Lili swallows. Esti needs a new ID. Perhaps she could pay the printer in Assisi to make her one.

"We're doing all that we can," the monk adds, "but still, it's impossible to keep up with the demand."

"Which is why you're so eager for Esti's help," Lili says.

"Exactly. From what I understand, your friend has mastered the process. It's laborious. Are you familiar with it?"

"I am." Lili says. "But it's always been Esti's undertaking, not mine."

"You understand all that goes into it though."

"I do. If there's anything I can do to help, Father, at least until she gets here . . ." Lili pauses, realizing the significance of her words.

"That's generous of you," Father Niccacci says. "There are many ways one can help. The risk involved is extreme though, as I'm sure you're aware. I appreciate the sentiment nonetheless, and I might take you up on it in the coming weeks. In the meantime, let's hope your friend gets here soon."

"Yes, let's."

Bells toll, a call for evening vespers.

"I'm sure you're eager to get settled," the monk says. "There's a woman in town, Isabella. You can stay with her. She can be trusted. Keep your ID on you at all times. Should anyone ask, Isabella will tell them you are her cousin."

"Okay. My habit—"

"You won't need it while you're here. The church community is small. I think wearing it would attract attention."

"All right."

"Isabella has a young son about Theo's age, Ricardo. Her husband, Tulio, was sent to Germany."

"Germany?"

"The Wehrmacht took his regiment. When Italy surrendered to the Allies."

"His whole regiment?"

"Have you not heard? Hitler's arrested and deported thousands of Italian soldiers. Along with anti-Fascists, prisoners of war, partisans—anyone he deems dangerous to the regime."

"I didn't realize."

"How Mussolini is able to stand by and watch his own countrymen get shipped off is a mystery to me."

"And the Jews? Are they being sent to Germany too?"

"The Jews, no. They are being sent east, to Poland."

"To Poland."

"Yes."

"There are rumors that the pope is protecting Jews who convert to Catholicism."

Father Niccacci frowns. "It's an option for some. But if the Germans catch us baptizing people by the dozens, they'll know what we're up to."

"So it's not something Theo and I should consider?"

"Not at the moment, no."

Lili thinks of the advice Dalla Costa gave, to obtain matching IDs upon arriving in Assisi. "Theo's ID has a different last name—Esti's. The cardinal recommended he have one made to match mine, that we can use until Esti gets here."

"Yes, I can arrange that. The cardinal is right—it's safer if the authorities think Theo is your son."

Though it feels strange, like a betrayal of sorts, to change Theo's name without asking Esti first, Lili agrees—she'd feel better pretending to be his mother than using the orphan alibi.

"I'm meeting with the printer next week," the monk continues. "If your friend is not here by then, you should join me. In the meantime, I'll have a courier deliver Isabella some extra ration cards."

"Thank you."

"Don't let your guard down even for a moment while you're here," Father Niccacci says. "The German colonel posted here seems a decent man—Müller is his name—but your enemies are never far from sight. Nazis. Fascists. Be prepared for them to arrive unannounced, to search Isabella's home. Tell no one of your true identity. I don't know of a civilian yet who's turned in a Jew, but the reward is significant; some, no doubt, will be tempted."

Lili pales.

"I don't mean to frighten you. Assisi is a welcoming place in general. Just . . . be vigilant."

Theo flinches in his sleep and his lamb drops from his hand. Lili catches it before it falls to the floor.

CHAPTER TWENTY-ONE

ASSISI

December 1943

Lili and Theo have been in Assisi for a week. Lili has sent letters to her father's uncle in Lausanne, to Sister Lotte at the convent in Florence, and to Niko in Salonica, begging for news. Every day, she reminds herself that even if her letters have reached their recipients, chances are it will take weeks, months even, for a reply to come back to her. She tells herself this, but the absence of news gnaws at her, as unshakable as the December cold. Meanwhile, the headlines are dire. Along with making arrests, there are reports of **carabinieri** continuing to confiscate Jewish property, seizing everything from businesses and bank accounts to dinnerware and bed linens. Lili goes to sleep every night imagining the contents of her home in Bologna being stripped away until the floors and walls and shelves are bare. The apartment is under Settimo's name, she reminds herself often. On the books, it's no longer Jewish property. There is hope.

A church bell rings—bells are always ringing in Assisi—and Lili counts the tolls. Seven in the morning. Unable to sleep, she'd risen before dawn and slipped out of the bed she and Theo share in Isabella's spare room. Now, she sits on the floor with a wool blanket wrapped around her, her back against the wall, a lantern at her feet and a book on her lap to serve as a desk as she writes another letter to Esti. This one, she's decided, she'll bring to Father Niccacci directly. He mentioned he had someone who carries photographs and IDs back and forth between Florence and Assisi. Perhaps it's Dalla Costa's same courier; perhaps, Lili hopes, he can deliver a letter for her.

From the bed, Theo rustles, makes a small humming sound. Lili climbs to her feet, moves to sit beside him. He rolls to face her, kneads at his eyes with the palms of his hands.

"Good morning, kiddo," Lili says, combing her fingers through his hair. His curls have grown into a wild jumble since leaving Florence; her attempt to tame them futile. Lili makes a note to ask Isabella for a pair of scissors.

"Is Ricardo awake?" Theo asks, and Lili smiles, grateful that his first thought of the day is a happy one. Isabella's son, Ricardo, and Theo are a year apart in age. They play well together. Lili often marvels at the ease with which the young boys, strangers just a week ago, have fallen into step.

"He is. I heard him downstairs a few minutes ago."

Theo grins and swings his legs over the side of the bed, and Lili watches as the bits of sleep that had clung to him a minute before fall away. He bounds toward the door in his pajamas.

"Hold on, tiger, let's get you dressed first," Lili says, laughing. She pulls out an armoire drawer and reaches for a shirt and a pair of pants. "Dry again today," she says, as she helps Theo out of his cloth diaper and into a pair of clean underwear. Theo will be three soon—the age, apparently, when a child can sleep through the night without wetting himself. Theo nods, puffing up his chest a little, then races from the room as Lili pulls the quilt back up over the bed, smooths it flat.

Downstairs, she finds Isabella in the kitchen, heating a kettle of water. Through the window over the kitchen sink, she can see a light snow falling.

"Sleep well?" Isabella asks over her shoulder.

"Well enough." In truth, Lili can hardly recall her last good night's rest. Whatever anxious thoughts she's able to keep at bay in the daylight come darting into her subconscious like a swarm of bees once the house is quiet, the room dark.

"Here," Isabella says, handing Lili an espresso cup filled with barley coffee.

"Thanks."

Isabella is small in stature, with delicate, birdlike features, but she carries herself in a calm, sensible way that Lili has come to admire. To make ends meet, she works at a leather shop in town, mending tack for the German cavalry. She and her husband had moved to Assisi from Naples just before the war broke out. Without family to help with Ricardo, she'd taken to carting her son to work with her, where, she says, he spends his days napping or entertaining himself under her desk with an old stirrup, a tin of nails, a picture book brought from home. **If you're comfortable with it**, Lili offered soon after she'd arrived, **I could watch Ricardo while you work. I'm sure he and Theo would enjoy each other's company.** It was the least she could do, Lili figured, to thank Isabella for taking her in. Isabella readily agreed, and Lili's days have since been consumed with overseeing the boys as they play in Isabella's living room, waving finger rifles in imaginary battles, building elaborate cities from wooden blocks, and kicking a pair of socks rolled into a ball back and forth in rowdy games of football.

"I've gathered some clothes for you, along with an old pair of Ricardo's boots, just there," Isabella says, nodding toward the kitchen table. "He's grown out of them. They're yours if you'd like them."

"Wow, thank you, that's kind of you. And perfect timing. I've just let the hem out of Theo's pants."

"Happy to put them to use. I'd hoped there might

be another baby by now. But . . . here we are." Isabella arches her eyebrows.

"Here we are," Lili echoes. She downs her coffee, then rinses the cup in the sink. "I was wondering if I might ask a favor this morning," she says. It's a Sunday, Isabella's day off. "I'd like to visit Father Niccacci at the monastery, to deliver a letter. Would you mind if I left Theo here with you for an hour while I go?"

Isabella places four plates on the table, each with a thin slice of peasant bread. "I don't mind. I'm also happy to take it for you, if you prefer. Or we could all go."

Lili hadn't considered the idea of making the walk together. She's barely left the house since she arrived. Her lungs are craving fresh air, her legs some circulation. She'd thought about taking the Giardinis' bike—she'd stored it beside Isabella's in her crawl space and written to Eva with an address for whenever Cenzo was able to come by for it—but the roads down to the monastery were steep and, with the snow, too slippery to bike. A walk, she realizes, sounds refreshing. It's twenty-five minutes to the monastery. And it would do Theo good, too, to get outside.

"Thanks," she says. "I'm eager for the exercise. Why don't we all go. That would be nice."

"Great. I'd love to get out. And we've got our story. If anyone asks, you're my cousin, from Lecce," Isabella says.

"Right," Lili says. "Your cousin from Lecce."

"And Theo is . . ." Isabella knows of Esti, of Theo's mismatched ID.

"My nephew," Lili says. "If anyone asks, I'll say his father was conscripted and his mother is sick and that I'm taking care of him until she's better." **Not a complete lie**, Lili thinks.

"It's done then," Isabella says, calling for the boys. "Let's put a little something in our stomachs before we go."

An hour later, wrapped in coats, hats, and gloves, Isabella, Ricardo, Lili, and Theo step out into the cold. Lili's breath catches as the icy air fills her lungs. She pulls the fur collar of Eva's coat up to her ears, grateful for its warmth. Fat flakes now tumble from the sky in earnest, carpeting the city and decorating their shoulders like sugar sprinkled over a **pasticciotto**. It's beautiful, and eerily quiet—the only sound the muted crunch of their footsteps. Lili takes Theo's hand, following close behind Isabella and Ricardo as they weave through a labyrinth of steep, narrow alleyways. When they reach the gate at the village wall, the view opens up and Lili takes in the sprawling Umbrian countryside below, its stone barns and hayfields and rows upon rows of olive trees, all filmed in white. She hadn't appreciated the view on the uphill walk from San Damiano when she and Theo first arrived in Assisi.

"It's so pretty here," she says, wiping a snowflake from her eyelash.

"Isn't it? Someday I'll be able to afford a flat in town with a view."

When Isabella tells her it's safe for the boys to explore, Lili loosens her grip on Theo's hand, and he and Ricardo take off, arms spread wide like wings, chins lifted to the sky as they carve serpentines with their footprints in the snow.

"Like this!" Ricardo instructs, pausing to catch a flake on his tongue.

Theo mimics, squeezing his eyes shut in the effort. "Got one!" he shouts a moment later.

"Stay close, please," Isabella calls as the boys skip ahead, dragging their mittened hands along the outer stone of the city wall. They bend every now and then to scoop up handfuls of snow and toss them in the air, shrieking as the soft, frozen powder falls over them, their laughter ringing like wind chimes through the frigid air. Lili looks ahead, wondering if she should tell the boys to lower their voices, but they're alone as far as she can tell, and she hasn't the heart to dampen the fun.

"I love your coat," Isabella says.

Lili runs a hand along her rabbit-fur lapel. "Thanks."

"It's gorgeous."

"It was a gift," Lili says, realizing how nice it feels to talk about something as frivolous as fashion. How normal. Bells sound in the distance. "The percussion is constant," she says. "I like it."

"Me too. I hear they're melting down church bells in other towns," Isabella says.

"Why?"

"To make weapons, I think. Ammunition, tanks."
Lili sighs. "Bullets from church bells."

"I know. Hard to believe it's come to that."

When they arrive at the monastery, Isabella
and Ricardo follow Lili and Theo through the portico to the arched entrance, where Lili stomps her feet
a few times, removes a glove, and raises a fist—but
before her knuckles strike wood, the door opens and
a man appears, carrying a bicycle over his shoulder.

"Well! Hello!" he says, seeing the surprise on
Lili's face. "Sorry for the scare—I didn't realize you
were there."

"It's okay—I was just about to knock is all," Lili
says, dropping her hand.

The man wears fitted beige trousers tucked into
knee-high socks, a woolen tunic, and a scarf. "After
you," he says, stepping aside. The women and boys
file in. Lili holds the door for him as he carries his
bike through, setting it down in the courtyard.

"Ragazzi," he says, winking at Theo and Ricardo.

"Are you going to ride through the snow?"
Ricardo asks.

The man glances skyward. "Appears so. It'll be
a chilly trip home, I'm afraid." He mounts his
bike, which, Lili can tell from its curved drop bars
and narrow saddle, is of the racing sort. There's

something familiar about him—his easy smile, his high cheekbones, his strong jaw—though what it is, exactly, she can't place. "**Ciao, amici!**" he calls, slipping his feet into his stirrups.

"**Ciao!**" the boys cry. They wave as he pedals away.

Isabella reaches for Lili's arm. "Do you know who that was?" she whispers.

"No, but I could have sworn I recognized him."

"That was Gino Bartali!"

Lili's eyes widen. "**The** Gino Bartali?"

"Yes!"

"Well, that would explain the racing bike."

Gino is Italy's golden boy, or had been, before the war. Lili doesn't pay much attention to the sport of cycling, but her father does, and Bartali is one of his favorites. He won the Giro d'Italia twice, even managed to clinch the Tour de France a few years back.

"What on earth is he doing **here**?" Lili wonders.

"I don't know. I thought he was from Florence."

"He must be a friend of Father Niccacci's," Lili says.

"Or maybe he has family in Assisi."

"I'm cold," Ricardo says, tugging on Isabella's coat sleeve.

"I'm cold!" Theo parrots.

"All right, all right," Lili says, letting the door swing shut as Father Niccacci appears, putting the subject of Gino Bartali to rest.

"**Signore!**" he says, greeting Lili and Isabella with

a small bow. "I wasn't expecting you. Is everything okay?"

"Yes, Father," Lili says, "apologies for coming unannounced. I know you have your services today."

"They're not for another hour." Father Niccacci turns to Isabella. "Isabella, it's nice to see you. How are you?"

"Fine as can be, thank you, Father."

"Any news from Tulio?"

"Not yet."

"Soon, I hope. And how about you, Lili. Are you settling in?"

"I am," Lili says. "Isabella has been so kind to us. Our boys are in heaven in each other's company."

"They look like trouble," Father Niccacci says, eyeing Ricardo and Theo, who giggle under his gaze. "You two aren't getting up to any mischief, are you?"

"No, Father," Ricardo says, shaking his head emphatically.

"Good. And how about your friend, Lili, any word from her?"

Lili feels Theo's eyes on her. She clears her throat. "Not yet. That's—why I'm here, actually. I'm afraid my letters aren't reaching her—or, perhaps hers aren't reaching me. You mentioned you had a courier making trips between Assisi and Florence. I wondered if I could leave something with you, if perhaps your friend could deliver it for me. I'd compensate, of course," she adds. She'd pay anything for news from Esti.

Father Niccacci's eyes flit to the door and back. "I'd be happy to pass something along. Do you have it with you now?"

Lili reaches into her purse, hands him the envelope she prepared that morning. The monk tucks it into his robe.

"What else can I do for you, **signore**? Can I take your coats? Offer you something to drink?"

"We'll let you prepare for your service," Lili says.

"Yes," Isabella agrees, "and be on our way before the snow gets much deeper."

"All right, then. I owe you a visit, Lili. I'll come by next week. Thursday night. Maybe by then I'll have some information for you from Florence."

"That would be wonderful," Lili says, her heart surging with hope.

"See you then," Father Niccacci says, as Lili and Isabella make their way back out into the courtyard.

Lili glances at the narrow tire marks left in the snow. "Father," she says, turning to face the young monk in the doorway, "the gentleman who was leaving as we came, by bike . . ."

"You never saw him," Father Niccacci says, his smile tight.

"Right," Lili nods.

ON THURSDAY, JUST BEFORE DUSK, FATHER NICCACCI appears at Isabella's door, as promised.

"Let's walk," he tells Lili.

"Sure," Lili says, reaching for her coat. Isabella was just home from work and had agreed to give the boys dinner and put them to bed, should Lili be out for more than an hour.

The young monk takes Lili's arm as she steps outside. "Do you have your ID with you? Theo's too?"

"I do."

"Good. How have you been managing?"

"Fine, actually."

"No one's given you any funny looks?"

"Just once. A couple of days ago, a woman behind me in line for rations struck up a conversation. Eventually she asked where I was from and when I told her Lecce she said she used to live there and then peppered me with questions about my family. It spooked me a bit."

"I don't blame you."

"I need to find a map of Lecce. Study the streets."

"Yes, that would be smart. Perhaps it's best to lay low for a few days. Let Isabella do the shopping." Lili had thought the same. "And how is the boy?"

"He's well. Let's hope behaving at the moment for Isabella."

Lili and the monk are quiet. Sunday's snow had given way to frost, the cobblestones now glazed in an invisible coat of ice. They walk mindfully, trying not to slip.

"Forgive me for being forward," Lili says, "but I've been aching to know if you've made contact with your courier."

"Yes, he came today. He didn't have any news from your convent in Florence, but I gave him your letter, and he said he would deliver it tomorrow. I mentioned your offer to compensate, and he refused, as I thought he might."

"That's very kind of him," Lili says. She pictures Esti with the letter in her hands. "Did he say when he'd return?"

"He'll be back on Sunday, if all goes as planned."

Sunday. In three days. This Lili can manage.

"Thank you, Father, for your help."

"I'm just the man in the middle," Father Niccacci says. "My couriers and my printer are the heroes of this story."

"I'm assuming that's where we're going? To meet with the printer?"

"Yes. I was hoping your friend would be here by now; since she's not, it's time we make you and Theo matching IDs. I'll warn you, Luigi's not the friendliest of sorts, but he's got a good heart."

They approach a large, empty piazza, decorated at its center with a dried-up fountain in the shape of a mushroom. On one side of the square is a row of single-story shops, and across from the shops a church—large and imposing with a pink-and-white banded facade. An intricately carved rose window over the doorway reminds Lili of the sunflower windows adorning the cathedral in Ferrara. On the other side of the square sits a long stone bench and, behind it, a wide-open vista of the valley below.

"Basilica di Santa Chiara," Father Niccacci says, nodding toward the church. If you're in the mood, you can visit Saint Clare in the crypt," he adds, with a trace of humor. "She's nothing more than a skeleton now, but her shrine is quite impressive."

Lili smiles. She likes this man.

"Luigi's place is just there." Father Niccacci gestures toward one of the shops. "We'll enter from around back." He guides her down a narrow side street to a nondescript door, looks around to be sure they are alone.

"I'm closed!" a voice calls from inside, at the sound of Father Niccacci's knock.

"It's Rufino," the monk replies, leaning his head close to the door.

He and Lili wait, and after a moment they hear the click of a dead bolt. The door opens a finger's width, and in the strip of light from within Lili can see the shadow of a man, then the white of an eye.

"So it is," the man grunts. A chain jingles and a moment later, Lili and Father Niccacci step inside.

The priest and the printer greet each other with kisses on the cheek. Luigi is a stout man of seventy, Lili would guess. He wears overalls and a beret and his hands are creased and stained black in the folds of skin around his knuckles.

"A pair of Germans came around yesterday, just before close. I was sure when you knocked they'd returned."

Father Niccacci frowns. "What did they want?"

"They were after a couple of souvenirs to send home to their wives."

"Ah. Well, that's a relief." Father Niccacci turns to Lili. "Luigi sells religious trinkets at the front of the shop. So—what happened?"

"I gave them a couple of carvings of Saint Clare. Told them it was a gift from Assisi to our German friends."

"Smart."

"I guess. Had to sit down for a bit when they left. This business we're in is hard on an old man's heart."

"And we are indebted to you for your help. You're saving lives, my friend. Just remember that."

Luigi glances at Lili.

"Luigi, this is Lili," Father Niccacci says.

Luigi nods. "**Piacere**."

"It's a pleasure," Lili replies.

"She's a friend of the counterfeiter I told you about, Ezratti."

"Ah. The illustrious forger. Has she shown up yet?"

"Not yet, unfortunately. She got held up in Florence. Lili brought Ezratti's child with her to Assisi. His ID should match Lili's, until his mother gets here. Can you make him a new one?"

"Let's have a look," Luigi says.

Lili removes her ID, along with Theo's, from her wallet and hands them to Luigi.

"These are excellent," he says. "I can make the boy a replica that matches yours. The only thing missing is a House of Savoy stamp. It's not required, but

you'll find it on some of the older IDs. I can add it.
That and some tags."

"Tags?" Lili asks.

"So it looks like you've been somewhere."

Lili recalls how her old papers, the ones she'd
traded in, were decorated with half a dozen postage-
stamp-size stickers, each in a different color, from
her travels. "Yes," she says, "of course."

"Just a final touch, for authenticity."

"How do you manage to come by such tags?"
Lili asks.

"We get Italian soldiers passing through here
every now and then, trying to make their way home.
It's remarkable what a hungry man will trade for a
slice of cheese, if you ask," Luigi says with a mis-
chievous smile. "I'll need a few days with these," he
adds, pocketing the IDs.

"That's fine," Lili says, though the thought of
leaving without proof of her Aryan identity gives
her pause.

"Thank you, my friend," Father Niccacci says. "I
believe you have some papers for me as well?"

"Yes, yes, I have a package ready for you."

Luigi leads them down a short hallway to a
cramped office. The space is poorly lit, the walls
stone, the floor made of rough wooden planks that
creak beneath their weight. At the center of the
room is a large black printing press, not unlike the
one Lili remembers from the offices of the **Ferrara**

Daily. A stool and an old phone book sit on the floor beside it. Lili examines the machine.

"A Felix," she says, admiring its many levers and rollers and ink disk. "Nice."

"It's refurbished," Luigi says. He removes a hammer from a desk at the far side of the room, lowers himself with a groan to his knees. Lili glances at Father Niccacci, wondering for a moment if the old man is about to offer a prayer. Instead, he pulls a loose nail, then another, from a floorboard, removing a plank of wood and setting it aside. From the hole in the floor, he retrieves an envelope, thick and cream colored. He replaces the wooden plank with a few quick taps of his hammer and stands, brushes the dust from his overalls, and hands the envelope to Father Niccacci.

"You've been busy," the monk says, grinning.

"I have."

"Thank you for this." Father Niccacci unbuttons his coat, slides the envelope into his robe, and adjusts the rope of his belt around it. "I should have some more photos for you on Sunday."

"You know where to find me," Luigi says, then looks at a clock on his desk. "Let me show you out."

They follow the printer back down the hallway. "It's nearly curfew," Luigi warns. "Better hurry."

"We will. Thank you again," Father Niccacci says, patting the spot where the envelope is hidden. "And Luigi . . ."

"Oh, here we go," the printer grumbles, but his tone is light.

"I know, I know, you're not a man of the church, but I can't help myself. God bless you, Luigi Brizi."

Luigi opens the door to let them out. "Damned ice," he says. "Watch your step out there." He nods in the monk's direction, then tips his hat to Lili.

CHAPTER TWENTY-TWO

ASSISI

December 1943

"Oh, that's an easy one. My mother's carbonara," Lili says.

She and Isabella are at the sink, Lili washing dishes, Isabella beside her with a drying cloth, discussing the meal they would choose, if given one wish.

"I love carbonara." Isabella glances at Lili. "Your family doesn't keep kosher?"

"No. My mother said she tried her first taste of pork at a friend's house when she was little." Lili laughs. "After that, she never looked back."

"A woman of my heart," Isabella says.

"She was an amazing cook," Lili says, scrubbing at a plate.

"How did she prepare hers? My carbonara's never as good as I want it to be."

Lili pictures her mother at her kitchen counter in Bologna, a dishcloth tucked into the waist of her pants, knife in hand, cutting block before her. "She'd slice the pancetta into little strips and fry it till it was crispy, then toss the pasta right into the pan, to soak up all the flavor. She knew just how many eggs and how much **parmigiano**, though she did it all by memory—I had to beg her to write the recipe down for me. Her secret was to whip the egg whites separately, then fold them in at the last minute." Lili's mouth waters. It was tantalizing as a kid, to smell the pancetta sizzling in her mother's cast-iron skillet. If she hung around the kitchen long enough, which she always did, Naomi would slip her a piece or two.

"Whipped egg whites," Isabella says. "I'll have to try that."

"How about you?" Lili asks. "What would your meal be?"

"In winter, my **nonna**'s minestrone **napoletano**. It's perfection. That with a loaf of just-out-of-the-oven bread, hard crust, soft in the middle." Isabella kisses her fingers, and Lili's mouth waters again. "I'm on a mission to perfect it."

"Someday you will," Lili says.

"Someday. When we can shop for what we please and not for what we're allotted. Thank you, by the way, for the carrots and onions today."

"Of course."

Lili has returned to the market with her ration cards, determined to do what she can to chip in, though she keeps an eye out for the woman from

Lecce. Most nights, she and Isabella combine provisions and get creative with the spices in Isabella's cabinet, culling together soups and stews from their food scraps. After dinner, when the children are asleep, the women come together in the kitchen to clean, a silent pact between them that neither will put their feet up or go to bed until the house is tidy. They try not to talk about the war, but instead of benign things: favorite songs and first crushes and the last good book they'd read—little reminders of the lives they hoped to return to someday.

"And for dessert?" Lili asks, handing Isabella a bowl to dry, thinking of her mother's sponge cake. "What would you have?"

"That's not so obvious, but if I had to choose—"

A rap at the door. Lili looks over her shoulder, freezes. Water drips from her hands into the basin. A knock after curfew can't be good. Who could it be? The only person who's dropped by since she arrived in Assisi is Father Niccacci. Once, to walk her to Luigi's, and then again a few days later, to deliver her ID along with Theo's new one—their last names match now. Lili's heart lifts. Could it be—Esti? She's dreamt the scenario so many times in the last six weeks, she's begun to wonder if she could will it true.

"Wait here," Isabella says, setting her cloth on the counter. Her footsteps retreat down the hallway. She returns a moment later, holding an envelope. "There was no one there. Just this," she says. "It's for you."

"For me?" Lili's fingers find the edge of the sink behind her. She makes no motion to take the envelope. "Who's it from?"

"I don't know." Isabella turns the parcel over in her hands. "The return address says Piazza del Carmine. Florence." She looks up at Lili. "Is that where your friend is?"

Lili grips at the porcelain, her knees soft. She nods.

"Would you like me to open it?" Isabella asks gently.

"No. No. It's all right," Lili whispers. She peels her hands from the sink, dries her palms on her trousers.

Isabella hands her the envelope. "I'll finish up here," she says.

"Thank you," Lili manages.

Time slows as she climbs the stairs, retreating to the privacy of her room. She moves silently so as not to wake Theo. At his request, to scare away the monsters, she'd left a lantern burning on the dresser at the foot of the bed. Now, she holds the envelope to its light, turns it over in her hands. She's tempted to rip it open and devour its contents, but something in her waits, wary of its message. The writing, she notes right away, is not Esti's. Perhaps it's Sister Lotte's. Maybe there will be a note from Esti inside. Or maybe it's from someone else at the convent, writing with news that Esti is finally on her way, that she'll arrive in Assisi in a day or two. Maybe— maybe!—Esti will arrive as early as tomorrow, on

Theo's birthday. What a surprise that would be! Lili hadn't made a to-do of Theo turning three, mostly because she'd told herself Esti would be there to celebrate, to make it special. Lili imagines them sitting down to share slices of the **torta alla panna** she'd planned to improvise, singing **Tanti Auguri**, Theo's face glowing in the halo of his candles and in the joy of having his mother back in his life. She pictures herself snuggled in bed with Esti, Theo between them, the two women taking turns reading aloud until Theo falls asleep, then talking late into the night, filling the gaps in the last month of each other's lives. **Maybe.**

She pushes a finger under the flap of the envelope, careful not to tear the paper, extracts a piece of parchment. She unfolds it, begins to read.

> **Dearest Lili,**
> I received your letter, thanks to a friend of Father N. You mentioned you'd sent others, but your last is the only one to reach me. I was so relieved to hear from you. You ask of Esti. I'm afraid the news is not good. There is no easy way to tell you this, Lili, so I will get straight to it.

Lili's hands begin to shake. She presses the paper onto the top of the dresser, holding it flat at its edges, her breath shallow.

Carità's gang returned to the convent
three days after you left. They found the
room where Esti and the others were
hidden and they took the women. All of
them. I have no idea where. I've spent
every day since searching for answers,
but the only morsel of information I've
uncovered is a rumor that a group of
women was arrested and moved from
Florence to Verona not long after the
raid. I've not yet confirmed if this is true
and if it is, I have no way of knowing if
they were the women from my convent.
I'll keep asking, and will write if I learn
anything new. But it is my belief that if
Esti were still in Florence, I'd have found
her by now.

One of Lili's hands finds her mouth. There is
more. She forces herself to read on.

I must tell you, Lili (for to not tell you
feels like hiding a truth) that Esti was not
in a good way when they took her. She
was still alive—I've seen too many dead
bodies by now not to know when a soul
has left one—but barely. I'm horribly
sorry to be the bearer of such news. I'd
have written sooner, but I didn't know
how to reach you. I will be praying for

you, Lili, and for Esti and for Theo. I'm
relieved to know that two of you, at least,
are accounted for.

May the Lord be with you,
Sister Lotte

Lili's breath is hot on her fingers, and she wonders
if she might be sick. She closes her eyes.

**I should have stayed, Esti. I'm so sorry. I never
should have left.**

She talks to Esti often, in her mind. It makes her
feel less alone, though she often feels like a mad-
woman doing so. Now, Esti's voice fills her head,
familiar as her own.

They'd have taken you too.

Maybe they would have, but at least we'd
be together.

You did the right thing.

I left you.

**Because I asked you to. It was my decision.
Not yours.**

But Theo . . .

**You've kept him safe. I owe you everything
for that.**

No! I should have stood up to you for once, held
my ground.

Leaving took more courage than staying.

Lili tries to picture Esti taking her last breath in
the filthy barracks of a detention camp in Verona,

but she can't. It's impossible. She opens her eyes, her lashes thick with tears. Maybe she should go, bribe a guard to find out if her friend is there. But the city is in the heart of the Salò. To travel there could be disastrous. And there isn't any proof that Esti was actually sent to Verona. For all Lili knows, she could still be in Florence. She could be anywhere.

"Where are you, Esti?" Lili whispers aloud. But this time, there is no answer, just the roar of silence in her ears.

CHAPTER TWENTY-THREE

ASSISI

January 1944

Theo sits up in bed. "Mama," he whimpers, still half asleep.

Lili feels around under the quilt for his lamb. When she finds it, she hands it to him. "Shh, shh, lie down, my love," she whispers. "It's the middle of the night."

Theo flops back onto his pillow.

"Turn over," Lili says, "I'll give you a tickle."

Theo rolls to his side, and Lili slips her hand under his night shirt, drawing her fingers along the short length of his spine, his satin skin warm to the touch. Her mother used to tickle Lili's back as a child; the before-bed ritual never failed to settle her into sleep. It works well for Theo, too, though it took a few weeks for him to get used to it—he dissolved into giggles the first few times Lili tried it.

"Can I have a song?" Theo asks.

Lili's repertoire of lullabies is small, but Theo doesn't seem to mind. She chooses a song she's heard Esti sing on occasion. She hums it first, then, searching for the words, pieces together a verse.

Zitto bambino, non piangere,
La mama ti canterà una ninna nanna.
Hush little baby, don't you cry,
Mama will sing you a lullaby.
Zitto piccolo tesoro, non dire una parola,
Papà ti comprerà un tordo.
Hush little darling, don't say a word,
Papa will buy you a mockingbird.

As she sings, the room contracts, and Lili feels the tears begin to gather, as they do in moments like this, when Theo is oblivious and when she has nothing to distract her—when loneliness wraps around her like a corset, siphoning away her hopes, her strength, the air in her lungs. She hums the verse a final time, letting her hand come to rest between Theo's shoulder blades, the bones sharp beneath his skin.

It's been more than a month since Sister Lotte's letter arrived. Lili has heard from the nun twice in that time, but there's still no news from Esti, no explanation of where she was taken, of what's happened to her. One of Sister Lotte's letters came with a few of Esti's things: a pouch of jewelry and a small leather-bound diary, embossed with a capital **E**, which Lili hasn't had the heart to open. She'd stashed everything, along with her own valuables, in the lining of her valise, which she keeps hidden in Isabella's attic.

Theo rolls to face her, his eyes closed, his breath sweet. Lili stares at his silhouette in the dark. She hasn't told him yet of Sister Lotte's news. She hasn't been able to bring herself to. What is she supposed to say? **Your mother was taken. She's missing.** How do you tell that to a three-year-old? Especially now that Theo's spirits are up. The last time he cried for his mother was weeks ago, on his birthday, when it set in that despite the special occasion, Esti wasn't there. Since then, he's stopped asking for her. He's happy here with Ricardo. Distracted. Perhaps, Lili thinks, he's grown tired of hearing the same ambiguous response when she tries to explain his mother's absence; perhaps he understands there's more to her story than she's willing to admit, and he knows better now than to pry. Whatever the case, it seems his parting wounds have begun to heal—outwardly, at least. If only her own memory were so short, Lili thinks. If only the ache of missing grew fainter, rather than deeper over time. The longing, the not knowing, the worry—it grows worse as the days pass, compounded by the fact that Niko and her father are also unaccounted for.

Theo's breath slows as he drifts back to sleep, and

she closes her eyes, pinching back tears. **I just want answers. I want to know that my father is safe, that Esti is alive. Niko too. I want to know that I'll sit with them again around a table, share a meal, a conversation. Please.**

CHAPTER TWENTY-FOUR

ASSISI

February 1944

Lili wakes to the hum of conversation a story below. She listens, her body rigid, wondering what time it is, and whether she should rouse Theo and climb the stairs to the attic to hide. Isabella hardly ever receives visitors. Surely she would have warned Lili if she were expecting someone.

She tiptoes to the window, pulls the curtain aside. A trace of morning light penetrates the night sky, barely illuminating the empty lane below. There is no sign of a bicycle, a wagon—whoever is here, it seems, has arrived on foot. The visitor is a man, this much Lili can decipher from the low timbre rising through the floorboards. Maybe it's Father Niccacci's courier. Maybe it's a friend of Tulio's. Whatever the case, she has her papers, her story. If she needs to, she can use them. Better to feign innocence than try to hide and get caught. She pads back to the bed, winces at the creak of mattress coils beneath her as she sits. Pulling her knees to her chest, she leans against the headboard and waits.

After a few minutes, Lili notices a shift in the conversation. Isabella's voice carries an edge, her words suddenly more audible. **No. Assolutamente no.** The man speaks next, his reply a jumble of consonants, his tone, too, escalated. The pair is arguing. **Non ne ho bisogno,** Isabella says. **I don't need it.** Don't need what, Lili wonders? This time, the man's words carry. **Nove mila, Isabella,** he bellows, and Lili inhales sharply. **Nine thousand.** She recognizes the number: the sum in lire the Nazis are offering in Assisi for a turned-in Jew.

This man, whoever he is, wants to turn her in. Lili's heart thumps at her ribs. Has someone tipped him off? She's been so careful. Or so she's thought. She glances at the window. They're two stories up; too high to jump. Blinking into the darkness, she practices her story—Isabella's cousin, a war widow—willing the visitor to leave. Several minutes later, the conversation finally ebbs and Lili's heart slows. She hears the sound of a door closing, and then, feet climbing the stairs, a tap at her door.

"Are you up?" Isabella calls softly.

Lili slides from the bed. She glances at Theo, still sleeping, and steps out into the hallway, closing the door quietly behind her. Isabella is wearing a dressing robe and slippers. She holds a candle, and in its shivering light, Lili can see the flush in her cheeks.

"I heard voices . . ." Lili says.

"A friend of Tulio's turned up, inebriated." Isabella pauses, purses her lips. "I never liked him, the Fascist bastard. I shouldn't have let him in."

"What did he want?" Lili asks, though she's fairly certain of the man's intentions.

"He lives across the way and says he's seen you, coming and going. He—claims to know that you are Jewish."

"What? How?"

"I don't know. I told him he was crazy. Explained that you are my cousin, that you have your papers."

"And he didn't believe you?"

"He's an ass. A greedy, selfish ass."

"He wants the reward."

"Yes."

Lightheaded, Lili leans into the doorframe for balance. "What should we do?"

Isabella's eyes fall. "He wants to turn you in. He said he'd split the reward with me. And that if I refused, he'd do it anyway, and keep the nine thousand lire for himself." She looks up. "I'm so sorry, Lili."

Lili shakes her head. "No, don't apologize. You've been good to us, Isabella. I know the danger we've put you in. I should be the one apologizing."

"You've done nothing wrong."

"Do you think he's told anyone?"

"I don't know. He was very drunk."

Lili swallows. "Theo and I should leave. As soon as possible."

Isabella exhales heavily, and Lili can see she wants to protest, but she doesn't. "I wasn't worried before," she says. "There are plenty of people in this town who are helping, who are turning a blind eye. But now . . ."

"I'll pack our things."

Isabella nods. "I'll prepare you something to eat. Why don't you wake Theo and send him down."

"Thank you."

Isabella turns.

"Wait," Lili says, touching her shoulder. "If I disappear, won't that implicate you?"

Isabella looks at her. "It might. I'll tell them you've left to help care for your in-laws."

"In Arezzo," Lili adds. A town north of Assisi she's certain she won't visit anytime soon but that makes for a good alibi. The truth is easier to bend, she's learned, when you're specific about it.

"Sure, Arezzo. Anyway, if it comes up, it'll be my word against Adolfo's. I have the Church on my side, and he's a drunk, with no proof to his theory."

Lili hates herself for putting Isabella in danger.

"Don't worry about me. I'll be fine," Isabella says. She smiles weakly, then retreats down the stairs.

In her room, Lili rests the back of her head against the door, trying to think. Where will she go? Luigi's printing workshop isn't too far. But it's so early, he's probably not there. And she won't risk drawing attention to the shop. She'd never forgive herself if she were the leak to Luigi's counterfeiting ring. She'll return to the monastery, she decides. Ask Father Niccacci for help.

Walking around the bed, she sits beside Theo, rubs her hand in a circle on his side. "Hey, kiddo," she whispers. Theo flinches awake, stretches his arms overhead. Lili's chest aches for him. He's been happy here. "Wake up, love. It's time to go."

It's just after dawn when Lili finds herself in the monastery refectory, sitting beneath the crucifix in the spot where she first met Father Niccacci two months before. One of the nuns had offered to watch Theo, and Lili is grateful now for the privacy.

"I'm very sorry this happened," Father Niccacci says, rubbing his chin. "You were smart to leave right away."

"I hope I haven't implicated you in any way."

"You haven't. But it isn't safe any longer for you and Theo to stay in Assisi."

Lili glances at her lap. "Even with another family?"

"Assisi is too small a town."

Lili knows this, but it's hard still to fathom the idea of another move. Of leaving the place she and Esti had agreed to meet.

"I know that's not what you want to hear," Father Niccacci says.

"No, you're right. I just . . . it's been nice here, with Isabella. I like it here. And I keep praying Esti will show up." Lili hasn't told him about the news Sister Lotte shared. Saying it out loud was too difficult.

"And I will be here to greet her when she comes," he says.

When. Lili holds tight to the word. "Thank you, Father," she says. "I worry, too, how Theo will manage, leaving this place. He's content, finally. He adores Ricardo, he's secure in his routine."

"He'll understand. Not today, but someday."

"I hope so."

Lili doesn't know yet how she'll explain to Theo the sudden change of plans. She'd told him nothing as she hugged Isabella and said a too-quick goodbye, as they slipped from her home, Lili's only thought to flee as quickly as possible, without being seen. Theo had asked where they were going in such a hurry with their belongings in tow, and she'd promised to explain once they reached the monastery.

"It's for his safety as much as yours," Father Niccacci says gently. "Where will you go?"

Lili has been rolling the question over in her mind. She has a few friends in Ferrara, and her father's neighbor, Settimo, in Bologna, although Bologna has been battered once again by Allied bombs. There's no telling if her apartment building still stands. She also runs the risk of being recognized in places like Ferrara and Bologna. Her instinct all along has been to make her way south, toward the Allies. Away from the Germans, the Blackshirts.

"I'll go to Rome," she says, the plan formulating in real time. "It's still an open city, right?"

"Technically, yes. The king declared it so—an attempt to preserve the city, to minimize casualties—but that hasn't stopped the Germans from rounding up Jews or the Allies from bombing it. It's occupied, as I'm sure you're aware. Most Jews are trying to get **out**, not in."

Lili thinks about this. "I was hoping we'd be able to blend in with our IDs, that it's a big enough city for us to get lost in the mix."

Father Niccacci rubs again at his chin. "I suppose there isn't a safe place for Jews anywhere in occupied Italy. And you're right, Rome is a big city. Your ID is good. You should be able to pass. But you'll have to keep your guard up at all times."

Bells ring overhead, filling the refectory with their deep, resounding toll, and Lili and the monk are quiet for a moment, waiting for the sound to pass.

"If I were you, I'd travel on foot," Father Niccacci says. "Avoid the train stations."

Lili looks up, wondering if he's serious.

"Last week a friend of mine accompanied a Jewish couple by train to Spoleto; they were arrested at the station when a German guard demanded IDs. A husband and wife. Their papers were good—all of Luigi's are—but they fumbled their story and the guard called their bluff."

"What happened to them?"

"They were sent north, to Fossoli. To a prisoner-of-war camp near Modena."

"A camp," Lili says softly.

"It was run for a while by Italians, but the Germans have taken it over. Apparently it can house thousands."

Lili lets that news sink in. "It'll take weeks to reach Rome on foot, Father—I don't know how we'd make it."

"It sounds daunting, but others have done it."

Lili tries to picture walking more than two hundred kilometers with Theo. The bike ride from Castelnuovo Berardenga had nearly done her in. How would she find the strength to make such a journey? How would Theo? "I understand the dangers of the train," she says, "but is it any less dangerous to be on the road, out in the open?" The Allies have been dropping bombs over all of central Italy, trying to push the German military north.

"It's safer than an interrogation. Than prison. I don't know what exactly is happening to the Jews in Italy once they're in German hands, Lili, but I've heard rumors. You must avoid the possibility of capture at all costs."

Lili senses that Father Niccacci is holding something back. Protecting her from a reality even darker than the one she knows.

"And it won't look suspicious, the two of us walking, with a suitcase?"

"Many have relocated from city to country and

vice versa—to avoid the bombing, to stay with family—and with railways an Allied target and petrol a thing of the past, it's not uncommon to travel on foot. But you should have a story nonetheless, in case. Maybe you're trying to reach Rome to be with your sister for the birth of a child, something like that."

"Right, yes. Perhaps from Rome," Lili says, "we can continue south, to Allied territory. The Allies are gaining strength, aren't they? If they keep advancing, we won't have so far to go to reach them."

Father Niccacci considers this. "It's not a bad idea," he says. "But entering Allied territory will be dangerous. You'll have to cross the front, and the fighting is intense. Several have tried and failed. For now, I'd just worry about getting to Rome. If—when you make it, you'll know whether it's safe to stay."

"That makes sense," Lili agrees. One step at a time.

"I can help you with directions," the monk offers. "I'll find you a map, and I'll mark the heavily occupied spots to avoid."

"That would be helpful," Lili manages. "Thank you."

"The penalty for harboring Jews is growing more dire. Not everyone will be welcoming on the road."

"I understand, Father."

"Do you have any money?"

"I have a bit, yes."

"Food?"

"A little. I left Isabella's in a hurry."

"I'll have the nuns pack some provisions for you."

"I appreciate that."

"There's a convent on Via Cicerone in Rome. When you arrive, look up Sister Natalia. Tell her I sent you."

"Sister Natalia on Via Cicerone," Lili says, repeating it in her mind, committing the name and the street to memory.

Father Niccacci's brow knots in concentration. "Actually . . ." he starts. "There's one other thing. A favor. If you're open to it."

Lili straightens. The monk's expression has changed; he looks upon her now not only with concern for her safety but with expectation. With trust. "Does your offer to help still stand?"

Lili blinks. "Yes, of course."

"I have a parcel that needs to reach Sister Natalia. Could you bring it to her?"

"I—what kind of parcel?"

"The less you know the better."

Forged IDs. It must be. Lili's thoughts swim as she chews on the risk of getting caught. The consequences. **Don't do it**, the rational side of her implores. It will be perilous enough to make the journey, let alone to carry contraband along the way. But how can she say no to helping this man, who's put his own safety at risk to protect hers?

She meets Father Niccacci's gaze with as much

conviction as she can muster. "I can take it," she says, knowing that if she thinks too much longer on it, she'll convince herself otherwise.

Father Niccacci's eyes brighten. "Thank you, Lili. You'll be doing a great service. This parcel will save lives. A great many, I hope."

"I'll do everything I can to deliver it," Lili says, clasping her hands together on her lap so he can't see them shaking.

CHAPTER TWENTY-FIVE

TORRE DEL COLLE

February 1944

My feet hurt," Theo whines. He kicks at a pebble with the toe of his shoe as he walks. "Mine too," Lili says. She's worn painful blisters onto her little toes and the backs of her heels and has been trying since noon to walk without a limp. "But you know what?"

"What?"

"You're getting stronger every day. We both are."

"I am?"

"Every time you take a step, your muscles are growing. You're getting tougher."

Theo looks up at her, his irises deep blue in the waning afternoon sun. "I'm getting faster too," he says.

"Oh? Let's see." Lili's learned that when Theo complains, of an empty stomach or of aching feet, often she can distract him with a challenge.

Pulling away from her, Theo sprints ahead, a cloud of dirt billowing beneath his feet as he pumps his knees, his elbows, his heels clipping his backside in the effort.

"That's too fast!" Lili calls, and Theo slows, turns, and waits for her to catch up.

They'd left the monastery early that morning, with some food hastily prepared by the nuns and Father Niccacci's secret parcel sewn into the lining of her valise beside her valuables, Esti's belongings, and what was left of Lili's lire. At the last minute, Lili had slipped Esti's ring from her necklace onto her finger. She's posing as Theo's mother now; it makes sense for her to be wearing it. **You'll want to take the back roads**, Father Niccacci said, tracing the path he'd marked for her that, as far as he knew, didn't require passing through German checkpoints. The route also skirts railroads and bridges—German supply lines that could be targeted by the Allies. **Of course**, he added, **locations of checkpoints and supply lines can change at any time. Stay alert.**

The snow had melted and, with the skies clear, the morning cold was tolerable. As they set off from the monastery to the peal of church bells, Lili had looked back. She hadn't meant to grow attached to Isabella, to Father Niccacci, but couldn't help it; she'll miss them both dearly. Ricardo too. It felt unsettling, irresponsible, to leave a place with a small network of people she liked and trusted—and even more so to leave without knowing where she and Theo would rest their heads that night—or any night for the foreseeable future. But what other choice did she have?

Now, with Theo's protests momentarily put to rest, Lili studies her map. She'd decided they'd try to walk as far as Torre del Colle, sixteen kilometers due south of Assisi. Father Niccacci had circled the town on the map, and she's pretty sure they're on the outskirts of it now. She hopes so, at least, with the sun now low in the sky and the temperature dropping.

"Are we close?" Theo asks.

"I think so."

"I want to play with Ricardo," Theo says, panting from the exertion of his run.

"I know you do."

"When can I play with him?"

"Someday soon, I hope."

Someday. Lili has found herself attaching the word to every other thought. She'd tried to explain to Theo that morning, once she'd sorted her plan, that they were better off in a big city, like Rome. She'd told him Ricardo was about to start at school and that he wouldn't be home to play much longer (a white lie but one that, she hoped, would dull the pain of leaving); begrudgingly, Theo believed her. **Will I start school soon too?** He asked. **Someday,** Lili said, then steeled herself for a question about his mother, but it never came, and Lili, still unsure of how to address the subject of Esti's absence, didn't bring it up.

"How much longer till we can stop?" Theo asks. A fair question. Lili checks her watch. It's nearly five. They've been on their feet for more than eight hours. The roads thus far have been quiet, the skies clear, thankfully—their only company a farmer who clattered by in a horse-drawn wagon. He'd lifted a hand as he passed, and Lili was tempted to ask for a ride but then thought better of it.

"Not much."

"How far have we gone today?" Theo asks.

"About fifteen kilometers, I'd guess."

"I think one hundred."

Only 175 more to go, Lili thinks. "Let's round the bend," she says. "Next place we see, we'll stop and have a rest, maybe even stay the night." She says this easily, as if knocking on a stranger's door was a normal occurrence. As if the thought of being turned away wasn't eating her up inside. "And just imagine, Theo, how strong and how fast you'll be by the time we reach Rome," she adds.

Theo flexes his arm and holds his breath, his cheeks reddening, and Lili can't help but laugh. She takes his hand, slows to a stop, and bends so their eyes are on the same plane.

"I need to tell you something, kiddo." Theo looks at her from behind his mother's long, dark lashes. "We're going to play a game, okay? From now until Rome."

"The animal game?"

"No, not that one."

"Which one then?"

"A game of make-believe." Theo blinks, waits for an explanation. "We're going to meet some strangers today, and in the coming days," Lili continues. "Several." She speaks slowly, holding Theo's gaze. "For the next while, it's important that we pretend you're my son. That I'm your mama."

Theo scrunches up his nose. "You're not my mama, silly! You're my **zia**!"

"I know! It **is** silly. But we're safer if people **think** I'm your mama."

Theo tilts his head. His expression is neutral, and Lili wishes she could step into his mind and read his thoughts.

"So. What do you say—can you play along?"

Theo squints at her. "Okay."

"That's a good boy." Lili brushes a piece of lint from his lapel. Theo's jacket, one of the hand-me-downs from Ricardo, sags at the shoulders. She's rolled up the sleeves so they don't hang over his mittens. "So. When someone asks, I'm going to tell them your name is Theo **Passigli**. Like me, Lili Passigli! Can you say it for me, Theo? **Passigli**?"

"Passigli," he tries. It comes out **Paseewi**.

"That's right. I know it's a strange thing, to pretend to be someone you're not. But it's better this way."

"So the bad guys don't hurt us?" Theo asks, and Lili's heart contracts. She asks herself constantly how aware Theo is about the war, about the dangers that lie ahead, wondering if he can see through her games, as he seems to see through her empty promises.

"It's just . . . safer. But I don't want you to worry about that," Lili says. "You're always safe with me, all right, kiddo? And if anyone asks a question you don't like, you don't have to answer. I'll be right here beside you, and I can speak for you. Sound good?"

Theo nods.

"**Bravo**," Lili says, standing. They walk on, the gravel crunching beneath their tired feet.

"**Zia**?" Theo asks after a while.

"What is it, love?"

Theo's smile fades. "Will my real mama meet us in Rome?"

The question Lili's been waiting for. "I hope so," she says.

"Where is she right now?"

"I—" Lili starts. She doesn't have a good answer. "I don't know," she admits, exhausted by the thought of another lie, of sugarcoating the truth. "I'm sorry. I wish I did. But I'm going to do everything I can to find her, okay?"

Theo nods, seemingly satisfied, and Lili breathes through the tug in her chest.

They walk in silence for a few minutes, until the dirt road curves and an old farmhouse comes into view, simple and square, perched on a plot of over-grown grass, a barn with a sagging thatched roof beside it.

"A house!" Theo cries, brightening. "You said we could stop. Can we?"

Lili eyes the property, wishing it looked a little less dilapidated. Its walls are built of stone, mismatched in size and each a slightly different shade of beige. Half a dozen tiles are missing from the roof, and one of the windows has been boarded up. Even from afar, she can see the weeds growing between the cracks in the brick walkway leading to the door. Lili wonders if the place has been abandoned and is about to suggest they keep walking when she spots the corner of a bedsheet strung from a clothesline in the back. "All right. Let's see if anyone's home."

They approach the house, and Lili rehearses her plea. At the door, she sets down her valise and fastens the top button of her coat, saying silent thanks to Eva—the fur-lined jacket has not only kept her warm but helped her to appear put together. Less desperate, at least, than she feels. And perhaps even a little bit more Aryan. She licks her lips and knocks. Three quick taps—not so hard to seem urgent, but loud enough, she hopes, for someone to hear.

"Theo Passigli," she whispers to Theo as they wait. He nods, his expression serious.

At the sound of a rustle, someone approaching from inside, Lili straightens. **Proud chest**, she tells herself, letting her hand fall to Theo's shoulder.

The woman who answers the door wears an oil-stained apron. Her hair is gray, her cheeks ruddy. She stares at Lili, her eyes wary.

"What do you want?" she asks, glancing at Theo.

"I'm so sorry to disturb you, **signora**. We've been walking all day. We left Assisi this morning. We're on our way to Rome, and—"

"To **Roma**?" The woman bunches up her brow.

"My . . . son and I, we haven't the money for the train, so we're making the trip on foot, and we've nowhere to stay tonight," Lili says quickly. "Would you consider allowing us in, **signora**? We—we could sleep in the barn, if you haven't the space in your home." With enough layers and a little bit of hay, Lili thinks, they might be warm enough.

The woman scowls as she studies her, and Lili shifts on her feet. A flock of geese passes overhead, the birds honking as they fly north in a V formation. **You're going the wrong way**, Lili thinks. Theo tugs on her hand. When she looks down, she finds him peering up at her, eyes wide as if trying to tell her something.

"You forgot to say please," he whispers.

"Oh! You're right," Lili whispers back. "**Per favore**," she adds, returning her gaze to the woman in the doorway, hoping Theo might help to soften her, but the woman pays him no attention. She looks past Lili to the dirt road from which they'd come.

"It's just the two of you?"

"Yes."

"You walked here. From Assisi."

"We did." Lili wonders if the woman can see

through her story; if she can sense that they're avoiding the train. That they are Jewish.

"I'm sorry, but—" the woman starts, then pauses, distracted by the sound of a motor. Lili turns. Two motorcycles approach from around the bend and the woman swears. "Quickly, then," she instructs, motioning Lili and Theo inside. Lili reaches for her valise as she and Theo step through the door. The woman locks it behind them and moves to the window, pulls the curtain aside a centimeter. The thrum of engines grows louder.

Still holding her valise, Lili clasps Theo's hand, the worn soles of her shoes rooted to the foyer floor.

"Germans?" Lili whispers.

"Yes. If they come this way, you'll want to hide."

She knows, Lili thinks.

"Do you think they saw us?" Lili thinks of the parcel hidden in her bag.

"I don't know."

"I—I have papers."

The woman raises a palm to silence her, and Lili counts the seconds, holding her breath. The revving grows louder and louder still, and then, finally, begins to fade.

"It sounds as if they've passed," Lili says. **Please, let them have passed**. The woman, still peering from the window, nods and Lili exhales.

"They have."

"Have they stopped here before?"

"Twice."

"What do they want?"

"They look around, check my papers, ask if I've seen anything suspicious. They must not have seen you. They'd be banging down the door if they had."

Lili looks down at Theo. His face is pale. She squeezes his hand to let him know he's okay. They're okay.

"Well then," the woman sighs. "This way. I don't have a spare bedroom. But you can sleep in the living room."

HOURS LATER, THE WOMAN WHO'D INTRODUCED herself as Anna helps Lili make a bed of blankets on the living-room floor. Theo is already asleep, curled up on the seat of an armchair.

"You are married?" Anna asks, stealing a glance at Esti's ring.

Lili shakes her head. "I was. I'm a widow." The lie comes more easily than she'd anticipated.

Anna nods, not surprised. She is a widow as well. "The boy must miss his father."

Lili can almost hear herself explaining. Telling Anna that Theo is not in fact her son but her best friend's. That her friend is missing and that Theo's father traveled to Greece to come to his parents' aid, then disappeared after a roundup of the Jews in his hometown. But her alibi and her ID tell a different story—one she'll uphold if she needs to, even if Anna suspects they are Jewish. "Yes," she says. "Although he died when Theo was just a baby. Theo has little memory of him. A blessing and a curse, I suppose."

Anna unties a seat cushion from a chair, hands it to Lili to use as a pillow.

"Thank you again for letting us stay," Lili says.

Anna shrugs. "It's not so bad to see some young faces," she says.

"How far are we from Torre del Colle?" Lili asks.

"It's a fifteen-minute walk from here to the town center."

"Do you go often?"

"Once a week, for ration cards, then to stand in line at the market. It's barely worth the effort though. Last week I waited three hours for a handful of lentils and one lousy egg."

"I see," Lili says. She needs ration cards. Badly. For dinner, Anna had shared her soup, and Lili insisted they eat the bread the nuns at the monastery packed for her. She has a few provisions left, but she'll need more soon. "And the Germans?" she asks. "Are there any living here?"

"They move around a lot. Here one day, gone the next. Afraid of another partisan attack, no doubt."

Lili knows of the partisans, has heard about the groups gathered in the countryside and in the forests—outlaws and anti-Fascists and ex-Italian soldiers who'd evaded capture after the German invasion, banding together to resist the Germans,

Mussolini, anyone in support of the Axis. "What do you mean, partisan attack?"

"They come through too. Hard to miss them in their rags and their red bandannas. Last time was a week ago. They attacked a German soldier in the village. Stabbed the man to death."

"They killed a German?"

"He fell asleep guarding a camp they'd set up for the night, apparently. When his body was found the next morning, the Nazis announced that a single German life was worth ten Italian lives, then sure enough, rounded up ten civilians from the village and killed them all."

"No."

"Shot them right there in the town square, in the middle of the day, then strung them up for the rest of us to see."

Lili shakes her head, the thought too brutal to process.

Anna speaks softly. "There were women in the group. A child too. A little boy. They say the Germans shot him last. That he had to watch his mother . . ." she trails off.

"I don't believe it," Lili says.

"I didn't either, until I saw the bodies. Days later, when I went to town for rations, they were still there. So. Forgive me if I wasn't so welcoming when you first arrived. This war . . ." she waves a wrinkled hand in front of her bosom in disgust.

"I understand. It's changed us all," Lili says.

"I just hope it ends in my lifetime. I'm tired of it all. Tired of being cold and hungry. And most of all tired of the Germans. No one thinks they can actually win this war, but they're still here, among us. Stealing our men, our women and children, our chickens, our sanity. Killing us. Why? What more do they want?"

Lili doesn't answer. **They want me**, she thinks.

CHAPTER TWENTY-SIX

UMBRIAN COUNTRYSIDE

March 1944

Hold on, kiddo. Your shoelace has come undone."
Theo groans. "Again?"

Lili grits her teeth as she drops to a knee beside him, the raw skin of her heel stabbing with pain. "I'll double knot it this time," she says, giving the waxy laces an extra tug. Like his coat, Ricardo's boots are a little big still, the leather scuffed to two shades lighter than it once was, but Theo loves them, calls them his big-boy shoes. Lili presses her palms into her knees as she stands.

"Do me a favor, would you?" she asks, reaching for her valise. Her palms are raw, too, from the hours spent carrying it.

Theo looks at her, skeptical.

"Stop growing, please." Esti's joke.

Theo smiles. "Never!" he cries, and they walk on, making their way slowly, steadily south.

An hour later, Theo declares he's hungry. It's nearly noon. They'd left Anna's cottage at seven that morning. Another thank you, another grateful smile, another goodbye, good luck to you. Lili's new routine. Now, their stamina is waning.

"Let's eat," Lili says.

They veer from the road into the brown grass, still brittle from the morning frost. At the trunk of a lone juniper tree, Lili pulls the provisions from her valise, lays the suitcase on its side. It's just big enough for the two of them to sit on if they squeeze, which they do, hip to hip, leaning into each other, their legs outstretched before them. The air is a few degrees warmer than it was the day before, though there are more clouds in the sky, which worries Lili—the gray makes it harder to spot planes. She hands Theo one of the hardtack biscuits Anna had given her as they left.

"Take little bites," she reminds him, glancing up at the cloud cover, "like a bird." A challenge, to encourage Theo to eat slowly, to make the meal feel more nourishing than it is. He nibbles from the biscuit, and she rescues a crumb from his lap, slips it into her mouth. It tastes like charred wood.

They eat in silence, listening to the chatter of finches in the tree branches overhead and watching the clouds drift lazily overhead. The scenery feels benign, picturesque in the simplest of ways. If Esti were with her, Lili thinks, she'd take a photo. Perhaps, Lili allows herself, her friend is somewhere looking up at the same sky. Or perhaps she's hidden away. The other options—that Esti is locked up in some awful prison, or worse—Lili refuses to consider. **She's alive. She has to be.**

Lili hates that leaving Assisi has put an even greater distance between Theo and his mother. She hates that Esti has no way of reaching them now and has vowed to write to Sister Lotte as soon as she reaches Rome. She'll send a return address, and perhaps by then the mother superior will have some news from Florence. She'll keep sending letters to Niko, too, and to her father's uncle in Lausanne. **Have you made it to Switzerland, Papà?** she wonders. **Are you safe?** She tries to conjure the sound of his voice, the sensation of his arm around her shoulder, the smell of his aftershave, and for a moment, she can feel him with her. She smiles.

"Someone's coming," Theo whispers. He jabs her with an elbow and Lili's smile vanishes.

"What? Where?"

Theo points. "There."

Sure enough, a man, approaching on a bicycle. **Careless**, Lili chides, straightening. Had she been paying better attention, they might have slipped behind the juniper, but it's too late for that now. She stands, tents a hand over her eyes as the figure nears. He moves at an alarmingly fast pace. Lili scans the road behind him to see if anyone is chasing him, but he's alone. He slows as he nears.

"It's him!" Theo cries. "The man from before, in the snow!"

And sure enough, Lili realizes, it is.

The cyclist brakes to a stop on the side of the road and waves. For as fast as he'd been riding, Lili notices, he's barely broken a sweat.

"**Buon giorno**," he says.

"Hello," Lili says.

"Hello," Theo says.

"I thought I recognized you," the cyclist tells Lili. "That purple coat. We met in Assisi, right? At the monastery?"

"We did."

"In the snow!" Theo says.

"That's right. It was a cold ride home." He turns to Lili. "You're a friend of Father Niccacci's, yes?"

"I am. Just recently so. You as well?"

"**Certo**, although we go way back. I'm Gino," the cyclist says. **So it's true.**

"I'm Lili, and this is my son, Theo. It's an honor to meet you, Gino. My father is a big fan."

"Well, that makes my day," Gino says, grinning.

"I like your bike," Theo says.

"Thank you, young man. How old are you?"

Theo waggles his three middle fingers.

"Three! So old. My son, Andrea, is two. You remind me of him. This is my racing bike—would you like to have a closer look?"

Theo glances up at Lili and she nods. He approaches

the bike, and Lili listens in as Gino points out its various parts: the saddle, the pump holder, the toe straps, brakes, stem, hubs, the double left axle caps.

"It's so dirty," Theo observes.

"Theo!" Lili scolds, even though he's right, the bike's frame is caked in mud.

Gino laughs. "Normally it's much cleaner. We had a run-in a few weeks ago with a bomber."

Theo's eyes widen. "You did?"

"Well, the bike did. Lucky for me I wasn't riding at the time."

"Where were you?"

"I was in Perugia, having a coffee. I'd leaned her up against the outside wall of the café, and the reflection of her frame in the sun must have caught the pilot's attention."

"And then what happened?" Theo asks.

"Well," Gino says, glancing at Lili. "He took some shots and missed the bike, thankfully. But the café—let's just say he left his mark."

"In broad daylight?" Lili asks, glancing overhead.

"No one was hurt, thankfully. After that, I figured I'd better make sure she wasn't so shiny." He pats the frame of his bike, then looks to Lili. "They fly over often, the Allies."

"I'm aware," Lili says.

"I heard a bomb one time," Theo says.

Gino arches his brows. "That must have been scary."

"The walls shook. Like this." Theo spreads out his arms and waves them, and Lili flashes to Aldo's basement, to the smell of damp earth, the thunder of explosives pulverizing the streets above.

"Are you still in touch with Father Niccacci?" she asks, eager to change the subject.

"All the time," Gino says. "I'm heading to see him now, actually."

"Really? Could you tell him we're all right— making progress?"

"Of course. Where are you heading?"

"South. To Rome."

"On foot?"

"That's the plan."

Gino nods, impressed. "Do you have a map?"

"I do."

"I've just come from that way, let's have a look. I can point out a few towns you're best to avoid."

"Oh, I'd appreciate that," Lili says. She moves to stand beside Gino, unfolds her map. "Father Niccacci flagged the towns he'd heard were occupied, circled the ones he thought were safe," she says.

"**Bene.** You've got all the right spots marked, though I'd avoid Torni as well."

"I will, thanks," Lili says, and in that moment, it dawns on her. The frequent rides between Assisi and Florence. The knowledge of which towns are safe. The longtime friendship with Father Niccacci. Could Gino Bartali be the courier the monk spoke of? It was possible, though he carries no bag, no satchel. If he's transporting papers, where is he keeping them?

"Do you have somewhere to stay tonight?" Gino asks.

"Not yet," Lili says.

"Well. I may be able to help with that too." Gino points to a valley on the map. "We're here," he says. "You're about three or—" he surveys Theo, "maybe four hours from the town of San Terenziano. There, you'll find a church in the center of the village, a big yellow one, you can't miss it. Ask for Sister Catalina, tell her you're a friend of mine. She can help you."

A smile spreads across Lili's face at the thought of having someone to call on, of having a plan. "I will," she says. "**Grazie.**"

Gino checks his watch. "I should head on. Tell me, Theo, do you think I can make it to Assisi in forty-five minutes?"

Theo nods enthusiastically. "**Si, certo!**"

"My record is fifty. But I think I can break it." Gino gives Theo a wink.

Lili folds the map, returns it to her pocket. "Thanks for stopping," she says. "And for the tips."

"Be safe," Gino says, slipping his foot into a stirrup.

"You as well."

Lili and Theo wave as Gino tears off, his figure receding quickly into the distance. They return to the juniper and finish their lunch, buoyed by the chance visit with the famous cyclist. Twenty minutes later, as they resume their walk south, Lili scripts a note in her head to her father. **You'll never guess who we ran into on the road. Gino Bartali! What are the odds?** She pictures the surprise on Massimo's face. **He's a nice fellow. You'd like him. I should have asked for an autograph, but I didn't think of it until—**

A deafening **boom** shatters Lili's train of thought. Twenty meters ahead, the road explodes.

Fumbling for Theo's hand, Lili steps in front of him to shield him from the spray of rock and sand falling at their feet. She scours the sky but the clouds are too thick to see anything. She searches the road ahead and behind. Nothing. Spinning around, she cranes her neck, desperate to find the source of the explosion, but there is no sign of life anywhere, just a shroud of ochre-colored dust mushrooming from the crater now blocking their path. Her mind reels. How could a shell just appear out of nowhere? Had they been targeted? Had Gino been targeted? He'd be several kilometers along, at least. She has to move. Find shelter. To her left, just beyond the meadow, is a forest. To her right, a small hill. She wishes she'd caught sight of the explosive's path before it struck ground, to know which direction, at least, it had come from.

They will go to the woods, she decides.

"What was that?" Theo asks.

"I don't know. Come, quickly."

They jog through the meadow toward the tree

line. There's no telling who or what might be lying in wait beneath the shadowed canopy, but at least, Lili rationalizes, she can see where she's headed. She can't see what's over the hill.

They walk several meters into the wood, until Lili is certain they're no longer visible from the road, then turn back to face the meadow. There, they wait, watching, listening. Five minutes pass, then ten. A light rain begins to fall, making a soft pattering sound on the leaves overhead.

"Can we go now?" Theo asks a few minutes later, growing impatient.

If they don't move soon, Lili knows, they won't make it to San Terenziano before dark. She searches the sky, the road for any sign of danger. "We can go," she says, "but we'll have to move fast." She takes Theo's hand. They hike back to the tree line and across the meadow, skirt the dusty crater and return to the road. Lili ignores the rain, feeling far too exposed to notice the wet on her cheeks. She spends the next several hours on high alert, pestering Theo to pick up his pace, her head a swivel on her shoulders.

THE RAIN HAS SOAKED THROUGH THEIR COATS when they finally arrive in San Terenziano at dusk, cold, famished, and exhausted. They walk to the center of the town, where Lili finds the big yellow church Gino described. She prays Sister Catalina will be there. Inside, they pause in the narthex, blinking as their eyes adjust to the dim interior. The church is modest, with gray stone floors and two rows of pews. There are no worshippers—it's too close to curfew. Behind the chancel, the glow of a pair of candles illuminates the altar.

"Can I help you?"

"Oh!" Lili jumps, turning at the sound of a voice behind her. "Forgive me," she says, a hand over her heart. "I didn't see you there."

The nun's gaze is stony, her aging face a map of creases.

"We've come to see Sister Catalina," Lili says.

The nun frowns. "It's late," she says. "You shouldn't be here. They are making arrests after dark."

"I'm aware of the curfew," Lili says. "It's just that we have nowhere to go. We're in search of a place to stay for the night. I was told Sister Catalina might be able to help."

"Who sent you?"

"**Signor** Bartali sent us."

This gives the nun pause. She softens.

"You are Sister Catalina?" Lili asks, and the nun gives a subtle nod. She looks over her shoulder, then motions with her chin for Lili to follow her toward the apse.

"Come. Let's pray."

At the altar, Lili and Theo kneel beside her.

"Do like me," Lili whispers to Theo, bowing her head and pressing her palms together, thumbs tucked beneath her chin. Theo plays along, his hands balled into a fist, his forehead resting on his knuckles.

Beside Lili, the nun speaks quietly into her hands. "Where have you come from?"

"From Torre del Colle. Before that, Assisi."

"You've traveled a long way."

"Yes."

Sister Catalina pauses, thinking. "There is a farmer who lives just outside of town," she says. "Giovanni. His wife is Luisa. You can stay with them."

Lili exhales. "Thank you, Sister."

"The main street is Via Roma. Follow it to Via Monte Pelato and bear right. Giovanni's farm is two hundred meters on the left. Look for the property with the barn beside it and the tractor out front."

"We will."

"Do you have papers?" Sister Catalina asks, and Lili hesitates. Is it so obvious that she's Jewish? She must not be the first to come through San Terenziano, she realizes.

"I do. We both do."

"Good. And ration cards?"

"A few provisions, but no ration cards. I can apply, though we won't stay long."

Sister Catalina shakes her head. "The town clerk won't be of any help," she says. "He's. . . . wary when it comes to strangers. Come back tomorrow, I'll see if I can round up a card for you."

"I appreciate that," Lili says. She shifts her weight, the cold stone floor unforgiving beneath her kneecaps.

"You should go now, before it gets any darker," Sister Catalina says, crossing herself. "Godspeed."

VIA ROMA IS NEARLY DESERTED, SAVE FOR A FEW shopkeepers locking their storefronts for the night. Lili nods to one of them as they pass, trying to project a facade of belonging, but her adrenaline is still swirling from the explosion, keeping her on edge. She shies at the flap of a flag, billowing on its pole, at the bark of a dog from a second-story window.

"I'm hungry," Theo says as they finally make the turn onto Via Monte Pelato.

"We're nearly there, love. We'll eat when we arrive."

The rain has turned to mist but still, Lili thinks, it will be a day before their coats are dry.

Theo groans, slows his pace. "I'm really, really hungry."

Normally, Lili would offer him something from their provisions bag. Anything to soothe his hunger, to appease him. But tonight, her nerves are frayed, her patience thin. She checks her watch. They've only a few minutes before curfew.

"I'm hungry, too, Theo," she says, walking on. "We'll be there soon, I promise. The faster we move, the sooner we'll put something in our bellies."

Theo falls behind. He takes a few more steps, then stops.

Lili turns. "Come on, Theo." It takes everything she has not to yell. "We haven't any time to waste."

Theo won't budge. He stands, staring at the ground, arms crossed in front of him.

Before she can help it, Lili snaps. "Dammit, Theo! Enough!" She regrets her words, her tone, immediately.

Theo looks up. He blinks at her and she watches as his face crumples. He begins to cry.

"Theo." Lili drops her valise and kneels beside him. The ground is wet and her knee is tender but she ignores the discomfort. "Theo, please," she says, her hands on his shoulders. "I'm sorry, kiddo. I didn't mean to yell. Please. Stop crying, love."

But Theo only cries harder, his wails like sirens, echoing down the street.

Lili takes a breath. "All right. All right." She wraps her arms around him, hoping a hug will help. She holds him, shushing him, and after what feels like a very long while, his sobs dissolve into quick, jagged sniffs. When he finally quiets, she pulls the sleeve of her sweater down from inside her coat and wipes the tears from his face with its hem. She looks around. Darkness is falling fast. They are the only ones now on the street.

"I know how hard this is, Theo," Lili says, her voice calm. "But we've got to stick together, okay?

I promise we'll eat. Very soon. It's dark now and I don't want to be out here when we can't see. We'll get in trouble."

Theo wipes at his nose with the back of his hand, his lashes matted with tears.

"We need to look for a house with a tractor in front of it," Lili says. "Let's see who can find it first."

Theo looks up. "Fine," he whispers, pulling away from her.

You're as defiant as your mother, Lili thinks as she stands. She lets him take the lead as they walk on. A few minutes later, Theo points. "There!" he calls, triumphant, his hurt feelings, along with his hunger, temporarily forgotten.

Lili and Theo trail the farmer, Giovanni, up a flight of creaky stairs and down a narrow hallway to a small bedroom. He lights a lantern then reaches for a broom in the corner and hands it to Lili. "You're under the granary," he says, "so you might need this. Our cat died, and ever since, the critters have been busy up there. If you give the ceiling a few knocks, it'll quiet them down."

"What kind of critters?" Theo asks.

"Mice, mostly. The occasional bird."

"Thank you," Lili says, stealing a longing glance at the bed, her legs suddenly heavy as lead.

"Can I try?" Theo asks, reaching for the broom.

"I'm not sure you'll be able to reach," Lili says, but she lets him take it anyway, worried if she says no, he'll make another scene. Gripping the handle, Theo stands on his toes, his tongue curled over his lip as he pokes the butt of it toward the ceiling.

"Here," Giovanni offers. Theo lifts his arms and the farmer hoists him up.

"Too hard, Theo!" Lili scolds as Theo pounds at the ceiling.

"It's okay," Giovanni says.

"No mices," Theo announces as he's returned to his feet.

Giovanni chuckles. "Well then, now that we've got that taken care of, I'll leave you to it. The door to the shelter is in the hallway by the kitchen, in case the sirens ring."

Lili nods.

"My wife would be happy to prepare a snack for you if you're hungry. We're luckier than most, living on a farm."

"That's very generous of you," Lili says. "Theo is starving and our provisions are nearly out."

"I'll bring up a plate."

"**Grazie, signore.**"

Lili listens to the sound of footsteps subsiding, aware that the farmer hadn't asked a single question about where she'd come from or where they were headed. He hadn't even asked her name. He'd simply opened his door. How many people had he taken in before her? She'd wondered the same about Aldemo and Eva. Were they part of some hidden network of helpers? Or were they each helping of their own accord, simply out of the goodness of their hearts? Whoever they were, Lili doesn't know where she'd be without them.

Theo yawns. His eyes are heavy. Lili hangs their coats to dry. She opens the provisions bag and they share another of the biscuits Anna had sent them off with, then devour the apple and baked polenta Giovanni brings a few minutes later. When they're finished, Theo asks for more. "We only have one biscuit left," Lili says. "We should save it for tomorrow. Come, let's rest our legs."

Theo takes off his boots and climbs into bed, pulling the quilt, a sunny, floral patchwork of yellows and blues, up to his chin. Lili retrieves his Nello from her valise, and he wraps it around his hand, bringing it to his cheek. She should remind him to use the toilet, to wash his hands, to brush his teeth, Lili thinks, but he's as limp with fatigue as she is. Removing her own shoes, she moans softly as she wiggles her toes, then crawls onto the bed beside Theo. Stroking his hair, she watches the contours of his face soften as he drops easily into sleep. Thirty minutes ago, she was furious with the boy. How easily, she thinks, she can forgive him.

"**Dormi bene,**" she whispers, kissing his cheek. She falls back onto her pillow. She, too, should undress, wash her face, brush her teeth. **I'll just rest** for a moment, she tells herself. She closes her eyes, vaguely aware of a light scratching sound, small feet scurrying overhead. **The broom. Use the broom.** But her lids are sealed stubbornly shut, her bones too heavy to move.

CHAPTER TWENTY-SEVEN

SAN TERENZIANO

March 1944

When Lili's eyes open, it's morning. She sits up, takes in the space around her: the simple oak dresser, set with a vase of dried lavender; the small mirror, framed in bronze, hanging by the door; the flecks of brown spotting the white paint on the ceiling, left, no doubt, from the butt of the broom handle. She crawls out of bed and limps to an armchair in the corner to inspect the blisters on her feet, dreading the idea of another day on the road. Perhaps, she rationalizes, if Giovanni will let them, they can stay the day in San Terenziano, stockpile some food, restore their legs.

She glances at her valise. The longer she holds on to Father Niccacci's parcel, she knows, the more lives are at risk. Still, it would do them both good, a day's rest. She'll return to the church this morning, she decides, in hopes that Sister Catalina might have found her a ration card. She doesn't want to depend on her hosts to eat, and she doesn't want to leave without replenishing her stores.

Theo wakes and downs the last of Anna's biscuits in two not very small bites. Downstairs, they wander into the kitchen, where they meet Luisa, a portly woman with broad shoulders and a kerchief over her hair. She doesn't ask of their plans, or of how long they'll be staying, just if they are hungry. Theo nods, and before Lili can stop her, Luisa sets out a cup of sheep's milk, a bit of cheese, and a boiled egg. A feast.

"Thank you for this," Lili says, grateful for the fact that Theo's hunger, for a few hours at least, will be quelled.

"A growing boy needs sustenance," Luisa replies.

"We appreciate you letting us stay the night. We'll be on our way soon," Lili promises, but Luisa has turned her attention to Theo.

"We could use a hand on the farm while you're here," she says. "What do you think, **bambino**, can I put you to work?"

Theo grins. "**Si, signora.**"

"We'd love to help," Lili says. Anything to feel like they're earning their keep.

Luisa leads them around the back of the house to the barn, a small structure of moss-dusted stone. They find Giovanni at the chicken coop, where a handful of hens sit, clucking softly, rustling their feathers.

"We used to have two dozen **galline**," Giovanni explains, "but the Germans came through a while back and took most of the brood. These lucky few we managed to hide up in the granary before the **ladri** could get to them."

"Do they lay eggs?" Lili asks.

"They sure do. And this young lady," Luisa says, opening a stall door, "gives us milk and cheese. We call her Dalila." A large sheep with a thick white coat lifts her head, turning at the sound of their voices and staring up at them with big, chestnut eyes.

"**Nello!**" Theo cries, pointing to a small woolly mound curled at Dalila's feet.

"That there's our newest addition," Giovanni says, smiling. "We inherited Dalila from a friend who moved away; we didn't realize she was expecting. The little guy arrived last week. We don't have a name for him yet."

"Can I play with him?" Theo asks.

"Go on," Giovanni nods, and Theo ventures into the stall, sits down beside the baby lamb.

"**Ciao, piccolino**," he coos, extending an upturned palm. The lamb sniffs his fingers then licks them, sending Theo into a fit of giggles.

"He likes you," Lili says.

"**Lucignolo** is a good name," Theo says, stroking the lamb's coat.

"Candlewick?" Giovanni asks.

"It's a character from **Pinocchio**," Lili explains, surprised Theo remembers the name from the story.

"Lucignolo is Pinocchio's bestest friend," Theo explains.

"**Best** friend. And he's a bit of a troublemaker, right?" Lili says.

"Oh, yes. A **piantagrane**."

"Lucignolo," Luisa says, trying it out. "I like that. He's a skinny little fellow, so it fits him. Candlewick it is."

Theo beams and Lili's heart warms—she hasn't seen this much joy in the boy's eyes since before they left Assisi.

LATER THAT MORNING, ONCE THEO HAS HELPED TO feed the sheep and collect the eggs from the hen house, he and Lili walk back into the town center. Lili wears two pairs of socks to pad the raw skin at her heels, but every step is painful. She makes a note to ask Luisa for some gauze when she returns. At the church, they spot Sister Catalina dusting the cross in the sanctuary. They catch her eye, and she motions with her chin for them to meet her at the altar. There, they kneel once again, assuming the position of prayer. Sister Catalina soon joins them, and after a few moments she slips Lili a Bible.

"The card is inside," she whispers. "Bring the Bible back tomorrow."

Lili nods. "I will." She tucks the book into her purse. It isn't until they've left the church and ducked into an empty alleyway that she opens it.

Sure enough, nestled between Proverbs is a ration card, good for the rest of the week. Lili holds the leather-bound Scripture to her breast. **Thank you, Sister.**

ONE DAY WITH GIOVANNI AND LUISA TURNS INTO two, then three. Lili thinks constantly of the package she's meant to deliver but tells herself at the end of each day that she and Theo will be stronger with the extra time to recuperate, with a little more sustenance in their bellies. Meanwhile, Luisa insists on sharing her food. **Save what you have for your travels**, she said, when Lili offered to dip into her own. **We have eggs and dairy and we make our own bread—last year's harvest was a good one, thank the Lord.** Lili returns to the town grocery each day, where she and Theo wait patiently for one hundred grams of dried fish, a wedge of dark bread—it's never much, but it's better than nothing, and it feels good to tuck it away, to know she and Theo will have something to reach for when they continue on their way. Back at the farm, Theo helps to collect eggs and tend to the hens, spending his free time brushing Lucignolo's soft coat and parading him around the property with a leash made of twine.

By her fourth day in San Terenziano, Lili knows it's time to resume their trek to Rome. Father Niccacci's parcel is burning a hole in the lining of her valise, and she doesn't want to outstay her welcome, or put Giovanni and Luisa in any more danger than she already has.

Theo bursts into tears when she tells him after breakfast it's time to say goodbye.

"Can we take Lucignolo with us?" he begs.

"No, love. He needs his mama. We can come back to visit when the war is over."

Theo sniffs, and in his somber expression Lili can see that her promise, like those before it—to visit Ricardo in Assisi, to find his mother—rings hollow. He understands as well as she that there's no telling when the war will be over, when, or if, they'll be back.

They depart with Lili's sights set on the hilltop village of Todi. This, at least, is a town familiar to her; she was pleased when Father Niccacci suggested it as a stopping point. She hasn't been there herself, but her mother visited once, before Lili was born, and the town had made a mark on her. Naomi used to go on about how beautiful it was, with its **palazzi** and belfries and narrow backstreets, how it was surrounded by not one or two but three concentric walls of stone. Lili liked the idea of spending a night there, of retracing her mother's footsteps.

They walk southwest in the direction of the Tiber, past long stretches of rolling farmland and abandoned vineyards. Lili scans the horizon, still skittish at the memory of their too-close-for-comfort explosion. So far, they've yet to see a soul, the only surprise a red fox that trotted across the road a few yards ahead of them, a pair of mangy pups chasing after her. Lili had hoped the sighting might lift Theo's mood, but it did little to cheer him up.

When they reach the Tiber, the road veers south, following the path of the river. Theo walks with his shoulders sagged, his gaze at his feet. He's said little since leaving the farm.

"Did I ever tell you about my pet turtle?" Lili asks, hoping a story might settle her nerves and coax him out of his slump.

In the distance, a wood pigeon calls to its mate. Theo shakes his head.

"I was five, six maybe, when I found him. He was just a baby. He was so small he could fit in my palm."

Theo straightens a touch and Lili can tell she's caught his attention. After a while he steals a glance at her. "Where was his mama?"

"I don't know. But somehow, this little turtle had made his way onto the street, and I was so worried he'd get stepped on or run over by a wagon I started crying. I couldn't stop. Finally, my parents told me I could bring him home, but **just for a few days**, they said. After that, they made me promise to set him free in the park."

"So you took him to your house?"

"I did."

"Did he like it there?"

"He loved it."

"Did you have to give him back? After some days?" Theo is looking intently now at Lili.

"Yes, I kept him for about a week, and then took him to the park. There was a big pond there, that's where I let him go."

"Before you put him in the pond, where did he sleep?"

"In a box. I collected moss and grass and sticks to make him comfortable."

"What did he eat?"

"I fed him carrots and radicchio. But his favorite were the zucchini flowers."

Theo is quiet for a moment. After a while he says, "Maybe we'll find a turtle on the road."

"Maybe."

Theo squints up at her. "Can you tell me another story?"

Lili smiles. "Sure." She thinks for a minute. "Oh, I know—I'll tell you about the time the circus came through Bologna. You know what the circus is, right?"

Theo's face lights up. "You saw one?"

"I did! Once. In the city where I grew up. The animals arrived by train, and my father took me to the station to watch them disembark."

"What kinds of animals?"

"So many kinds. Horses, elephants, monkeys. Even a tiger."

Theo's mouth drops. "A **tiger**?"

"Yes!" Lili relays the story of how her father had purchased front-row seats for the show as a special birthday surprise for her, how she was so close to the action she could feel the heat on her cheeks when the circus master lit a ring on fire for the tiger to jump through. She tells him about the men who walked on tightropes and the women who swung from giant hoops and about the monkey that played the trumpet. She tells him every detail she can remember, painting an especially unsavory picture of how an elephant chose to relieve himself just in front of her seat, which makes Theo laugh.

"Another one," Theo says, when she quiets.

They pass the hours this way, with Lili telling stories. Each time one ends, Theo asks for another. Lili is happy to oblige. Theo is content, and she doesn't mind the distraction, the excuse to relive her younger years. With every story, she's reminded of just how normal her childhood was in comparison to Theo's. How carefree.

By the time they arrive in Todi, Lili is parched, and it's almost dark. Theo yawns as they climb the stone stairs leading to the outermost of the city walls.

"Careful now," Lili says.

The steps are precariously steep; she can barely keep her balance with her suitcase in one hand and Theo's palm in the other. She looks down, so as not to trip—a fall would be treacherous. At the top of the stairs, they reach the outermost of the city's walls. They pass through one brick doorway, and then at the next wall, a second. At the third, final entrance to the village, Lili grins at Theo.

"We made it," she says, her breath heavy from the climb. But Theo says nothing. He looks past her and as Lili follows his gaze, she realizes they're not alone.

"Shit!" she breathes. A group of German soldiers is gathered within a stone's throw of where she and Theo stand. Lili's mind whirls. Todi wasn't one of the towns marked as dangerous on the map. Why are there Germans here? **Why not**, she scolds herself. **They're occupying half of Italy. They're everywhere.** Quickly, she rearranges her expression to read surprise, rather than fear.

One of the soldiers—there are at least ten in the group—peels away from the others and approaches her. He's tall, with blond hair shorn close to his scalp, a square jaw. Lili eyes the rifle slung over his shoulder, the swastika stitched onto his armband.

"**Anhalten!**" he barks. He tosses the butt of a cigarette onto the ground, stomps it out with his toe. "**Papiere.**"

Sweat beads on Lili's brow. She was warm before but now, suddenly, her skin is blazing. She fumbles through her purse, hands over their IDs. It's the first time she's used Theo's new card. She prays Luigi's work is convincing. That Theo will remember his last name is **Passigli** if he's asked.

"**Ihre Haus**," the soldier says, narrowing his eyes. "**Adresse**."

Willing her voice not to catch, Lili recites her false address in Lecce. The soldier purses his lips, and she feels a drop of sweat trickle down her temple. Had she gotten the street name right? The number? She thought she'd memorized the details, but suddenly she's unsure.

"I lost my husband," she says. She has no idea how much Italian, if any, the soldier will understand. "We are . . . going to see family in Rome."

"**Warum nicht mit dem Zug?**" the German says, and Lili nods, trying to understand. She knows a few words in German, and **Zug**, train, is one of them. Maybe he wants to know if she is traveling by train.

"**Nein Geld**," Lili says. I have no money. She opens her near-empty wallet, grateful she'd hidden all but a few of her lire into the lining of her valise. Her answer, however, doesn't seem to satisfy. The soldier gestures toward her suitcase. Lili pauses for a moment. He gestures again. She hands it to him.

"**Bewegen Sie nicht**," he orders, pointing at her feet, and Lili understands: stay put. The soldier walks back to the group, carrying her valise. They'll find her valuables and see she was lying about the money, she thinks, feeling the blood drain from her cheeks. Worse, they'll find Father Niccacci's parcel. They'll realize she's helping Jews by shuttling papers in the underground. This is it. It's over.

A tug at her coat. Lili looks down to find Theo gaping up at her. "It's okay," she whispers. A lie. Nothing about the moment is okay.

The soldier kneels, flips open her valise, and begins rooting through its contents. She can't see much, just his arms moving, a few pieces of clothing hanging over the edges of their compartments. After a while he goes still, holds something up for his colleague to see; Lili can't tell what. She counts her breaths, sickened by the thought of what will happen to Theo when she's arrested. Of what will happen to her. And then, when she can't bear it any longer, she hears two sharp snaps. The soldier stands, struts back to her. Lightheaded, she squares her shoulders as he approaches.

"**Das ist alles**," he says, handing Lili her valise along with the IDs. He dismisses her with a flick of the wrist.

Lili pauses, taking a moment to breathe. To gather herself.

"**Andiamo**," she tells Theo as she reaches for his hand.

They continue on, past the Germans with their cigarettes and sideways glances and their olive uniforms, toward the town center. As she walks, two words ring in her head. **It worked.** The false IDs, her valuables, the parcel, hidden away . . . she'd fooled them. She'd lied, and they'd believed her. **It worked.** Did she get lucky? Will they see through her the next time? Every hour has begun to feel like a gamble.

"Come," she says, lifting her chin and picking up her pace, as if she knew exactly where her path would lead her.

CHAPTER TWENTY-EIGHT

TODI

March 1944

Todi, the town Lili's mother once recalled so fondly, is overrun with German soldiers; Lili knows she and Theo must leave as quickly as possible. She'd dipped into her savings to rent a room in an apartment off Piazza del Popolo, the main village square. Lili had barely slept, her mind too consumed with the question of where they'll go next.

Glancing at Theo, asleep still in bed, she pads to the window and opens her map, tracing Father Niccacci's route, wondering if she can trust it any longer. She's hesitant to move on to the next village he'd circled without knowing if it, like Todi, is now occupied. The devout, thus far, have been good to her, she thinks. Perhaps one of the clergy in town will be able to offer some counsel.

An hour later, standing with Theo in the nave of the Cathedral of Santa Maria Annunziata, Lili summons the nerve to approach a priest after his morning service.

"Excuse me, Father?"

The priest turns.

Lili takes a breath. "My son and I have come from Assisi and are trying to make our way to Rome. I'm hoping you might have advice on a safe route to the capital." The request is blunt, she realizes, but there isn't any point in skirting around the subject.

"Do I know you?" he asks coldly.

Lili shrinks under his gaze. "No, Father. I've just arrived last night. Stopping through on my way to Rome." The priest takes a small step toward Lili.

"You are traveling on foot?"

Lili shifts her weight to her heels, feeling suddenly as if she's walked into a trap. "We are."

"Why not take the train?"

"I—we—" Lili is about to say she can't afford to when the priest interrupts her.

"Who are you running from?"

Lili opens her mouth, a slew of answers at her tongue. She's running from the Germans. But also from Mussolini's acolytes, and from the Italian gangsters, out for blood. She's running from the traitors—the people so desperate they'll do any-thing, no matter the consequences, for a reward—and from Allied bombs. But none of these answers will serve her well. "I—" she fumbles. "I just need to get to Rome, Father."

The priest's expression darkens. He glances

over Lili's shoulder as someone enters the church. "What's your name?" he asks.

A buzz between Lili's ears, like a brood of cicadas. Should she tell him?

"I—"

"Get out of my church before I have you arrested," the priest hisses. He stares hard at her then swivels, disappears into the presbytery.

Lili can barely breathe. Her chest is tight, her abdomen flexed, as if bracing for a punch. Theo looks up at her, questioning.

"Why did he—"

"Shh, love. Let's go."

She turns and hurries toward the door, trying to understand what just unfolded. Could a **priest** be collaborating with the Nazis? Why else would he interrogate her like that? Whatever the case, he knows her face. She's been marked. Her thoughts cartwheel as she tries to sort a plan. Who can she turn to, if not the Church? Should she try someone else, perhaps—a different priest? Maybe if she mentioned Father Niccacci's name, or Cardinal Dalla Costa's, she'll be better received. Or maybe she's better off leaving Todi as quickly as possible, following her original route and hoping for the best. Maybe they're better off on their own.

At the entrance to the church, a monk passes by and glances in her direction. Lili meets his eye, and he looks at her for a beat too long. The buzz in her ears grows louder. There is no safe option, no obvious answer. **Think, Lili**, she wills, summoning Esti's nerve. They'll leave, Lili decides as they exit the church. They'll continue south. Knock on more doors. Hope for the best.

On the street, she tenses at the sound of footfall behind her. She doesn't look back, doesn't want to appear suspicious, but the cadence of the footsteps matches hers, and she can feel it in her bones; she's being followed.

"This way." She ducks down a side street. The footsteps trail her.

"**Mi scusi, signora!**" The voice behind her is hushed but urgent.

Lili spins around, pulls Theo to her. It's the monk from the church. She doesn't know how to react—angry, for being accosted? Surprised? Should she beg forgiveness? **You are innocent**, she tells herself, her breath quick.

"What is it?" she asks.

The monk leans toward her. "I heard you talking in there, with the priest."

Lili replays her words in her mind. She'd said nothing revealing. Just that she needed help. A safe route to Rome. "I'm not sure what you heard, but I have nothing to hide."

The monk glances behind him, lowers his voice. "There is a man."

"What?"

"Someone who can help."

Lili stares at the clergyman, wondering if it's a setup. She says nothing. She will disclose nothing.

The monk presses his palms together. "Forgive me if I've scared you," he says. "I mean no harm. There is a band of **partigiani**. They've been escorting refugees south. They live in the woods and move around a lot, but often send a scout in the evening. We've been . . . I've been . . . helping to coordinate."

"Partisans?" Lili's mind turns to the attack Anna had described in Torre del Colle. She's always pictured partisans as outlaws—the kind of men capable of murdering a German in his sleep—not the kind to escort Jews to safety.

"**Si**. You are aware, there are many groups . . ."

"Yes, yes, of course."

She studies the monk, searching for his motive. There is an intensity about him, the way he carries himself.

"You want to help us," she says.

"Yes."

"Why?"

The monk looks at her. "Why? It's . . . the right thing to do." There is a note of defiance in his voice. Of a man straying from his orders.

Lili adjusts her purse on her shoulder, weighing the monk's offer. She'd do anything to get out from under the noses of the Wehrmacht in Todi. But was sheltering with a group of partisans any less dangerous than traveling the streets alone? Sleeping in the woods and foraging for food was one thing, but putting herself and Theo in the middle of an anti-Nazi, anti-Fascist group was another. Should the enemy come upon them in the company of the **partigiani**, they'd be butchered without a second thought. She looks at Theo.

"What are **partigiani**?" he asks, and Lili shakes her head, the message clear. Not now.

A young woman turns down their street, and Lili waits for her to pass, trying to quiet her thoughts, to plan her next steps. What would Esti do? It's the question, always, at the back of her mind. Joining up with the **partigiani** was dangerous. Very. But then again, isn't she already technically a resister, in lying to the authorities about her identity? In carrying Father Niccacci's parcel? At least with the partisans, she allows, she wouldn't be alone.

"There have been many arrests made in Todi," the monk tells Lili. "Some of the clergy here are . . . not so sympathetic toward newcomers. If it were me, and my child, I would leave. Quickly."

Lili meets his eye. His words, his expression, feel genuine. She makes a choice.

"How do I find him?" she asks. "This man?"

"Come back at dusk. There is an alleyway behind the church, and off of it a small courtyard. I will be waiting."

"The courtyard, at dusk."

The monk nods, then turns and walks hastily

back toward the church, leaving Lili and Theo alone on the street.

"Are we going to the woods?" Theo asks.

"Not yet. Later, maybe. Right now we're going to the market."

They're low on food, and Lili doesn't dare ask anyone else for ration cards. She'll draw again from her lire to purchase provisions if she can find any on the black market. She'll buy enough for a few days, just in case. And she'll find a quiet spot to hide out until sundown.

LILI AND THEO SPEND THE LAST FEW HOURS OF daylight tucked away in a cemetery, sitting atop the valise as they nibble breadsticks and play tic-tac-toe in the dirt, keeping a close eye out, always, for Germans.

"How long will we be in the woods?" Theo wants to know. All Lili had told him of her plan was that they were going to meet some people in the forest.

"I don't know yet, love."

"Will the people there be nice?"

"I think so. I hope so. You can let me do the talking at first, all right?" Lili says.

"I like the woods," Theo says.

"I do too. It'll be an adventure."

At dusk, they retrace their steps to the church. Lili keeps her chin low, terrified of running into the priest from earlier, as they walk around back to a skinny alleyway. When she finds the courtyard, she waits for a moment on the narrow street, listening. All is quiet. She swallows, steps inside.

Two figures emerge from the shadows.

"This is Ziggie," the monk says, nodding toward the large, bearded man beside him. "He's a part of the group I mentioned." Ziggie. **What kind of a name is that?** Lili stares up at him. He looks to be ten years her elder. His eyes are hard, his clothes ragged. He wears a maroon handkerchief around his neck. There's something about his scowl, about the rifle and the rounds of ammunition slung across his chest, that gives Lili pause. She nods hello. "You'd best be off then," the monk says, and without a word, Ziggie turns.

"Thank you," Lili calls over her shoulder as she and Theo hurry after him. But the monk has disappeared.

"Stay close," Ziggie orders, a few paces ahead. "And stay quiet."

Theo looks up at Lili. "It's okay," she whispers.

Ziggie moves at a fast clip; it's an effort to keep up. Lili's knees ache as they descend the precipitous steps they'd climbed the day before when they arrived in Todi. At the bottom they turn and walk east, toward a holt of evergreens. Thirty minutes later, when they reach the forest, Lili pushes away a sickening thought—if anything should happen to them, who would ever know?

They follow a dirt path in single file beneath the

tree canopy, Ziggie in the lead and Lili at the rear, Theo in between.

"Are we almost there?" Theo whispers after a while.

"I'm sure we're close."

They plod on. The deeper they get into the wood, the harder it becomes to see. Overhead, a quarter moon casts a faint blue light through the branches, and the shadows at the forest floor play tricks on Lili's eyes. She steps carefully, trying to avoid the roots and rocks and sticks that poke at her ankles, threatening to roll them over.

Finally, the path widens and Ziggie slows. Lili smells smoke. She takes Theo's hand. Three small fires burn up ahead; she can make out the silhouettes of bodies sitting around them. Several look up as they near, and Lili can see they are all men, and they're all wearing the same maroon handkerchiefs. Two of them stand. Lili straightens.

"Settle down, boys, they're from the church," Ziggie says, motioning for the pair to return to their seats.

Lili lifts a hand in greeting. "Hello," she offers, hoping the simple gesture might win them over. The words feel stiff on her tongue. Theo wraps an arm around her leg, rests his head on her thigh. The men stare. A foul odor orbits the group, of vinegar and tobacco and days-old sweat.

"Oy, **amici! Benvenuti.**" Lili's ears perk up at the greeting. The voice belongs to a woman. She turns to find its owner striding toward them, wearing a camouflaged tarpaulin and wool pants tucked into a pair of sturdy black boots. Her hair is parted down the middle and braided in two long plaits that hang over her shoulders and fall at her chest. Everything about her is dark—her eyes, her hair, her dirt-smudged cheeks.

"I'm Matilde," the young woman says, hands on her hips.

A woman. It hadn't even occurred to Lili that she might not be the only one. "Lili. And this is Theo."

"Welcome to camp," Matilde says, as if she'd been expecting them.

Lili smiles. "Thanks."

"Are you hungry?"

"Always."

"**Vieni**, I have just the thing."

The men in the group watch as Matilde guides Lili and Theo to the far side of one of the fires.

"Don't be afraid of these guys," she says, jabbing a thumb at one of the partisans as they pass. "They reek like hell, but they won't do you any harm." She pulls three crates up to the fire, then digs a hand into her tarpaulin and removes something lumpy, wrapped in a handkerchief. "Have you ever had a roasted chestnut?" she asks Theo.

He shakes his head.

"Well. You're in for a treat. There's a process to it though. You have to score them before you roast them, see?" She slides a jackknife from her pant pocket, flips it open, and carves slits into the flat sides of the shells. Matilde is skilled with the blade, Lili notices. When she's through scoring, she reaches for a shovel from beside the fire and dumps the chestnuts carefully into its iron blade. "How'd you like to roast them yourself?" she asks.

Theo looks to Lili and Lili nods. "Okay," Theo says, pleased, it seems, to have been given the job.

"**Bene**. Here you go, then."

Theo stands and wraps his hands around the shovel's thick wooden handle, spreading his feet wide for balance.

"That's right, hold it just over the fire. When your arms get tired, give them a rest, all right?"

"I will."

"You're doing great, kiddo," Lili says.

"We'll know they're done by the smell," Matilde says. She pats his shoulder as she steps away from the fire.

"He's precious," Matilde says as she and Lili sit down on the crates.

Lili looks at Theo, taking him in as if through Matilde's eyes. "He's a sweet boy."

Matilde produces a small tin flask, and Lili wonders what else she has stashed in the folds of her clothing. She takes a swig and hands the flask to Lili. "**L'chaim**," she says and Lili pauses, the drink halfway to her mouth. Matilde is Jewish.

"**L'chaim**." The metal is cold on Lili's lips, and the

alcohol burns as it travels the length of her throat. She coughs. "Sorry," she says, returning the vessel. "I'm out of practice."

Matilde laughs. "So. You came from Todi?"

"We did. Though we were only there for a day. We were interrogated, our belongings searched when we arrived—I wasn't expecting the town to be occupied. It's not such a friendly place at the moment." Lili looks around the camp. "Are there any other women here?"

Matilde takes another swig. "There were." She says this quietly, and Lili senses there are stories to tell, for another day. She doesn't press.

"I heard you were scouting routes to Allied territory. Have you had any luck?"

"We're trying. Nazi bastards are on the move though; the route's always changing."

"I'm hoping to make it to Rome," Lili says.

"That's where we're headed. The underground in the capital is struggling. You have papers, I assume?"

"We do."

"Good. There are still hundreds, maybe even thousands of Jews in hiding throughout the city. I'm hoping we can help a few of them, at least. If we can keep them from the camps, they might stand a chance."

"The forced labor camps in Poland, you mean?"

Matilde looks at her. "Oh, you—haven't heard."

"Heard what?"

Matilde licks her lips, lowers her voice. "They're

not work camps. Chelmno, Belzec, Treblinka, Auschwitz. They're death camps."

Lili shakes her head, uncomprehending.

"The Jews sent east are being killed," Matilde says. "Exterminated. By the thousands."

"What? No."

"Some are spared, if they're able to work. But the rest . . ."

"That's—that can't be true," Lili manages.

"They've built gas chambers. Ovens to burn the bodies after. It's monstrous, Lili."

An acidic taste, at the roof of Lili's mouth. Her stomach turns. It's an effort, suddenly, to breathe.

"It's a lot to process, I know," Matilde says gently.

Lili grips the corners of the wooden crate beneath her. She thinks of Esti. Of her father. Of Niko. All unaccounted for. "I don't believe it," she says, her voice hoarse.

"I didn't at first either," Matilde says. "I'd heard whispers. Refused to think it possible. But then a prisoner at one of the camps found a way to sneak messages—smuggled them out with the SS's dirty laundry—and one of the notes made its way to the underground. Word spread quickly about what was happening. It's . . . part of the reason I'm here. To try to help where I can."

Lili sips at the air, forcing it down into her lungs. She can comprehend being taken prisoner of war. Arrested, deported. Made to work. But mass murder? For simply being Jewish? She looks over at

Theo, his small figure silhouetted by the fire. It doesn't make any sense.

Matilde offers her flask again. This time, Lili embraces the burn. She has no words. She wraps her arms tight around her chest.

"I see some cracks," Theo says, swinging the shovel around for Matilde to have a look.

"**Bellissimo**," Matilde tells Theo. "Just a few more minutes and they'll be ready." Theo guides the shovel carefully back to the fire.

When the chestnuts are fully roasted, Theo settles himself cross-legged at Lili's feet as Matilde shows them how to cut the nuts open. Lili isn't hungry, but she forces herself to eat once the nuts are cool. The meat is soft and sweet. She feels herself come back to life a little, after her second.

"How did you end up here?" Lili asks Matilde.

"Me? I was arrested in Turin at the start of the war. Not for my religion—that was when it didn't matter much that we were Jewish—for being the daughter of an openly anti-Fascist professor. He and my mother moved to Palestine before the war, but with his work I knew they'd come for me."

"Who came for you?" Lili asks. She glances at Theo, wondering how much of Matilde's story he'll be able to follow. "The Germans?"

"The **carabinieri**."

"Italians arresting Italians. I still can't get used to that."

"They sent me to prison on some made-up charge,

but I argued my way out and decided if I wanted to be a part of something I'd better do so more discreetly. So when I heard about this group, I joined."

It sounds like something Esti would do, Lili thinks. "Courageous of you," she says.

"Courageous, risky, whatever you want to call it."

There's a distinction, Lili supposes, though it's almost impossible now to differentiate between the two.

"Being a partisan suits me," Matilde says. "It feels good to fight back. To live outside. To not know where I'll end up tomorrow, or how I'll fare. It's invigorating. I didn't used to think that way, but I've come around to it."

Lili considers this. There's hardly a part of the last few months that she'd describe as invigorating.

An owl screeches in the distance. Matilde points at Lili's feet. "You need some better shoes," she says.

Lili looks down at her battered oxfords. "I know."

"I have new shoes," Theo says. "Ricardo gave them to me."

Matilde makes a point of giving his boots a good once-over. "Those are some great boots, my friend."

Theo smiles and moves closer to the fire, arranges a small pile of twigs.

"And you?" Matilde asks, "Where were you before Todi?"

Lili glances at Theo, who's begun throwing his twigs in the fire. He seems to have lost interest in the conversation. "We lived in Ferrara at the start of the war," she says. "We stayed there for a while, then moved to Nonantola, near Modena, then to Florence, then Assisi. We've been on the road since."

"Is your family from Ferrara?" Matilde asks.

"No, I grew up in Bologna. My mother passed before the war. Last I heard, my father was leaving for Switzerland though I don't know if he actually made it. I haven't heard from him in months."

"You'll find him once you get to Rome."

Lili admires Matilde's certainty. She's reminded again of Esti.

"Do you have any family in the city?" Matilde asks.

"No family. Just a name, someone to contact when I arrive."

"Sister Natalia?"

"How did you know?"

"We've been working with the underground for a while now. There are only so many people we can trust. Sister Natalia is one of them."

"So the underground and the partisans work together?" Lili asks.

"Sometimes. When we have the same purpose, like trying to save Jewish refugees. I know, it's confusing. Some groups are fixated on fighting Fascists, others on incapacitating the German army. Not all partisan groups have the same goals we do."

Lili reflects on this for a moment, trying to process the complexity of the various factions operating in the shadows of this war. She looks back at Matilde.

"A priest in Assisi gave me Sister Natalia's name," she says, omitting the bit about the parcel she's supposed to deliver.

"Perhaps we'll meet her together," Matilde says.

"Yes, maybe." Lili tries not to think about how far they have to travel to make that happen.

"And Theo's father?" Matilde asks.

Lili reaches instinctively for Esti's wedding band, twists it around her finger. "He went back to Greece to find his family two years ago, but the news he was sending from Salonica wasn't good. The BBC reported a roundup last March, and then there was . . . nothing. We've lost touch."

Matilde clucks her tongue. "I'm so sorry."

Lili stares at the dwindling fire, at the feeble lap of its blue-tipped flames, the soft crimson glow of the logs at its base. "It's all right," she says. She can feel the two gold hands of the **fede** ring making indents on her finger pads.

"No, it's not," Matilde replies. "None of it is all right."

CHAPTER TWENTY-NINE

UMBRIAN COUNTRYSIDE

April 1944

Lili has been with Matilde for nearly three weeks. Every day, the band moves south, taking care to choose a safe place to make camp at night. Lili carries a knife strapped to her thigh (**Just in case,** Matilde said on her first night, **we aren't the only ones in the woods**), and sleeps in a tent with Matilde and Theo, on beds of pine needles and leaves. They eat roasted chestnuts, foraged honeyberries, and the occasional river carp—Lili refuses the stolen horse-meat she's offered. It's never much but it's something, and she's grateful not to have to rely on ration cards for sustenance, to share the responsibility of cobbling together their next meal with the group.

Most nights, once she's settled onto her makeshift bed, she's so spent from the day's hike that sleep, which eluded her for months, comes easily. And most mornings, she wakes refreshed despite the cold, uneven ground beneath her. She's grown accustomed to rising with the sun, enjoys it, even. Theo wakes happy too. He seems to like being with the partisans. A few boys in the group have taken to him. The youngest, Rafa, is fourteen. He told Lili that Theo reminded him of his younger brother, whom he hasn't seen since he left home a year ago. In their downtime, the boys play pass-the-pinecone, or swing branches at rocks in a game they've coined stickball. At first, when Theo grew tired of walking, the older boys took turns giving him piggyback rides. But Theo tires less and less. Lili often finds herself watching him, in awe of his endurance.

Lili's body has changed, too, since they left Assisi. Her legs can sustain her now throughout the day. Her back no longer aches as it once did after hours of walking. Her shoulders have grown brawny, the palms of her hands hardened, like leather, from carrying her valise (though Matilde had helped her fashion ropes around the suitcase, so when her arms tire, she can strap it to her back). She wears a pair of boots now that Rafa had outgrown—she'd nearly cried when he gave them to her, so relieved she was to slide her feet into them, the lining of her oxfords having worn through to the sole.

Lili may be stronger than she was when she left Todi, but she's no less wary. **Don't let the serenity of the forest fool you into thinking you're safe**, Matilde said. **If there's one thing I've learned out here, it's to expect the unexpected.** In the hours they've spent walking, Matilde has chronicled the last year of her life for Lili—the mishaps, the adventures, the close calls. Some stories were almost comical, like the time she woke to a bear cub in her tent, rummaging through her pack for food scraps. Others, not funny at all—like when she veered off trail to try to find a place to relieve herself and came face-to-face with a German soldier crouched behind a boulder. They'd stared at each other for a moment, looking equally shocked, until Matilde had simply walked away. **Thankfully, he didn't follow. He was a deserter, I think**, she said.

Now, Lili listens as Matilde shares another memory—this one about a mother cat snake that attacked her after she'd mistakenly walked over its nest.

"You should have heard it hissing at me," she says. "I was sure she was going to bite my foot off."

Through the trees, Lili can see a patch of farmland. A barn, a small pasture with a wooden fence around it. Something about the fence, though, doesn't look right. She squints at it, and as they near, others seem to notice too. They slow to a stop, staring.

"Jesus," Ziggie mutters.

"What the . . ." Matilde says.

It takes Lili a beat to process what she's seeing. The fence posts are crowned with **heads.** Human heads. She can tell by the red bandannas tied up beneath their chins that they are partisans. She looks at Rafa and he meets her eye, then leads Theo into the woods, picks up a couple of sticks, and challenges Theo to a swordfight.

"Do we know them?" Matilde asks Ziggie.

"Hard to tell," he says.

"We made camp for a few nights with another group before you joined us," Matilde tells Lili. "Could be them."

"Who do you think did it?" Lili asks, turning away.

Matilde shrugs. "My guess is Germans. But could have been Mussolini's ISR, acting for the Nazis. Or a mob of fed-up civilians. The country's at war with itself now. Whoever it was, they wanted to make a point," she says, taking Lili's arm.

"Well, they made one," Lili says, trying to will away the gruesome image, though she knows it will stay with her. She watches Theo and Rafa waving sticks in the woods. How much of the death, the trauma, she wonders, is Theo taking in? It's nearly unfathomable, even for her. Vicious gangsters. Bombs raining from the sky. Heads on fence posts. Gas chambers. She'll have to explain some things to him eventually. If she doesn't, someone else will. But what will his young mind do with this information? What does anyone do with it?

They walk for an hour along the edge of the forest before passing another parcel of farmland with a small, run-down home, a plot of tilled earth beside it. It's the kind of place they've stopped at before, to forage for food.

"Looks abandoned," Matilde tells Ziggie.

"Looks like a garden," Ziggie says with a smile. "Potato crop's my guess."

Lili scans the property, searching for signs of life. She sees none.

The partisans drop their belongings. A few pull spades from their duffels. Matilde and Ziggie untie the shovels they keep tethered to their packs.

"Come on," Matilde says. "Let's forage."

They jog thirty meters through overgrown grass to the property, then disperse around the garden and get to work digging. Sure enough, Ziggie was right.

"Got one!" Rafa yells.

"Hush, fool," Ziggie whispers.

Lili glances at the farmhouse. There are four windows at the back, facing toward them. One, she realizes, is missing a pane. She stares at the empty space behind it, trying to shake the feeling that something, someone is in there. That they're being watched. She's grown to appreciate the camouflage of the forest; she doesn't like being out in the open.

Beside her, Theo squats, his knees spread wide, scooping dirt by the handful. A small pile grows beside him as he excavates, and within minutes, his fingers are black. Lili's are too. Kneeling, she brushes a stray hair from her forehead with the back of her hand. "Here," she calls quietly, motioning Theo over so she can roll up his jacket sleeves.

They stay only a few more minutes before Ziggie gives a whistle, indicating that they'd better move on.

Lili stands, pockets the two potatoes she'd found. She claps the earth from her hands and knees. There is dirt still between the folds of her fingers and in the creases of her palms, but she lets it go—she'll rinse in the river later. They wash up when they can. It's too cold to bathe properly though, and over the last couple of weeks their skin has darkened a few shades—their hands and cheeks, especially—the bits exposed to sun and dirt. She'd pay anything for a shower, she thinks. She's nearly forgotten what it's like to be clean.

She takes Theo's hand, and as they begin their trek back to the forest, she looks behind her again at the farmhouse. This time, a flash catches her eye, in the open window. She stares as something long and skinny pokes from the empty space. The barrel of a rifle. And then, a millisecond later, a shot. A bullet whirs past, and a mound of dirt beside her jumps from its impact.

Someone up ahead shouts. "Run!"

Lili takes off, pulling Theo with her. A second shot fires. Then a third.

"Faster," she yells. "Pick up your feet." She considers hoisting Theo onto her back, but she'd have to stop to do so, and anyway he's too heavy. They're quicker on their own.

She runs as hard as she's ever run, tugging Theo along beside her, and soon they are ten meters to the tree line, then five, and then they are there, beneath the canopy. But the bullets keep coming.

She weaves to her right, looks frantically for the others. The group is scattered. Will the shooter— shooters, if there are more than one—follow them? Where is Matilde? They sprint on, deeper into the woods. Don't stop, Lili tells herself. Don't let go of his hand. Just keep going.

CHAPTER THIRTY

UMBRIAN COUNTRYSIDE

April 1944

Seems as good a place as any," Ziggie says, letting his pack fall from his shoulder. It lands with a thump at his feet.

Lili surveys the small clearing in the woods, wary of the open space. They'd skirted the bullets at the farm—barely—and they've seen no more evidence of violence in the week since, but still, the close call rattled her. The clearing is small, at least, with no homes in sight. It will do.

She drapes her coat over the top of her valise. The days have begun to warm, finally. She wears her heavy layers in the evenings and mornings, but by noon she strips them off. An aluminum canteen hangs from a leather strap across her chest—a gift from Matilde. She brings it to her lips before realizing it's empty.

"Come, Theo. Let's refill our water."

While the others set up camp, Lili and Theo walk to the riverbank. They've been following the Tiber since leaving Todi. **The river is our guide**, Matilde said, **it'll take us all the way to Rome.** They can't always see it, but more often than not they can hear it, the distant sound of moving water.

"This way!" Theo cries. The scare at the farm had shaken him, too, though only for a day. By the following morning, he was back to his bright self. The others hadn't made a big deal over it, which helped. Now, he runs ahead and his legs disappear in the thick tufts of soft, golden heather flanking the river. Lili glances overhead, scans for planes, picking up her knees as she walks and praying a foot doesn't land on a snake.

At the riverbank, she removes the cap from her canteen and dips the copper canister into the river, watching as the frigid water carves an eddy around her wrist. She waits for the last of the trapped air to bubble to the surface then stands, tips the thermos back, and takes several long pulls.

"Have a drink," Lili calls, and Theo trots over.

"Can we play for a little?" Theo asks, wiping the water from his mouth with his arm once he's had his fill.

Lili looks back at the group. "Why don't we follow the river to that big chestnut tree over there. We can hunt for some kindling." Theo's been delegated the responsibility of gathering firewood each night and takes great pride in the task.

"I bet I find the most," he says and takes off, elbows swinging, curls bouncing as he trots downriver.

Lili follows. Overhead, a pair of kingfishers circle the river, searching for their dinner.

"Found one already!" Theo thrusts a small stick in the air, an Olympian holding his torch.

"Excellent!" Lili calls. "Now find another."

The river shines iridescent black beneath the day's last rays of sun. Lili follows its gentle curve, admiring a patch of snowdrops poking their heads from the thawed, damp earth, the welcome pop of white reminding her of the hikes she and her mother used to take into the hills outside Bologna. They'd walk the Via degli Dei, the Route of the Gods, gathering stems of gentian, campion, primrose, and saxifrage, carrying the flowers home in a basket. There, Naomi would arrange them in a crystal vase at the center of the dining table and eventually hang them upside down to dry so she could preserve **the magic of spring**, as she called it, for months to come.

"**Guardami!**" Theo calls, and Lili looks up to find Theo strutting toward her along the riverbank, a pile of sticks in his arms.

"Watch your—" **step**, Lili tries to warn, but she's too late. Theo's toe catches a root and he stumbles. He cries out as he falls, and in the next moment he's splayed out on the dirt, his kindling scattered around him. Lili jogs over, kneels beside him.

"Are you okay?"

"It hurts."

Lili can tell from the quiver in his chin that he's holding back tears. "Show me where."

Theo pats at his foot. She pulls up his pant leg and rolls down his sock to get a better look, pressing gently on the skin around his anklebone.

"It hurts a lot," he whimpers.

"Let's get you back to camp," Lili says. She positions her arms beneath his and lifts him to his feet. "Can you walk?" Theo tries to take a step, shakes his head.

A pang of worry. "I'll carry you, then." She lifts him to her hip and walks, slowly, toward the others.

"What about my sticks?" Theo asks, looking over her shoulder.

"I'll come back for them, don't worry."

Hours later, Lili and Matilde sit by a fire, Lili's map spread across their thighs. Theo is asleep behind them, his leg propped on a rolled-up blanket. His ankle has swollen to nearly twice its normal size; he hasn't been able to bear weight on it since the fall. Lili has made a bandage from one of his too-small shirts, torn into strips. She hopes that elevation, along with the pressure of her dressing, will help with the swelling. Still, she worries.

"What if he still can't walk in the morning?"

"It's probably just a sprain," Matilde says.

"And if it's not?"

"Boys trip and fall all the time. Trust me. I have three brothers. At least two of them were limping on any given day."

Lili has no experience with brothers or with sprains. She's never broken anything, never even pulled a muscle. "If he can't walk in the morning, I think he should see a doctor."

"We'll sort something out," Matilde says.

Lili looks down at the map. "Where exactly are we?"

Matilde runs her finger south along the path of the Tiber. "The river is wide here, see? We passed Orte a day ago. So that puts us about . . . **here**, I believe." She points to a town called Scalo Teverina.

Lili tucks a lock of hair behind her ear, brittle as straw from weeks without a wash. She traces her own finger to Rome. They're three, maybe four days from the capital. "We're so close," she sighs, trying not to sound bitter.

Matilde leans into her. "Look at how far you've come, Lili. You'll make it to Rome. With or without us. Just tell yourself you can, and you will."

You sound like Esti, Lili thinks.

"Get some sleep," Matilde says. "Let's see what tomorrow brings. Theo's a tough little boy. I bet he'll be back on his feet."

Lili pushes away a twinge of panic at the thought of leaving the group. Of setting off again on her own. "Yes, let's see."

CHAPTER THIRTY-ONE

UMBRIAN COUNTRYSIDE

April 1944

Theo's ankle is swollen and hot to the touch the next morning, the skin around it a bright, angry purple. When he tries to stand, he crumples, and Lili and Matilde share a knowing look. He needs a doctor.

"Ziggie and I will take you as far as the tree line," Matilde tells Lili. "If all goes well, you'll only be a day or two in Scalo Teverina. We'll meet up again in Rome."

Lili would do anything to know for certain that this would be the case. A familiar sense of dread roots at the base of her spine, begins its slow crawl upward. She tries to ignore it, for Theo's sake, airing a veneer of confidence. Theo is in a foul mood. He'd been up most of the night, too uncomfortable to sleep. He sulks when she tells him they will split off from the group.

"At a clinic you might even have your own bed," Lili says to lift his spirits.

But Theo only frowns. "I don't want a bed. I want my tent."

Rafa gives him a hug before they go. "**Arrivederci**," he calls after them as they set off. **Until we meet again.** The word lands like a lump in Lili's chest.

Ziggie walks with Theo on his shoulders. It takes them about fifteen minutes to reach the edge of the forest. There, they pause. The trees are on the crest of a hill; down below, Lili can see clay-tiled roof-tops, a church dome, a stone bell tower.

"That road there," Matilde says, pointing, "should lead to the village."

Lili follows the road with her eyes as Matilde reaches for Theo. He slides from Ziggie's shoulders into her arms, and she hoists him onto Lili's back. Lili wraps one of her arms behind her, slipping her hand under his bottom to support him. She holds her valise with the other.

"Do you have some money?" Matilde asks.

"I do."

"Good. Here. Something to tide you over." Matilde drops a handful of roasted chestnuts into Lili's coat pocket.

"Thanks," Lili says.

"If I'm not there when you arrive in Rome," Matilde says, "I'll leave word for you with Sister Natalia." She gives Lili a tight hug, pats Theo's knee. "I'll see you soon, **piccolo uomo.**"

"**Ciao**, Matilde," Theo says softly.

Lili swallows a wave of sadness. She takes a few unsteady steps into the meadow, then looks over her shoulder. What are the odds that she and Matilde will be together again soon? Or ever? The confidence she'd feigned earlier dissolves.

"Thank you again," she says, fighting tears. "For everything."

"**Ciao, amica, ciao,**" Matilde says, blowing her a kiss, her dark eyes shining.

LILI WALKS SLOWLY, AWKWARDLY, AWAY FROM THE protection of trees, praying there aren't enemy eyes watching them from afar, rifles scoped at their heads. When she turns back once more, Matilde and Ziggie have disappeared, and Lili feels more alone than she has in months. She takes a breath, then another. **One foot in front of the other.**

"How long till we get there?" Theo asks.

"I don't know, ten minutes? Fifteen?"

"That long?" Theo huffs. Lili grits her teeth. Normally, she'd tell him to watch his tone, remind him that complaining won't help. But the boy is sad too. And in pain. She lets his question rest.

"Not so tight," she pleads a few minutes later, prodding his forearm with her chin. He loosens his grip and Lili bends at her hips to take some of the weight from her lumbar. She walks like this, half stooped, until they reach the outskirts of the town and the first glimpse of village life—a man sitting on a stool outside his door, an old woman rolling a small cart behind her. She doesn't see any uniforms. A good sign. She does a little hop to adjust Theo on her back. What a sight we must be, she thinks. They hobble to a large piazza at the center of the town, where Lili searches the square for a friendly face.

"Excuse me," she calls when she spies a young woman walking toward her, holding the hand of a girl who looks to be about Theo's age. "Could you tell us if there is a clinic here? My son needs to see a doctor." She's marked herself a visitor, and this is a risk, Lili knows. But she can't fathom walking every block of the village with Theo on her back, searching for some sign of medical care. That would only draw more attention.

The woman stops, unsure, Lili can tell, of what to make of her. "There's a hospital three blocks south," she says, motioning to the far side of the piazza.

Lili gives a grateful nod. "**Grazie mille**," she says, then continues on; if she stands for too long, she'll lose her momentum, and she doesn't want to answer any questions this stranger might have. A few steps later, however, she feels a body beside her, fingers next to hers on the handle of her valise. She starts, then realizes it's the woman, who's turned to follow her.

"Here," she says. "Let me help."

The weight of her suitcase melts away. Lili wraps

her free hand beneath Theo, grateful to use the strength of both arms to carry him. "Thank you," she says.

The woman nods and the little girl at her side looks up at Theo. "What's wrong with him?" she asks Lili.

"Sofia!" the woman scolds. "Be polite."

"He's twisted his ankle," Lili says. "But he'll be okay, won't you, Theo?"

"Yes," Theo says, and Lili can feel him shifting his weight to get a better look at the girl.

They walk past a bakery, a fabric shop, a tobacco store.

"I'm Felicia," the woman says.

"Lili. **Piacere.**"

"I like your coat," the little girl says.

"Thank you," Lili says. "It was a gift."

"The color is pretty."

"Here we are," Felicia says as they reach a building marked **Ospedale.**

Lili hikes Theo higher up on her back, and Felicia hands over the valise. "Thanks again," Lili says. "I appreciate the help."

"Take care," Felicia says, and Lili can see from the worry in her eyes—a mother's worry—that she means it.

"You as well." Lili turns to climb the stairs to the hospital, ignoring the ache in her tired legs, the rabbit fur stuck to the sweat at the back of her neck.

CHAPTER THIRTY-TWO

SCALO TEVERINA

April 1944

From a chair beside his hospital bed, Lili watches Theo sleep. He hasn't broken his ankle, as she'd feared. **It's a sprain**, the doctor said. Matilde was right. **It'll be sore for a while. He'll need to stay off his feet for a few days, at least.** He asked Lili where she was from—**This is a small town**, he said, he could spot an unfamiliar face from afar—and Lili told him a partial truth: that she'd come from Assisi, and they were on their way to Rome. She said they'd been traveling for the most part on foot, and when he raised an eyebrow, she explained she was nervous to take the train, as she's heard the Allies were targeting stations. And besides, she added, since her husband passed, money was tight; she couldn't afford the tickets. **You've been on quite a journey**, the doctor noted, then told her she could stay at the hospital while Theo healed, or until they got some wounded soldiers in from the front—whichever came first. That was three days ago though, and Theo still can't walk.

While she waits, Lili debates how to reach Rome. The safest route, she knows, would be to continue on foot. But at the moment, that's not an option. Even if Theo is well enough to walk in a few days, he won't make it far on a newly sprained ankle. And she can carry him only for short distances. Taking the train would be faster, though far more dangerous. Was it worth it to risk the checkpoints, a German arrest? Would their Aryan IDs be as convincing the next time they're scrutinized? Matilde's words are never far. Deportations. Camps.

Lili closes her eyes. She has to make a decision soon, but her options are so limited. There is no good solution. Unless. She opens her eyes, straightens.

What if—? She stops herself, tries not to think it. No. She couldn't. Not possible. But it's too late. Her mind has already turned the corner. The thought is there, dangling before her, waiting for her to reach for it.

She could leave. Set out on her own.

A rush of guilt. She sits with it. Lets the idea settle. Theo is safe here at the hospital, she rationalizes— safer at least than out on the streets with her. Safer than at a train station checkpoint. He'd be better off, and she would be too; she could move faster, more stealthily, without him in tow, the risk of getting caught hers and hers alone.

Lili holds her breath, at once paralyzed and electrified by the plan as it solidifies. She could leave **now**, she tells herself. She could be in Rome in a few hours. Deliver her parcel to Sister Natalia and begin her search for Esti, for her father, for Niko. She'd come back for Theo, of course, when it was safer. Surely, someone would take him in. The doctor— he seems kind enough—would help to find him a good home. She could leave his ID, and a note by his bedside, a promise to return, perhaps even mention the name of the woman who'd carried her bag, Felicia.

Lili stands, too agitated suddenly to sit, and slinks from the room. In the hallway, she paces. When a nurse gives her a curious look, she finds a washroom, steps inside, locks the door behind her. She moves to the sink, props her hands on the steel basin, stares at herself in the mirror. The image is jarring. Her sun-streaked hair hangs well past her shoulders, matted and frayed at the ends. Her lips are cracked, her cheekbones too pronounced. There's a smear of dirt at her forehead, a spot she must have missed when she first arrived at the hospital and the nurse gave her a cloth to wash herself clean. She leans closer, staring at the flecks of gold in her hazel eyes—the only part of her she recognizes. Should she leave him? Could she? She splashes water on her face and steps back out into the hallway.

A familiar voice sounds from behind her and Lili jumps. "**Buon giorno**. Didn't mean to sneak up on you," the doctor says. "Just making my morning rounds. Everything all right?"

"Yes, **Dottore**," Lili says. "Yes. I was just freshening up."

"How's my patient today?"

"Still sleeping."

Lili follows the doctor back to Theo's room, stands at the foot of the bed. "His spirits have improved," she says quietly. "But as of last night, he still wasn't able to walk."

"I see. Give it another day or two," the doctor says. He places the diaphragm of his stethoscope on Theo's chest, listening, then presses his fingers to Theo's wrist, taking his pulse. Lili waits for Theo to blink open his eyes, but his face is slack. It's as if the comfort of a real bed, the luxury of sleep when he wants to sleep, has put him into some kind of coma. "He should rest," the doctor says. "I'll come back when he's up to look at his ankle."

"Thank you, doctor," Lili says. She expects him to turn and leave, but he doesn't. Instead, he lowers his voice.

"I wanted to let you know—I'm expecting a delivery from Rome. Medical supplies. I've been waiting on it for weeks, but I'm told it'll be here any day. If my driver makes it, you might ask if you could return with him to the capital. You mentioned you're traveling on foot, but I imagine Theo won't soon be fit to walk such a distance."

A ride to Rome. "That's—" Lili looks at Theo,

watching the mound of his belly rise and fall beneath his bedsheet, his eyes flit under his lids. His lips are full and parted, and there's a new outcrop of pale freckles on his cheeks, from his days under the sun. One of his hands is curled around his Nello. Lili swallows, feeling her heart fill with shame, then resolution. They've come so far, the two of them. She'd tried to tell herself that leaving him was the smart choice, as selfish as it felt. That he'd be sheltered here at the hospital. That Esti would understand. But she knows now she was wrong. She can't leave him. Of course she can't. Not because Esti wouldn't want her to—and she's certain Esti would not—but because he's all she has. The one good thing left in her life. There's no certainty any longer in her war-torn world, her future. The ground is no longer solid beneath her feet. But Theo—loving him, protecting him—this at least is real. Something she can hold on to with focus, with clarity. And she can't protect him if she's not with him.

She looks up at the doctor, nods. "That's wonderful," she says.

Four days later, Lili sits propped against the inside wall of a truck bed, Theo's head in her lap. He'd fallen sick thirty minutes into the trip, woozy from the constant jostling and from the musty scent filling the dim, cramped space. At least they're on their way, Lili thinks. And at least he can walk again, albeit with a limp. They'd left the hospital in Scalo Teverina some three hours before, as soon as the doctor told Lili to prepare her things. At the last minute, unable to leave without offering something in thanks, she'd pressed her father's gold cufflinks into the doctor's hands. He'd tried to refuse them, but Lili insisted. **For your kindness**, she said.

The Dovunque, a transport truck with a canvas top, rumbles south. When she met the driver, he told her she and Theo were better off hiding in the back. **We may pass through some checkpoints**, he said before they left. **If they see you up front, they'll be suspicious.** Lili hadn't anticipated checkpoints. She'd nearly backed out of the ride. So far though, the truck hasn't made any stops.

She wishes she could move around, stretch her legs, but Theo's head is heavy on her thigh and there isn't any room, anyway—the truck is filled with now-empty crates, which the driver had stacked between her and the rear door in an effort to conceal his human cargo. Lili sways along with the motion of the vehicle, breathes deeply to keep her nausea at bay. They must be close to the capital by now. She lifts an arm to check her watch (pointless, as it's too dark to see the time) as the Dovunque slows, then stops, and for a moment she wonders if they've made it. But then she hears voices, snapping orders in German.

"**Dein Zweck!**"

Lili stiffens.

"Medical supplies," she hears the driver shout in Italian, over the drone of the idling engine.

A reply comes in German but it's garbled. Lili imagines the door being thrown open, the cavity searched. There's a padlock on it—she'd heard the clack of metal as the driver fastened it when they set off—but if the Germans want to see what's inside, there's no stopping them. Straining for clues as to what's happening, she catches fragments of conversation. **Papiere. Destinazione. Krankenhaus.** And then, the driver's voice rings clear and Lili's throat seizes.

"See for yourself," he says.

The truck bed wobbles as he gets out, slamming the cab door behind him. The padlock rattles and a moment later the space around Lili lightens several shades as the tailgate drops open. She stares at the flimsy wooden barrier between her and the enemy, at the narrow openings between the crates, trying to breathe without sound and imploring Theo not to wake with a noisy start. One of the crates at her feet moves as another is pulled aside.

"See? Just boxes," the driver says.

A shout, in German. Wood scraping metal as more crates are pushed aside. **Please, please, please.** And then, silence. Lili tries to breathe without a sound. Finally, the doors slam shut, and once again she's enveloped in darkness. She listens as the padlock is secured into place. As the driver returns to his cab. As a German voice calls from outside: **"Heil Hitler!"**

"**Heil** Hitler," the driver echoes, then shifts the vehicle into gear. They lurch forward and lumber on, Theo still soundly asleep on Lili's lap. She exhales, lets her head fall to the wall of the truck bed behind her, and closes her eyes.

WHEN LILI AND THEO FINALLY STUMBLE FROM THE back of the truck onto Via Cicerone, they are pale-faced and disoriented. Theo looks around, squinting, still half asleep. Lili blinks several times into the too-bright daylight, relieved to find there are no uniforms in sight. She inhales, savoring the sensation of pavement underfoot, of clean air in her lungs. The driver bids her a quick goodbye, not wanting to chance another run-in.

At the door to the convent, Lili takes a few deep breaths before ringing the bell. On the street, a horse trots by, pulling a wagon, his rib cage protruding beneath a dull chestnut coat. Lili waits a long moment, then rings the bell again, staring at the heavy oak door. Finally, it opens. "**Buon giorno.** I'm looking for Sister Natalia," Lili says.

The nun in the frame looks from Lili to Theo, her lips drawn into a tight, thin line. "I am Natalia. What do you need?"

"I have a delivery for you, from Father Niccacci in Assisi."

The nun's eyes dart to the street. "I see," she says.

She takes a step back, holds the door open for Lili and Theo to enter.

They follow her through the convent to a small, empty chapel. They stand at the back, in the aisle between pews.

"A woman came by a few days ago," the nun says, studying Lili's face. "She asked for a friend by the name of Passigli."

"That's me!" Lili says. "Was it Matilde?"

"Yes, that was her."

At the mention of Matilde's name, Lili laughs. She can't help it. Matilde was **here**. Just days ago! The knot in her chest loosens and it's easier, suddenly, to breathe.

"She's a friend. We were supposed to arrive in Rome together, but—it's a long story." Lili props her valise on a bench, opens it. Removing the clothes from one side, she runs a hand along the lining. When she finds what she's looking for—a thread— she tugs, and a small hole opens at the seam, just large enough to poke her fingers inside and pull. The thread makes a succession of **pops**, and a second later the parcel she's carried since Assisi falls into her hands.

As she stands, her heart begins to race. She's made it. She's kept her end of the promise. She turns the envelope over once before handing it to the nun. The gesture is a small one, but it feels monumental, like the passing of a baton.

Sister Natalia unties the string around the parcel, pulls back its top flap, and peers inside. "I've been waiting a long time for this," she says.

"I know. I wish I could have gotten it to you sooner. We came most of the way on foot, and arrived just now."

Sister Natalia holds the envelope close to her chest. "Did Father Niccacci tell you what you were carrying?"

These papers will save lives, he'd said. "No. Just that it was important." Lili assumed they were identification papers, but she never asked.

"**Molto importante**. Thank you."

Lili stands a little taller. "Of course."

"I should tend to these," Sister Natalia says, tucking the parcel under her arm. "I'll send word to Rufino that his delivery has arrived." She fishes beneath her robe and produces a slip of paper. "Your friend left you this." She hands the paper to Lili. On it, Matilde has written an address: **3 Vicolo del Giglio, Piazza Farnese**.

"Did she say what it is?" Lili asks.

"It's a place to stay."

Lili laughs again, this time at her good fortune. **Thank you, Matilde.**

CHAPTER THIRTY-THREE

ROME

May 1944

The second-story flat Matilde arranged for Lili on Piazza Farnese has a bedroom, a kitchen with a single-burner stove, a bathroom as broad as Lili's shoulders, and a living area just big enough for a two-person settee and a round bistro table where she and Theo take their meals. It's tiny, but it suits them, and Lili appreciates the fact that the space has two windows overlooking the square. Lili had found a note tucked into the spout of a teakettle when she first arrived. **My colleagues and I used this as a place to meet. A safehouse, Lili understands. It's small but should do! And cheap, 1000 lire per month. The landlord, Giacomo, is old and half-blind; he doesn't care who comes and goes, just that we're not late on rent. He lives on the third floor, apartment D.** Lili knew she'd be responsible for the rent—a nerve-racking prospect as her savings will last her another month, maybe two if they can get by solely on ration cards for their food—but she'd smiled faintly at the word **we**. She and Matilde, part of something together now. **Be safe, Lili,** Matilde signed off. **Rome is not a friendly place. Trust no one. I'll check in when I can.**

With the capital occupied by German troops, Lili has taken Matilde's warnings to heart in the weeks since she and Theo arrived. Petrified of getting stopped and questioned, they leave the flat only for ration cards and provisions, or to visit the post office or the Red Cross office. Lili thinks often about trying to make her way to Allied territory. But American and British troops, according to the papers, are battling hard to push the Germans north—and to walk blindly through hostile territory, without any advice on where to try to cross the front, seems foolish.

Matilde was right. The city is not a welcoming place. There are posters plastered all around offering rewards for turning in Jews, and she'll be arrested if she's stopped and the authorities see through her false ID. But at least in the capital, she has an apartment, a bed, access to ration cards. They are the most basic of things, but a means to survival. And so, she's stayed. She keeps a low profile. She blends in.

Theo darts across the room to the window, reaches for the sill, and bounces on his toes to try to see out. "Can we go outside?" he asks, for the third time that morning. It took a while, but his limp has finally disappeared.

Lili picks him up so he can see out. They peer down at the piazza, deserted but for a pair of fountains in the shape of bathtubs at either end, their waterspouts long dried up. Lili had cracked the window earlier that morning, and she pushes it farther open now, feeling a rush of spring air flow over her fingertips. The sky is a pale, crystalline blue, the temperature inviting. Normally, they'd spend the afternoon reading, or practicing numbers, or playing endless games of make-believe and patty-cake and "would you rather." **Would you rather have twenty fingers or twenty toes? Which animal would you rather be—a bird or a fish?** But Theo's attention is short, his energy high. With the partisans, he'd grown used to being out in nature; he complains often now about being cooped up all day. Lili can't blame him. She doesn't like it either. Perhaps today, for a special treat, they could take a quick walk to the Borghese Gardens, stretch their legs. If they spot any Germans, she tells herself, they'll turn around.

"Okay," she relents. "Let's go to the park."

"Yahoo!" Theo celebrates with a happy dance and Lili smiles.

They leave their building hand in hand, cross Piazza Farnese, then pass through an adjacent square called Campo dei Fiori, where there's a market in the mornings and where Lili does her shopping. At the main thoroughfare, Corso Vittorio Emanuele II,

Lili finds a line of donkey carts waiting at the curb. She's tempted to ask for directions—it's been years since she was last in Rome, and her memory of how to reach the gardens is vague—but she's fearful of talking to a stranger. She hesitates, trying to get her bearings, and the driver closest to her looks her way, tips his hat. She nods a polite hello.

"Need a ride?" the driver asks.

"Just directions," Lili says.

"Where to?"

"The Borghese Gardens."

The driver explains the route, then cranes his head to survey the carts lined up in front of him. "**Perché no**," he says to himself, and then to Lili, "I'll take you there."

Theo claps his hands. "Can we? Go for a ride?"

"We can't afford it, love," Lili tells Theo, even though she always carries a few lire on her. But the money is for necessities, not for frivolous rides in donkey carts.

"For the pretty lady, it's on me," the driver says. "Federico here needs the exercise, anyhow, huh, Fed." The donkey blinks a big glassy eye, his long ears twitching.

"Please, Mama, can we?" Theo begs, pulling on Lili's sleeve.

Mama. The word rolls so easily now from his tongue.

"It's a long way to walk," the driver says, and

when he smiles the corners of his eyes wrinkle in a way that reminds Lili of her father.

"All right," she says finally, and Theo claps again. "If you insist." She hoists Theo into the cart and climbs up behind him.

"You from here?" the driver asks as they clip-clop up Via dei Baullari.

"No. I'm from Lecce."

"Well then," the driver says. "Welcome to Rome."

Lili looks around at the boarded-up storefronts, at the apartment windows masked in thick curtains and long, black strips of tape, at the occasional bombed-out building, casualties of an Allied battering. Rome, once a thriving metropolis, is falling to pieces.

"Thank you," she says, wrapping an arm around Theo and pulling him to her.

THE BORGHESE GARDENS, LILI IS HAPPY TO FIND, have been spared from bombs and axe-wielding civilians in search of firewood. In fact, the park looks very much as Lili remembers it from her visits as a child—lush and sprawling, with emerald-green ponds, ornate stone villas, and ancient statues around every corner. They choose a sunny path, passing a group of schoolchildren sitting in the shade of a chestnut tree, each with a drawing slate before them.

"I used to come here when I was little," Lili tells Theo, "with my parents."

"What did you do?"

"I'd see a puppet show. Visit the stable—I loved watching the horseback riders trot by in their fancy clothes. Sometimes I'd eat gelato, or climb up the Pincio, where, from the top, you can see all of Rome."

"What's gelato?" Theo asks, and Lili glances at him. "It's a sweet treat, love. I can't wait for you to try it." There is so much he doesn't know. "One time," she adds, "and you'll like this—my parents took me to a museum where I saw a **dinosaur bone**."

"A **real-life** dinosaur bone? How big was it?"

"Bigger than me," Lili says.

"Wowza."

The air smells of pine needles and rain-dampened grass. Lili breathes it in, grateful for the change of scenery. They can live for only so long in captivity. She narrates as they walk, pointing out a cinema, painted green and shaped like a chalet. At the grand Galleria, she tells Theo about the time she visited, and how she circled the statue of **Apollo and Daphne** over and over again, enamored by the soft appearance of Daphne's marble figure, the delicateness of the leaves around her. "I couldn't believe she was made of stone," Lili says.

They pass a lake with an island at its center, home to a small white-columned church, and pause to admire the reflection of the steeple on the glassy water. When they turn, Lili's stomach flips at the sight of two uniformed men walking in their direction. She can tell from the shape of their black uniforms and peaked caps that they are Guardia Nazionale Repubblicana, GNR for short—former **carabinieri** that make up Italy's new gendarmerie force, an infamously violent militia. She searches for a way to veer from the path, to avoid a run-in, but there isn't one.

She takes Theo's hand. "If those soldiers up there stop us," she tells him quietly, willing her voice to be calm, "remember: you are Theo Passigli, and I am your mother. Got it?" Theo's smile wilts as he registers the officers' presence.

The men stare at her as they approach, and Lili knows they will be stopped. **Proud chest**, she tells herself, pinching her shoulders down her back.

"Just a minute, **signora**," one of the officers says, stepping into her path. He is tall, thin, his partner the opposite—small and square.

"Gentlemen," Lili says.

"Your papers, **per favore**."

Lili hands their IDs over, and as the tall one inspects them, his partner turns his attention to Theo. He takes a step closer, props a meaty hand on Theo's shoulder; it takes every ounce of Lili's self-restraint not to pull him away, to hiss **get your hands off him**. But the officer is smiling, and not in a menacing kind of way, so she bites her tongue and waits.

"I see the making of a fine Figlio della Lupa here," he says, giving Theo's upper arm a squeeze as if testing it for strength. The Sons of the She-Wolf is a branch of Il Duce's Operazione Nazionale Balilla—his version of the Hitler Youth—that begins recruiting children at six. Lili finds the name, inspired by the statue of Romulus and Remus suckling a mother wolf, as disturbing as the organization itself. Theo, not understanding the reference but sensing a compliment, puffs up his chest and the soldier laughs. **Never**, Lili thinks, but she smiles, hoping the officers won't notice the perspiration gathering at her hairline.

"If only we should be so lucky," she says smoothly, which seems to please the soldier.

"How old are you, son?" he asks Theo.

Theo holds up three fingers.

"A few more years, then." The officer pats his head.

The skinny officer eyes Theo's identification card. "Can you tell me your name, son?"

Lili's throat turns to paper. She looks down at Theo. He glances up at her and she nods.

"My name is Theo," he tells the officer.

"And your surname?"

Lili holds her breath. A second passes, then two. She licks her lips, ready to answer for him.

"Passigli," Theo says softly. Lili could hug him.

"You're a long way from home," the officer tells Lili.

"Yes, sir."

She waits before elaborating—it wasn't a question, and she senses the less information she gives the better. The officer nods, seemingly satisfied.

"Thank you," Lili says as he returns their papers, her tone casual, as if accepting a cappuccino from across the bar.

"Enjoy your afternoon, **signora**," he says.

"See you in a few years, little cub!" the stout officer tells Theo with a wink.

As the pair walks off, Lili bends as if to tie the lace of Theo's shoe. She brings a hand to his cheek. "Good boy," she whispers. "Good boy."

She rights herself and they walk on in silence. Behind her, as their voices recede, she can hear one of the officers make a joke, the other howling with laughter.

CHAPTER THIRTY-FOUR

ROME

May 1944

It's mid-May, and the capital, as if to defy its depleted, war-torn state, is drenched in wisteria, purple and fragrant. Lili and Theo walk their usual route along Via Giulia to the post office— it's a bit out of the way, but the street is quieter than the main thoroughfares, and one of the city's most beautiful, Lili's decided. Most days, she walks slowly, peeking through the palazzo gates flanking the street, imagining what it might be like to live in such luxury. Today, however, her thoughts are occupied by the dwindling number of clothes Theo can now wear. Despite their meals of watery soup and bread made with rye, sugar beets, and straw, the boy keeps growing. The hems of his pants, which she's let down to the last millimeter, hang at his ankles, the cuffs of his sleeves well above his wrists. She'll need to buy him a new outfit soon. She wonders what it will cost. If they're going to stay on in Rome, she knows, she'll need to look for a job. But how can she work with Theo at home? She can't bring him to work with her. And he can't stay alone in the flat. She can sell some of her jewelry, or her grandmother's silver, she tells herself, if she has to.

Lili wishes Matilde would check in. Perhaps she's joined the underground in Rome, or returned to the forest, to another band of partisans. Surely, her friend would send word or come back for her if she were to find safe passage to Allied territory. The Americans and the British are close now, the headlines report. They're battling at the German Gustav line of defense, less than one hundred fifty kilometers south of Rome. If the Allies break through, they could be in the capital in a matter of weeks.

"I smell something sweet in my nose," Theo says, and Lili smiles. Theo is good at this—breaking her worry spells with an innocent observation.

"It's the wisteria," she says, taking notice of the colorful display. She guides him to a vine, lifts him up so he can put his nose to one of its violet flowers. When she sets him down, she spots a poster on the mottled ochre wall, half obscured. She leans to have a closer look. It's a warning, she realizes, issued by the Germans.

"From the cave incident," someone says, and Lili startles. The woman behind her is older, in her sixties maybe. Well dressed. She must have come from one of the palazzos.

"What cave incident?" Lili ventures.

"You don't know?"

"We're new to town."

The woman lowers her voice, whispers out of Theo's earshot a story about a partisan attack in March that killed thirty German soldiers, about how, in retaliation, the Nazis murdered three hundred Italians. "Shot them dead in a cave up in the hills over Rome."

Lili thinks of Anna's reprisal story, of the villagers rounded up and hanged in Torre del Colle. The ratio is consistent. Ten to one.

"That's—horrendous," she says, the wisteria's sweet scent suddenly making her sick.

"They are barbarians," the woman says, matter-of-fact, then continues on her way.

Lili pulls her gaze from the poster, reaches for Theo's hand. It takes all her willpower to push the image of the cave, the dead bodies, out of her mind.

"Come. Let's get to the post office before it closes."

She's received one letter since arriving in Rome, from Father Niccacci in Assisi. Nothing from Sister Lotte in Florence or from her father. The mail is more unreliable than ever—she reminds herself of this often when it feels like she's sending messages into an abyss—but every week still, she writes. For not to, she knows, is to give up. And that's not an option. Father Niccacci didn't have any news to report on Esti, but he told Lili that Isabella and Ricardo were fine, that the "incident" with her neighbor—the drunkard who had threatened to turn Lili in—had been brought to the attention of the police and dismissed. He told her, too, he'd heard from Sister Natalia how grateful she was to receive his parcel. **Thank you, Lili**, he wrote, **you have no idea how valuable your help was in that matter**. This, at least, had brought Lili some comfort. Maybe this afternoon, she thinks, as she and Theo walk beneath Via Giulia's arched entrance, the clerk will smile and hand her a letter as she steps to the front of the line, rather than shake his head with his usual apologetic **nothing today**.

She checks her watch. "We'd better hurry," she says, picking up her pace.

Theo skips beside her, his body quivering with unspent energy. "I can run!" he says. A request. He knows he needs permission.

"Let's just walk quickly."

"But I'm fast!" Theo cries. "I'll show you. I'll run just a little bit, then I'll run back." Lili surveys the street. There are only a handful of people out and about, and none appear to be a threat.

"Fine. Just a few steps ahead though."

Theo pumps his fist and takes off.

"That's far enough," Lili calls. He stops, bounds back to her, then sprints ahead again. "You're like a puppy," Lili says as he trots a loop around her. She should rein him in, she thinks, but it's obvious he needs to move, so she lets him run, hoping the exertion will tire him.

A few blocks from the post office, they pass a **tabaccaio** on the corner of Piazza Colonna, and Lili glances inside, where a woman stands at the counter, tall and lean with long, auburn hair. Her build and posture remind Lili of Esti's. She slows to have a closer look, feeling her pulse stir as it does when she spots a look-alike. The woman turns and Lili glances at her feet, embarrassed to have gotten her hopes up. It's not her, of course. It never is.

She walks on, then stills as she realizes suddenly—Theo is gone.

"Theo!" she cries. She spins around, scouring the intersection. "Theo!" He's vanished. Panic spreads through her, hot and fast. She jogs several meters toward the tall marble column in the middle of the square and then stops, spins around again. "Theo!"

A truck motors by, followed by an ambulance. Two horses pulling carts plod in the opposite direction. But there's no sign of the boy. "THEO!" she screams, and heads begin to turn. She's making a scene, shouting like this, but she doesn't care. **He has to be close.** She retraces her steps, back to the **tabaccaio**, to the intersection where she'd last seen him, her brain spinning as she curses her negligence. "THEO!"

And then, she sees him. A block west on Vicolo dei Bovari. He's—with someone. A man. "Oh dear God no," she whispers as she realizes the man is wearing a German uniform. She hurries toward them, adrenaline skating in her veins. When Theo sees her, he runs to her. She pulls him close, lifts him from the ground.

"Oh, my sweet boy," she whispers into his ear. "I was so worried." She holds him for a moment before setting him down, then lets her eyes fall over him, tracing his cheeks, his hands, the length of his torso. No scratches. No marks. **He's okay.** "Don't ever do that to me again, my love."

"I smelled chestnuts," Theo says. "There's a cart," he adds, pointing.

Lili takes Theo's hand, vowing to never again let it go, and makes eye contact, finally, with the German soldier. "My apologies, sir," she says. "Let's go, Theo." But as she turns, she feels a hand on her arm, the grip firm.

"**Scusi**," the soldier says. He pulls Lili back down the street.

"Please let go," Lili says, but the soldier ignores her. When they reach an alley, he ducks into it, towing her with him. They walk another few steps before he loosens his grip. Lili pulls her arm from him, considers running. He might chase her. And to run, she realizes, is to admit some sort of guilt. So she stands, doing everything in her power to keep a brave face.

The soldier removes his cap. "Please," he says, in English. "I didn't mean to scare you."

Lili blinks, thrown off guard. He's not German. She'd studied English in high school, had taken a few classes at university—she was proficient by the time she graduated and knows enough to understand that the soldier is apologizing. **Who is this man**, she wonders. **Is he a spy? Why is he dressed as a German?** She keeps quiet, her emotions in check, vowing not to reveal anything he could use against her.

"You see," the soldier continues, his tone hushed, "I'm an American soldier. **Americano**." He pats at his chest. "I am . . . I was **prigioniero**. I escaped."

A prisoner of war. Lili stares at him. His words feel forced, preposterous. She thinks of the posters on Via Giulia, of Matilde's warning: **Trust no one**.

"I don't believe you," she says, in English.

"Oh! You—you speak English!" the soldier says, brightening. He returns his cap to his head and smiles. Dimples form on his cheeks and suddenly his face is open, handsome—as if it belonged to a different person entirely.

"A little," Lili says.

The man dressed as a soldier holds up a finger, then squats, unlaces one of his boots. Lili takes a small step back, pulling Theo with her. She watches as he extracts a metal token from the toe of his boot. He stands, holds what appears to be a necklace for Lili to see.

"This is me," he says, running his fingers along the embossing on the rectangular-shaped pendant. "Thomas Driscoll. 6957765—that's my service number. I'm a Ranger with the United States Army. This is my address in Virginia." He swallows, closes his fingers around his tag, his blue-gray eyes steady on

Lili's. "I've been living on the streets," he says. "But if the Germans, they find me, well, that's the end. I hate to ask, but . . . I'm wondering, ma'am, if you might be willing to help me. I need a place to hide."

Lili can't believe what she's hearing. The man must either be deranged or desperate, or both. No man with decent intentions would ask a stranger— especially a woman—on the streets of Rome to hide him.

"I'm sorry," she says. "I can't help you."

The soldier nods as if he understands exactly what she's thinking. He pauses before continuing. "I know how bad this must look. Perhaps . . . I can explain?" Lili says nothing so he continues. "I'm searching for my regiment, you see. I don't know exactly where they are. I was captured near Naples and sent to a prison called Marina-something, outside of Rome. As soon as I can locate the unit, I'll be on my way."

Lili tries to follow but his words come fast. "You are American soldier," she says.

"Yes."

"And you are . . . **perduto**. Lost?"

"In a way, yes."

"How did you **scappato**?"

"How did I escape?"

Lili nods.

"We dug a tunnel," he says, miming the action of digging and crawling. He speaks more slowly now, so she can understand, his words long and soft at the edges. "From the floor of our barracks to the border of the prison. We burrowed through, then ran. Haven't stopped running since."

"We?"

"Me and two others. The guards spotted us, unfortunately, and started shooting. My pals . . . they didn't make it."

"Your **uniforme**." Lili eyes the swastika beneath the eagle emblem on his helmet.

"I borrowed it from a German. A dead one, of course," he says, then glances at Theo. "Sorry," he adds. He pulls a photo ID from his shirt pocket, shows it to Lili. "Horst Krüger. Twenty-two years old, from a town called Holfgeismar. I know it's sinister and I probably smell like bratwurst, but I needed the disguise."

Lili's eyes flit from the photo on the ID to the soldier's face, finding no resemblance. She shakes her head. She wants to call the man's bluff—this dirt-caked person claiming to be an American called Thomas, posing as a German soldier, telling her he's tunneled his way out of prison—it sounds like a scene out of a movie. But there's something about him that seems genuine. She feels herself softening.

The man drops his tag into his tunic pocket, bends to address Theo. "I have a nephew about your age," he says, his hands on his knees. "He lives in America, in a town called Richmond, where I'm from. His name is Steve."

Theo looks up at Lili. She translates, knowing the

word **America** will mean nothing to him. If the soldier is telling the truth, she can't help but feel sorry for him. He's a wanted man, and he's chosen a Jew, of all people, to beg for shelter. He'd be no safer with her than he is on his own.

"**Perché io?**" she asks, bringing a hand to her chest. The soldier looks at her, shakes his head. "Why ask of **me**?" Lili says, in English.

"Why you? Well," he starts, dipping his chin. "I suppose it's that I've seen you a few times, you and your son, walking through the market together, once in Piazza Farnese. You look . . . I don't know, kind. And then this little one came wandering down the street here and when I recognized him, I took it as a sign. Figured it was my opportunity to talk to you, that I should seize the moment and not let it pass."

Theo wraps an arm around Lili's leg and pulls at the belt loop of her trouser. "What is he saying?" he whispers.

Lili brings a hand to the back of his head. "**Un secondo, amore.**" She looks up at the American, taking in his sideburns and his days-old beard and his eyes the color of a winter sky. He doesn't look at all German. He looks like a cowboy from the American western films Esti liked to drag her to in Ferrara.

"Please, **signora** . . ." he says.

"Liliana."

"Please, Liliana. I just want to find my regiment.

And then I want to go home. Alive." He looks up quickly, as if asking the gods to grant these not-so-simple wishes. "I can go out at night to scavenge for food, you won't have to feed me. And I have a few lire I can offer." He pats his pocket. "They came with the uniform." He ventures a smile.

Who are **you?** Lili wonders again. How can she trust this man? **He could be lying**, a voice inside warns. **You owe him nothing.** She checks the time. The post office will have closed by now. **Wish him well and go home.** Lili opens her mouth but the words don't come. He's a hideaway. An enemy of the Axis, pretending to be someone he's not in order to survive. He has no one to turn to, no safe haven. He's just like her.

Lili thinks of the countless people who have taken them in since the start of the war. Who've given them food, clothing, a ride, in exchange for much less of an explanation than he's given her. The people to whom she may well owe her life.

"You are called Thomas," she says, pronouncing it toe-**maz**.

"That's right. Thomas Driscoll. But my friends call me Tommy."

"All right, Thomas," she sighs, "follow me."

WHEN THEY REACH THE NORTHEAST CORNER OF Piazza Farnese, Lili stops, looks around. Thomas's is the only uniform in sight.

"It will be **sospettoso**," she tells him. "For a German soldier to walk in beside us."

"Suspicious. Yes, of course," Thomas agrees.

"Five minutes," Lili says, holding up a hand and spreading her fingers wide. "Floor two, **appartamento B**." She enunciates slowly, hoping he'll understand. "I leave the door open for you. **Intendi?**"

Thomas gives her a quick nod and a thumbs-up, and Lili turns, feeling his eyes on her as she and Theo cross the square.

"The soldier is coming to our house?" Theo says.

"Yes. He's an American, love. I know he looks like one of the bad guys but he's not. Americans are good. He's just pretending to be German."

"But why is he coming?"

"It's dangerous to be an American in this town."

"Like it is for us?"

"Exactly."

"He needs help."

"He does."

"How long will he stay?"

"Not long."

Lili's heart pounds as she wedges a pebble into the doorframe at her building's entrance to keep the door from locking behind her. She climbs the stairs to her flat, Theo a step ahead, as usual. What has she done?

Inside, she paces, peering every now and then through the window overlooking the piazza. Finally, she spots Thomas's lanky figure walking toward her building.

"He's coming," she whispers. She waits, barely breathing. A minute later, a soft tap-tap at her door sends a shock of apprehension down her spine. She adjusts the collar of her blouse.

"Stay behind me, Theo," she says, a hand on the doorknob. She takes a breath, then opens the door a crack, and even though she's expecting him, the sight of the nice-looking, swastika-laden soldier in the hallway gives her a jolt. She pulls the door wider. "**Vieni**," she says, a finger to her lips, and Thomas removes his cap as he steps inside.

"Thank you," he says, once Lili has locked the door behind him.

"Did someone see you?" she asks.

"I don't think so."

"**Bene**."

An awkward silence falls over them as Thomas looks around, and Lili follows his gaze, seeing the flat through his eyes, wondering what he had expected. "Your things," she says, motioning to his pack. She moves to the table, pulls out a chair.

"Actually, I thought I might put on some different clothes," Thomas says, glancing down at his uniform.

"**Si. Certo.** You maybe would like a shower too." Lili wonders when was the last time that the American had bathed.

"Oh, that would be great," he says. "I'd do anything for a shower."

Lili shows him to the washroom, where, over the toilet, a hand-held hose is attached to the wall. She demonstrates how to turn it on, warning that the hot water will last only a minute or two and pondering how, with a frame as tall as his, he'll manage in such a small space. She shows him the drain on the floor. "Water goes there," she explains. She considers offering him her bedroom to change his clothes when he's out of the shower, but the idea of a strange man undressing in her room makes her uneasy. He'll survive in there, she decides, as the bathroom door closes behind him.

Thomas emerges fifteen minutes later, his cheeks neatly shaven. He wears a pair of olive-green pants and a long-sleeved cotton undershirt with three buttons at the neck, the top one, Lili notices, left open. He looks younger. More boyish. Lili finds herself wondering his age, and what he did for work before the war dragged him overseas.

"I feel like a new person," Thomas says, depositing his pack on the chair Lili had pulled out for him. Theo climbs into the chair beside it. "Thank you, Liliana."

"Do you have thirst?" Lili asks.

"Some water would be wonderful," Thomas says. "But I can get it."

"Sit," Lili says, motioning to the table.

In the kitchen, Lili fills two glasses. Standing at

the sink, she drinks one quickly then sets down her glass, closes her eyes. The presence of the American has unnerved her. But what did she expect? She's barely spoken to a man who wasn't a priest or a partisan in months. And now she's agreed to harbor one—a stranger—in a space barely big enough for her and Theo. She rests her palms on the rim of the sink and waits for her pulse to steady.

Finally, she refills her glass and returns to the living room, where she finds Theo with his elbows propped on the table, staring at a deck of cards in Thomas's hand.

"He was curious to know what was in my pack," Thomas says, motioning to Theo.

"His name is Theo," Lili says.

"Theo! I have an uncle named Theodore. Pleased to officially meet you," Thomas says, extending a hand. Theo takes it tentatively and Thomas pumps it a few times. "Do you know any card games, Theo?"

"He speaks no English," Lili says. "And he knows no cards."

"Well, my deck's been around the block, but it'll do the job. Mind if we play?"

Lili's shoulders relax a degree. "Yes, **va bene**." She sets his water on the table.

"Great. We'll start with an easy one. With the game of War."

Fitting, Lili thinks, then explains to Theo. "Thomas is going to teach you a game, it's called **la guerra**."

"War!" Theo repeats in English, delighted.

"Does Theo know his numbers?" Thomas asks, and Lili nods. "I wonder if he'd teach me how to say them in Italian."

Lili translates and Theo bobs his head emphatically.

"I'll tell him the names," he says, and Thomas understands, or pretends to at least, and deals out a hand.

Lili watches them for a minute, her thoughts twisted into a jumble of remorse and relief. Theo hasn't been entertained by someone other than herself since their time with Matilde and the boys in the forest. It's good to see him smile at someone else's coaxing, to hear the excitement in his voice.

"Would you like to play?" Thomas asks.

Lili is still standing. "Oh. No, thank you."

"It's you and me then, son," Thomas says, dealing his cards.

Lili watches them for a moment before realizing, suddenly, she's gone the length of the day without even a glance in the mirror. She excuses herself to freshen up before dinner, but neither Theo nor Thomas seems to hear her, so caught up they both are in their game.

THAT NIGHT, AFTER BOWLS OF POTATO SOUP (MADE a bit more nourishing thanks to a pair of onions Thomas produced from his pack) and a thin slice each of bread sprinkled with water and toasted carefully over the burner (a trick, Lili has discovered, to make stale bread edible), Lili puts Theo to bed.

"Can Thomas stay?" Theo asks, as she pulls a blanket over him.

"No, the army needs him. He'll leave when he finds his unit."

Theo rolls to his side. "What if he doesn't find them?"

"He'll find them," Lili whispers. She strokes his forehead until he closes his eyes, then kisses his cheek and tiptoes backward out the door, closing it quietly.

Thomas is still at the table, bent over a pocket-size notebook, pencil in hand. He stands as Lili approaches, flips the notebook's leather cover closed, tucks the pencil behind his ear.

"Please," Lili says, not wanting to interrupt.

Thomas nods and lowers himself back down to sit. Lili rolls up her sleeves and steps into the kitchen to rinse the bowls she'd left to soak, but when she peers into the basin, it's empty. She opens the cupboard and stares at the neat stack of dinnerware. He's washed and put away their spoons, too, along with the cutting board and knife. A damp dish towel hangs on a hook by the stove. She pads back into the living room, unrolls her sleeves, and sits down at the table.

"The dishes," she says. "Thank you."

"Sure. It's the least I can do."

"What do you write?" Lili asks, her curiosity getting the best of her. "If it's okay for me to ask."

"Oh, just a few notes. Sometimes I jot down things I don't want to forget, like an address or a name, but now mostly I record where I've been, what I've done—helps me to keep track of the days, pass the time. I figure if I can live to see the end of the war, I'd like to have a story to tell. Something to share with my kids, you know?" Lili nods, thinking of Esti's diary, hidden, unread, in the lining of her valise. "A few days ago," Thomas adds, "I caught a pigeon, ate it for dinner. See?" He turns back two pages to show her his entry: **Pigeon dinner.** "I roasted it over a fire first."

"A pigeon?"

"You know, the birds you see everywhere." Thomas licks a finger then pages to an empty sheet. He plucks the pencil from behind his ear and sketches a quick outline of a pigeon. He adds a big, terrified eye at the side of the bird's head, then draws a bubble over it. In the bubble, he writes: **Don't eat me!**

"Ah. **Una picciona.**" It's a good drawing. Lili suppresses a laugh. "And today?"

Thomas slides the little book across the table and Lili reads his note, the lead smudged where the edge of his palm has rubbed over it; he's left-handed. "This is as far as I've gotten."

May 15, 1944, Rome. Met a girl. Liliana. And a boy named Theo.

Lili smiles. "So you have **bambini**?" she asks.

"No kids, just my nephew, Steve. The one I mentioned." He reaches into his pack, removes two photographs from an inside pocket. "This is my family. He slides the faded, sepia-toned photos toward Lili. "My sister, Sue, her husband, Walter, and here's my nephew. This is my mother, Ethel, and my father, Francis." Lili stares at the tall, dark-eyed gentleman, with his neat mustache and pressed three-piece suit, at the pretty, curly-haired blonde beside him, wearing a string of pearls and a pair of dimples that match her son's.

"How many years has he, your nephew?"

"He's five," Thomas says softly, and when he looks up Lili can recognize it, the longing in his eyes. "How old is your son?" Thomas asks.

"Three," she says, then clears her throat. "Four in December."

"I enjoyed playing with him."

"He enjoyed too," Lili says.

Thomas twirls the pencil in his fingers. "Does Theo have a father?"

Lili blinks, gathers her thoughts before answering. "His father is in **Grecia**. But we have no news from him. For three years."

Thomas's tone shifts. "I'm very sorry to hear that." He sounds like he means it.

Lili nods. "I will find a **coperta**. For sleep," she says. She retrieves a quilt from the linen closet and hands it to Thomas. "Here," she says. "It is all I have."

"It's all I need," Thomas says, grateful.

"I will retire now."

"Good night, Liliana," Thomas says. "And thank you. For the meal, for the place to stay. I promise I won't be in your way for too long."

"**Buona notte**," Lili says, lifting her hand in a quick wave before turning. She enters the bedroom quietly, pausing for a minute with her back to the door. **It was the right thing to do**, she tells herself. **A few days. Then he's gone.**

CHAPTER THIRTY-FIVE

ROME

June 1944

May has folded into June and the American is still there. He's left Rome on four separate occasions in an effort to reach his unit, but each time he returns to the flat within a few days. Once, he came back with deep red scratches on his face and hands. He'd had a run-in, he said, with some Germans, though he didn't elaborate. He talks little of the army, but every now and then Lili catches him lost in thought, and she can sense from the distant look in his eye that he's thinking about his regiment, his responsibility to them and to the war effort. Surely there is a part of him that's relieved not to be dodging bullets at the front. The other part, she realizes, must hate being stuck in hiding, just inside the enemy's line of defense.

Thomas has offered to find another place to stay. He understands the risk she's taking in putting him up. **I'm a liability**, he's told her twice. **You can kick**

me out, anytime. But Lili doesn't have the heart to make him leave. He can't speak Italian (although, thanks to Theo, he's learned to count to twenty), or a lick of German for that matter, and he hasn't any papers other than for the young man whose uniform he'd stolen. Out on the street, even posing as German, he's a walking target.

So, she lets him stay, learning to maneuver around him in her too-small flat. Thomas, too, goes out of his way to give her space. And though she's hesitant to admit it, Lili appreciates the company. The sound of his gentle drawl. The playfulness with which he interacts with Theo. The fact that he doesn't ask to help, he just **does.** Around him, she finds, she's at ease. She treats him as she would a stranger, of course—politely, and with a proper amount of distance—but as time passes, the worry and the self-consciousness that had gripped her when he first arrived begin to wane. It helps that her English has improved dramatically; speaking it every day, the language has come back to her. Perhaps, Lili tells herself, she's just incredibly lonely. Whatever the case, since Thomas stepped into her life, she's begun to look forward to, rather than to dread, facing each day. This comfort alone, she's decided, is worth the risk of harboring him.

With her new flatmate, the days take on a different kind of rhythm. When she wakes, Lili watches with hidden amusement from behind her teacup as Thomas takes his exercises, often with Theo by his

side, imitating his push-ups and sit-ups and counting out repetitions—in Italian and, more recently,
in English, for Thomas has insisted if he's going
to learn Theo's language, the boy must also learn
his. Thomas refuses breakfast (**You've only rations
for two**, he says), and after Lili and Theo have eaten,
he holds open the door as they set out for the post
office, or to collect provisions, locking it behind
them. While she's out, Lili makes a point to read
the headlines at the newsstand, hoping for a bit of
information on the whereabouts of the U.S. Army,
which continues to forge its way north, into Axis
territory. Every few weeks, they move slowly up the
shaft of Italy's boot. The biggest breakthrough came
at the end of May, when the Allies, despite several
failed attempts and severe casualties, finally captured the German stronghold of Monte Cassino.
The victory, the papers reported, allowed the Allies
to penetrate the Gustav Line at last, opening up
access to Via Casilina, a highway that leads directly
to the capital. The Allies' arrival in Rome, the article
pronounced, was imminent. Lili wishes she understood what that means exactly.

When Lili and Theo return from the market,
Thomas is there to greet them. After lunch, which
Thomas also often refuses, Lili sits with Theo to
work on his lessons, and Thomas observes, his notebook splayed out before him, taking notes. Both are
avid students. Afterward, Lili settles herself back
at the table with her sewing kit, or with a pen and

paper, determined, still, to continue her search for her father and for Esti and Niko. As she mends and writes, Thomas and Theo play cards or make-believe (Thomas's imagination is as vivid as Theo's) or take turns trying to roll Theo's marble into the bull's-eye Thomas has fashioned from three concentric loops of thread on the floor.

At sundown, Lili insists they share a meal, and Thomas insists on cleaning the dishes. Once night has fallen, he slips out. It's dangerous to be on the streets after curfew, but with the blackout in effect, he assures her, he can steal through the shadows unseen. He doesn't tell her where he goes, although Lili knows while he's out, he's hunting for food scraps—he often returns with a chicken bone or a turnip, which Lili adds to their soup—and for information on the Allied advance toward Rome. She doesn't pester him for details; the risk, she figures, is his to take. Before he gets back, Theo is asleep and Lili, rather than lingering, has turned in. Most nights she's still awake though, propped up in bed reading, listening to the rhythm of Theo's breath, and for the sound of Thomas's spare key in the lock as he returns to the flat, for the shuffling just outside her bedroom door as he settles in for the night. Like clockwork, by the time Lili emerges the next morning, Thomas is awake, his makeshift bed put away, the blanket folded and placed in the linen closet.

Now, Theo and Thomas are huddled on the settee

reading **Pinocchio**. Theo narrates as best he can as Thomas thumbs through the book's worn pages. Lili listens from the kitchen, wondering how much longer Thomas will be with them. Rome is flooded now with displaced German troops—men who've been pushed north by the Allies. Would there be a battle for control of the city? If so, would Lili and Theo be safe? And what would an Allied occupation of Rome mean for Thomas? He hasn't mentioned another attempt to leave, to find his unit, but Lili can sense that his time in the capital might be coming to an end.

"Fifteen minutes, Theo," Lili calls, poking her head out from the kitchen. "Then we'll head out." She can see the top of Theo's head, his curls jostling as he mimes the phenomenon of Pinocchio's growing nose. Returning to the sink, she strains a handful of fava beans she'd soaked the night before. Perhaps she'll get lucky at the market today and bring home some dried fish and a potato, to make stew for dinner.

"Can I stay here? With Thomas?" Theo calls.

Not expecting the question, Lili hesitates. She returns to the living room, drying her hands on a dish towel.

"I heard my name," Thomas says, eyeing Theo with mock suspicion. Theo giggles.

"He asked to stay here while I go to the market," Lili says, dismissing the idea.

"That's fine by me."

"Yes, but—"

"Please?" Theo begs.

Lili purses her lips. It would be easy to leave Theo home with Thomas. But what if someone comes while she's out? The landlord, or worse—a German soldier or a member of the GNR, checking papers. Then again, she could argue that Theo is safer in the flat than out on the streets with her. They've witnessed the Wehrmacht making arrests in the city. For what, Lili can never be certain.

"I have to go to the post office, as well," Lili says. "So I might be awhile."

"Pleeeease, Mama?"

"I don't—" Lili stumbles.

"It'll be fine," Thomas says, ruffling Theo's hair. "We'll stay out of trouble, I promise."

Lili hasn't left Theo's side since . . . Florence, she realizes. For months, he's been her only constant, and she his. She hesitates, racking her brain for an excuse to say no, but she can't think of one. "**Bene**," she relents. "If you are certain."

Theo shoots his arms overhead, quick to perceive her consent, and Thomas laughs.

"I'm sure," he says.

Lili procrastinates for as long as she can before leaving, then hurries to the market, where the line for produce is impossibly long, and then to the post office, where there is another line. **Theo's fine**, she tells herself. It feels wrong though, to be out and about without him.

She half jogs home, climbs the stairs quickly. **He's fine**, she tells herself again as she pushes her key into the lock. But rather than catch, the door swings open on its own accord. Lili freezes. Had she forgotten to lock it behind her? Could she have been that careless? No, she'd locked it, she's sure of it. Beneath her blouse, her heart beats rapidly, a metronome set to a too-fast tempo. Had Thomas left? Had someone come while she was away? Was that someone inside **now**? She stands motionless, unsure of whether or not to enter, holding her breath, listening. And then, the sound of Theo's voice, counting in English. Laughter. He sounds happy. She pushes the door open, steps inside.

There are three figures at the table in the living area, playing cards divided into piles between them. Thomas and Theo look up and a woman with long braids spins around in her chair. Lili gasps at the familiar face.

"You're back!" Matilde calls.

"Matilde?"

Matilde stands, charges over, and envelops Lili in a hug. "It's so good to see you!" She takes a step back. "Theo's teaching me how to play War. Wait— what's wrong? You look like you've seen a ghost."

"The door. I thought—" Lili starts.

"Don't worry," Matilde says, pulling Lili over to the table. "Thomas didn't let me in. I let myself in—there are a few of us with keys to this place. He nearly took my head off though when I walked through the door." She throws Thomas a look of admiration. "Till I explained to him as best I could—which wasn't easy with his elbow around my throat—that I was a friend."

Lili glances at Thomas, then back at Matilde, trying to picture the scene, Matilde in a headlock. "Where was Theo during all of this?"

"Under the bed," Matilde says. "Came crawling out when Thomas told him it was okay to do so."

"A **few** of us?" Lili asks. It would have been nice to know there were a handful of keys to her flat floating around.

"You got my note, right? This place was a safe-house. It's not anymore—we never keep the same address for more than a month or two. But yeah, I've had a key for months."

"I see," Lili says. She glances at Thomas, wondering how much of the conversation he's followed, then back at Matilde. She exhales, feeling her pulse slow, then smiles. Her friend—sitting beside her. "How long will you stay? You'll join us for dinner, I hope." She holds up her bag of provisions.

"I'd love to. I need to move on later today, but I'll wait until dark."

Lili has a dozen questions for her friend, about the partisans and about what Matilde is doing in Rome, but she'll wait till Theo is asleep to ask. She looks again at Thomas. "So it was not the afternoon we planned," she says in English, with a small laugh.

"No. Though we did learn some new phrases,

right, Theo?" He leans over, whispers something in Theo's ear and Theo grins, turns to Lili.

"What's up?" he croons, in English, then bursts into laughter.

Lili looks up at the ceiling, confused.

"It's how we greet each other sometimes, where I come from," Thomas says, then whispers again in Theo's ear.

"How **are** you?" Theo says, once again in English, pronouncing each syllable carefully. Lili's eyebrows lift.

"**Sto bene.** I'm well, thank you," she says.

"I didn't know you spoke such good English," Matilde tells Lili. "You, too, young man," she adds, looking to Theo. "I'm impressed."

"We've been practicing, haven't we, Theo?"

Theo grins. "Every day!"

"Theo's been teaching me Italian too," Thomas says. "Though I'm not as fast a learner as he is." Lili translates for Matilde.

"Want to see what else we did today?" Theo asks, looking from Lili to Matilde, excited to have the attention of an audience of three.

"**Si, certo,**" Matilde says, nodding.

"Show us," Lili says.

"We made an **automobile.**" Theo slides out of his chair and runs to the bedroom. He returns with a toy car, holds it out for Lili and Matilde to see. It's crafted from a cork, a piece of tin, and four green buttons.

"**Che bello**," Matilde says.

"I love it, Theo," Lili says, in English. "Where did you get . . . **il tappo?**" she asks, pointing.

"The cork? I found it a few nights ago, on my walk," Thomas says. "On the street."

"And the buttons?"

"Those I borrowed from Herr Krüger," Thomas replies, sheepish. "I was hoping you could help me sew them back if I need to wear the tunic again. I saved the thread."

"And Mama, watch this!" Theo calls. He kneels on the floor, driving the toy car in a circle, then speeding it toward a small black book propped open in the corner, spine up on the floor. "It can jump too!" He lets it go and the toy launches off the book's cover, landing with a clatter on the hardwood floor behind it.

Theo hoots and Lili cocks her head. "Is that . . . ?" she starts.

"It's a Bible," Thomas says. "Army issued. This's the most use it's gotten, I'm ashamed to say," he adds, and Lili smiles. Anything that brings the sound of Theo's laughter, she thinks, is a godsend.

LATER THAT NIGHT, AFTER DINNER, THOMAS offers to put Theo to bed so Lili and Matilde can catch up. Lili pours them each a glass of water and they settle themselves at the dining table. She can

hear the murmur of Thomas's voice through the bedroom door, mingling with the high pitch of Theo's.

"So," Matilde says, coy. "Thomas."

"It's not what you think," Lili says.

"Sure."

"It's a long story, really."

"I love a good story."

Lili smiles. "I found him on the street, posing as
a German. Or rather, he found Theo." She fills in
Matilde about her unlikely encounter. "He said he'd
escaped a POW camp and needed a place to stay. I
couldn't say no."

"With a face like that, I don't blame you." Matilde
fans herself with her fingers and Lili laughs.

"He's been good company. That's all."

"Right. Well, **Theo** adores him, that much is
obvious."

"I know. It's sweet."

"Whatever he is, I'm glad you're not alone,"
Matilde says. "I've met someone as well, believe it
or not."

"Oh?"

"Matteo Finzi," Matilde says with a flourish. "I
met him here, through the underground. In the
sewer, of all places!"

"That's a first," Lili says, amused. "Why on earth
were you both in the sewer?"

"We were scouting. Turns out Rome is full of
secret tunnels that can take you from one end of

the city to the next. Which comes in handy in our line of work."

"**Really.**"

"Really. We met beneath Saint Peter's. It was quite romantic, actually."

"I'll take your word for that," Lili says. "Tell me, what else have you been up to, besides traversing the romantic underbelly of our country's capital?" Lili leans in, eager for details, her existence over the last several weeks suddenly mundane in comparison to Matilde's.

"I've been in Trastevere, mostly. Finding hiding places for Jews; passing along information and weapons to the partisans. I'd have come by sooner, but I'm so busy I hardly have time to sleep. Lately I've been helping to write and distribute newsletters. Anti-Fascist, anti-Nazi material, that type of thing."

"What **don't** you have your hand in?" Lili jokes.

"Most days I wish there were six of me, so I could be everywhere at once. There's always something to do, somewhere to be. Which reminds me."

Matilde jumps to her feet, pulls a small duffel from the top shelf of the linen closet. She rummages through the bag and sets a rag on the table, something hard and lumpy wrapped inside. Lili eyes the mystery object. "I hid it up there so little hands wouldn't find it," Matilde says. "I've got to clean it and deliver it tomorrow." She unfolds the rag and Lili recoils at the sight of a small black pistol.

"Oh-kay . . ." she says, staring.

"Problem is, I also have to get a message to one of our contacts. I was planning to deliver this and the message myself, but one of our commanders got himself arrested this morning and the underground wants me to help negotiate his release."

"You can do that? Negotiate with the Nazis?"

"I have an ID, I speak a little German. And I know how to flatter the bastards just enough to get what I want."

"You're out of your mind," Lili says. She's silent for a moment, reflecting on the risks Matilde takes every day to try to save innocent lives, to shorten this seemingly endless nightmare of a war. **You and Esti are so much alike.** She stares at the gun on her table. It's the closest she's ever come to a weapon. She takes a breath, a thought forming. "What do you need?" she asks.

"For what?"

"To deliver the message. To your contact."

Matilde looks at Lili, registering the meaning behind the question. She hesitates. "You don't have to do that. I didn't come here to ask any favors."

"I know," Lili says. "But maybe I can help." Lili blinks. The audacity. It's not like her. "You can at least tell me what would be involved."

After a beat, Matilde nods. "It's not as hard as it sounds," she says. "There's a guy who runs a news-paper stand by the big fountain just over the Ponte Sisto in Trastevere. He's in our circle." Matilde fishes into her bag again, extracts a spool of yellow thread and some coins. She bites off a piece of thread. "Here's how it works. You stand in line to buy your paper. You pay him with this." Matilde pushes the lire across the table. "But you also leave him this." She ties the thread into a small bow. "It's a sign, see? A yellow thread means a delivery."

Lili follows along, aware of the seconds ticking by. A familiar voice inside urges her to snap out of it. If she speaks up now, she can retract her offer. It's too irresponsible. Too risky. But Lili says nothing, so Matilde continues.

"When my guy sees the thread, he'll hand you a newspaper. Take it, walk to the base of the steps in front of the fountain, and sit." Matilde retrieves a small envelope from the duffel. "Set this envelope beside you—you can tuck it under your purse or your newspaper. When the time is right, he'll come, sit down next to you. He'll probably ask for a cigarette or make some small talk. You chat for a minute, then just stand and go, leaving the envelope behind. That's it."

Only that. Lili nods. "You've done this before?"

"Many times. It's routine."

"Your guy—the vendor—he won't know me."

"Doesn't matter. He sees new faces all the time."

"He's expecting this tomorrow?"

"He is. First thing, between seven and eight."

Lili tries to picture herself at the steps of the Fontana di Ponte Sisto in Trastevere. What if there are **carabinieri** nearby? Wehrmacht? Would her expression give her away? Would she lose her nerve?

Matilde senses her hesitation. "I don't want to force you into anything," she says. She picks up the pistol, rubs it with the rag. "Maybe"—she glances at the door to the bedroom—"maybe if you're not comfortable with it, Thomas would be? I trust him if you do . . . it's just that the authorities are more suspicious of men in general. We ladies can get away with more."

As if on cue, Thomas steps from the bedroom. He takes a seat beside Lili. "Interesting centerpiece," he says. "What did I miss?"

Lili looks at him, considers Matilde's question. He'd make the drop if she asked, she's certain. He'd do it without hesitation. But Matilde trusts her, and like she said, as a woman, her odds are better. **You've helped before**, she reminds herself, **with Father Niccacci's parcel**. It had felt good to bring those papers to Sister Natalia. This might feel good too. If she can pull it off. "I'll do it," she says.

Matilde grins. "That's my girl."

Lili goes still, processing the implications of her offer.

Thomas nudges her elbow with his. "You okay?"

"Yes," she says. "I'll explain."

Thomas turns his attention to the pistol. "May I?" Matilde hands it over and he studies it closely. "Beretta?"

Matilde's English is rudimentary, but she understands, replies in Italian. "M1934."

"Nine millimeters?"

"Seven rounds."

Lili looks between the two, flummoxed. They're
speaking another language entirely.

"Can I help you clean it?" Thomas asks, miming
the cleaning motion.

"**Perché no?**" Matilde says. "Have at it."

Within seconds, Thomas has emptied the pistol's
magazine and disassembled it. He wads up one end
of Matilde's rag and twists it through the barrel. "If
you have some olive oil, you could give it a swab," he
says. "If not, this should work just fine. It'll be slow
to reload, but that's just the way it's manufactured."

Matilde raises a brow as he puts the pistol back
together, sets the safety, reloads it, and slides it back
to her. "**Grazie**," she says.

Lili watches her wrap the gun in its rag, wondering whose hands it will eventually fall into, whose
lives it might take before war's end.

"How are you feeling?" Thomas asks. It's just
after seven the next morning. Theo is still asleep.

"I'm fine," Lili says.

In truth, she feels the opposite of fine. Her anxiety
is bunched like a ball of barbed wire at the base of her
gut, and the roof of her mouth is so dry her tongue is
sticking to it. She'd barely slept the night before, her

brain too busy imagining all the ways Matilde's plan could go wrong. Now, she stands at the door, an umbrella folded under her arm. Her purse is looped over her shoulder, the envelope inside, Matilde's change and the yellow thread stashed carefully in her wallet along with her false ID. She knew better than to ask Matilde what was inside the envelope. **You can do this**, she tells herself for the seventeenth time. She'd relayed the plan in detail to Thomas, who, as she suspected he might, offered to make the delivery for her. But Lili knew it was more of a risk for Thomas than it was for her; it felt selfish to let him go in her place. **I've got it**, she said.

"Ponte Sisto," Thomas says.

"Yes." The pedestrian bridge that connects central Rome to its western neighborhoods. Lili had shown him her route on the map. It's not far, thankfully. Just five or six blocks and across the river.

"If you're not back in an hour, we'll walk that way."

"I'll be back."

"Be safe," Thomas says, opening the door for her. He steps toward her as if to hug her then checks himself, straightening. "If something doesn't feel right, just turn around. You don't need to be a hero."

Lili nods.

A light rain is falling as she leaves the building. She's grateful for the umbrella, not because it keeps her dry, but for the anonymity it offers. She feels slightly hidden beneath it. She walks quickly—too quickly—reminding herself often to slow to a normal pace. At each corner, she tilts the umbrella upward just enough to check for men in uniform. When a military truck passes her and pulls to a stop a block ahead, she detours.

It takes Lili ten minutes to reach the Ponte Sisto. Halfway across the river, she spots the newspaper kiosk. The vendor, she can see from afar, is old, with a scruffy gray beard and a frayed cap. She pauses on the side of the bridge and pretends to check the time, scanning again for uniforms. The area is busy, but she sees only civilians—mothers walking with their children, middle-aged men making their way to work. Several customers approach the newsstand. Nothing seems unusual or suspicious, so she continues on, keeping her composure despite the chatter in her head. What if the vendor doesn't recognize the yellow thread? What if he doesn't trust her? What if Matilde's regular contact isn't there today at all? What if this guy is not **her** guy?

Enough, Lili scolds. She forces a deep inhale, reminds herself there's no time to waste; she needs to get back to the apartment before eight or else Thomas will come looking for her—and she doesn't want Theo walking around in the open with Thomas. **This will work**, she tells herself. **Just be calm.**

The rain has let up. Lili closes her umbrella, folds it under her arm, and steps in line at the kiosk. When she reaches the front, she lifts her chin slightly as she slides the coins and yellow thread across the small counter. The vendor scoops them up and hands her today's **Corriere della Sera** without a word or the slightest gesture of acknowledgment, without even meeting her eye. Lili waits a beat, realizing she was expecting—what? A wink? Some signal that the plan was working? She says a quick thanks and walks to the fountain. There, she sits on an ancient marble step, still damp from the rain. As discreetly as she can, she pulls Matilde's envelope from her purse and tucks it between the folds of her coat tail, so it won't get wet. And then she waits.

She opens her paper, skims the headlines, though they are nothing to her. She can't possibly absorb the words. The vendor's back is to her. She tries not to watch him too closely. Ten minutes pass. Then another ten. A group of German soldiers walks by, passing close enough that Lili can smell the smoke from their cigarettes. One of them flicks a butt at the fountain. Lili keeps her expression neutral, exhaling once they are out of sight. Meanwhile, the vendor sells a dozen papers, at least, though there are pockets of quiet between transactions—windows when he could step away. Still, he makes no motion to join her. Lili checks the time. It's twenty to eight. Thomas will have started to worry. She contemplates leaving, giving up for today, then stills when she notices a figure moving toward her. She looks up as the vendor saunters over and takes a seat on the step next to her.

"Morning," he says.

"Morning," Lili nods.

The vendor pulls a silver case from his pocket, offers her a cigarette.

"No, thank you," Lili says. She doesn't smoke, and the last thing she wants is to start hacking from the burn. They sit quietly for a moment, their shoulders nearly touching, as the vendor smokes. After a while, Lili shifts her weight subtly, keeping her eyes ahead as she pulls her coattail aside an inch, so the corner of Matilde's letter is visible. The vendor returns his cigarette case to his pocket, and when Lili gets the courage to look down at the small space between his body and hers, the envelope is gone.

"Have a good day," she says as she stands. He nods and for the briefest moment their eyes meet, and just like that, she leaves.

BACK AT HER APARTMENT, THOMAS MEETS HER AT the door.

"Two more minutes and we'd have come looking for you," he says, his face flushed.

"Mama!" Theo calls from the table, a pencil and drawing paper in front of him.

"Good morning, love." Lili hangs her purse on the hook by the door. Thomas helps her out of her coat.

"How did it go?" he asks.

"Somehow . . . exactly as Matilde said it would," Lili says.

"Really?"

"Really."

Lili looks up at Thomas. He's smiling, his expression a mix of relief and also of something else—of respect, Lili realizes.

"Well done, Liliana," he says.

Lili gives her hands a shake, feeling her jitters melt away. She'd done it.

"Thanks," she says, returning the smile.

CHAPTER THIRTY-SIX

ROME

June 1944

Highest goes first," Thomas says, fanning the deck and holding it out for Lili to choose a card. She selects one, glances at it. Thomas does the same.

"Jack of hearts," he says. "What've you got?"

Lili lays a queen of diamonds beside his jack. "Sorry," she says, though she doesn't mean it.

"Unbelievable," Thomas says, laughing to himself.

A few nights earlier, Lili, unable to sleep, had risen from bed for a glass of water and found Thomas at the table, a candle before him, playing solitaire. He invited her to join him for a game of rummy, pulling out a chair before she could decline. **Come on**, he said, **it'll be fun.** And so, not wanting to be rude, Lili sat, cradling her water, grateful she'd wrapped her dressing robe over her nightgown. She'd played rummy a few times with Esti and Niko, but this version, which Thomas called "gin" rummy, was new to her. Thomas was a patient coach, and she caught on quickly. They played for an hour that night, and each night after.

Now, Thomas counts aloud in Italian as he distributes them each ten cards, placing a three of spades face up in the center of the table. His accent is still awful, but Lili would never tell him so. He's trying. She arranges her hand.

"Pass," she says.

"I pass too."

Lili draws a card from the deck, keeps it, discards another. She has a decent hand, but she'll need to play smart to win. They trade turns in silence for a while, Lili stealing looks at Thomas's discards, and occasionally up at him. Every now and then their eyes meet and Thomas smiles, his dimples carving shadows in his cheeks, and Lili's stomach contracts and she looks away.

"What did you do before the army?" she asks, picking up a discarded eight of diamonds. Lili's English is nearly fluent now.

"I went to college in Virginia, thinking I'd study business. My father's a banker and had high hopes for me to follow in his footsteps."

"But . . ." Lili says.

"I hated my classes. I'm not cut out for finance, accounting, that sort of thing. My favorite subjects were art and writing."

Lili discards. "So you will not be a **banchiere**."

"A banker? No. Much to my father's dismay. I ended up majoring in fine arts." Thomas takes her ten of hearts. "Probably sounds crazy," he adds, "but I've actually always wanted to be an actor."

Lili glances up at him. He certainly has the looks to be an actor. "It doesn't sound crazy," she says. "Have you done this before? Acting?"

"Just in school plays."

Thomas throws a five of clubs and Lili takes it, arranges it carefully between the four and the six she holds of the same suit. "Well, that's something," she says.

"How about you?" Thomas asks. "Did you have a career before the war?"

"I worked at a botanical garden after university," Lili says. "But that was never . . . how do you say it . . . **il mio sogno**." She pats at her chest.

"Your dream?"

"Right. It was never my dream."

"What's your dream?"

Lili tilts her head. It's been years since anyone's asked her about her passion, her goals. Even longer since she's asked herself. Her dream since the start of the war has been for peace, for safety, for shelter, food, anonymity. For the chance to once again feel the warmth of her father's hand in hers, to hear the sound of her best friend's laughter. Before the war, though, she dreamed of writing. Of traveling.

Of someday starting a family of her own. "I like to write too," she says. "I studied journalism in school. I love the . . . **la ricerca?**"

"The research."

"Yes. I worked a little for a newspaper before the war."

"Why did you stop?"

Lili studies her cards, considering her reply. Thomas has asked of her family, and until now she's told him the simplest version of the truth: that her father and her best friend have disappeared and that Theo's father is missing—but she hasn't explained how or why any of this is true. Part of her assumed he'd have pieced it together by now—the fact that all the important people in her life are gone; that her safety, too, depends on the arrival of the Allies. They've never spoken of her religion, though, and while she knows she'd be smart to keep it that way, the thought of lying about her upbringing, of coming up with some excuse for why she was fired from the newspaper, is exhausting.

"I stopped when the Racial Laws came into effect," she says.

Thomas looks up.

"You've heard of the Racial Laws, yes?"

Thomas shakes his head.

"The Nuremburg Laws, then?"

"Sure. Those I've read about."

"Same idea. Just Mussolini's **interpretazione**. His way of creating a divide between Italy's Jews and non-Jews. We are of our own race now." She says this last bit with two fingers bunny-eared into quotation marks. "And not worthy, apparently, of regular jobs. My father had to give up his business too. Everyone with a decent profession lost their jobs. Even the children were dismissed from the public schools."

Thomas lowers his cards. He looks at her intently. "I had no idea you were Jewish," he says.

"I didn't see the point in telling you earlier. If anything, I imagined it would make you nervous to be living here."

"I understand," Thomas says. He flexes the muscles in his jaw. "It's horrific, what's happening to the Jews in eastern Europe," he says. "I didn't realize it was happening here in Italy too."

Lili wonders what Thomas knows. Whether he's aware of the camps, the gas chambers. "I don't think it's exactly the same here," she says. "We're not hemmed in as the Jews are in the north and in the east. And the arrests didn't start until last year, when the Germans came. We had a little time to prepare. Some, like my father, fled. Others, like me, had false identities made, or hid. So, we're lucky in that way."

"But if you're caught . . ."

"My papers say I'm Aryan. Theo's too." Lili thinks of Luigi, of his printing press in Assisi. "They've worked so far," she says.

In the quiet that follows, Lili shifts in her seat,

drawn, suddenly, to tell Thomas everything. Before she can stop herself, she says, "There's something else you should know." Thomas looks up. "About Theo. He's . . . not mine. He's my best friend's son. The one I've been looking for, Esti."

"Wait—what?" Thomas blinks.

"I haven't told anyone but you. We have IDs with the same last name in case we're questioned. It's . . . safer that way."

"But your wedding ring," Thomas says slowly, processing.

"I wear it for the alibi. It's Esti's. It's her husband, Niko, who's missing in Greece."

"I—had no idea. You seem like such a good mother."

Lili smiles. "I've been with him for so long. I think it was strange for him to call me Mama in the beginning—it was strange for **me**—but he's used to it now. I am too."

"Does he remember her? His mother?"

"He does. Or at least I think he does. He doesn't talk about her much anymore."

"What happened to her?" Thomas asks.

Lili takes a breath. "She was hurt. **Gravemente**. It was her idea for me to take Theo and run. I tried to talk her out of it, but . . . here we are."

"Who hurt her?" Thomas asks, bristling.

Lili looks down at her hand. "The convent where we were hiding in Florence was raided by a gang. They were savages, these men. I was hidden but Esti was caught. She was trying to help a friend. Another mother, at the convent."

"She sounds very brave."

"She was. She is."

"And you haven't seen her since you left?"

"The nuns at the convent said the gang came back and took her. I never heard from her after that."

"That's awful," Thomas says. "I see why you're so determined to find her."

When Lili looks up at him, his eyes are shiny. "I didn't mean to upset you."

"No, it's—I just—I have a hard time accepting that we live in a world where such cruelty exists."

"I know," Lili says. "Me too. Sometimes I imagine explaining this war to my late mother, telling her about what's going on around us, and I can't. She'd never believe me."

"Thank you, Liliana," Thomas says.

"For what?"

"For telling me."

"It felt like time," Lili says. "I feel better now that you know." And she does. Her real identity, and Theo's too, are no longer secrets for her to harbor alone.

They play on in silence, the only sound between them the soft **fwip** of cards being drawn and discarded.

"The world will right itself," Lili says after a while. An echo of her father's sentiments. And when it does, she tells herself, she'll find her father, her best friend, maybe even Niko too. She'll gather up the tattered scraps of her old life and stitch them together into some semblance of normalcy. What her new tapestry will look like, she has no idea. But at the moment, that's the least of her worries. For now, her only thought is to keep herself and Theo safe. And, she thinks with an inward smile, to win her next hand.

"I hope so," Thomas says.

"It will. And then, in some years from now, I'll look for you on the big screen."

Thomas smiles. "And I'll look for your byline in the paper."

Glad to have steered the conversation toward a lighter subject, Lili asks, "So you like to write?"

"I love to write," Thomas says. "I used to write for my college paper. Editorials, that kind of thing. And draw cartoons. For me, writing, art, acting, they have a similar appeal."

"What's that?"

"They're an escape."

"I've never been on a stage," Lily says. "How is it?"

"For me it's scary, but freeing. I like the idea of creating a world that's new and unfamiliar on the page too."

"So you are a writer of . . . **finzione**, then."

"Fiction! Yes. Well, an **aspiring** fiction writer," Thomas says, patting the notepad in his shirt pocket. "Many of my ideas are in here. Who knows what'll come of them."

"Can you tell me about one of your ideas?" Lili asks, discarding a two of diamonds.

Thomas grins. "You really want to know?"

"I do."

Lili listens as Thomas describes an end-of-the-world scenario where a small pocket of humans is left to defend against an army of deadly beasts.

"Beasts?" Lili interrupts. "What kind of beasts?"

"You know, monsters. Human in stature but otherwise grotesque, covered in slime, yellow teeth, the works." Thomas splays his fingers into a claw. "If you get attacked by one, you become one of them," he says, with a hint of menace, and Lili laughs. This, coming from a soldier. An Army Ranger who dreams of a life in the arts. It's no wonder he didn't make it in finance. "And you?" Thomas asks. "Would you ever want to write a book?"

"Sure," Lili nods. "I think it's the dream of every writer."

"What would you write about?"

Lili thinks for a minute. "I'm not sure. Maybe I'd write about the war."

"You could write a memoir," Thomas says. "**The Extraordinary Life of Liliana . . .** "

"Passigli," Lili says.

"**Passigli**. I like that. So tell me, **Signorina** Passigli, where would your story begin?"

Lili thinks back to her earliest memories and tells Thomas about the haircut she gave herself at three, with a pair of her mother's scissors stolen from an open mending kit, and of the time at five when she stepped barefoot on a bee, and how when she sat down, teary, to inspect her throbbing foot, she landed on a second bee, who stung her again—in the bottom. Thomas laughs and the sound fills Lili with warmth.

"And you? Where would your story begin? Your **Memorie di un Artista Americano?**"

Thomas leans back in his chair, rubs his chin. "My first memory is of running away when I was two."

"You ran away? Your poor mother. She must have been beside herself."

"She was. That wasn't my **intent**, of course, I just wanted to float my toy boat in the James River. It was just before dawn and I was the only one awake in the house, so I let myself out—the door must not have been closed all the way. My mother found me at the riverbank, ankle-deep in mud. She gave me a hiding I'll never forget."

Lili laughs, even though she's not sure what a **hiding** is. They play on, swapping stories. It's after eleven when Lili checks the time. "**Allora,** it's late. We should sleep," she says.

"Finish this hand?"

"All right."

"Whose turn is it?"

"Yours, I believe. The seven was mine."

"Right." Thomas draws a card, taps it twice against the table—a habit—then discards it. Lili grins.

"Thank you for that." She takes the card, an eight of hearts, and slips it next to a pair of eights. She sets one card face down on the discard pile, then spreads her hand.

"You're knocking?" Thomas asks, incredulous.

"I'm knocking," Lili replies, pleased at the prospect of ending the night with a win.

Thomas fans his own cards out on the table in front of him, counting out the score. "Lili Passigli, you've done me in," he says with a sigh. He reaches his hand across the table in defeat. "Good game."

His hand is warm when Lili takes it.

"Good game," she says.

CHAPTER THIRTY-SEVEN

ROME

June 1944

Lili is in line for bread at the market in Campo dei Fiori when something in her periphery makes the hair stand up at the back of her neck. She glances behind her and meets the eye of a woman toward the back of the line, recognizing her as one of the tenants in her apartment building. Older, hard mouth, cinnamon hair. She stands beside a man in a peaked hat and an all-black uniform—GNR, like the officers she'd encountered at the park—and she is pointing at Lili.

Lili sucks in a quick breath and turns to face the bakery stall, trying to recall her last interaction with the woman. She lives down the hall, though the few times Lili has said hello, she's replied with a curt nod, or not at all. Lili had told herself the sullen woman was a widow scarred by the war. Rome was a city full of haggard, resentful widows.

It takes everything for Lili not to look again over her shoulder. She shuffles forward, debating whether or not to step out of line. The square is full at this time of day with locals—mostly women and a few elderly people—coming to and from the market. If she's quick about it, she could wend her way through the crowd; she'd be difficult to follow. But would running make her look guilty? Just last week, she'd watched a pair of GNR officers chase a man from the back of a shop and beat him to near death in the street. Lili didn't know if the man was a Jew, or simply anti-Fascist—just that he had tried to run. Theo was with Thomas in the flat at the time, and Lili had decided then that Theo was better off staying behind while she went out for provisions. She's grateful he isn't with her now.

She'll keep her place in line, she decides. Stand her ground. At the counter, her ration card is stamped and she's handed her allotment of bread. Perhaps, Lili tries to convince herself, the woman was pointing at someone else. She slips the bread into her provisions bag, her eyes flitting to the line of people behind her. Her neighbor has vanished, but the officer in black is still there. He looks her square in the eye, then makes a move in her direction. **Get out of here**, Lili tells herself, her skin crawling. She turns—the rest of her rations, she decides, can wait—and sets off toward Piazza Farnese. This time, she can't help but look behind her. The officer is closer now, moving with intention, and she knows—he's following her.

She weaves quickly through a swarm of bodies, keeping her gaze forward, her ear tuned to the strike of boot soles on the cobblestones trailing her. It's all she can do not to break into a run. **Just get home**, she thinks as she enters Piazza Farnese. There, she slows, realizes her mistake. She'll lead him straight to her flat. Panicked, she debates where to go, what to do, but it's too late. The footsteps are upon her.

"**Stop!**" the officer orders. A hand, rough on her shoulder.

Lili wheels around.

"ID," the officer says. Lili recoils. His breath smells of alcohol. She twists out of his grip. There will be a bruise on her shoulder tomorrow, she realizes, as she roots through her purse for her wallet.

Lili shakes her head, feigning confusion as she finds her voice. "Have I done something wrong?" she asks, handing the officer her ID. Her chest rises and falls with her breath. The officer ignores her. Behind his scowl, Lili senses, there is something more. She can see it in the pallor of his complexion, in the way his eyes dart across the piazza. There is desperation.

Steady. Steady.

"Your address," he says. "It says Lecce."

"Yes. I grew up in Lecce and moved to Rome to study, just before the war began," Lili says. "I've requested a change of address on three separate occasions, but the registrar keeps telling me to come back when they are not so . . . preoccupied."

The officer glowers at her. "Your neighbor says you are harboring someone—a man—that she's heard his voice from your flat."

"What? That's ridiculous."

"She says you are hiding a Jew."

Lili laughs, indignant. The irony. "She lies."

"She says you have a young boy too. Where is he?"

"This much she is right about, sir. My son is at home. He's not feeling well. I didn't want to subject him to the heat today."

"You left him alone."

"He has a fever. He's not fit to be outside."

The officer nods in the direction of Lili's flat. "This is where you live?"

She could lie about her address, but it occurs to her now that her neighbor has likely told him where she lives. She follows his gaze, looks up at the building, then goes rigid at the sight of a figure in her window. Thomas. Panic builds inside her like a wave, powerful and all-consuming. **Move, Thomas**.

"Take me to your flat."

Lili tries to smile, to emote confidence, but her mouth won't cooperate. Her legs are soft, her heartbeat too quick.

"Listen," she says, collecting herself. "I'm a single mother. I met my husband my first year in university. I was pregnant when he was called for service. He died in the field a month after our son was born; the boy has no memory of him. Please—there's no reason to startle him by showing up at our flat. We have nothing to hide. You must believe me."

"Bring me to your flat or I'll arrest you and you can explain yourself at the station."

Lili swallows, shifts on her feet. She'd hoped to trigger an ounce of sympathy, but she can see now that tactic won't work. She makes a split-second decision. She will play his game.

"Fine," she says, her lips tight, her voice low. "If you don't believe me, give me back my papers and let me be, and I'll give you something in return."

The officer glares and Lili glares back. When he says nothing, she reaches for Esti's ring, twists it from her finger. She pauses for the briefest moment, her throat tight. **You must**. Holding it between her thumb and forefinger, she thrusts the ring at the officer. "My wedding ring. It's very expensive."

The man's gaze volleys from Lili to the gold band in her hand. He looks over his shoulder. "Well," he grunts. "Let's have a look."

Lili drops her arm, makes a fist around the ring. "First, my ID," she says, pulling her shoulders back.

The officer brings his hand to the pistol at his belt, and Lili wonders whether he would shoot her here, on the spot, in the middle of a public square. His expression is cold, unfeeling. She doesn't move. She watches him closely, refusing to cower. A pigeon lands with a noisy flutter on the cobblestones at their feet, pecking at invisible crumbs, oblivious to the tightrope of tension overhead. The soldier shoos it away with the toe of his boot.

"Give me the ring," he says.

"My ID," Lili insists.

The officer wraps his index finger around the trigger of his pistol, still holstered. "If you run, I shoot," he says through his teeth. Slowly, he extends his arm, hands her back her ID.

Lili drops it into her purse, bites down on the insides of her cheeks as she passes him the ring. I'm sorry, Esti. The officer turns the fede over once in his hands, then brings it to his mouth, curls his lips back, and clamps the beveled hands between his teeth.

"It's real," Lili says.

The officer grunts again, drops the ring into his pocket. "I'll be watching out for you," he warns, then turns and strides off.

Lili waits until he's long out of sight before walking slowly toward the entrance to her building. When she glances up again, Thomas is still there in the window.

He meets her at the top of the stairwell.

"What the hell happened out there?" he asks, his voice flooded with apprehension. They enter the flat quickly and he bolts the door, follows her to the kitchen, where she sets down her provisions bag and fills a glass with water, gulps it down. Her whole body is shaking. She can hear Theo playing in the living room.

"One of the neighbors," she says. "She said she overheard a man's voice here in the flat. She accused me of harboring a Jew."

"No."

Lili nods.

"We've been so careful." Thomas's voice is barely above a whisper.

"I thought so too."

"It was all I could do not to run down there, when I saw that officer follow you into the square."

"I'm glad you didn't."

"What did you tell him?"

"I told him it was a ridiculous accusation."

"And he believed you?"

Lili refills her water, takes a sip, the absence of Esti's ring burning a hole in her chest.

"No. He wanted to search the flat. I didn't know what else to do, so I bribed him with my ring."

"Your best friend's ring?"

Lili nods, tears brimming.

"Oh, Lili. I'm so sorry." Thomas's eyes search hers, heavy with guilt.

"It's okay," Lili manages. "It's . . . just a ring."

Thomas reaches for her and she lets him pull her to him, wrap her in a hug.

CHAPTER THIRTY-EIGHT

ROME

June 1944

Lili wakes to shouting. What now? Since the confrontation with the GNR officer, she and Thomas have spoken in whispers, and she's left the apartment only for food, hurrying home and avoiding eye contact with Italian authorities and with the German military who seem to be stationed now at every street corner. Yesterday, on her return to the flat, she had to wait for a column of Panzers to roll down the Corso Vittorio before she could cross. Tension in the city is high. **The Allies must be close**, Thomas said, when she told him of the tanks.

Lili dresses quietly, slips from the room. Thomas is up, too, standing by the living-room window, wearing his olive pants and a T-shirt.

"Good morning," Lili says, in English, moving to stand beside him.

Thomas smiles. **"Buon giorno."**

Outside, several women from the adjacent flats and from the buildings next to theirs lean from their balconies overlooking the piazza. They wave handkerchiefs, calling to one another. Lili slides the window open a crack. It takes her a moment to understand what the women are saying, as they are speaking over one another, praising the Lord between their cries. **Gli americani sono arrivati . . . prega al Signore!** Lili stares, listening. Could it be true? Have the Allies finally made it to Rome? She watches as more balconies begin to fill.

"Are they saying what I think they're saying?" Thomas asks, and Lili nods.

"It sounds as if your army has arrived."

They are quiet for a moment, neither sure of what to say.

Theo pads sleepily from the bedroom and wriggles his way between Lili and Thomas. "What's happening?" he asks. He grips the windowsill with his fingertips, stands on his toes to try to see out. Thomas slides a dining chair over. Theo climbs up and they watch, shoulder to shoulder, as a small crowd of Italians—men, women, skipping children—trickles into the piazza.

"**Gli americani?**" Theo asks, overhearing the shouts.

"Yes," Lili says.

Theo turns to look at her, his eyes wide. "They are here? Now?"

"From the sound of it." Lili wishes she knew someone with a radio.

"Where? I don't see them."

"I don't know, love."

A megaphone sounds from below. "The German army has retreated," a voice trumpets. "I repeat: the Germans have retreated. The city is no longer occupied. Rome is free!"

Lili's heart cartwheels. Free.

"**Libera?**" Theo asks. "The war is done?"

"Rome is free, yes," Lili says. The words feel surreal, made up. "But the war's not over. Soon, we hope."

"Can we go out there?" Theo asks.

Lili and Thomas share a glance. Could it really be possible the Wehrmacht had left without so much as a shot fired? They haven't heard any gunfire, explosions. But it feels too soon to Lili to take to the streets. Even if the Germans had left, surely there were still GNR.

"Please?" Theo begs, his forehead pressed to the glass.

Lili squeezes his shoulder. "Let's wait a little," she says, and Theo groans.

By nine in the morning, Piazza Farnese is filled with people. Lili, Thomas, and Theo gather once again at the window. Shouts of victory float from below. **The tides have turned! Fascism has been defeated! Roma is free!** The crowd, Lili notices, has begun moving, funneling slowly from the square.

"Where are they going?" Thomas asks.

"I'm not sure."

"Let's go see!" Theo says. "Please? Can we?"

Lili looks to Thomas.

"We'll stay close together," he says.

"All right," Lili says.

"Yahoo!" Theo scrambles across the room toward his boots, laid neatly beside Thomas's by the door.

"Slow down, **tigre**," Lili says. "How about some pants first?"

LILI LOCKS THE DOOR BEHIND HER AND THE THREE of them descend the building's stairwell—together for the first time. As they step through the entrance into the morning sun, they are swept into a sea of ebullient Italians. Lili tightens her grip on Theo's hand. Up ahead, a cheer erupts as someone rips a poster of Mussolini from a storefront. **Maybe this really** is **the beginning of the end**, Lili thinks, glimpsing half of Il Duce's face staring up at her from underfoot as she steps over the discarded poster a moment later. Two decades of Fascist rule. Four years of war. Nine months of German occupation in Rome. Lili glances at Thomas, taken aback for a moment by how familiar his face has become. His cheeks are glowing from the heat, or perhaps from the hum of excitement, palpable in the air. He turns, sensing her eyes on him, and smiles, and Lili's throat tightens. He'll be reunited soon with his unit. **He was always going to leave**, she reminds herself. **It was just a matter of time.**

"Do you think your regiment is here?" she shouts over the din, her voice artificially bright.

"If not, I'm sure they will be soon."

The crowd swells, and beyond the cries of **Victory!** and **Viva l'Italia!** Lili hears the roar of engines.

"I can't see!" Theo shouts, hopping up and down.

"Here," Thomas says, hoisting him onto his shoulders. He holds Theo's ankles with one hand and motions with the other for Lili to walk ahead of him.

"Now I can see!" Theo shrieks, pointing. "**Mama!** Look!"

"What is it?"

"Soldiers!"

They push on until they've reached the Corso Vittorio, then pause, watching as a column of battered trucks and dirt-caked tanks rumbles by, each with a five-pointed star painted on its side and packed with uniformed Americans. **They're really here**, Lili thinks, absorbing the sight. The locals flanking the thoroughfare roar in approval as the motorcade passes, waving flags, pumping their fists, their fingers pronged in the sign for victory. The Americans smile broadly, tossing metal tins and packs of cigarettes into the crowd. When one of the tins clatters to a stop by Lili's foot she picks it up, turns it over. Its label reads **Wieners**. She hands it to Thomas.

"Look at that!" he laughs. "Lunch! It's our lucky day."

Lili has no idea what kind of food a **wiener** is, but the idea of a meal in a tin appearing at her feet after so many years of standing in line for scraps feels too good to be true. Thomas pockets the gift, and as the last of the Americans file past, the locals close ranks behind them, tanks and trucks and bodies moving as one.

"Where's everyone headed?" Lili asks, touching the arm of a woman walking beside her.

"To the Vatican!" the woman replies. "**Piazza San Pietro.**"

"Saint Peter's?" Thomas asks, overhearing.

Lili nods. "The pope must be getting ready to speak."

Thomas's eyes pop. "The pope?"

Someone in the crowd hands Theo a tiny Italian flag. Still straddling Thomas's shoulders, he grins, waves it overhead.

"To the Vatican?" Thomas asks, offering his arm. Lili nods, hooking her elbow through his, and they press on toward the Holy City.

When they arrive twenty minutes later at Saint Peter's Square, they find a spot to stand along the tiered base of a massive obelisk. Together, they listen and watch as thousands of Italians stream into the piazza, cheering for the motherland, for the Allies, for the fact that the Germans had finally, inexplicably, fled without a fight. **It's a blessing**, they cry. **The miracle of Rome.** Lili scans the sea of faces around her, wondering for a beat if she might spot

Matilde's. It's unlikely. Her friend had sent a letter saying she and Matteo were north of Rome—she didn't say where, just that she'd likely be incommunicado. There's a good chance, Lili realizes, Matilde is somewhere sabotaging the German army in its retreat.

As the celebration escalates, Lili quiets, withdrawing into her thoughts. She should be happy—she **is** happy—Rome is free. Finally. But Bologna is not. The land north of the capital is still occupied. Will the Allies succeed in liberating the rest of the country? She scans the giant piazza, letting her eyes fall on the marble colonnades arching outward from the world's most beloved basilica. **What comes next?** she wonders. She's a stand-in mother to her best friend's child. Her father, her friends are unaccounted for. Even if she were to find them, her old life—the one she led before the war—is gone. There is no going back. She recalls the hatred in the GNR officer's eyes, the contempt in his voice when he accused her of harboring a Jew. Fascism may be declared a thing of the past, but Esti was right—**people are set in their ways,** she'd said in Nonantola, when Mussolini was first removed from power. Beliefs don't shift overnight. Just because the capital is no longer occupied doesn't mean she and Theo are safe.

She looks up at Theo, whose eyes are wide as he takes in the revelry, the sudden turn of events. She'll continue to use their false IDs, Lili decides. If

Hitler and Mussolini are defeated—if all of Italy is liberated—then, perhaps, she'll let her guard down. Then she'll call herself **free**.

"You all right?" Thomas asks, giving her a nudge.

"Yes. Yes!" Lili smiles, not wanting to taint the moment.

"**Ho fame**," Theo says. Of course he's hungry. They'd left the flat in such a hurry she'd forgotten to pack him something to eat.

"Here," Thomas says. He swings Theo from his shoulders, sets him on the ground and pulls the metal tin from his trouser pocket. **Ho fame** are words he's heard before; he knows what they mean. "How about a wiener?"

"What's a wiener?" Lili asks.

"A wiener? It's a hot dog!" Thomas says.

"What's a hot dog?"

"I'm not eating **dog**!" Theo says in Italian, sticking out his tongue, and Thomas chuckles.

"No, no, it's not **un cane**. It's beef. And pork." He offers his best moo and an oink, and Theo laughs as Thomas turns to Lili. "You can't walk two steps in New York City without running into a vendor selling these things."

"Hot dog," Theo says, tasting the words in his mouth as Thomas peels open the top of the tin with a pocket knife.

"Here, have one," he says.

Theo pulls one of the little pink logs from the tin, sniffs it, wrinkles his nose. "Smells funny."

Lili agrees. She's eaten pork in her mother's carbonara, or occasionally as prosciutto sliced thin over melon, but it didn't smell anything like this American version.

"We can't be picky," Lili says, half to herself, as she sizes up the tin.

"**Signora**." Thomas tips one of the hot dogs upright with his knife. It looks disturbingly like a small finger. Lili takes it tentatively.

"Go on, you two," Thomas coaxes. "I don't know a soul who isn't a fan."

Theo takes a bite. "**Strano**," he says as he chews. "I kind of like it."

Lili tastes hers. The consistency is off-putting but the flavor is decent. Mostly, she tastes salt. "Not bad," she says, and Thomas beams. He and Theo take turns popping the miniature links into their mouths, and Lili translates as Thomas tells stories about American ballparks, where hot dogs are called franks, and about the time he saw Joe DiMaggio hit a home run at Yankee Stadium.

When Pope Pius XII finally steps out on the balcony of the Vatican Palace, the crowd—there must be some two hundred thousand in the square—thunders in approval. The cheers go on for a full minute, vibrating the ground beneath Lili's feet, until the pope finally signals for quiet. A hush falls over the square as the Pontiff speaks.

"Yesterday," he begins, "Rome was still trembling for the lives of its sons and daughters. It can now look with new hope and a renewed faith toward its salvation." The pope crosses himself, raises a palm in blessing, and the ovation once again is deafening. Lili claps along but inside she's hollow; the pope's words feel disingenuous. What had Pius done for Italy's Jewish sons and daughters? Where was he when Mussolini began stripping away their rights, judging them less than human? Where was he when the Germans came and, with the help of his own people, rounded up thousands, right here in the capital, sent them away to the east? Matilde had said she'd heard rumors there were Jews hidden inside the Vatican, but if the pope was sympathetic to the Jews, why had he never publicly condemned the Nazi persecution? Or Mussolini's for that matter? He could have discouraged his fellow Italians from cooperating. He could have saved countless lives.

A spray of confetti blooms over the square, and Theo stretches out his arms, determined to catch a scrap of tissue paper. Lili lifts her chin, watching the colors of Italy rain from the sky. After a moment, she feels Thomas's hand in hers.

"Big day," he says.

Lili forces herself again to smile. It **is** a big day. She should enjoy it. She squeezes Thomas's hand and he grins, then bends to plant a kiss on her cheek. The gesture comes as a surprise to Lili, but she accepts it, turning her face for a second kiss to follow on the other cheek and remembering too late that this is not the American way. Her lips sweep across Thomas's and she draws back, flustered.

"Sorry!" she says.

Thomas laughs, unfazed. "Don't be." He extracts his hand from hers and cups it around her cheek, bringing his lips to hers again, with intention this time. The kiss is short, sweet, and for a moment, Lili is weightless. When Thomas pulls away, he laughs, then wraps his arm around her waist. Lili blinks, her cheeks hot, her insides humming.

"**Roma Libera!**" Theo chants along with the crowd, bouncing in place as if on springs. His smile is as wide as she's ever seen it, and Lili wonders if this is a scene Theo will describe someday to his children—the moment in time he'll recall when asked of his earliest memory. It's a good one to have, she thinks, and as Thomas holds her close, she leans into him, embracing the sensation that, for the moment at least, she is safe.

LEAVING SAINT PETER'S, THEY CHOOSE SIDE STREETS to avoid the enormous crowd. Theo skips between Lili and Thomas, a hand in each of theirs.

"Want to play a game I used to play when I was your age, Theo?" Thomas asks. Lili translates, but Theo answers before she's finished.

"Yes!"

"Okay. On the count of three, we'll swing you

up. All you have to do is kick your feet in the air. Got it?"

Lili smiles. She'd played a similar game with Theo on their walk south, though it usually lasted only a few tries before her shoulder gave out. "We'll swing you, okay?" she tells Theo. "Hold tight to our hands."

Theo nods and Lili and Thomas count to three then swing him off the ground and he shrieks as the soles of his shoes fly skyward. "Again!" he cries as soon as he's found his footing.

They are half way across the Ponte Mazzini when Thomas slows. "Hold up," he says, reversing direction and pulling them toward the center of the bridge, where a motorcycle inches forward among the vehicles and foot traffic. "I know him," he tells Lili. "Captain Hughes!" he shouts.

A man in a khaki uniform with sand-colored hair and a dimple in his chin turns. His eyebrows jump when he sees Thomas. He motors over. "I'll be damned," he says, when they're within arm's reach.

Lili watches the men slap each other a few times on the back as they embrace. So this is it, she thinks. **This is when he leaves us.** She tucks a flyaway behind her ear, suddenly lightheaded.

"Liliana, Theo, this is my captain, William Hughes."

"Billy," the captain says, extending an arm. He pumps her hand up and down, his grip firm. A strange way to greet someone, Lili thinks.

"Nice to meet you," she says, in English.

"Hello," Theo says with a wave.

"Pleasure's mine." The captain has Thomas's same smooth drawl. He turns to Thomas. "Tommy! I'd taken you for dead."

"Chances are I would be, if it weren't for this kindhearted woman. Long story, for another time."

William Hughes tips his helmet to Lili. "We're setting up headquarters a few blocks from here," he tells Thomas. "Hop on, I'll take you."

Thomas looks at Lili, hesitates for a moment. "All right," he says, and Lili takes a breath, feeling her chest begin to deflate, a balloon with a pinprick leak.

"I'll be back," Thomas tells her. "Once I get my orders. I'll need to . . . collect my things. I'll be home before dark, I hope."

Home. He'd said it so casually. Like it was theirs.

"**Stai partendo?**" Theo asks. He, too, looks like he's had the wind taken out of him.

Thomas squats beside him. "I'm not leaving yet, buddy. Just taking a little detour, is all. I'll see you back at the **appartamento. Va bene?**" Theo nods, understanding enough to know that it's not a forever goodbye. Not yet.

Thomas stands, gives Lili a nod, then steps over the back of the motorcycle as if mounting a pony— his feet touch the ground, even straddling the saddle. "**Italia Libera!**" he calls, and Lili watches as he motors away, the bike threading between Italians still holding flags, cheering. Within seconds, he and the captain are out of sight.

LILI AND THEO RETURN TO THE FLAT, WHERE LILI spends most of the afternoon at the window, watching the piazza. As darkness falls, she feels her chest tighten with worry. Has something happened? Has Thomas been sent to the front already? It's plausible. The war is still going on and the Allies need all the help they can get. But would he really leave without collecting his things? Without saying goodbye? Lili chews her bottom lip, trying to put a finger on the feelings welling up in her.

She'll miss him, she realizes. Not just his smile, the gentle cadence of his voice, his company, but the way she feels when she's around him. She's never met someone so helpful or so honest—with himself or with her. Someone so comfortable in his skin. She worries less when she's with him. Smiles more. What would have become of them, she wonders, if they'd had more time?

She sighs as she moves away from the window. She can still feel the warmth of his lips on hers. Maybe that's what's throwing her. Why did he have to kiss her? What did it mean? Nothing, probably. She'd watched thousands of people kiss at Saint Peter's today. It was a moment that called for embrace. Whatever these feelings are, she tells herself now, they're not worth dwelling on. Even if Thomas does return, he'll be off again soon.

Night falls, and she tucks Theo into bed.

"Where is he?" Theo asks. "He said he would come back."

"He did," Lili says, her tone stolid. "He must have gotten held up at his headquarters."

"He left all his clothes here. And his cards."

"I know."

"Will you wake me up if he comes?"

"Sure." Lili kisses his forehead, turns out the light. But Thomas doesn't come.

CHAPTER THIRTY-NINE

ROME

June 1944

Two days pass. In the papers, Lili reads about an Allied invasion in Normandy, the largest, apparently, in military history. There's a chance, she realizes, that Thomas has been moved north for support. Lili tells herself not to worry. She does her best to stay busy, refusing to sit around waiting for Thomas to appear, but it's hard, the weight of his absence exacerbated by Theo's persistent questions. This morning, growing tired of his probing, she'd broken down and told him that Thomas may not be returning after all. Theo spent the rest of the day in the bedroom, complaining of a stomachache.

Now, it's nearly midnight. Lili, unable to sleep, is on her settee with her mother's book of Rilke on her lap when she hears footsteps in the hallway. Then, a knock. She stands, tiptoes to the door. The knock comes again, a decibel louder this time.

She takes a breath, leans her head toward the door. "Who's there?"

"It's me."

Lili exhales, then feels her lungs expand as she takes a long, full breath—her first in days. Thomas.

"Come in," she says, stepping aside as he enters. She closes the door, turns to face him.

"Hi," he says, removing his hat. The room is dimly lit by the single lamp Lili was using to read by. She can see though that he's dressed in a new, neatly pressed cotton-khaki uniform.

Lili wants to be angry with him for disappearing, but instead finds herself resisting the impulse to wrap her arms around his shoulders, to bury her face in his chest. "Hi," she says. "You didn't use your key."

"I wasn't sure if you'd be asleep. I didn't want to scare you, coming in at this hour. I'm so sorry I didn't make it back sooner."

"I was a little worried," Lili says. An understatement. "Especially with the news from Normandy."

"I just learned of the operation yesterday. The army kept it top secret, hoping it would come as a surprise. I hear the fighting has been fierce."

Lili is quiet for a moment, processing the enormity of the invasion and wondering of its impact on the war.

"Did you find your Rangers?" she asks.

"Unfortunately, no." Thomas's face drops. He blinks

several times, and Lili knots her hands together at her waist, wondering if he might cry. "My regiment didn't hold up so well, I'm afraid. Turns out there are only a few of us left."

"Oh. That's terrible. I'm sorry, Thomas."

Thomas looks up, brightens. "The good news is the major I report to here wants me to stay in Rome, to help him train a new company. We've already recruited some guys from Fort Benning."

"So—they're not sending you north?" Lili tilts her head, not sure she's understanding him right.

"Not yet. They're only dispatching units that are intact. Guys who are used to fighting alongside one another. Since my unit has disintegrated, we're starting over, in a sense. Once we have enough men, we'll ship out, probably in July."

He's not leaving yet. "July. So you'll be around for a little while."

Thomas nods, spins his cap in his hands. "Would it be all right if I stayed here for one more night, Lili? I don't have to report back until the morning." Lili's pulse stirs. When did he stop calling her Liliana and start calling her Lili? She can't recall.

"Of course." She watches his hat move in his hands. A few awkward seconds pass.

"Lili," Thomas says. "I want to apologize."

Lili lifts her gaze. "What could you possibly need to apologize for?"

"For kissing you the other day, out of the blue like that. It wasn't very . . . gentlemanly of me."

Lili blinks. "Oh—that. You were caught up in the moment. Everyone was. I was—it was—I didn't mind."

"I should have asked you first."

Lili pauses. Her heart dips in her chest. "You can ask me next time," she says.

Thomas swallows. "Next time?"

"You can ask me now." Lili's voice is barely above a whisper. She's never been so forward with a man.

Her words seem to bolster Thomas's confidence. He takes a step toward her, closing the space between them, and Lili's hands move to his freshly shaven cheeks. He holds her gaze, folding his arms gently around her waist, and Lili feels her body come alive.

"May I kiss you, Lili Passigli?" Thomas asks, and Lili smiles. She wants nothing more, suddenly, than to be with him.

He bends and she meets him halfway, standing on her toes. His lips are soft on hers, sending a current, warm and powerful, through her veins. She lets the kiss linger, an invitation.

"Are you sure—" Thomas whispers, pulling away.

"Yes," Lili manages. She's never slept with anyone before. And she and Thomas are—what—friends? But in this moment, she couldn't be surer of anything. She presses her body closer to his and closes her eyes. Time stretches out, and the next thing she knows she's fumbling at the buttons on his tunic.

AFTER, LILI MAKES TEA AND THEY SIT ON THE settee, talking.

"Where will you stay after tonight?" she asks.

"The army's put up some barracks near the Vatican. They make this place feel like a palace," Thomas says with a laugh. "I've gotten permission to visit, though, when I can." He runs his hand through his disheveled hair.

"I like the sound of that," she says, playing with the belt of her dressing gown. "Theo will too. I've lost count of how many times he's asked about you."

Thomas's eyes light up. "I can't wait to see him."

"How is it out there?" she asks, glancing toward the window overlooking the square. "We haven't been much farther than the market. There were American soldiers asleep on the streets this morning. They looked pretty ragged."

"Our guys are exhausted. But morale among the locals seems to be growing. A few of the cinemas and clubs have opened back up. I imagine folks are eager to get back to some sense of normal."

Lili ponders the word. In a different life, normal was a morning bent over a cappuccino and **cornetto** at Café Savona with Esti by her side. It was an evening at the theater, a walk through the park with her father, the sturdy feel of his arm in hers. There is no such thing anymore, Lili realizes, as normal.

"Have you thought about where you'll go from

here?" Thomas asks. Lili bites her lip, considering her reply. They haven't broached the subject yet of what will come next for her. A part of her wishes he'd offer to join her on wherever **next** is from here. It's easy to imagine them traveling together. She shakes off the thought. It's not an option; Thomas is on active duty, following his army's orders.

"I think about it all the time," she says. "I need to know where Esti is, and if my father has made it to Switzerland. I have to keep searching for Theo's father too."

The odds of learning anything new have begun to feel impossibly small. But somewhere, Lili tells herself, there are answers. There have to be. Even just a morsel of information would help. Anything to make sense of the enigma of what's become of her friends, her father.

"I have a contact in Florence whom I haven't heard from since I left," she says. "A nun, at the convent where Esti and I stayed. There's a chance she might have some information for me." She pauses, trying to picture herself on the road again with Theo. "I thought I'd go see her and then return to Bologna. My father has an apartment there. At least I think he still does. Bologna is—well, it's home. And it's the place he and Esti will know to find me."

"Bologna. That makes sense," Thomas says. "When would you go?"

Lili shrugs. "As soon as it's safe. Although with our papers, I suppose we could leave any time."

Thomas sets down his tea and leans in, closing the space between them. "You and Theo will be better off here in Rome for a little while longer," he says. "The Wehrmacht may not have put up a fight when they left, but from what I understand that's only because the capital was designated an Open City. I'm told the fighting north of us is worse than ever. That the Germans are destroying everything in their wake as they retreat. Villages, bridges, churches. Resisters. Innocent people. You don't want to get caught up in that."

Lili nods. He's right. It would be irresponsible of her to leave too soon, to make a decision that would put her and Theo in danger. A little longer in the capital, she rationalizes, won't do any harm. And if it means more time with Thomas, she's all right with that.

"You'll stay here then?" Thomas presses. "Until it's safer to travel?"

"I'll stay," Lili says and Thomas smiles, sits back, happy with her answer.

Lili glances at his uniform, lying in a heap on the floor. He'd put on his olive pants and the undershirt with the three buttons at the top. "I like your new ensemble, by the way," she says. "The color suits you."

"I should probably hang that up," Thomas says,

but makes no move to retrieve the clothes. "The army doesn't look highly upon wrinkles."

"And how will they look upon your German uniform?"

Thomas laughs, sips his tea. "That we can burn before I leave tomorrow," he says.

CHAPTER FORTY

ROME

July 1944

Over the next two weeks, amid a sweltering summer heat, Thomas pulls together a company of Rangers while Lili considers the right time to leave Rome. Meanwhile, rhythms of life from before the occupation gradually reappear in the capital. The locals ease back into their jobs, their routines. Restaurants reopen, with limited menus. And little by little, Campo dei Fiori boasts a new array of colors, as market stalls are decorated with peaches and gooseberries, zucchini flowers and Castelvetrano olives—delicacies once allocated only to the Germans and the Fascists.

Lili walks the streets more freely now, though always with her ID and her alibi at the ready. Around every corner, there are signs, reminders, of what the city has endured. The streets near the Tempio Maggiore di Roma, the Great Synagogue, are still empty since its residents were rounded up last October. Neighborhoods destroyed by bombs are littered with rubble. Countless shops are boarded up, their owners' whereabouts unknown. There is chatter among the women at their stoops who, while mending socks or peeling potatoes, compare notes about their families, watching with dimming hope for the return of their sons, their husbands, their brothers. The city is recovering, but the effects of the war cling to it stubbornly.

Thomas drops by as often as he can, usually as soon as his shift has ended, for dinner, with treats from the army commissary: a packet of bouillon powder, a can of biscuits, a bar of soap, a stick of chewing gum. Theo lives for his visits, for the surprises he extracts each time from his pack. They draw pictures and play cards, and it's Thomas now who puts Theo to bed when he's around. Sometimes Lili joins him, sitting at the edge of the bed and listening as he tells a story, beginning each time with the same, **Once upon a time, there was a . . .** and letting Theo fill in the blank. Lili marvels at Thomas's ability to spin such engaging tales at a moment's notice. Theo's favorite story of Thomas's is about a curious duckling who flies into a magic cloud and emerges on the other side in the Jurassic era. Lili has committed it to memory. **You should write a children's book**, she told him once.

Lili and Thomas are never physically affectionate in front of Theo—it doesn't feel right to be—but

Lili relishes her time spent with him alone, once Theo is asleep. Their games of rummy. Their conversation. His touch, which she's come to crave like a glass of water on a hot, hot day.

"You're here early," she says when Thomas shows up at the flat one afternoon.

"We've gotten the order," he says, a hint of disbelief in his tone, as if he himself is still absorbing the news.

A tightening in Lili's abdomen. "To leave?"

Thomas nods.

"When?"

"Tonight."

"Tonight."

"At six o'clock," Thomas says quietly, and Lili can tell from his expression that it hurts to say the words.

Lili glances at her watch. "That's—in two hours."

"It's safer for us to travel through the night."

Theo, who's been listening but not quite following, dissolves when Lili explains that Thomas will be leaving soon, for the front. Thomas picks him up and holds him for a while, rocks him gently while he cries. When the tears fade to hiccups, he peels Theo's arms from around his neck and sets him down in a chair at the dining table.

"I brought my cards," he says, extracting his deck from his trouser pocket. "Will you play with me?"

Theo nods.

"What do you want to play?"

"Five hundred?" Theo suggests, in English.

"You got it."

Thomas shuffles. As he deals, Lili prepares a snack and tidies the flat, doing her best to keep from hovering. At five thirty, Thomas checks his watch.

"It's time, buddy," he says.

Theo's chin wrinkles. "Stay," he says. "Please?"

Thomas glances at Lili.

"He can't stay, love," she says.

"I wish I could, my friend," Thomas says. "I tell you what though, I'm going to leave my cards here with you—can you take good care of them? Teach your mother some of the games we've played?"

Lili translates. Tears pool in Theo's eyes. Thomas tousles his hair, then stands to gather the few things he's left in the flat—a shirt, a toothbrush, a razor. Lili and Theo trail him to the door. There, he pauses, removes his notebook from his shirt pocket, flips through it until he finds the page he's looking for. He tears it out and hands it to Lili.

"This is my APO address. Will you write? Let me know how it goes with your search?"

"Of course."

"I'm not sure how much longer this war will go on, but . . . if I make it home, and if you ever come to America, I . . . I hope you'll visit." Thomas's voice sounds strange. Measured.

Lili looks at the address he's written, then back up at him. "I'd like that," she says. "Here." She motions for the notepad. "I'll write down my father's address in Bologna."

Thomas fishes the stub of a pencil from his pocket. "Thanks," he says, when she returns the pad. He drops it, and the pencil, back into his shirt pocket, then digs into his pack. "I want you to have this too."

He hands Lili a small leather pouch. Inside is a roll of United States twenty-dollar bills.

"They gave it to me a few weeks ago," he says, before she can object. "But I don't see why I'll need it, now that I'm back with the army."

Lili shakes her head. "This is too much."

"It's not enough. Please, take it. Use it to find your father, your friends."

Lili cinches the pouch shut, nods. "Thank you."

Thomas turns to Theo. "Theo. I'm going to miss you, pal." He props himself on one knee and stretches his arms wide and Theo disappears into them. Lili hears a muffled cry. When they part, Thomas stands, looks to Lili. She gives a small smile.

"I owe you, Lili Passigli," Thomas says.

"You don't."

"I do. You trusted me. You let me into your home. I'll never forget what you've done for me."

"You'd have done the same for me."

"Yes. I guess you're right."

"Be safe, Thomas," Lili says. For the last few weeks, she's tried not to think about what he'll be asked to do once he's forced back into battle. She refuses now to consider the possibility that he may never make it home to Virginia.

"You as well. Please."

A silence hangs over them as they stare at each other, delaying. Finally, Thomas draws her to him for a hug, and Lili closes her eyes and lets her arms fall around his waist, her cheek rest beneath his collarbone. She wonders if he can feel the punch of her heart through her blouse, the quick, steady beat. She pulls away and Thomas holds her by her shoulders. He clears his throat as if to say something more, then pauses.

"I thought I'd be better at this part," he says, his eyes damp.

"Me too." Lili can feel her throat closing. "I hate goodbyes."

"Till next time, then?"

Lili nods. "**Arrivederci** is how we say that here." She opens the door for him, takes Theo's hand.

Thomas slings his pack over his shoulder. "**Arrivederci**, Theo," he says, offering Theo a Ranger salute. "Stay strong, young man." Theo returns the salute and Thomas turns once more to Lili. He dips his chin.

"Good luck, Lili."

"Same to you, Thomas."

And then, he's gone.

Lili and Theo move to the window, where they watch the piazza for Thomas's figure. When he emerges, he looks up, sees them, waves. Lili slides the window open and Theo hollers another farewell. Thomas yells back, swings his cap overhead, then walks on, his pace brisk, disappearing a moment later from the square.

Theo doesn't say much for rest of the evening. "Can I bring them to bed with me?" he asks, clutching Thomas's playing cards to his chest when it's time for bed.

"Of course," Lili says.

Theo holds the cards as she reads to him and as he rolls over for her to tickle his back. When she kisses him goodnight, he tucks the deck beneath his pillow.

Later, at the kitchen sink, Lili picks up a scrubbing brush and washes and puts away their dinner plates. Drying her hands, she feels in her pocket for the slip of notebook paper Thomas had left her, reading it for the second time. His handwriting is fluid, messy. Nothing like hers. It was a nice gesture, she thinks, exchanging addresses. But there won't be a next time. This much she knows. Promises made in the uncertainty of war—they're simply a means to get through. To make leaving easier. She sets the paper down. Tomorrow, she decides, she'll begin making arrangements for their trip north, keeping a close eye on the dailies for updates on the German position. If the Allies can force the Germans out of Florence, if the city is liberated, she and Theo will leave. And from Florence, with luck, she'll continue north to Bologna. She'll go home.

PART IV

CHAPTER FORTY-ONE

FLORENCE

August 1944

When Lili and Theo arrive at the train station in Rome, a **carabiniere** at the ticket office orders Lili to show their papers. She produces her false ID, Theo's, too, wondering why the police are still checking now that the capital is free. When he's slow to return the documents, she lifts her chin and stares at him, unblinking, until he waves her by.

In Florence, they stop at a bakery for a loaf of peasant bread and to ask directions to the Ponte alla Carraia, the bridge they'll need to cross to get to the convent on Piazza del Carmine.

"Ponte alla Carraia is gone," the man behind the counter tells Lili. "They're all gone. Only way to cross is the Ponte Vecchio. The one Hitler must have deemed too beautiful to take down."

Lili knew the Germans were ordered to destroy the city before they left—she'd read about how they'd blown up pasta works, flour mills, and leather factories, razed telephone exchanges and set railway tracks on fire. Still, looking around at the decimated city, she realizes nothing could have prepared her for the aftermath. She presses a handkerchief over her nose and mouth as she and Theo walk toward the Ponte Vecchio, stepping around mountains of garbage and the occasional horse carcass rotting in the street.

"Eyes down," she instructs as they pass a building on whose steps the dead have been collected, arranged into piles, and sprinkled white with lime. Lili averts her gaze, too, sickened by the sight of the pale, speckled corpses and fighting off the thought that Esti's could be among them.

When they reach the bridge, they fall into step behind a pair of middle-aged women. "They took everything," one of them says. "The watercolor hanging on the wall, a rug. Dinner plates. They took the coverlet from my bed!"

"At least they didn't take the bed itself," the other replies. "The Napoliellos are sleeping on the floor."

Theo tugs at Lili's hand. "How much farther?" It's been a long day. He's been grumpy since they left Rome.

"Not much. Ten minutes?"

Lili had told Theo of her plan, explaining they'd travel by train this time. When he asked her why they were leaving Rome, she told him the truth, which was that Rome was expensive, and that they had a place to stay for free in Bologna. (She chose not to tell him that there was a chance her old home had been bombed, and that if it **hadn't** sustained any damage, it may well be occupied now by a stranger—these were possibilities she'd face once she arrived.) **It's a place for us to live while we wait for the war to end**, she said. **And it's much bigger than our flat in Rome. You'll have lots more room to run!** Theo had asked if there were toys in Bologna, and Lili said she thought so. **There are definitely books**, she said. **Lots of them.**

"I came here to Florence once with my mother," Lili tells Theo as they cross the bridge. "Before the war. We walked and walked, even went to the top of that big dome over there." Lili points to the brick-orange cupola of the cathedral, protruding over the northern horizon, relieved the Germans had left it intact.

"Are we going to find my mother?" Theo asks, and Lili's stomach drops. She wasn't expecting the question.

"I—I hope so, love."

"I don't think we will," Theo says, matter-of-fact.

"Don't say that. We might. Do you remember Sister Lotte?"

Theo shrugs.

"She was with us in the convent, where we're headed now. Maybe she'll have some news for us."

Theo stares at the ground as he walks, his jaw set, eyes hardened, his expression a replica of the frown Esti used to give when something was bothering her.

"She said she would meet us in Assisi and she never came."

Lili slows. He remembers. She pulls him to a stop, drops her valise, and bends so their eyes are level.

"I'm certain that she tried. It's all she wanted, to find you. To find us."

"But she didn't."

Lili takes both of his hands in hers. "I know you miss her," she says. "I miss her too. Terribly. Almost as much as you do." Theo blinks several times in succession, his blue eyes magnified suddenly behind a wall of tears. Lili waits for him to look at her, keeps her voice steady. "You have to understand, Theo, that if she could have made it to Assisi she would have. I don't know what happened. That's what we're trying to find out. I'm doing everything—**everything**—I can to search for her, okay? I'm going to need your help though. I'm going to need you to be strong, like Thomas said. Can you be strong for me? And for your mama?"

A tear spills over the freckles on his cheek. Lili wipes it away with her thumb. She knows his pain. She'd do anything to make it go away. Theo is silent.

"Come here," Lili says. She holds him close as he cries. Strangers file around them. Someone bumps her shoulder, but Lili doesn't move, doesn't look up. She hugs him for several minutes, until he stops shaking and his breath evens. "I love you," she whispers, cradling his head to her chest. "We're in this together, you and me," she says when she finally loosens her grip. "Whatever happens, okay?"

Theo sniffs, nods.

"Okay." Lili stands, reaches for her valise.

Slowly, they walk on, across the Arno, past the vendors selling meager offerings of leather goods and overpriced fruit, the surface of the river beneath them a mirror image of the silver clouds above.

WHEN THEY REACH THE CONVENT ON PIAZZA DEL Carmine, Lili stops in the square. **Esti.** She can almost feel her. She glances up at the convent's white stucco facade, at the small wooden cross on its roof, silhouetted against the overcast sky. It all looks as it did almost a year ago, when they first left Aldo's bombed-out block to come here, praying the nuns would let them in. What if they'd been turned away? Where would they have gone? Would they have fled Florence? Would they still be together? Lili pushes the thought aside. She's made countless decisions since the start of the war, of where to go, of whom to pretend to be, of whom to trust. There's little point in second-guessing them now.

She steps up to the convent's heavy door, taps the mottled brass knocker twice, and waits. After a while, a young nun appears. Lili recognizes her, but only vaguely.

"Sister," she says, a hand over her heart. "My name is Liliana Passigli. You took us in at the start of the war. I'm not here to stay, just to ask about a friend we left behind. May I speak with Sister Lotte?"

The nun steers Lili and Theo inside. "This way," she says, and they follow her through the cloister. When they pass the door to the storage closet—the place they'd seen Esti last—tears prick at Lili's eyes, the memory of her goodbye still acute.

"Wait here," the nun says, when they reach the refectory. It's three in the afternoon, between meals. The room is empty. Lili and Theo sit down at a long, wooden table.

"I remember this place," Theo whispers. He looks up at her, his eyes tired, his cheeks pale.

"Rock Paper Scissors?" Lili asks.

Theo nods.

"Quietly, okay?"

They play several rounds before Lili hears some-one approaching. They stand as Sister Lotte enters the room.

"Liliana?"

Lili is taken aback by the sight of the old woman. She looks as if she's aged five years in the months Lili has been away. "Sister. It's so good to see you."

The nun draws Lili into an embrace. Lili holds her gently, her shoulders sharp beneath her habit.

"And you as well," Sister Lotte says. She pauses, as if to say something, then steps away to have a look at Theo. "What happened to the small boy I taught when he was here?"

Theo looks down at his feet, suddenly shy.

"Are you doing all right, Sister?" Lili asks.

"I'm fine, all things considered. We've had food, shelter."

Sister Lotte summons the young nun who'd fetched her. "Would you take this young man to the kitchen for a snack?" she asks. "You can have anything you'd like," she tells Theo.

Theo looks up at Lili and she nods, then watches him as he walks away. He's in good hands but still, she doesn't like not being the one by his side.

Sister Lotte turns back to Lili. A shadow crosses her face, and Lili feels suddenly as if she's sinking. She takes a deep breath.

"I have news," the nun says, the skin between her eyes folding into creases.

"Tell me," Lili whispers.

"Let's sit." Lili returns to the table; Sister Lotte sits down opposite her. "Do you remember Zaira?"

Lili searches her memory. "Yes. Small. Redhead."

"That's the one. She was with Esti when Carità came back around for the second time. When all the women were taken. As I wrote to you, no one in the group returned, which led us to fear the worst. But Zaira came back, just a few weeks ago . . ."

Sister Lotte pauses as if to gather the strength to go on, and Lili waits, until she can't any longer. "What did she say, Sister?"

"She told us that—when they were taken from the convent, they were locked up, as I'd suspected, in a prison in Verona, with hundreds of others. That one day the Italian police came and piled them all into trains and sent them north, to a place called Auschwitz."

Auschwitz. One of the Nazi death camps Matilde had mentioned, in Poland. Lili's hand is at her mouth.

"Zaira was able to escape the camp—she wouldn't say how, I think she was too ashamed. Maybe she got close with one of the guards, I don't know. She said when they arrived, they were divided up. She and a few other able-bodied women were put to work. The rest, who weren't fit for physical labor . . ."

Lili sits stone-still, barely breathing. Esti couldn't walk when Lili left her. She wasn't fit to work. What use would the Germans have had for her? "Did she say what happened to the others?"

"Just that she didn't see them again." Sister Lotte shakes her head. "Esti, she wasn't . . ."

"I know," Lili says. Tears streak her cheeks. She stares over Sister Lotte's shoulder, unable to focus. "Is there a way to retrieve information from the camp?" she asks, her voice hoarse. "Through the Red Cross, maybe?"

"I've tried."

"And Dalla Costa? Have you been in touch with him?" The cardinal is well connected—to the authorities, to the pope, to the underground. He'd be privy to information others were not.

"We're in touch. I ask him often of the women who were taken from here. I wrote to you, Lili, when Zaira returned," Sister Lotte says. "You must not have received my letter."

"No," Lili says. She feels as if she's left her body; she can't tell if her mind is moving too fast or too slow. "No, I never got it."

CHAPTER FORTY-TWO

BOLOGNA

August 1944

Lili stares through a dirt-speckled train car window as they trundle north toward Bologna, wondering how, with Sister Lotte's news, she'll hold it together, how she'll occupy her time, her mind. Theo is asleep, his head on her lap. Every time she looks at him, her heart constricts. How do you explain the concept of a death camp to a three-year-old? The fact that, in all likelihood, his mother is gone? Lili chews her lip, her thoughts wheeling. Even if it's true, there is a part of her, she knows, that will never believe it. Esti—fierce, defiant, beautiful Esti—meeting her end at the hands of the enemy. It doesn't add up. **She could have escaped, too**, Lili tells herself. **There's a chance.** Zaira hadn't actually **seen** Esti die. But then, if she'd escaped, wouldn't she have sought out Dalla Costa? Or Sister Lotte? Or Father Niccacci? Wouldn't she have sent word? The landscape spools by, a blur of dried-up hayfields and run-down farmhouses. Lili hardens. She'll keep searching. She can't not try.

She lets her thoughts turn to Thomas. Had he and his Rangers helped to liberate Florence? Or was he farther north in the Apennine Mountains, fighting to breach the latest line of German defense? He could be anywhere. He could be in battle, or laid up in a medical tent. He could be lying lifeless on the side of a mountain. She's thought about writing him on several occasions, but sending a letter felt like holding on to a thread of hope—and what was she even hoping for? That he'd survive the war? That they'd see each other again? There was no sense wondering what might have become of them, if they'd met under different circumstances. If they'd had more time. What hope she has left in her, she decided, she'll devote to Esti, to her father, to Niko. The question that should occupy her mind, Lili tells herself now as the train begins to slow, is what their existence will look like in Bologna.

Despite months of Allied air attacks—the Americans and the British hell-bent on pushing the Germans out—her hometown is still occupied. It's a risk to return. She's acutely aware of this. But she's heard the Germans are posted largely on the out-skirts of the city, that the center itself was so badly bombed, there is little left of interest to them. Still, she'll need to be careful, should the air raids continue. Should someone recognize her. She and Theo will use their Aryan IDs, along with her familiarity of the city she's known for most of her life, to help maneuver the streets.

Combing her fingers through Theo's curls, Lili calculates how much longer they'll be able to survive on the lire and the U.S. dollars stashed away in her valise. She's been chipping away steadily at her cash reserves. She won't be able to afford many more train tickets, and certainly won't be able to pay for rent, at least not without a job. **Please**, she prays, **let my home be standing**.

The train slows to a crawl as they approach the Bologna station. Theo sits up and leans into her. Lili wraps an arm around him. He didn't press her for details about his mother in Florence. He must have known, from Lili's ghostly expression when he was returned to her at the convent, that she didn't have any good news to share. But it wasn't right to say **nothing**, Lili decided, so as the train had pulled away from the Florence station, she told him Esti had been taken away from the convent not long after she and Theo left, and that she hadn't returned. **I wish I knew more**, she said. Theo had accepted this, as if his prediction was proven right, then retreated inside himself.

"Are we there?" he asks now, his voice still caked with sleep.

"Almost."

The clerk at the ticket office had warned Lili that the rail line outside of Bologna, like the one in Florence, had been destroyed, that the track ended some four hundred meters from the terminal. They'll have to walk an extra kilometer, at least, to reach her block.

"I'm hot. And tired," Theo says. "Will you carry me?"

He's talking now, at least, Lili thinks. "You're too heavy, love. I'll carry your coat though." Theo slumps, but doesn't argue.

They step off the train into a wall of humidity. Lili drapes their coats over an arm and begins sweating immediately. It was warm inside the train car, but the windows were open, the air circulating. Now, the air is stagnant, thick in her lungs. She scours the road for Germans, the sky for bombers as they pick their way toward the city center, climbing over burned-up railroad ties and mounds of rubble. There are no enemies that she can see, but there is also no path, just obstacles of cement, stone, and debris.

When they finally reach the edge of her neighborhood, Lili looks around, feeling as if she's lost her bearings. The streets are in complete disarray. Every third building has been severed in half, or gutted. Some are missing roofs, their walls reduced to piles of broken brick. Hardly anyone is out, Lili realizes, save for a few harried women trudging by. For a city that once bustled with people and energy, Bologna feels eerily vacant.

Her heart leaps when she spies her old apartment

building, a block ahead on the corner. Her home, still standing. It feels like something of a miracle. Two of the four on the intersection are in ruins. She wonders how many of her neighbors had made it to a bomb shelter before the buildings fell, whether the shelters had done any good.

"This way," she tells Theo. They step around a smattering of bricks on the sidewalk to enter her building, then climb the stairs to the fourth floor. At her door, Lili drops her valise, panting, praying as she fishes her old key from her purse that it will still work. That she won't be met at the door by a new tenant. She slides the blade of her key into the lock, holds her breath, and turns. The key swivels ninety degrees. The lock clicks open.

"Hello?" Lili calls as she steps inside, holding tight to Theo's hand, ready to exit quickly if she has to. There are no shoes at the door, no coats hanging up on the wooden rack in the corner. She looks around the foyer. Dust motes circulate overhead. The beige paint on the walls feels tired. But—it's **her** tired paint. **Her** dusty foyer. She takes it all in: the glass table shaped like a half-moon, where her father kept a bowl for his keys; the round, brass-framed mirror hanging over it; the red Persian rug underfoot—the one her mother had bought on a trip to Turkey. The familiarity of it almost brings her to tears.

"Hello?" she calls again, for good measure.

When a voice rings out in reply, she stumbles backward.

"Hello?" the voice comes again.

Lili fumbles for her valise, pulls Theo toward the door. She hears the voice again, closer this time, accompanied by footsteps, moving quickly in her direction.

"Hello? Who's there?"

In the doorway, Lili freezes. She knows this voice. Her chest thrums. She braces herself for it all to be a dream. But in the next moment, he's there.

"Papà!"

Massimo makes a strange sound when he sees her. His eyes grow big, and then bigger still as shock, then recognition, grip him.

"Lili!"

He brings his palms to the crown of his head, closing his fingers around clumps of silver-streaked hair, as if his legs might give way and he has to hold himself up.

Lili reaches for him, and in her next breath his arms are around her and she's sobbing silently. She feels the warmth of his cheek at the top of her head, the accordion of his ribs beneath her hands, and she can tell from the rocking of his shoulders he's crying too. They stand like this for a long moment.

"Papà," Lili says again, stepping away, taking him in.

"Lili. You're here."

"**You're** here."

He is not the same man, Lili realizes. He's diminished—his waist, his neck, his hairline. He looks like a smaller, frailer version of his old self. But he's alive.

Lili shakes her head. "You look thin, father. Are you well?"

"I'm fine." Massimo smiles and Lili warms at the crow's feet flanking his eyes. Later, she decides, she'll see what kind of produce she can find, prepare him a proper meal. She lifts Theo to her hip, catching a glimpse of herself in the mirror—her too-sharp cheekbones, her eyes, rimmed in shadows, her own narrow waist. She is not the same person either.

"Don't tell me this is . . . **Theo**," Massimo says.

Lili nods. "Not so little anymore," she says, turning so her father can have a better look at him. He's getting too big to hold like this, legs looped around her waist, arms around her neck, but she doesn't care; in this moment, she can barely feel the weight of him. "Theo, this is my father, Massimo. You've met him before, but it was a long time ago, when you were only two, so you probably don't remember him."

Theo says a soft hello.

"Hello, son," Massimo says. "My, you certainly have grown."

Theo nods. "I'm big."

"I can see that." Massimo looks to Lili. "But where is—" Lili cuts him off with a quick shake of her head and his face falls, understanding. A conversation for later. "Come," he says. "Leave your luggage, I'll get it."

Lili makes her way down the hall toward the living room, Theo still in her arms, her father following close behind. Massimo! Here, in Bologna. Under the same roof. She's spent so long imagining what it would feel like to step into her old apartment, into his arms, and now, here she is. She inhales fully, letting the smell of old books and tobacco fill her lungs. It's a scent Lili could recognize blindfolded, that could be described only with one word: **home**.

CHAPTER FORTY-THREE

BOLOGNA

August 1944

The streets are empty when Lili, Massimo, and Theo venture out for a walk early the next morning. They leave their apartment building, turning north toward the Giardini Margherita.

"Are you sure it's safe to be out?" Lili asks, glancing reflexively up at the sky.

"Safe from Allied bombs or from the Germans?"

"I don't know—either? Both?"

"I've only been here for a few days but I've yet to run into any Germans," Massimo says. "And there's nothing left to bomb in the center. If we listen for the sirens, we should be okay. There's a bunker in the park. And the one in our building."

"All right," Lili says, satisfied.

Before they left, Massimo had found an old football at the back of a closet. He'd showed Theo how to juggle it, promising to play a game of pass with him in the park. Theo holds the ball now, close to his chest as he might a teddy bear, cherishing the new toy.

The night before, Lili and her father had talked for hours, filling each other in on the trials of the last year. Massimo described how, when he left for Switzerland, he was turned away twice at the border—once for no reason, and once for looking like a Jew, or so he was told, despite the fact that his papers stated otherwise. **If it weren't for the ID Esti made me, I don't think I'd ever have made it,** he said. **And for my watch,** he added, tapping his bare wrist. **The Fascists were turning everyone away. Only a lucky few were able to cross—posing as Aryan, and most, like me, carrying something valuable to proffer as a bribe.**

Once he finally reached Lausanne, Massimo said, he learned that his uncle had moved his family to the countryside outside of Bern. He found them there and wrote a dozen letters to Lili at the address she left for him in Nonantola, but by then, of course, Lili had moved to Assisi. **No wonder my letters never reached you,** Lili said. Massimo had decided a few weeks ago to make the trip to Bologna. **It was awful not hearing from you,** he said. **I knew there was a chance you'd come back here.**

Lili gave her father the abridged version of her own journey. She told him first about Florence—about Aldo and Cardinal Dalla Costa and the nuns at the convent across the river, and then about Esti, relaying the story of the Carità gang, the prison in Verona, the camp in Auschwitz. It didn't feel real, hearing the words from her mouth. She cried, and Massimo cried too. She told him about Adelmo and Eva Giardini and their beautiful estate in Castelnuovo Berardenga, about her frigid bike ride to Assisi, where she met Father Niccacci and Luigi Brizi, who printed papers at the back of his shop and who'd changed Theo's ID to match hers. She told him about Isabella and Ricardo and the drunk who'd threatened to turn her in to collect a reward, about her long, endless walk south, and about her surprise run-ins with Gino Bartali, first at the monastery and then again on the road. (**The** Gino Bartali? Massimo marveled, his face lit in disbelief.) She described the close call with the Wehrmacht and the unsympathetic priest in Todi and told him about Matilde and her time with the partisans in the forest, omitting the part about the stray bullets and the decapitations. **You slept in the woods?** he asked, incredulous. She told him how Theo had twisted his ankle by the river and about the doctor in Scalo Teverina who arranged a ride for her to Rome, and she admitted that, in her broken state, she'd nearly opted to leave Theo under the doctor's care. She explained about the papers she'd delivered to Sister Natalia in Rome, and, only briefly, about Thomas. When Massimo raised a brow and asked for details, she brushed him off, worried he would judge her for allowing a man—a foreigner, and a soldier to boot—into her home. Massimo didn't press. It was after midnight when he and Lili finally turned in. There was still much to discuss, but Lili's adrenaline had faded, her exhaustion from the last several days of travel having finally caught up with her. She fell into bed, her old bed, and for the first time in weeks, slept a deep, dreamless sleep.

Now, as they enter the Giardini Margherita, Lili loops an arm through her father's. Theo walks a few paces ahead, tossing up his ball and catching it in his arms.

"I still can't believe you walked all that way," Massimo says. "To travel so far, on foot—it must have been grueling."

"It was," Lili says. "But I've already forgotten the worst of it. Strange how the mind works like that."

"A testament to your strength," Massimo says.

Lili motions toward Theo, lowers her voice. "I told him it's my mission to find Esti," she says. "But I'm scared, Papà. I have a terrible feeling about it."

Massimo is quiet for a moment. "This war has torn so many of us apart," he says. "Maybe she managed to find a way into hiding. Maybe she's waiting for the war to be over before she finds **you**."

"Maybe. When I left her, our plan was to meet in Assisi. But I know her. She'll come to Bologna if she's alive."

"Just as I did."

Lili looks at her father.

"You're brave to have left Switzerland," she says. "It's not safe to be crossing borders."

"Not without an ID, no. But mine has served me well."

"Mine too."

"Have you written to the Red Cross?" Massimo asks.

"Yes, many times."

"Nothing?"

"No. I've been hard to reach though."

"Very," Massimo agrees.

They walk on in silence, listening to the wail of a far-off siren, the gong of a church bell. Lili glances over at the dusty shell of a bombed-out apartment building. "The city feels like a ghost town," she says.

"It's barely recognizable."

"Why are the Germans still here?" Lili wonders aloud. "Territories north of us have been liberated. It doesn't make sense."

"I don't understand it either." Massimo squeezes her arm. "It was torture being away from you, Babà. Not knowing if I'd see you again."

"I know, Papà."

When Massimo speaks again, his voice is timid. "I haven't been well, Lili."

She glances at him. "None of us are well, Papà."

"I mean, I've been sick."

Lili looks closely at him now, but his expression is hard to read. "What do you mean?"

"The doctors in Switzerland thought it was ulcers, but they're not sure."

"It's your stomach?"

Massimo nods, and Lili can see how much it distresses her father to admit this.

"We'll go see Dr. Aloni right away," Lili says. "Are you in pain?"

"Nothing I can't manage with medicine. But Dr. Aloni and his family . . . I stopped by the clinic as soon as I returned. The space is abandoned. There aren't so many of us left in Bologna, it seems. I tried to look up the Laffis, the Segres, the Zevis—they're all gone. The Mosseris fled to Palestine. The Kleinmans are still in confinement, apparently. The others, I'm told, were arrested."

A lump at the back of Lili's throat. It's no surprise that there are few Jews left in Bologna, but it's jarring still to hear father speak the names of so many old family friends who have disappeared.

"We'll find another doctor, then," Lili says, determined to lift her father's spirits. "You can use your false papers."

"We can try."

"We'll figure something out, Papà. Don't worry."

Massimo smiles weakly and Lili regrets her words. There's no such thing anymore, as a life without worry.

"Can I kick it now?" Theo asks, holding up the football.

"Sure," Lili says. "On the grass there, not on the path."

Theo runs to the grass, drops the ball, and gives it

a kick, chases after it. Lili and Massimo watch him, calling for him when he runs too far.

"Tell me more about Bern, Papà," Lili says after a while.

Massimo smiles, genuinely this time. "Things are different there," he says. "Safe. Stable. It helps to have family nearby. I've made a few friends. I've been painting a lot. And I've found a part-time job—at the local bookstore, believe it or not."

"That's wonderful, Papà."

"It suits me."

"Are you planning to return? To Bern?"

"I was. But seeing you here . . ." Massimo looks at her. "I think I'll stay for a while. Unless—would you and Theo come to Switzerland? You could join me, Lili. Life is better there."

Lili sits with this invitation, tries to imagine a life in Bern with her father, her cousins. "I can't leave, Papà. Not yet, at least."

"Because of Esti."

"Yes. If there's a chance she's still alive, I have to find her."

"You're right, Lili," Massimo says gently. "Of course you do."

They walk on in silence.

"Massimo! Here!" Theo cries. He kicks the football and Massimo jogs ahead. Lili watches them in their game of pass. They move like opposites: Theo with the playful, fluid gait of a Border collie, her father stiff and awkward, a scarecrow version of his old self. **Sick,** he'd said. **Ulcers. Maybe.** What if it's something worse? Surely, Bern has good doctors. She imagines him painting by the window of his room, reading behind the counter of the bookstore where he works, sharing a meal with his uncle. He's happy in Switzerland; he'd told her so. He's safe. **He has to go back.** The thought solidifies quickly. He will fight her. He'll tell her he can't. But he'll be better off in Switzerland. He'll have his family, his friends, his job. He'll have medical care. If he stays in Bologna for her and her alone, and if something were to happen to him—she can't even think it. She'd never be able to live with herself.

"I'm open!" Lili calls, raising a hand in an invitation for Theo to pass her the ball. They'll discuss it later, she decides. She glimpses again at the sky. They should turn around soon. But her father is enjoying himself, and Theo, too, and it feels good to move her body this way. To play. They form a triangle, passing and laughing, and Lili wishes Esti were there with her camera, to capture the moment.

"LILI, YOU'RE ALL I'VE GOT. I DON'T WANT TO LOSE you again."

Lili had waited until Theo was asleep to suggest to her father that he return to Bern alone.

"You're not losing me, Papà. You can come back to Bologna, once the war is over. Once you're feeling better."

"The city is occupied. It's not safe," her father argues.

"You said yourself you haven't seen any Germans in the city center. And my ID says I'm from Lecce, remember? If I get questioned, I'll tell the authorities I'm renting from the owner, a gentleman a floor down. Settimo can vouch for me."

In the end, Lili convinces her father it's the right decision for him to go, and for her to stay. **We will write to each other constantly**, she promises. **You'll be sick of my letters come fall.** She'll breathe easier, knowing her father's whereabouts, knowing they can write. It won't dull the pain, though, of another goodbye.

CHAPTER FORTY-FOUR

BOLOGNA

December 1944

It's not easy, living in Bologna. There are still Germans stationed on the outskirts of town. There's still a reward for a turned-in Jew. Every now and then, the Wehrmacht show up in the dilapidated city center and Lili hears shouts, once even gunshots, as someone—a Jew, a partisan, an anti-Fascist—is arrested and carried away. These sporadic attacks terrify her, as she has no choice but to brave the streets for ration cards and for food. She's on constant alert for Germans, for nosy neighbors, for the high-pitched warning of a raid siren. The Allied air raids are relentless. Twice, she and Theo have sprinted for shelter in one of the city's bunkers. She's memorized the locations of all of them.

Some days, Lili questions her decision to stay. But there's comfort in being surrounded by a shadow of her old life. Her bed, her kitchen, her dining room table with its polished oak surface and its various divots and ring marks, little mementos of happier times. Here, Massimo knows where to reach her (he writes often, as promised) and most important, if Esti is alive, she'll know where to look for her.

A few days ago, Theo turned four. Lili had made a thing of the milestone, worried he was growing despondent. Since Massimo left and they'd settled into their routine in Bologna, he'd smiled less, complained more—of having no one to play with, nothing to do. Lili hoped a celebration might give him something to look forward to, lift his spirits. She'd invited Settimo to join them. He brought a small cake with four candles, and Lili made hot cocoa from a bar of chocolate her father sent from Bern, melted over the stove and mixed with water and a splash of cream purchased on the black market. For a gift, she found a wooden yo-yo at a second-hand shop, which, to her delight, Theo loves. He safeguards it now as if it were made of gold and has spent countless hours in his room, standing on the edge of his bed, his mouth twisted in concentration as he spins the toy up and down, up and down, determined to master it.

Lili visits the resurrected post office twice a week, sending off inquiries to the Red Cross, to the Greek embassy in Rome, even to the mayor's offices in Rhodes. She's lost much hope of locating Niko, but she writes to the Italian consulate in Salonica anyway, to feel like she's done something. And she continues to reach out to Father Niccacci in Assisi and to Sister Lotte in Florence, begging for news by telegram, should they have any. Thus far she's found nothing, heard nothing.

Massimo, at least, is managing well. His doctor in Bern is good, he says, his medicine is working, he's feeling better. In his last letter he even alluded to a new female acquaintance—he was vague about it, but Lili read between the lines, and was happy for him. He was set to make a trip back to Bologna over the winter but the snow has made the barrier of the Alps, towering between them, impossible to cross. The trains aren't running—nor are many armored vehicles, the Italian campaign forced into a stalemate thanks to the inhospitable winter weather conditions. Massimo had postponed his visit, promising to come as soon as the mountains were passable. Perhaps by then, Lili prays, the stubborn, straggling German army will have raised a white flag and the war will be over.

And then, one snowy afternoon, a bump in their usual routine, in the form of a letter. Lili recognizes the handwriting immediately. **Thomas.** She scours the envelope for a return address, but it simply reads AE, Italy, and beneath that, a number: 09629.

"Who's it from?" Theo asks as they leave the post office, curiosity piqued.

"It looks like it's from Thomas, love."

"Thomas!" Theo's smile is so big Lili can see both rows of teeth. "Open it!" he pleads.

"Let's read it at home."

A dozen scenarios spiral through Lili's mind as Theo asks again and again, **What do you think it says?** Perhaps Thomas has written to tell her he's hurt. He's been demobilized. He's going home. She tears open the envelope as soon as she's closed the door behind them, and reads it out loud.

> Dear Lili,
> If you're reading this, you've made it safely back to Bologna, which I pray is the case. How are you? How is Theo? I think of you both every day, and of our time together, which feels surreal, as if I'd dreamed it—do you ever feel that way? Anyway, I suppose nothing about the last few years feels real. Have you learned anything of your father? Your friend? I hope so. And I hope the news is good, as rare as that is to come by these days.
> We are moving every day, on the heels of the Germans. The fighting is bad. I wish I could unsee the things I've seen. We're all freezing and bone-weary, but we keep pressing on. I pray we prevail in the end.
> On a lighter note, I've been drawing at night, in my tent. Cartoons, mostly, to pass the time when I can't sleep. I've

included one for Theo, which I thought
he might enjoy. Have you been writing
at all? Made a dent in your memoir?
Tell Theo I miss him, will you? I miss
you, too, Lili. More than you can
probably imagine.

Take care.
Love, Thomas

Thomas's cartoon is a sketch of the toy car he
and Theo made on the afternoon Lili first left them
alone together in the flat in Rome—the afternoon
Matilde showed up unannounced. The young man
at the wheel is clearly meant to be Thomas, his passenger, Theo. They're waving. The tires of the car,
like the toy that still sits on Theo's bedside table,
are rendered as buttons, and there is a bubble over
Thomas's head, the words within written in all
capitals: **ARRIVEDERCI!**

"Let me see, I want to see," Theo says, standing
on his tiptoes. Lili hands it to him.

"That's us!" Thomas says, grinning.

Lili smiles, buoyed by Theo's excitement. She
reads the letter again, to herself.

She'd done her best to put Thomas out of mind
since she got to Bologna. Now, though, with his
playful drawing, his words in hand, she softens, and
it occurs to her that the effort of not thinking about
him has taken a toll on her.

She folds the letter, slides it back into the envelope. **I miss you**, Thomas had written. He'd signed off with **love**. The words settle over her and she feels the air in her lungs grow a little crisper, a little lighter. **I miss you too**, she thinks.

CHAPTER FORTY-FIVE

BOLOGNA

January 1945

S now dusts the cobblestones underfoot. Lili takes Theo's hand as they leave the vegetable stand. They walk carefully toward home.

"I wish there was more snow," Theo says. "Then I could make a snowball."

"I'm sure there's more on the way," Lili says, distant. Her mind is occupied by the fact that the Germans had recently set up a new line of defense just south of Bologna. How much longer, she wonders, will their fortifications hold? Why haven't the Allies broken through?

They round the corner and she eyes a crowd gathered around a newsstand across the street from their building. There's something about the way the men stand with their shoulders bent, the women with their arms wrapped tight around their chests, that gives her pause.

"This way," she says, guiding Theo over. They weave through the crowd until Lili finally sees what the group is fixated upon: the front page of **La Stampa**. She picks up a copy. AUSCHWITZ DEATH CAMP LIBERATED, the headline reads.

Lili blinks. Auschwitz. Liberated. She almost smiles. If Esti is alive, if she's been locked up in the camp this whole time . . . but then her eyes drift to the subhead—NAZIS EVACUATE THOUSANDS, LEAVING BEHIND ONLY THOSE TOO SICK TO LEAVE— and then to the photo beneath it, and her stomach curdles. In the forefront of the photo is a gate made of tall metal beams and chicken wire, a sign hung at its center painted with the words HALT: AUSWEISE VORZEILN. Behind the fence, depicted in grainy black dots, are the vacant faces of half a dozen prisoners. Two women, three men, a young boy. They wear striped tunics that hang loosely over a protrusion of bones, their shaved skulls too big for their emaciated frames, their sockets too big for their eyes. One of the men leans on a crutch. The boy, who can't be more than seven, holds the wire fence with his good hand, the other wrapped in a dirty bandage and pinned to his chest with a rudimentary sling. One of the women looks down, the other into the camera. Lili can't tear her eyes from the photo.

She pays the vendor, folds the paper in half, and tucks it under her arm. "Let's go," she says.

"What's everyone looking at?" Theo wants to know.

"Nothing, love."

They bump into Settimo in the lobby of their building. He holds a copy of the same paper. He glances at Theo, forces a smile and a wink.

"You okay, kiddo?" he asks Lili.

No, she wants to say, but she nods. "I will be."

IN THE WEEKS THAT FOLLOW, LILI OBSESSES OVER the news. Each morning on her way back from the market she buys a paper and pores over the latest headlines. At night, once Theo is asleep, she listens to the radio, tuning in to Radio London. Every few days, it seems, a new Nazi death camp is discovered, and the estimated number of Jews murdered climbs exponentially. In Poland, and in other parts of Eastern Europe, the numbers are staggering. In Greece too. Last week, Lili learned that Salonica was one of the cities hit the hardest. To think now that Niko and his family might have been sent to a death camp is horrifying.

As the days pass, more photographs surface, many from Auschwitz: a collection of teeth, from which, the paper noted, gold fillings had been extracted; a room overflowing with sacks of shorn hair; a mountain of old clothing beside a barrack—adult and child size, along with suitcases, eyeglasses, and prayer shawls, brought to the camp by prisoners who believed, as they'd been told, that Auschwitz was a stop along the way to being resettled. There are photos of survivors, too, some so skeletal Lili could wrap her hand around a thigh and her thumb and forefinger would touch. Many, the papers say, died when the Red Cross attempted to feed them, their bodies, after such deprivation, rejecting the calories. Others succumbed just days after liberation, of dystrophy, typhus, typhoid, tuberculosis. Lili writes almost daily to the Red Cross with Esti's name, begging for information. At home, she scours the papers, looks for her face in every photo, praying to find her among the survivors. But she is not there.

CHAPTER FORTY-SIX

BOLOGNA

April 1945

I'm making another picture for Thomas," Theo announces from the dining table, where Lili has set him up with pencil and paper. She sits across the room at her writing desk, penning a letter to her father in Bern.

"I can't wait to see it," she says over her shoulder, wondering if it's fair to let the boy believe his picture might actually make its way into Thomas's hands. The chances are slim, she expects. The newspapers report that American forces are scattered throughout northern Italy, spanning the top of the boot above Bologna from coast to coast. But Theo's spirits have been up since Thomas's note arrived, and she doesn't want to take that from him. He's hopeful. And isn't that the thing she's relied on all these months to keep going when all else failed—hope?

A week ago, the Allies finally pushed the Germans

out of her hometown. Most of the fighting, thankfully, took place south of the city. The few pockets of Wehrmacht who were stationed in Bologna fled without resistance. The Polish army arrived first. Lili and Theo had watched from their fourth-story window as a battalion of armored tanks rolled down Via Rizzoli, swarmed by applauding Italians. Theo asked why some of the tanks were draped in branches—for camouflage, Lili presumed; they looked like giant, rolling bushes. The U.S. Army followed shortly after, though within days the tanks and soldiers were gone, in steady pursuit of the retreating German army. Lili wondered if Thomas might have been among the units passing through.

She returns to her letter, imagines her father opening it, reading it. The act of putting words to paper has become precious to her. It's not a conversation, but the closest thing to it. **Bologna somehow feels much as it did before,** she writes, **aside from the fact that we no longer have to worry about air raids. I still walk outside and look skyward though—I'm not sure I'll ever break that habit.**

Her city may be liberated, but there is still no end in sight to the war. **No news on Esti,** she writes now. **I've inquired with the Red Cross, but I can only imagine how overwhelmed they are.** She'd read that the Germans were destroying records as they fled the camps—which meant that even if Esti's name had been noted on a list, there was a possibility that list no longer existed. **I keep trying to convince myself** there's a chance she may still be out there, Papà—Niko too. It's becoming irrational, I realize this. It's just that, when I think about giving up, I get this feeling inside, and all I can think is—if our roles were reversed, if it were me who was missing—I'd want my best friend to keep searching.

And Esti would. She'd face the horrific odds and the terrifying unknown, and she'd do everything in her power to find her.

"Do you like it?" Theo asks, and Lili looks up, jolted from her train of thought. Theo holds up a piece of parchment for Lili to see.

"Wow," she marvels, setting down her pen. "It's quite good, Theo. Tell me about it."

Theo lays the paper on the desk. "Well, this is me here, by the river. This is Thomas. He's fishing."

"It looks like a sunny day in your picture," Lili says, pointing at the concentric circles Theo's drawn in the corner. "What's that there? Up in the clouds?"

"An airplane."

"Oh! Yes, of course. Who's flying the airplane?"

"You!"

"A pilot. I like it."

Theo traces his finger along Thomas's figure. His face grows serious. "Will he come back?"

Lili hesitates. "I don't think so, love. His home is in America." When Thomas's letter arrived, Lili had pulled an old atlas from the bookshelf to show Theo a map of the world, pointing out Italy, Switzerland, and the United States.

"America is far away."

"Yes."

"Maybe we can go see him."

"I'm sure he'd love that." **If he's still alive**, Lili thinks.

"Do you think he got my picture?"

"I don't know. The mail is tricky. I hope so."

"I bet he did. I hope he liked it."

Theo's first drawing was of a young boy and a tall strapping soldier, playing football. Theo had labeled the figures with arrows and Lili helped him to write out the letters, spelling **Thomas** and **Theo**. Both wore smiles that stretched from cheek to cheek.

"If it reached him, I'm **certain** he loved it," Lili says. She'd addressed the letter simply to Captain T. Driscoll, AE, Italy, 09629. At the last minute, she added her own postscript, short and sweet, double-checking her vocabulary in the dog-eared Italian-English dictionary she found among her high school textbooks. **I appreciated your letter**, she wrote. **It's awfully quiet without you. Do let us know if you make it out of this mess unscathed.**

"Maybe he'll write again," Theo says, half to himself.

Lili tucks a curl behind his ear. His hair is longer than it's ever been. She thinks often of cutting it, but with the images from Auschwitz still seared in her mind, she can't bring herself to do so.

"Maybe," she says. Maybe.

CHAPTER FORTY-SEVEN

BOLOGNA

May 1945

It's the eighth of May, a Tuesday. Lili has propped her father's radio on the coffee table. Harry Truman, the United States' new president, is expected to speak momentarily. She fiddles with the dial then stands, too antsy to be still. Theo, oblivious to her angst, lies on his stomach on a rug by the fireplace, legs bent at right angles, his socked feet swaying as he plays with his toy car, singing the tune to "Hush Little Baby" under his breath.

Just over a week ago, Lili learned that Mussolini was captured by a mob of Italian partisans. He and his mistress, Clara, were discovered attempting to flee north toward Switzerland—Mussolini had tried to pass himself off as German in a Luftwaffe helmet and overcoat, but the partisans who stopped his convoy at the border saw through the disguise. Unfortunately for Il Duce, whose portrait had been plastered across Italy for decades, his high cheek-bones and square jaw were unmistakable. He and his lover were hidden in captivity for a night, then executed by shotgun and brought to Piazzale Loreto in Milan, where their bodies were hung up for the public to see. When the paper published a photograph of the dictator, his bullet-wracked body dangling upside down by the ankles, Lili looked hard at the image, angry and disgusted, but also relieved. Never before had an image so distinctly symbolized the end—not only of a life, but of an era.

In the days following Mussolini's death, there was still no sign of peace. Hitler, from his bunker in Berlin, continued to order his men to fight, despite the fact that victory for the Germans now felt unattainable. Why then, Lili wondered, would the Führer waste more supplies, more lives, when he could concede and put an end to it all? And then, remarkably, he did. He gave up. With Soviet troops some five hundred meters from his bunker, he and his own mistress took their lives. HITLER DEAD, the papers pronounced on the thirtieth of April. An official surrender and proclamation of peace, however, didn't come until yesterday, a full week after Hitler had died. In that time, there were reports of the Wehrmacht still battling, refusing to lay down their arms in Italy, and across Europe.

Out of a hiss of static, a voice emerges. Lili adjusts the radio's antenna. She sits, crosses her legs, and jiggles her heel, trying to picture the American president, secreted in the depths of the White House, an ocean away.

"We interrupt our program to bring you extraordinary news," an Italian broadcaster announces. "Please stay tuned." A moment later, another voice, in English. Truman.

"This is a solemn but glorious hour," the president proclaims. "General Eisenhower informs me that the forces of Germany have surrendered." He pauses, then adds, "The flags of freedom fly all over Europe!" A few notes of **Bella Ciao** play in the background, fading as the Italian broadcaster returns.

"As you've just heard from the president of the United States, German forces have capitulated. The high command has signed a complete and unconditional surrender to the Western Allied forces. The war in Europe is over. I repeat, the war in Europe is over."

Cheers reverberate from the apartment above. Theo looks up at the ceiling then at Lili. He climbs onto the sofa to sit next to her. She turns the radio off.

"The war is finished?" Theo's eyes are bright.

Lili takes a long breath, allowing the news to settle. "There is still a war," she says, thinking of the headlines she'd read recently about the fighting in Japan. "But it's very far away. Here where we live, the war is finished."

"Did the good guys win?"

"We did."

Theo grins, and Lili manages a smile. There is still too much to grieve to be truly happy—too many unknowns, too many decisions to make—but it's a momentous day. The Allies have prevailed at long last. She needs to acknowledge it, for Theo at least.

"Wait here," she says. In the kitchen, she prepares two small glasses of milk, then shuffles through her mother's old recipe tin for her secret supply of chocolate, breaking off the corners of a bar. She returns to the table and hands Theo a glass and a piece of chocolate.

"Chocolate!" he cries.

"Special treat. Before you eat it, though, do you know what it means to make a toast?"

"A toast?"

"It's something like a celebration. Words to commemorate something good. Here, lift your glass up like this, next to mine." She holds her glass out and Theo does the same. "To the end of the war, Theo. To the good guys, who never gave up. To us. We had to travel a long way, didn't we?" Lili had shown him their route when they were looking at the atlas one day. "We were hungry all the time, and tired. We lived in the woods!" Lili pauses. "But we made it. You and me."

"Me and you," Theo says.

Lili smiles, in earnest this time. "And now we bring our hands together, like this." She touches the rim of her glass to Theo's. "And you say, **cin cin.** And you take a sip."

"**Cin cin!**" Theo parrots. He sips his milk then pops his chocolate into his mouth and Lili does the same, letting the morsel melt on her tongue for a moment before chewing.

"Yummy," Theo says, and when he smiles his front teeth are smudged brown.

LILI CRAWLS INTO BED WITH THEO SHORTLY AFTER eight that evening and falls asleep. She sleeps and sleeps, and it's Theo who wakes her the following morning, with a glass of water in hand.

"I brought you this," he says, tapping her shoulder.

Lili rubs her eyes. "I didn't hear you get out of bed," she says, sitting up.

Theo shrugs.

"Well, thanks for the water—and for letting me sleep." Lili takes the water and sets it on her bedside table. She looks sideways at Theo. "How did you fill this?"

"I climbed onto the counter."

"Oh? I didn't know you were tall enough to do that."

"It was easy. I used a chair."

Lili cups a hand around his cheek. "Stop growing, please," she says.

"No!" Theo yells with a devilish smile, then climbs into bed with her. She moves so he can rest his head on her pillow. "Is the war really over?" he asks.

Lili rolls to her side, props her head in her hand.

She runs the backs of her fingers along Theo's cheeks. His freckles have grown more pronounced, his eyes somehow bluer, since he turned four.

"It's really over," she says.

"Finally," Theo huffs, in an exasperated tone that Lili recognizes as her own.

"Finally."

"Does **Nonno** Massimo know it's over?" Theo asks, and Lili's heart expands. They speak of her father often, but she's never heard Theo describe him as grandpa.

"Oh yes, the whole world knows."

"Will he come home now?"

"I think he's going to stay in Switzerland," Lili says. "But we can visit him there. Would you like that?"

"Yes," Theo nods. "When can we go?"

"Soon," Lili says. She waits for a question about Esti, grappling with how she might answer, but Theo's mind is elsewhere.

CHAPTER FORTY-EIGHT

BOLOGNA

May 1945

L ili is brushing her teeth at the bathroom sink when she hears the knock. She looks at her watch. It's after nine. A bit late for Settimo to stop by, she thinks, dropping her toothbrush in a cup and dabbing her mouth with the corner of a hand towel. Settimo drops in often, to deliver a piece of mail, or to borrow a splash of wine or a sprig of basil from the pot that Lili's revived on the kitchen windowsill. Mostly, though, he comes to say hello. Lili suspects her father has asked him to check in on her, but whatever the case he seems to enjoy the visits and so does she.

"Coming," Lili calls, pinning her hair into a bun at the nape of her neck. She wears her mother's gray linen slacks and a white linen shirt, buttoned to her collarbone. Her father never had the heart to purge Naomi's closet, and neither has Lili, so her clothes have stayed, just as they were, just as Lili remembered them. Which has worked out well for Lili, as she'd arrived in Bologna with next to nothing. Most of what she wears now, in fact, was her mother's.

"Is everything all right—" she starts as she opens the door, then brings a hand to her mouth. It is not Settimo.

Thomas smiles when he sees her, removes his cap. He wears his khaki uniform, his pack slung over his shoulder. His hair is cut short, his cheeks neatly shaved.

Lili laughs through her fingers. She motions him inside, and as he steps into the foyer he drops his duffel and Lili moves toward him as if it were the most natural thing, to step into his arms.

"It's you," Thomas says into the top of her head.

Lili breathes him in. He smells just the way she remembers, of leather and soap. She lets her cheek rest on his chest for a moment, then steps away. He looks the same, albeit a few kilos lighter, and with the mark of a newly healed scar on his forehead.

"What happened?" she asks. Without thinking, she lifts a hand to his face, traces her fingertips around the scar.

"Shrapnel."

"Ouch. Does it hurt?"

"Not anymore."

Lili lets her hand fall. "I didn't think I'd see you again."

"Didn't you receive my letters?"

"We received the one with the drawing," Lili smiles. "Theo loved it. We sent a reply. I'm guessing it didn't reach you."

"You wrote?" Thomas looks surprised.

"Yes. Theo drew a picture for you."

"I didn't know if—" he shakes his head. "No, I didn't get it."

A warmth builds in Lili's chest.

"How is Theo?" Thomas asks.

"He's—he's well. He'll be thrilled to see you tomorrow." In her answer, Lili realizes, she's extended an invitation for Thomas to stay.

"I can't wait to see him."

Lili shakes her head. "How are you, Thomas?"

"Lili . . ." His eyes are soft, but clear. He looks at her closely. "I haven't stopped thinking about you since I left."

"I—" Lili takes a breath. "I missed you too," she says. The words feel even more true than when she'd written them. She wants nothing more, she realizes, than to hold him. To feel his skin against hers. She meets his gaze, her eyes flashing. "May I kiss you, Thomas Driscoll?"

Thomas laughs, dimples framing his mouth. "I thought you'd never ask."

"ARE YOU HUNGRY?" IT'S NEARING ELEVEN. LILI walks barefoot into the living room, wearing her white shirt and her underwear. She's opened a bottle of wine, poured two glasses. She hands one to Thomas, who'd lit a small fire.

"Famished."

"I am too."

Lili disappears into the kitchen, returning with a plate of sliced bread—real bread, which she now considers a delicacy, along with a wedge of asiago cheese and jar of fig jam. They sit at the sofa and eat in contented silence.

"This sure beats a can of beans," Thomas says.

"How about a **wiener**?"

"That too."

Lili reaches for the blanket at the back of the sofa and pulls it over their laps. Thomas wears his underclothes—white cotton shorts and a T-shirt. He drapes an arm over the sofa and turns to look at her.

"So," he says, and Lili smiles at his easy warmth.

"So."

"Fill me in. On everything. Have you found your father?"

Lili smiles, nods. "I have! He was here in Bologna, believe it or not, when Theo and I arrived."

"After all that searching!"

"I know, I couldn't believe it. Neither could he."

"Incredible. Is he—oh my—is he here now?" Thomas looks over his shoulder, his posture suddenly broom straight.

Lili laughs. "No, no, he's gone back to Switzerland.

He made it across more than a year ago. That's home for him now."

Thomas exhales. "Phew. I mean, I'd love to meet him," he adds quickly. "Just, you know, under different circumstances."

"I think the two of you would get along," Lili says. In fact, she's thought quite a bit about what Massimo and Thomas would make of each other. Thomas would appreciate her father's thoughtful, considerate manner. And her father, she's certain, would see what Lili sees in Thomas: a man with an open heart, a kind soul. He'd see himself, Lili thinks.

"A toast then, to your father," Thomas says.

Lili lifts her wine and her ears are filled with the chime of glass touching glass.

"What about Matilde?" Thomas asks.

"I haven't heard from her since we saw her in Rome," Lili says. "I think about her all the time though." Lili can't walk past a sewage drain without wondering if Matilde might pop up out of it, all dark braids and impish eyes, a pistol concealed in her purse. "I hope she hasn't gotten herself into too much trouble."

"She seems like a woman who can hold her own."

"She does."

"And . . . Esti?"

Lili's smile dims. "No. I went back to Florence, to the convent where I left her, and one of the nuns there told me she and the rest of the women had been sent off to a prison, and then to Auschwitz." Lili studies her wine as she says this.

"Auschwitz?"

Lili nods, unable to lift her gaze. If she sees the shock in Thomas's eyes, she'll cry. "I've been trying to find out more, but they haven't released any records yet."

"Oh, Lili, I'm so sorry."

"The camp was liberated months ago. I think I've been a fool for holding out hope for so long."

"No. Don't say that. I know it's hard, the not knowing—but it's better to hope for the best than to expect the worst, right?"

Lili glances up at him. "That's what I keep telling myself."

"They told us that thousands of prisoners from Auschwitz were evacuated just before the Reds arrived—maybe Esti was among them?"

"The infamous Death March, yes, I read about that. Maybe."

"It's unfathomable, what the Nazis have done," Thomas says. His voice breaks, but he makes no effort to hide his emotion.

"I just can't comprehend it," Lili says.

"There's a lot, I think, we won't ever understand about this war."

Lili sips her wine. For years, she's refused to believe that when the war ended, she'd be left without resolution. But the possibility of having to live with the uncertainty, without any sort of concrete explanation, is there, undeniable.

"It's over, at least. Thank God," she says.

"You're right. That's something." Thomas swirls what's left of his wine in his glass, swallows it down.

"It's from Montepulciano," Lili says. She doesn't want to talk about the war any longer, to ponder the myriad of mysteries still left to be solved. "The wine. It was one of my mother's favorites." She lifts her glass to her nose, inhaling a simple note of clove.

"Naomi, right?"

Lili smiles. She'd told him about her mother in Rome. He'd remembered her name. "That's right."

"Where's Monte . . ."

"Pulciano. South of here. Tuscany."

"The last drink I had was at the start of the war," Thomas says. "Right when we got to Italy."

"Where were you?"

"In a town just north of Salerno—I can't recall the name of it now. We'd made camp by a country road and ended up helping an old man fix his truck when it broke down nearby. Nice fellow. He insisted we come to his home and try his grappa."

"And?"

"It reminded me of the moonshine my buddies used to make me drink in college," Thomas says, sticking out his tongue.

Lili laughs. "Grappa isn't for everyone. Fortunately—or unfortunately, depending on who you ask—I grew up on it. My grandfather used to distill his own as well. When I was a girl, he'd sneak me sips after dinner. I hated it at first, but after a while I got used to it. Now, I don't mind it."

"Well, you're a whole lot tougher than I am."

"I don't know about that."

"I'd love to go back to that little town some-day," Thomas says, looking at the fire. "I'm not sure I've seen a prettier coastline. It's a pity we couldn't enjoy it."

"Salerno, you said?"

"Near there. That's where we landed."

"You were on the Amalfi Coast, then. I've never been. We always vacationed on the Adriatic side. But I hear Amalfi's spectacular."

"It is."

"How far are you from the coast in Virginia?" Lili asks.

"About an hour. I spent my summers as a kid pick-ing crabs on the Eastern Shore—my parents have a place on an off-shoot of the Chesapeake Bay in a lit-tle town called Matthews. But the coast there looks nothing like it does here. It's flat, and the water's dark as mud." Lili tries to imagine it, the Eastern Shore with its low-lying coast and brown water and its crabs. It sounds altogether foreign to her.

"When we landed in Salerno, I drew a picture of the towns hanging from the cliffs and sent it to my mother, told her I wanted to bring her there some-day," Thomas says.

"You must be counting the minutes till you see her," Lili says.

"I sure am."

"When will you go home?"

"My ship's due out of Naples next week." Thomas pauses, sets his empty glass on the table. "Come with me, Lili." The words come so quickly Lili wonders if she's heard him right.

"Excuse me?"

"Come with me. To the States."

"Thomas—"

"I know, it sounds crazy. Italy is home for you. You've got your father, and of course Theo too. But I've had a lot of time to think about it—about **you**. And in that time, I realized I've never felt this way about anyone in my life, and I—I want to be with you. And Theo."

Lili puts down her glass beside Thomas's and stills, absorbing the weight of his question. His eyes are wide, alive with hope.

"I don't expect you to agree to it, of course, at least not right away. But maybe you could—think about it? Will you do that?"

Lili's head starts to spin. "I'm not—I haven't—"

"We can keep looking for Esti from the States. For Theo's father too. I have contacts in the army who might be able to help. And we can come back as often as we like, to visit your friends, your father."

"I wasn't expecting this," Lili says finally. The

most she'd allowed herself to hope for after Thomas's letter arrived was that they'd keep in touch by mail. She never thought he'd show up at her home. And while she knew what they had was real—is real— she'd chalked it up to the fact that they were two lonely people whose orbits had crossed at what felt at once like the exact right and exact wrong time.

Thomas scoots closer to her on the sofa, takes her hands in his. "I know, I'm sorry. I should have waited to ask you. That was my plan, originally—I told myself if I was lucky enough to find you here in Bologna that I'd give it some time, sort out my thoughts. But seeing you, it feels so good—so **right**—I can't explain it. It's like you've filled a piece of me that was missing. And I guess I couldn't wait to ask." He looks at her and Lili studies him, searching for a sign that his invitation is a rash one, one he'll regret in a day's time. But his face is open, his blue-gray irises now focused, calm.

She shakes her head, unsure of what to say.

"Just—promise you'll think about it," Thomas says. His fingers are warm. She can feel his pulse beating gently beneath his skin.

Lili takes a breath. "I will," she says. "I'll think about it."

CHAPTER FORTY-NINE

BOLOGNA

May 1945

Lili stares bleary-eyed from the living-room window, contemplating a walk. Outside, the sky is heavy with clouds. She moves her chin in circles, stretching out her neck. She's barely slept in the four days since Thomas returned, and she's begun to feel disoriented, as if her life belonged to someone else and she's watching it unfold from several meters above. She's tempted to take a nap, but she'll feel better, she knows, if she gets out. She needs some fresh air to fill her lungs, clear her mind.

"Oh, that one's swell," Thomas says, from down the hall. "He's a beauty." He and Theo must be drawing, Lili thinks. She can still hear the elation in Theo's voice from the morning after Thomas arrived, when she told him there was a surprise waiting for him in the spare bedroom; he'd bounded out of bed, and Lili was certain he'd wake the neighbors with his shrieks: **THOMAS! Thomas is here!** The pair has been inseparable since, their days spent in perpetual motion. Yesterday, they entertained each other for an afternoon at the Giardini Margherita, kicking the football and searching for frogs down by the canal and building elaborate cities of sticks and rocks, while Lili watched from a nearby bench with a book in hand. At home, they play round after round of War, they read and they draw. When Theo learned that Thomas hadn't received his pictures, he drew them again. Thomas taught Theo how to sketch a baseball diamond, a jeep, an eagle. Every day it's something new.

All the while, Lili observes, turning Thomas's invitation over in her mind. She hasn't brought it up and Thomas hasn't asked about it, but the proposition is there, dangling between them, impossible to ignore. It feels ridiculous to consider it. And even if she **did**, what would her father say? Putting the distance of the Atlantic between herself and Massimo felt too far, too bold. And what would a move to the States mean for her and Thomas? Would she be agreeing to **marry** him? It sounded like something out of a romance novel, to run off and wed a man she met during the war. Like a made-up love story. Was it though? They'd spent only a few months together, but those months were important. They'd dodged an enemy together, shared the singular mission of staying alive.

In the kitchen, Lili makes herself a cup of tea. Maybe it's not their relationship that's giving her pause, she thinks. Maybe it's her. The fact that if she followed him to the States, she'd be putting her life, her future, her fate—Theo's too—in his hands, relying on him for everything. And for the last year and a half, every decision, every move, every measure to keep herself and Theo safe, has been hers and hers alone. Is she even capable any longer of trusting her fate to someone else? She wishes she and Thomas and Theo could just live in this moment together, without obligation, without talk of what's next. But Thomas is due in Naples in three days. With every passing hour, Lili's heart grows more twisted, her thoughts more jumbled.

Carrying her teacup, she follows the sound of Thomas's and Theo's voices to the dining room.

"Hey there," Thomas says, standing as she enters.

"Hello," Lili says, resting a hand at the back of Theo's chair. "Don't let me interrupt." Thomas slips back into his seat, glances up at her before returning his attention to Theo. They haven't so much as brushed shoulders since the night Thomas came back. Lili has slept in her bed with Theo as always, Thomas in the spare room that used to be her parents'. Lili told him she needed her space, emotional and physical, in order to think about his invitation. It's taken a surprising amount of strength to ignore her own wishes—her insides burn at the thought of being with him—but she's held her ground and kept her distance, and she appreciates that Thomas has done the same.

"Look at my horse!" Theo cries, and Lili leans to have a closer look.

"Surely someone else must have drawn that," she says, teasing.

"No, it was me! Thomas teached me. See, he's galloping. It's the same word in English, you know, **gallop**."

"Thomas **taught** you. I love it."

"I'm drawing a **leone** now," he pronounces. "In English you call it **lion**. It almost sounds the same! Not like **cavallo**. Horse is different."

Lili smiles, impressed with Theo's growing vocabulary. "I can't wait to see." She turns to Thomas. "If it's all right with you, I'll step out. I need to run a few errands. I'll be back in an hour, two at most."

"Of course," Thomas says. "Take your time."

Lili reaches into the closet for her mother's old trench coat and an umbrella. As she leaves the building, she inhales the cool, damp air and pauses, considering where to go. She hasn't any real errands to run. In fact, she has nowhere to be; she's just hoping some time on her own will help her to think. She loops her purse over her shoulder and heads west, toward the university.

A light mist gathers on her cheeks, though Lili

is too caught up in the question nagging at her to notice. Why hadn't she simply told Thomas **no** in the moment? It would have been easy to do so, and the decision would have been made. They could put it behind them and simply enjoy their few days together. Now, though, because she hadn't turned him down straightaway, she's begun to consider it: A future together. A clean start. A safe haven for herself, for Theo. She can almost picture it. But then her breath catches. How could she move so far from her homeland and from her father, especially after all she went through to find him? And what if—somehow, by some miracle—Esti came looking for her in Bologna?

Lili sighs. When she looks around, she realizes she's passed the university and is a block from the Jewish cemetery. She hasn't been back to her mother's grave since returning to Bologna; she'd thought about visiting on several occasions, but posing as Aryan, she didn't want to chance it. Her feet guide her to the tall brick entranceway, and as she walks the familiar pebbled path to Naomi's plot, she feels a drop on her shoulder, and then another on her nose. She unfurls her umbrella.

The sky opens, and Lili listens to the sound of the rainfall around her. Maybe it's the ache of sadness, of missing her mother. Maybe it's the solitude, or the feeling of being cocooned beneath her umbrella, protected. Maybe it's fatigue. Whatever the case, she's relieved to feel her mind finally start to settle. She comes to a stop at Naomi's headstone. It's too wet to sit on the nearby bench, so she stands, staring at the sleek marble glistening in the rain and wishing she'd brought flowers.

Mammina, she says silently. **I wish you were here.** If she could talk everything through with her mother, she'd feel better. She'd be able to make some sense of her situation. Lili had considered calling her father for advice, but the conversation required more than the few minutes she was able to afford with him on a telephone, and anyhow, Lili knows the decision of what to do, of which path to take, is up to her. It's a choice, like the ones that came before it, she'll need to make on her own.

The rain comes harder now. It bats at her umbrella and splashes from the patch of scrub grass beneath her feet onto the toes of her leather loafers, speckling them dark brown. She should move before she's soaked, take shelter beneath the branches of a cedar, or return home, dry off. But she's just gotten here. She watches the rainwater gather and curl at her feet, and as it seeps through the seam of one of her shoes, a profound sorrow rises from the base of her gut, climbs up into her chest. When it reaches her throat, she tries to swallow it down, as she has before—she's grown adept over the years at keeping her grief at bay—but the pain has been building, she realizes, surprised by its force, and now it's greater than she can manage.

Alone in the cemetery, Lili cries. She closes her

eyes and opens her throat and lets the sadness flood through her. Hot tears stream down her cheeks and fall in heavy drops into the cold wet below. She cries for Esti. For Niko. For the Jews all over Europe. For the soldiers and civilians and the partisans and the resisters and the women and men and children and elderly who've suffered and lost their lives, or the lives of loved ones. She cries for the life she thought she'd lead. And she cries for Theo. For the fact that his childhood has been wracked by war, that he knows nothing of stability, of safety, of normalcy—and that despite the Allies' declaration of peace, his earliest childhood memories will forever be of bombed-out cities and severed families, of fighting and loss and hunger and destruction. She cries for it all.

When she has nothing left, Lili blinks open her eyes. Bringing a hand to her belly, she breathes in a lungful of air, then releases it slowly, feeling her shoulders drop in the process. She inhales again, and then again, until her breath steadies. **What would you do, Mama, if you were in my shoes?** she wonders. She glances down at her rain-splattered loafers—her mother's—aware of the irony. Reaching under her collar for her pendant, she holds the gold flower between her fingers. The blossom of an almond tree. A symbol of renewal, as Naomi told her all those years ago when she gave it to her. Of hope. Would you spend the foreseeable future raising Theo on your own in Bologna,

Mama? Searching for answers, knowing that you may come up empty—or that when the answers **do** surface, they likely won't be the ones you'd hoped for? Would you move to Switzerland, to be near Papà and what's left of our family? Or would you consider trailing a man you've just met across the Atlantic, starting a new life, a new family, giving yourself the chance to love—to be loved? Lili stares at her mother's headstone, willing it to produce the answers she needs, willing Naomi's voice to whisper some sage advice in her ear. But the only sound filling the space around her is the drum of raindrops deflecting overhead.

She licks her lips, salty from her tears, and wipes at her eyes.

"I love you, Mama," she says.

She nods, then turns, walking slowly in the direction she'd come.

CHAPTER FIFTY

BOLOGNA

May 1945

Lili wakes to the lilt of conversation. She sits up in bed, rubs the sleep from her eyes, and when she listens closely, she can hear Theo coaching as Thomas reads aloud in Italian from **Strega Nona**, one of her old childhood books, a family favorite. She pads to her armoire, slips her dressing robe from a hook on the inside of the door. As she ties the belt around her waist, a glint of metal catches her eye. She bends to have a closer look, realizing it's the brass corner of her valise. She'd stashed it at the back of the wardrobe when she arrived in Bologna. She reaches instinctively for the handle, cracked and worn and loose now at the hinges. How far had she carried this bag, she wonders, setting it on the bed—a thousand kilometers? Two thousand? The metal clasps make a familiar snapping sound as she unlatches them.

She'd left Esti's things tucked away in the lining of the valise, which she'd sewn back up in Rome after delivering Father Niccacci's parcel. She told herself they were safe there, that she'd return them once she reunited with her friend, refusing to consider the possibility that the keepsakes she shuttled up and down Italy's boot might be all she has left of her. Now, she stares at the hidden compartment, a part of her feeling guilty for not opening it sooner, the other part terrified of the emotions Esti's belongings might evoke in her. She pauses, takes a breath, then plucks at a thread and pulls. The seam separates easily. She slips her hand into the lining.

Her fingers find the lump of Esti's jewelry pouch first. She removes it, lays it on the bed, then feels around for the diary, extracting it slowly, carefully. Lowering herself to sit on the edge of her bed, she props the book on her lap, runs a finger over the **E** embossed on its leather cover.

A small stack of photographs falls from the diary onto the bed when she opens it. Lili picks them up. The first is a photo she took, of Esti on her wedding day; Esti is laughing, her eyes closed, mouth wide. Niko is beside her, dapper in his three-piece suit, his arm around her waist. The next photo is of Theo, swaddled, asleep in his bassinet, his cheeks round, his lips a perfect cupid's bow, his dark hair poking out from beneath a white knit hat. The third is of Esti with her parents, standing in bathing suits in front of their beachfront cabana in Rhodes, their feet hidden in the sand. And the last—the last is of Lili and Esti, seated next to each other at Al Brindisi in Ferrara, each with a glass in hand, the candle at the center of the table burned to a nub. It was taken the night they celebrated Esti and Niko's engagement. Their smiles are carefree, their cheeks flushed. Lili studies the photo, the evening still sharp in her mind: the hours-long dinner; the slow walk through town after, to the city walls; the surface of the Po River from their perch on the **bastioni**, a perfect reflection of the stars above; the tang of Lambrusco at the back of her throat; the sound of Esti's voice, like a balm, insisting Mussolini's new manifest was just a formality, nothing to worry about.

Lili arranges the photos into a pile on the bed, then returns to the diary. The few times she was tempted to read it—anything to feel closer to her friend—she resisted. It felt like an invasion of privacy. She'll just skim an entry or two, she tells herself now, holding her breath as she flips to the first page. The words, the loose familiar handwriting, are so distinctly **Esti**. She exhales.

Antonia, from art history class, Esti writes in the spring of '39, **has stopped speaking to me. I suppose it's because I'm Jewish, although I'll never know, because she's grown skilled at putting the width of the classroom between us. Every now and then, I sneak up on her as we're being dismissed, just to see the expression on her face when I ask, brightly, "How are things?" then laugh as she**

ducks her head and scurries out the door like a spooked little rat.

And then, in December of '40: **How does something so little consume so damn much? This baby never stops eating! Why didn't anyone warn me about the pain? My nipples are so sore I've begun walking around the flat shirtless. Poor Niko isn't sure what to make of it. A friend suggested I line my brassiere with cabbage. Cabbage! I suppose I should give it a try, but it sounds ridiculous to walk around with leaves stuck to your breasts, if you ask me.**

Lili thumbs through the weeks leading up to their decision to leave Ferrara, to live in Nonantola, to move to Florence. She knew Esti kept a diary, had fallen asleep on many occasions to the scratch of her pen on paper, but she didn't realize the extent to which she'd recorded her life—their lives. She flips to the last entry. It's from the day Lili and Theo left Florence. The day Carità's gang stormed the convent. Esti's handwriting is distinctly different, and Lili tries to recall which hand was injured in the attack. It must have been her right, from the look of her jagged penmanship. The words are barely legible. Lili summons the courage to read on.

Lili left with Theo today, Esti writes. **She left because of me. It was the hardest thing I've ever done, sending them away.**

Lili's eyes well. She'd thought so much about her own gut-wrenching experience that night, she hadn't considered how impossible it must have been for Esti to force her plan upon her, to decide—hope—her son would be safer in her hands.

Lili tried to convince me she couldn't go it alone, but she can. She will. She's so much more capable than she thinks. I could hear Theo crying outside the door when they left. It was all I could do not to claw my way to him. I hate that it's come to this. But it's the only way. And there's no one I trust more than Lili to keep my son safe. If I die in this godforsaken convent, I'll die at peace, knowing he's in her hands.

A tear slides down Lili's cheek and onto the page. She wipes at it with her finger, smudging the ink in the process, then curses. She reads the entry once more and stands, holding the diary to her chest as she paces the length of her bed, her heart knocking at her ribs. She braces herself for the onslaught of dizzying, unanswerable questions she knows will come—but rather than spinning into an incoherent blur, her thoughts begin to slow, playing out before her with startling clarity. She moves to the window, peers down at the brick frame where a neighboring building once stood.

All this time, she thinks, it's been one or the other: the chance at a new life for her and for Theo, or the chance to find her friend. But—what if she doesn't have to choose? What if starting over doesn't have to mean giving up? What if it simply means moving forward? It's what she's done since setting off on her own. She's kept moving. Pressed on, day after day, week after week, month after month. The weight of loss and uncertainty has been unbearable at times, but she's carried it. She continues to carry it. And she's persevered, in a way she didn't know she could. She's survived.

Esti's words ring in her ears. **There's no one I trust more than Lili to keep my son safe.**

Lili turns the diary over in her hands. If she were to agree to go with Thomas to the States, she'd be stepping again into a succession of unknowns. She can barely place the state of Virginia on a map. And she certainly can't predict what might become of her and Thomas. But she would be safe. Secure. She'd be building a new foundation, on solid ground. Theo would have the chance at a normal childhood, would grow up in the comfort of a single home, where he could learn and play and start anew, too, with a father figure who would love him as if he were his own son. Who already does.

Outside, a sparrow flies by. It disappears then circles back, lands at the top of a wrought-iron streetlamp, cocks its head. Lili swallows. Thomas leaves in two days. She'll spend the next twenty-four hours, she decides, opening her heart to the idea of a move. She'll sit with it, see how she feels in the morning. Give it one more day, she tells herself. You'll know what to do. Your body will tell you. Just listen.

CHAPTER FIFTY-ONE

BOLOGNA

May 1945

The next morning, Lili lies quietly in bed, waiting for Theo to stir.

"Hello, sweet boy," she says when he wakes.

"Hi," Theo says in English. He smiles. She's seen much more of his dimples since Thomas stepped back into their lives.

Lili sits up, crosses her legs in front of her. She pats the bed for Theo to do the same. "I have a question for you, love," she says. "An important one."

"Okay." Theo's knees brush hers, his expression suddenly serious.

Lili has spent the last hour practicing the conversation in her mind, certain she'd be anxious in this moment. But her breath is steady, her voice calm.

"You know how Thomas has to leave soon, to return to America . . ." Theo's gaze falls to his lap.

He nods. "Well, he's . . . invited us to go with him." Lili pauses, letting this settle.

Theo looks up, eyes wide. "Really?"

"Really. He wants to take us to his home in Virginia. And the thing is," Lili says gently, "he's invited us to go there not just to visit, but to stay."

Theo tips his head. "To stay?"

"To live there."

"Together?"

"Yes. Together, the three of us. You could go to school. We would meet his family."

Theo blinks twice, scratches at his temple.

"There's a lot we don't know about life in America," Lili says. "Everything will feel new. But we'd be safe there. And I think happy too. And . . . I want you to know, Theo, that if we go, I'd keep looking for your mother while we're there. Thomas could help. And if we miss home, Italy will be here. We could come back whenever we want."

Theo reaches for his lamb, half hidden under a pillow. He tucks it into the space between his legs. "When would we go?" he asks.

"We'd leave soon. In a couple days, maybe. But Theo, before we decide, I want you to tell me how you feel about it."

Theo looks away, staring for a moment out the window. Outside, the spring sky is a pale blue. The birds have taken up their morning chatter. "Will I have friends in America?" Theo asks.

"I'm sure you'd make plenty of friends. Thomas's nephew, Steve, for one."

Theo's eyes find Lili's again. "Would **Nonno** Massimo come with us?"

"Maybe. To visit, at least."

Theo nods. He sits up a little taller. "I want to go."

His words land with a conviction that reminds Lili of Esti's. She smiles.

"Do **you** want to go?" Theo asks.

"I—" It hadn't occurred to her that Theo would care about what she wanted. "I appreciate you asking me that, love. I've been thinking long and hard about it, and, well—if you want to go, then yes, I'd like to go too."

A smile stretches across Theo's face, broad and toothy. "It will be an adventure," he says, and Lili laughs.

"It will be."

"I'm going to tell Thomas!" Theo cries, on his knees suddenly, twitching with energy.

"Let's tell him together," Lili says. "Will you let me do the talking first?"

THEY FIND THOMAS AT THE BREAKFAST TABLE IN the kitchen, a book open before him.

"Morning," he says, standing.

"Good morning." Lili rests a hand on Theo's shoulders. Theo glances up at her.

"Tell him," he whispers.

Lili gives his shoulders a squeeze. "Theo and I have been talking," she says, knowing if she waits to share her news, Theo will do it for her. "And we were wondering if your offer still stands." She pauses, watching Thomas's face closely.

"You mean—the offer to come home with me to the States?" His eyes jump from her to Theo and back.

"Yes. That one."

Theo bounces in place. "We go to **America**!" he cries, in English, and Thomas claps his hands once, throws his head back, and laughs as his surprise melts into joy. Lili laughs too, and before she can say any more, Thomas's arms are around her. He pulls her close, then reaches for Theo, spinning them both around in a circle. Theo squeals.

"So that's a yes?" Lili asks, when they finally part.

"Yes! Yes. Of course, yes." Thomas is crying. Lili is too.

"Happy tears," she tells Theo, wiping them away.

America. She'd woken that morning knowing she would go. And now that Theo is so excited, any remaining doubt in her mind has evaporated.

"You have no idea how happy this makes me," Thomas says, rubbing at an eye with the heel of his hand.

"We can talk more in private," Lili says. It will be nice, she thinks, to have a moment with him alone.

"About the . . . planning of it all. I'm sure there will be plenty to do, to prepare."

"I'll take care of everything," Thomas says, and Lili smiles at the prospect of him sharing the weight of decision-making.

Theo climbs into the chair where Thomas was sitting. "What is this book?" he asks. Now that his future has been decided, he's on to more important things.

"I was looking for something to read this morning and found it in the living room," Thomas says. He flips through a couple of the pages, and Lili recognizes it as a collection of images by a photographer named Ansel Adams. A gift to Massimo from Esti, from before the war.

"They're photos from America," Lili says.

"Can we go **there**?" Theo asks, pointing to a photo captioned **Half Dome, Yosemite.**

"Sure, buddy," Thomas says. "Anywhere you wish."

CHAPTER FIFTY-TWO

BOLOGNA

May 1945

Thomas was meant to depart from Naples with a group of fellow Rangers on a military transport ship, but instead requested permission from the army to travel with Lili and Theo on a passenger liner leaving the following week. Their ship, the S/S **Campagna,** will take them to New York, then they'll continue by train to Virginia. Lili has no idea what kind of strings Thomas had to pull to secure three tickets on the **Campagna** so last minute, but she's grateful for the effort as it's allowed them to travel together, and it's given her a few extra days in Bologna to get packed.

She's filled two of her parents' old trunks with the things she hopes will be useful in the States: her nicest clothes (most of which were her mother's), her purple coat, which she'd carefully washed and hung to dry, and a new pair of pants, a shirt, and some shiny new shoes for Theo, purchased with the help of one of Thomas's twenty-dollar bills. She's packed some sentimental things as well: the floral cotton pillowcase she'd slept on since she was a child, its crimson petals faded to pink; her mother's book of Rilke poetry; the sheet music for Scarlatti's **Sonata in D Minor**—she'd played the piece once in a high school recital; perhaps she and Thomas will own a piano someday, she thinks, and she'll relearn it. She brings one of Massimo's handkerchiefs, embroidered with his initials, along with his Tuscan landscape, its canvas rolled up in a scarf. She'll reframe it in Virginia. Of her mother's belongings she's packed the silk dressing robe—her own threadbare cotton one she'll leave behind—along with the photo album Lili had brought from Ferrara, the five photos she carried with her throughout the war slipped back into their empty spaces.

Now, she ambles through the apartment, reaching for last-minute additions, convincing herself they're small enough to stow in what little space her trunks still offer: a few spice jars; her favorite set of espresso cups; her mother's recipe tin; an unopened bottle of her grandfather's grappa—a suitable gift, she hopes, for Thomas's parents. She laments the things that are too big to bring: the dining table, the Persian rug in the foyer, the antique mirror—each with a lifetime of memories attached to it. In the living room, she pauses to run her hands along the patina of her father's favorite wingback armchair. How easily, she realizes with a pang of longing, she can picture him there, sitting with his familiar loose posture, legs crossed, a newspaper in hand.

The day before, Lili had borrowed Settimo's telephone to call her father. It pained her to tell him from such a distance about her plans, but she knew she couldn't leave without his blessing. He listened while she tried to put to words, as succinctly as possible, her decision. When she was through, he asked her only one question: **Are you happy?** She told him she was, and he replied, **Well then, I support you, wholeheartedly. You deserve all the happiness in the world, Babà.** After that, Lili felt better. The call was expensive—she had time to share only the highlights—but she promised to call again from the States and told him to expect a letter in the coming weeks, explaining everything.

She's scripted that letter a dozen times over in her head. In it, she's decided, she'll include the details of how she and Thomas met and how easily they got on, right from the start; how he took immediately to Theo and Theo to him; how empty she felt when he was called back to duty and how surprisingly full when he returned; how he was a writer, too, and an aspiring actor and how she appreciated his kindness, his honesty, and how he wore his emotions unabashedly on his sleeve. She'll describe how she resisted the idea at first, when Thomas proposed she return with him to the States, but then realized the opportunity—for stability, for love—was too great to turn down. **I have to give this a chance**, she'll say. **Whatever** this **is. It's hard to describe at the moment, just that it feels right.**

Lili is still standing at the back of her father's armchair when she hears the door open and close— Thomas and Theo, home from the park. "In here," she calls.

"Just me!" a voice hollers in reply.

"Oh! Settimo! Be right there." Lili hums under her breath as she makes her way to the foyer, where she finds Settimo standing by the door with a funny look on his face. "Hello," she says.

"Special delivery," Settimo replies, grinning as he steps aside. Lili stares.

"Papà?"

Massimo drops his suitcase and takes two giant strides toward her, and it's not until he's holding her that Lili truly believes it's him. "Papà!" she says again, laughing into his shoulder. "What are you doing here?"

"I couldn't let you leave without a proper good-bye," he says, holding her at arm's length.

"But—how did you get here so quickly?"

"The train! How else?"

It's a foreign concept now, Lili realizes, the ease of train travel. She points an accusing finger at Settimo. "You knew he was coming?"

"He phoned me yesterday, told me when he'd be in."

"But how did you manage to keep such a secret?"

Settimo raises his palms to the ceiling. "It wasn't easy."

Lili shakes her head. "Come in, both of you."

"You have some catching up to do," Settimo says. "I'll leave you to it."

Lili doesn't argue. She'd love nothing more than a few minutes with her father before Thomas and Theo burst in. "Come back for dinner then?" she suggests.

"I'd love to."

Settimo leaves and Lili and Massimo move to the living room, where Lili deposits her father on the sofa. She fetches them both a glass of wine.

"Where's Theo?" Massimo asks. "It's too quiet in here."

"Thomas took him to the park so I could pack," Lili says. "They should be back any minute. Theo will be over the moon to see you! Thomas too."

Massimo smiles. "The excitement is mutual."

"I can't believe you came," Lili says, lifting her glass.

"I had to see you, Babà. And to hear more about Thomas, and about your plans." He brings his glass to Lili's. "Tell me everything."

WHEN THOMAS AND THEO RETURN THIRTY MIN-utes later, Lili hurries to the door to greet them, whispering the news of her father's surprise arrival in Thomas's ear and watching his eyes go wide.

"Here? Now?" he says. Lili nods and takes his hand.

"There's someone here to see you," she tells Theo. "In the living room. Go ahead, we'll be right behind you."

Theo dashes off and his shrill **Nonno!** upon discovering Massimo travels down the hallway and into the foyer. Lili turns to Thomas. "Ready?"

Thomas clears his throat. He glances at the mirror, smooths his hair, adjusts his collar. "Ready as I ever will be," he says.

They walk hand in hand to the living room, where they find Theo sitting on Massimo's lap, regaling him with a story about the salamander he and Thomas had found under a rock in the park.

"You'll have to take me back and show me," Massimo says. He glances up at Lili and Thomas, shifting Theo onto the sofa as he stands. "You must be Thomas," he says, surprising Lili with his English. She knew he could speak the language, but it's warming, hearing the words from his mouth.

Thomas extends a hand, his posture military straight. Lili can tell from the way her father's arm moves up and down that his shake is robust.

"**Signor Passigli. Molto piacere!** It's an honor to meet you."

Lili smiles at the two men greeting each other in their respective languages—a show of respect.

"The pleasure is mine," Massimo says. "You speak Italian."

"**Un poco**. Lili and Theo are excellent teachers."

Massimo glances at Lili and she shrugs. Despite his best efforts, Thomas can't for the life of him roll his r's. But his vocabulary is on par with Theo's now, and that is something.

"I hope you don't mind the intrusion," Massimo says.

"What? No! It's your home, sir."

Massimo looks around. "A home from another lifetime." He says this without sentiment.

"**Nonno**, I have something to show you," Theo says, an arm curled around Massimo's leg. "I'll be right back. In **one minute**," he adds, showing off his English, and Massimo arches his brow, impressed.

Lili, Thomas, and Massimo are quiet for a moment, listening to Theo's footfall as he races from the room.

"I'll be right back too," Lili says. She steps into the kitchen and returns a moment later with a third glass of wine. "**Cin cin**," she says, handing the glass to Thomas and raising her own. She, Thomas, and Massimo touch rims, take a sip. Theo darts back into the room with his drawings and his pad.

"You really made all these pictures yourself?" Massimo asks, admiring Theo's creations as Lili and Thomas look on.

"Thomas taught me," Theo says.

"They're wonderful, Theo. Can I take one home with me to Switzerland?"

Theo thinks hard about this, his tongue curled over his lip. He shuffles through his drawings, selecting one of a striped, four-legged animal with a long tail and a circle around it.

"Here," he says, handing the drawing to Massimo.

"Thanks," Massimo says. "Is it a tiger?"

"He's jumping through a ring, see? He's at the circus."

Lili's throat tightens. She'd told Theo only once about the tiger she'd seen when her father took her to the circus. He'd been listening that day on the road.

Massimo glances at Lili, and she can tell that he remembers too. "I love it." he says.

"Theo, why don't you draw us something new," Lili says. "Maybe another animal from the circus?"

"How about an elephant?" Thomas suggests, reaching into his shirt pocket for his pencil. He hands it to Theo, who, excited to have been given the challenge, settles himself at the coffee table with his pad of paper. Around him, the adults fall into conversation.

"You traveled from Switzerland?" Thomas asks Massimo.

"Just got here a half hour ago. Settimo picked me up at the station."

"You can imagine my surprise when he walked in," Lili says.

"I bet. So you've had a moment to catch up?"

"We have. Though I feel like we've barely scratched the surface," Lili says.

"Your English is so good," Thomas tells Massimo.

"It's improved of late," Massimo says. "The bookstore where I work in Bern sells a few English editions. I picked one up a couple of months ago and couldn't put it down. Helped to bring the language back, I think."

"Which book was it?" Thomas asks. "If you don't mind me asking."

"It was **A Farewell to Arms**."

Thomas smiles. "Hemingway. My mother loved that book. She gave me her copy; I haven't read it yet but it's waiting for me on my bookshelf in Richmond."

"I hope you enjoy it as much as I did," Massimo says.

They talk about favorite titles and favorite films. Eventually, the topic shifts to the war.

"Did Lili tell you she saved my life?" Thomas asks. Lili shakes her head.

"She didn't mention it, no," Massimo says, intrigued.

"He's exaggerating," Lili says. "Thomas is a writer—of many things, including fiction."

"True," Thomas admits, turning to smile at her. "Though it's not an exaggeration."

Massimo crosses his legs and leans back in his chair. "Well," he says. "It sounds like there's a story there. I'd love to hear it."

MASSIMO HAS PLANS TO STAY FOR THREE NIGHTS. HE sleeps a floor below, in a spare bedroom of Settimo's (much to Thomas's protest, though Lili doesn't mind the privacy). The days pass in a blur of laughter and conversation and meals and long walks in the park. Life, despite the backdrop of the war-torn city, feels strangely benign. Lili has to remind herself often that it's all about to change.

On Massimo's last night, she finds him in the kitchen, leaning against the counter. Thomas is putting Theo to bed, so it's just the two of them, the apartment quiet.

"What are you thinking about?" Lili asks, moving to stand beside him.

"Your mother," Massimo says, looking around, and Lili smiles. "She was so happy in here with her sleeves rolled up to her elbows, her apron a mess. She loved to cook."

"I've been dreaming of her carbonara," Lili says, picturing her mother at the stove, a slotted wooden spoon in hand, her fingers dusted with grated Parmesan.

"There was nothing better."

Lili leans into her father. "What will you do with this place?" she asks.

"I'll sell it. It's time. We don't need it any longer."

It makes sense to sell the apartment, Lili knows, but it saddens her to think of it no longer being theirs. It's the only home she's ever known. "You don't think you'd ever move back?" she asks.

"I don't. But I'm okay with that. Are you okay with that?"

Lili nods, realizing she is. "I am."

"I'm going to ask Settimo to list it when you leave. You and Thomas can use the money to put a down payment on a house in Virginia."

"No, Papà. The money's yours. You keep it, you'll need it."

"I won't. My life is simple, love. You'd be surprised how little I need to get by."

"Thomas will support us," Lili says. Thomas had made a list of the various positions he could take in Richmond—he'd pursue his writing and acting on the side, he told her, until they'd saved enough to feel secure, settled.

"Of course he will."

"I love him, Father."

"I know, Babà."

Massimo's shoulder is warm against Lili's. "I missed you so much during the war, Papà," Lili says. "I worried about you. It's hard to imagine being so far apart again."

Massimo takes her hand. "I know."

"Do you think I'm crazy to leave? It feels like such a leap. It feels . . . unlike me. And Theo—to take him away, not knowing for sure what's happened to either of his parents. Not having any definite answers . . ."

"I think you'd be crazy not to go," Massimo says.

"Really?"

"Really. You can't put your life on hold forever. And—I know this isn't what you want to hear,

Babà, but you may never find the answers you're looking for."

Lili knows in her heart this is true. But still, it's almost impossible to fathom it. Not knowing. Ever.

"You're doing the right thing," Massimo says, and Lili nods, wipes a tear from her eye. "I don't think I'm supposed to mention this," Massimo says gently. "Apparently it's an American custom to keep it secret, but . . ."

"But what?"

"Thomas asked for my permission to marry you, Babà."

Lili's heart somersaults. "He did? When?"

"Yesterday, while you were giving Theo a bath. He promised he wouldn't rush it—he knows it's still new, and the move will be a lot on you. But he said he's loved you for a long time. That a part of him knew he'd marry you the day you let him into your apartment in Rome."

"And what did you say?" Lili asks.

Creases form around Massimo's eyes. "I told him you'd come into each other's lives for a reason. And that I hadn't seen you this happy in a very long time."

Lili smiles. It's true.

"He's a good soul, Lili," Massimo says.

"Thank you," Lili whispers.

"For what?"

"For coming here. And for saying that. About Thomas. It means a lot."

"Well. I wouldn't miss sending you off. I'm happy for you, Lili. Truly."

They are quiet for a moment.

"This isn't a goodbye," Massimo says after a while. "It's **arrivederci**. Until we see each other again."

NAPLES

May 1945

Lili moves steadily with a throng of bodies along a pier in Naples harbor, one hand snug around Theo's, the other around the handle of her valise. Thomas follows a few paces behind between a pair of porters he hired to transport Lili's trunks. He'd offered to carry her valise, but Lili insisted she could manage. As much as she'd cursed its weight over the last year, the old leather bag, with its scratched-up surface and its dented brass corner plates and its handle worn smooth from overuse, feels almost like an extension of her. She'd packed it with her most important things—items she wanted to keep close so she could reach them at any moment if she needed to: Theo's lamb, his marble; the deck of cards Thomas had given him; **Pinocchio** and **Strega Nona** and a picture book from Switzerland that Massimo brought from the bookshop in Bern; her fountain pen and some parchment, so she could write to her father from the ship. Even though there was no reason any longer to hide her valuables, she'd sewn her grandmother's silver, her own bracelets and earrings, along with Esti's jewelry and her diary, back into the lining of the valise—it's habit now, she can't help herself.

She'd spent the evenings before they'd left writing notes to the people who had helped her when she had nowhere else to turn—to Adelmo and Eva (making a point to thank Eva for the treasure of the purple coat), to Aldo and Sister Lotte and Cardinal Dalla Costa in Florence, to Father Niccacci and Isabella in Assisi. She wishes she'd recorded addresses for the farmers in San Terenziano, Giovanni and Luisa, and to the widow, Anna, in Torre del Colle, who had taken her in while she was on the road. She wishes she had a way to reach Matilde. It didn't feel right, somehow, to leave Italy without a goodbye, a word of thanks. She gave Thomas's address in the States to the cardinal, Sister Lotte, and Father Niccacci, asking for what felt like the hundredth time to write with news of Esti should they learn anything.

Now, she stares up at the S/S **Campagna** as they near, awed by the ocean liner's imposing prow, by its massive anchor, by the neat row of portholes along its gleaming white side. Overhead, the sky is clear, the late spring sun warm on her cheeks. She glances behind her and catches Thomas's eye. He grins and she smiles, curious if his heart is beating as fast as hers.

"Let's make our way to the bow," Thomas says once they've climbed the gangplank and Lili's trunks have been stowed.

Lili turns to Theo. "What do you think, love, shall we go to the front of the ship?" She speaks in English, so Thomas can follow.

"**Andiamo!**" Theo cries.

They snake their way across the ship's crowded deck and find an empty spot by the railing. Lili sets down her valise and squints into the sun, taking in the steady, salty breeze. An hour passes, and then another, as more and more passengers pile onboard. Women and children outnumber the men. Most speak Italian but some converse in other languages: French, German, Polish, Dutch. Their tones are hushed, saturated with a sense of nervous anticipation. Of nostalgia. Of hope. Lili wonders how many are carrying one-way tickets, as she, Thomas, and Theo are. She wonders about the lives being left behind.

Finally, the ship's horn sounds.

"Loud!" Theo yells, in English, his hands pressed to his ears.

"Wait till you meet my nephew," Thomas jokes, and Theo smiles. He knows the word **nephew**. In the last several days, he's talked constantly of Steve, whom he calls **Stefano**, giddy at the prospect of a boy, a friend, his age.

The horn sounds again, long and throaty, and as the ship's engines rumble to life, Lili watches the water below churn turquoise. Finally, they push away from the pier.

"And, we're off," Thomas says.

Lili lifts Theo to her hip, and Thomas wraps an arm around her shoulder. They stand together leaning into the rail, and into each other, watching a pair of gulls circle overhead.

"Are we going to go any faster?" Theo asks. He looks at Lili and blinks his thick lashes, his eyes—Esti's eyes—startlingly blue in the light of the sun, looming large in the western sky.

"Once we get out of the harbor we will," Lili says.

"How many sleeps till we get to New York?"

"Seven."

"And then how many to **Ginia**?" Theo talks as if he's been to these places before. As if they were already a part of his vernacular.

Lili looks to Thomas.

"Just one," he says. "Unless we stay a night or two in New York. It would be a shame to pass through without exploring a little."

"You understood all of that," Lili says, brows arched.

"Most of it." Thomas's face is open, his eyes bright. He looks handsome—more alive than she's ever seen him.

"I'm hungry," Theo says, and for the briefest moment Lili's heart sinks. How many times she's heard those words—and how she's dreaded them! **You will not go hungry any longer**, she reminds herself. She'd packed some bread and cheese and the ship has a dining lounge, where they will take their meals. Lili checks her watch. It's almost five.

"Why don't we find something to eat?" Thomas asks.

Lili lets Theo slide from her hip, and Thomas takes his hand. "If it's all right," she says, "I'll stay here." She isn't hungry, and she's not ready yet to venture indoors.

Thomas looks to Theo. "What do you say, captain, shall we go scout out the dining options, find you a snack?"

"**Si!**" Theo says, and then in English, "Let's go!"

"We'll be back," Thomas says, and Lili nods, smiling as she watches them zigzag through the crowd, then disappear.

She turns to the sea, rests her hands on the white metal rail, cold and smooth beneath her fingers. The wind picks up, blowing a long strand of freshly shampooed hair across her face. They're gaining speed now as they leave the harbor, the coastline slipping away. Soon, it'll be gone. Her life. Her Italy. **If you're listening**, she thinks, sending a silent message toward the peninsula, **I'll keep him safe. I promise.**

The ship rocks gently beneath her. She brings a hand to her throat, finds her mother's gold pendant. Rubbing the coin between her fingers she closes her eyes, feels her mind float back in time—to Naomi on a mountain trail, waving her over as she plucks a pair of daisies to fold into Lili's braids; to her father, skin bronzed by the summer sun, as he shows her how to skip a stone at the beach in Rimini. She can see Niko, just home from a game of football, his hair a sweaty tangle of curls as he holds his six-month-old son overhead. And she can see herself—sprawled beside Esti on a blanket atop Ferrara's walls with a baguette and a bottle of wine; wearing her chartreuse dress on a rooftop restaurant in Rhodes, her hand stretched across the table to meet Esti's; pressed close to her best friend's side in the maternity ward hospital bed, watching Theo's back rise and fall as he sleeps soundly, safely, on her chest. These are the memories, she tells herself, she'll hold close. The ones she'll turn to when she misses home, and that she'll share with Theo and with Thomas too, when the time is right.

She opens her eyes, lets the pendant fall back to the hollow of her neck, its metal warm from her touch. Behind her, the land has disappeared, the only contrast on the horizon the ocean liner's frothy wake, painting wide, curved stripes on the surface of the sea. She turns away from the mainland, toward the dipping sun, listening to the chatter of conversation, the slap of water against the hull, the faint call of a gull from high above, letting her gaze come to rest on the infinite expanse of blue ahead.

ACKNOWLEDGMENTS

Book writing tends to be a solitary act, but there are parts of the process—the brainstorming, the research, the editing, for example—that, for me, are very much a collaboration. I'm indebted to the people who offered their time, insights, and resources to help bring this project to fruition.

First and foremost, **One Good Thing** wouldn't be what it is today without the help of my mother and thought partner, Isabelle. My mother fielded countless questions, joined me in Italy for my research travels, and read every line of every draft of my manuscript a dozen times over (there were many, many drafts). Her sharp eye for detail and honest feedback buoyed me from start to finish. I also want to thank my late father, Tom, who passed along his love of writing and whose cinematic voice still rings clear every time I imagine how a scene might unfold.

The bones of Lili's narrative were pieced together over a lunch with my literary agent, Brettne Bloom, when the idea of writing a second novel was almost too daunting to fathom—her compassion and gentle critique were a constant source of comfort and inspiration and took my work to another, better level. I'm forever grateful for Brettne's friendship, as well as for the support of DJ and all the wonderful women of The Book Group.

My friends at Penguin have worked tirelessly behind the scenes to bring this book to market. Thank you to my brilliant editor, Pamela Dorman, who believed in **One Good Thing** from its inception and whose instincts around plot and pacing are invaluable. Thanks to Marie Michels for the spot-on editorial input, as well as to Andrea Schulz, Brian Tart, Kate Stark, Patrick Nolan, Rebecca Marsh, Julia Rickard, Mary Stone, Ryan Boyle, Nayon Cho, Jason Ramirez, Tricia Conley, Claire Vaccaro, Jane Cavolina, Natalie Grant, Chantal Canales, Kristina Fazzalaro, and Becca Stevenson—I'm overwhelmed by the constant support from this extraordinary team.

Partway through my work on **One Good Thing**, I joined the writers' room for the television adaptation of my first novel, **We Were the Lucky Ones**, where I was introduced to the talents of now-dear friends Erica Lipez, Adam Milch, Eboni Booth, Anya Meksin, Jonathan Caren, and Tea Ho. I'm beholden to this group of remarkable humans for the master class in screenwriting. I've learned so much from each of them.

John Sherman, Jonathan Caren, and Robert Farinholt were among my inner circle of early readers whose vision and encouragement gave me just the motivation and the confidence I needed to keep going. Thank you to fact-checker Carl Schulkin for lending a keen eye to my historical detail, to friends Amanda and Craig, for offering the perfect quiet refuge to put the finishing touches on my manuscript, and to Andrea Carson, once again, for her photographic artistry.

Thanks as well to Jenny Meyer and Heidi Gall for shepherding **One Good Thing** into the hands of readers around the world with such passion, and to Sylvie Rabineau for believing deeply in me and in the relevance of Lili's story today.

Rachel Silvera was a wonderful host during a visit to the Museum of Italian Judaism and the Shoah in Ferrara. Holocaust exhibits in Assisi, Bologna, Florence, and Rome also provided valuable background and visual references. I'm deeply appreciative of Centro Primo Levi, the United States Holocaust Memorial Museum, the Shoah Foundation, Yad Vashem, the Museum of Jewish Heritage, and the New York Public Library for making their extensive texts, records, and interviews available. My research drew me to countless books, representing various viewpoints, including **The Italians and the Holocaust** by Susan Zuccotti;

The Italian Executioners by Simon Levis Sullam; **Road to Valor** by Aili and Andres McConnon; **The Pope at War** by David Kertzer; as well as to the works of Joshua D. Zimmerman, Renzo De Felice, Nicola Caracciolo, Florette Rechnitz Koffler, and Joseph O'Connor, among others.

Finally, a heart full of thanks to the boys I'm lucky enough to come home to every day. To Robert, for the constant outpouring of love and support—the road to publication is long and winding, and I felt your energy and your optimism at every hill and around every turn. And to Wyatt and Ransom—watching you grow into the kind, curious, and courageous souls you are today continues to be the joy of my life. I can't wait to see what the next chapter will bring for all of us. As Lili would say, it'll be an adventure.

AUTHOR'S NOTE

Age three, with my father in Rome

I'm always fascinated by the origin story behind a novel. My own debut, **We Were the Lucky Ones**, was inspired by the discovery, at fifteen, that I came from a family of Holocaust survivors. Unearthing and recording that story took nearly a decade—it was, in every sense, a labor of love. When the book was released and my publisher asked "What's next?," I was at a loss. I knew I wanted to keep writing, but I wasn't sure how to follow a project that felt so deeply personal. I took my time to consider what kind of material I was drawn to, where I'd like to allot my headspace, my heartspace, and I kept coming back to Europe, to the Second World War, and to the untold stories of the Holocaust.

I was drawn to Italy as a setting for many reasons. Although Italy's Jewish community is one of the oldest in Europe, its Holocaust history is relatively unknown. I loved the idea of bringing that narrative to life through the eyes of an ordinary young woman—someone readers today could relate to.

Italy is also the place I credit as the reason for my existence, thanks to the fact that my parents' orbits first crossed in Rome in the early 1970s. My mother was running a clothing business, and my father was in the arts—an actor, director, and writer. Both were American. They met through the expat community, fell in love, and stayed for a combined seventeen years. In the summers, they bounced between Rome and a village on the Mediterranean called Sperlonga, where my mother opened a trattoria. I grew up hearing stories about life in Italy—the food, the culture, the coastline, the energy that was somehow chaotic and laid-back all at once.

I took the first of many trips to Italy at three and spent a college semester abroad in Rome. Today, despite the fact that my bucket list is never-ending, Italy is a country I return to again and again. My most recent visit was in 2021, to research **One Good Thing**. My mother flew over with me, and we traversed the peninsula in our rented Fiat, tracing Lili's footsteps from Ferrara to Nonantola, Bologna, Assisi, Florence, and, of course, Rome.

While Lili's story is imagined, it was important to me to weave as many real-life people and places into her journey as possible. Early on in my research, for example, I was moved to learn about a group of Jewish refugees hidden at a villa in Nonantola, and about how willingly the locals had protected them in their homes when a German invasion was imminent. My heart raced for them as I imagined their middle-of-the-night escape, and I thought, **Now, there's a story I want to tell.** Thanks to the efforts of many volunteers, seventy-one children from the villa made it safely to Switzerland. One young boy, Salomon Papo, was sick in the hospital when the group escaped. He and staff member Goffredo Pacifici were arrested. Tragically, both were killed at Auschwitz.

Gino Bartali was another character I stumbled across in my research. One of Italy's most decorated and beloved cycling champions, Bartali helped to save more than six hundred Jews during the war by smuggling false identification papers in the frame of his racing bike. He never spoke about his heroism. Bartali worked with Cardinal Elia Dalla Costa, the archbishop of Florence, and with Father Rufino Niccacci of the Franciscan Monastery of San Damiano in Assisi, who partnered with local shopkeeper Luigi Brizi to print and distribute the

IDs Bartali carried. Brizi's press, a refurbished Felix hidden at the back of his shop, is now on display in a small museum nearby.

Eva and Adelmo Giardini are based on a real couple from Castelnuovo Berardenga who took in a young Jewish boy, Ettore, during the war. They introduced him to their neighbors as a relative, brought him to church, and treated him as family. Ettore remained with the Giardinis for two years until Italy was liberated in 1945.

Matilde's character is also loosely based on the real-life Matilde Bassani Finzi, one of many young Jewish women to join the Italian resistance. Her work included writing anti-Fascist material, negotiating with Germans, crossing the front lines, and smuggling weapons to partisan groups. I was so impressed by Finzi's courage and ideals, I knew she'd make a cameo in Lili's story.

The characters in **One Good Thing** were inspired by a myriad of individuals rooted in history, but also by people I know and love. I drew many of Esti's traits, for example, from my grandfather's younger sister, Halina, whom we meet in **We Were the Lucky Ones**. Esti's Greek heritage was seeded by a trip I took in 2011 to the island of Rhodes, where, upon getting lost in a cobweb of winding, cobblestoned streets, I stumbled across a beautiful little synagogue—the oldest in Greece. I fell in love with the temple as well as with the island. Years later, in my research for **One Good Thing**, I met a survivor named Stella Levi, who talked about what it was like to grow up on Rhodes and about the fate of the Jews in Greece during the Holocaust (horrific, I learned—the percentage lost near that of Poland's Jews). Several of the details Stella shared are woven throughout Esti's backstory.

Thomas and Massimo were inspired by my own late father, Tom, and by my husband, Robert, both southern gentlemen and two of the kindest, most loving men I know; Theo by my sweet, adventurous boys, Wyatt and Ransom. Lili is a mix of people, including my mother and myself, and in the end, it was Lili's story that kept me going when the writing felt especially challenging. The more time I spent with her on the page as she struggled to cope with the events of the war, as she was forced to summon the strength to press on without any certainty as to what lay ahead, the more deeply I cared for her, the more desperately I wanted her to find a place of happiness. Lili's loyalty to Esti—the sisterly, I'd-do-anything-for-you kind—was also a guiding light, their friendship a reincarnation of the bond I share with my own dearest girlfriends.

It's worth mentioning here that Italy's World War II history is rife with perplexing and contradictory twists and turns, in politics, military tactics, legislation, and leadership—historians still debate the why and the how of what happened. There is much controversy, especially over the role of non-Jewish Italians in the Holocaust. Many see them as resisters, saving lives; others refute the "myth of the good Italian," pointing to the part some played in persecuting their Jewish compatriots. Countless individual churches harbored and protected Jews, but whether the pope could have used his influence to save more lives is also still under discussion. I tried, in my narrative, to make sense of it all and to tell both sides of the story, reminding myself often that the confusion, the murkiness of what was taking place, of what to believe and what not to believe, was very much a part of Lili's own worldview.

I hope that, in **One Good Thing**, I've shed some light on Italy's Holocaust-era past, as well as on what it was like to experience history as it unfolded—not in sepia or in black and white or with the benefit of hindsight, but in the moment, in vivid color. I hope, too, that Lili's story sparks some conversation, perhaps even moves readers to ask, as I did many times over, what they'd have done had they found themselves in her shoes. Or in the shoes of a stranger on the other side of one of the doors Lili knocked on in her struggle to survive. We'll never know, of course. But I can't think of a more important time than now to ask the questions, to imagine. In doing so, we begin to relate. To understand. To empathize. And what a beautiful place the world could be with a bit more understanding, a bit more empathy.

ABOUT THE AUTHOR

When **GEORGIA HUNTER** was fifteen years old, she discovered that she came from a family of Holocaust survivors. Years later, she embarked on a journey of intensive research, determined to unearth and record her family's remarkable story. The result is the **New York Times** bestseller **We Were the Lucky Ones,** which has been published in more than twenty languages and adapted for television by Hulu as a highly acclaimed limited series. **One Good Thing** is Hunter's second novel. She lives in Connecticut with her husband and their two sons.

georgiahunterauthor.com

Instagram GeorgiaHunter

Facebook GeorgiaHunterAuthor